FOREVER HIS

"I want to know who you are, how you came to be in Desiree's house that night a week ago, and for whom you work," Brady demanded. "It will all go easier on you if you tell the truth."

Julie sat down, but it was with exasperation. He still didn't believe her!

"I have told you the truth. I don't know how I came here. I am not a spy."

Brady yanked her up off the bench. "I'm afraid I have good cause to disbelieve you, my dear."

"Let me go," Julie said. "Let me go!"

Brady released her ever so slightly and looked into her face. Then he bent down and pressed his lips to her.

Julie doubled her fists and started to hit him, but his kiss was deep and passionate and the heat of him against her caused an unfamiliar feeling she could not even define. She could only feel the maleness of him as he pressed against her, his mouth moving hungrily on hers.

It was a wild, wondrous kiss . . . a kiss like none other she had ever had.

It was a kiss taken, and at least for the moment it was a kiss that conquered . . .

Books by Joyce Carlow

TIMESWEPT

A TIMELESS TREASURE ✓

TIMESWEPT PASSION ✓

Published by Zebra Books

TIMESWEPT PASSION

Joyce Carlow

Zebra Books
Kensington Publishing Corp.

http://www.zebrabooks.com

ZEBRA BOOKS are published by

Kensington Publishing Corp.
850 Third Avenue
New York, NY 10022

First Printing: February, 1997
10 9 8 7 6 5 4 3 2 1

Printed in the United States of America

Chapter One

Spring 1992

Julie Hart brushed a damp strand of her golden blond hair off her forehead and silently cursed the humidity that always enveloped St. Louis. No matter the season, it was always there. It was spring now, and though the breeze off the Mississippi was cool, the air was still laden with moisture.

In spite of its climate, Julie had always thought St. Louis was a wonderful city, a city of contrasts—contrasts that seemed dictated by its history and weather.

Since its founding in 1763, this city, in which she had grown up and lived for so many years, had dual influences. In the beginning those influences were French and English, then in the 1800's they became the influences of North and South. East St. Louis, just across the river, had been in the Free State of Illinois before the Civil War; the rest of St. Louis was in Missouri, admitted to the Union as a slave state. North and South met and sometimes clashed in St. Louis. Oddly, the mores of North and South now seemed to shift with the seasons. In the winter, St. Louis was a northern city with northern rhythms. Its streets and sidewalks were often coated with thin ice as the ever-present moisture rising from the Missouri and the Mississippi, which joined at Alton just above St. Louis, froze, causing a penetrating damp cold, a fog of tiny ice crystals. In the winter, wealthy women dressed in furs from the city's fine stores, while those less affluent bundled up in man-made imitations, or Alpaca coats and jackets. In the winter, skaters often covered the pond at Forest Park; in the winter, people hurried, business flourished, time was of importance. In the winter, St. Louis could have been Chicago or New York or Boston.

But in the summer the rhythm of life slowed and everything changed. In the summer, St. Louis was a southern city. Warm breezes floated off the Missouri and the Mississippi, the tempo of life slowed, and people who had run now strolled. It was as if time no longer mattered, as if everything were suspended only to be awakened with the setting sun and the sound of the jazz bands that toured the river cities from New Orleans to Chicago, their music evoking another time, another place.

At this moment, St. Louis was a city in transformation. It was spring, and warm summerlike days mingled with cool, damp days, so that winter was still a vivid memory and the long, lazy days of summer were yet a sweet promise.

Julie peered out from beneath her broad-brimmed straw hat, her deep blue eyes surveying those present in the chapel adjacent to the cathedral.

Her father's elder brother, Henry Hart, sat with his wife Sylvia in the pew to one side of her. Her cousins, on her father's side, George, Gwyn, and Gleason sat just behind their parents, Henry and Sylvia. There was no one from her mother's side of the family because her mother was an only child whose parents were long dead.

To her regret, her family was almost nonexistent. She always kept in touch with her aunt, uncle, and cousins, but she had little in common with them and, as a result, they were not close.

Now that she lived in New York and they lived here, in St. Louis, she almost never saw them. Moreover, she thought with some amusement, they regarded her with an odd mixture of awe and disapproval. She was what they called "artsy," and for them her chosen profession of costume and set designer for the theater was viewed as more of a hobby than a livelihood.

Julie did not think of herself as artsy or at all bohemian, which she suspected was what her relatives really meant. She dressed well because she designed and made most of her own clothing. She worked hard and read and researched carefully. She did not live in a commune, but rather in her own small apartment. Most of all, she was careful and thoughtful about forming relationships with men. She supposed she lived a more conventional life than many of her classmates who had remained in St. Louis. Still, she knew it was the fact she worked in the theater that they all found so unique, so puzzling.

But then, Julie thought, suppressing a smile, her mother had been no less of an enigma to her father's relatives. Her mother, who had died last year, and for whom this memorial service was being held, had worked for the St. Louis Museum of Fine Art. It was from her mother that she had first become interested in costume and design.

She glanced around the chapel and could not help but think that her mother had made so many good friends. The remaining twenty or so people in the chapel were all from the museum and the midwestern art world. They were co-workers and art dealers; people who had known her mother well and who respected her.

At that moment, the priest finished the service and slowly people got up. Some of those who had not done so before the service lit votive candles and placed them on the side altar, in memory of her mother, Louisa Landry Hart.

Julie walked to the door and positioned herself next to Father LeBlanc, who, like her mother, had roots that were buried deep in the history of North America—Acadian roots. Roots yanked from the soil of Nova Scotia and transplanted from the Carolinas to Louisiana.

"It's so nice to see you, dear." Mrs. Cartwell, one of her mother's many co-workers at the museum, grasped her hand.

"It's nice to see you. Thank you for coming."

Mrs. Cartwell leaned close. "Please call me before you leave the city, Julie. I'd love to hear about New York and your work."

Julie squeezed her hand gently. "Maybe we can have lunch."

Mrs. Cartwell laughed. "Do lunch," she said, smiling. "I've heard people in New York *do* lunch."

Julie smiled back. Mrs. Cartwell was nearly seventy, but she liked to be up to date. She was an enchanting woman who had, for many years, taught history and art history. "I guess I'm not a complete New Yorker yet," Julie replied.

"That might be for the best, dear. Please do call me."

"I will, I promise.

With variations, it was to be an oft-repeated phrase as Julie stood by the door and she and Father LeBlanc shook hands with all those who had come to the service. And there were all the usual statements and questions: "Are you moving back to St. Louis?; Don't you miss the Midwest?; Isn't New York too fast paced?; We'd love to have you come home."

Then there was only her aunt and uncle, Henry and Sylvia Hart, left in the chapel. Their children, her three cousins, had disappeared, no doubt to return to their insurance offices. The entire family—father, mother, and children—all seemed locked into one business, a single enterprise—that of insuring, what seemed to her, to be a risk-ridden future. Still, had her own parents not availed themselves of so much advice and bought so many insurance policies, she supposed she would be far less independent and indeed would not have been able to pursue her dreams in New York.

"Are you staying in town long?" Aunt Sylvia prodded gently, her expression concerned.

"The annual awards of the American Playhouse Academy are being held here on Saturday. Remember? I told you I'd been nominated for best historic costume design. I planned this service to coincide with the awards banquet."

"Oh, yes, I do recall your mentioning them. Does that mean you're leaving Sunday?"

"No, I guess I'll be here at least till Monday or Tuesday."

Father LeBlanc leaned across them, a hand on each of their shoulders. "Forgive me for interrupting. I have to say good-bye now, I have a baptism in half an hour."

"Thank you for being here, for having the service."

"My pleasure, Juliet. My pleasure. Mr. and Mrs. Hart." He smiled and nodded at her aunt and uncle, then turned and hurried away, leaving the three of them framed in the doorway to the side chapel of the Great Cathedral.

"You don't have to stay in a hotel, dear. You know we have plenty of room," her aunt continued.

Julie smiled. "I know. But the hotel came with my registration for the awards banquet. There are people coming from all over the States. I've been attending the awards ceremonies for two years. I have friends coming who I haven't seen in a long time."

"Besides, the hotel is air conditioned," Uncle Henry said with a grin. "Climate-controlled for our unpredictable days and nights."

"You have such an unusual job," Aunt Sylvia half-whispered.

"If she were getting an Emmy you probably wouldn't say that," Uncle Henry muttered.

Julie smiled. She was always grateful for his understanding comments. Neither his wife nor children seemed to believe theater was as important as TV.

"Come along, Sylvia. And we'll see you on Friday for dinner? Right?"

Julie nodded. "Yes, of course. Friday night."

For a moment she watched as Uncle Henry guided her aunt Sylvia away, toward the parking lot. Then he turned, remembering she had no car. "Can we give you a lift?"

"No, it's only a short walk." Then she, too, turned, and with a final wave to them, began walking up Lindell Avenue, toward the Chase Hotel.

The avenue was wide and the sun glared up off the sidewalk. The sights, the sounds, and the smells were all familiar to her, yet she felt consumed with an extremely odd feeling—a feeling that she was seeing St. Louis for the last time; a feeling that this was her last visit home. It was peculiar. She had felt this way since she arrived, but now that sensation seemed stronger, and she thought she must really look around, look around and commit it all to her memory. She vowed to walk the wide avenues, visit the wonderful park and zoo, go to the museum that her mother's talents had helped to build, and visit the law courts where her father had dedicated himself to defend justice. The feeling seemed to propel her, to guide her. This was the city of her youth, a city she wanted to remember.

Yes, something inside her demanded she realize that her future was elsewhere.

Julie slid into a booth in the air-conditioned coffee shop of the Chase Hotel. It was a sunny room filled with plants. Even the booths were covered with green leather. Outside it was a cool spring day, but inside it was like a summer day in the park. Floor-to-ceiling mirrors on one end gave the room depth and made the plants seem even more plentiful.

She ordered some iced coffee and a club sandwich. Again she acknowledged the fact that she felt otherworldly and yet filled with earthly emotions. She knew full well that the vague depression gnawing at her was because of the memorial service, perhaps that was why her inner feelings seemed at war. One voice said, "Slow down, look around, you won't pass this way again." At the same time another voice urged her to run, to take leave of all that was familiar.

"Julie? Julie Hart? Is that really you?"

At the sound of her name, Julie awakened from her self-analysis with a start. She looked up and into the wide, questioning eyes of Kathy Charles.

"It's really me," Julie said.

"A ghost out of the past!" Kathy sat down opposite her and smiled warmly. "It's been ages! Let's see—oh, at least five years."

"Exactly five years," Julie replied with a smile. "Your nineteenth birthday, as I recall."

Kathy blushed. "Oh, yes. The spring of '87—the spring of Brad Barton." She shrugged. "Well, next week I'll be twenty-four and Brad Barton is long gone."

"I thought you'd marry him."

"Brad? Oh, no! Never."

That spring Kathy and Brad had carried on a torrid affair. It had shocked their friends because both of them were so young and because it resulted in Kathy dropping out of college.

"I don't think that's how you felt then."

Kathy giggled. "Well, I suppose not. But enough of me. What brings you to town? Visiting your mother?"

Julie shook her head. "My mother died last year. In fact, I was just here for her memorial service."

"Oh, I'm so sorry. I didn't know. That must be rough, I mean, your dad died when you were twelve and you don't have brothers or sisters."

"Yes, I'm alone, but I'm used to it—it's been a year. I'm

okay now, really." It was not the total truth. She never got used to not making weekly calls to her mother or of having her mother fly into New York to visit. They had been more than mother and daughter, they had been best friends.

"Still living in New York? Still trying to break on to Broadway?"

Julie nodded. "My last job was for an off-Broadway production of the Beggar's Opera. It was really well reviewed, especially the costumes."

"I've never been much on opera," Kathy admitted.

"It's not really an opera," Julie replied. She thought of giving an expanded explanation, but then decided not to bother. There was hardly any point in telling Kathy things she probably didn't want to know.

"So, you do like New York," Kathy pressed.

"I'm doing well, I love my work. I love New York!"

"I'm glad. Guess you'll be glad to get back. It's a long way to come for a memorial service."

"I'm also here for an awards banquet."

"That sounds exciting. What kind of awards?"

"Small Theater Awards for costume and set design."

"I remember when you won that dress design contest. Remember, your mother took us all out for a party."

"Quite a party," Julie added as her mind traveled back over the years. She sipped some of her iced coffee and looked across at her old high school friend. Kathy was the same age as she, a pert little redhead with green eyes and a bubbly personality. On the surface, she didn't appear to have changed at all. She was still very much the cheerleader she had been.

"How about you?" Julie asked earnestly.

"I'm in advertising. In fact I've got a great new job. I'm about to leave for New Orleans."

"That sounds exciting."

"The best part is that I'm driving down and I'll get there in time for Mardi Gras! My job doesn't start for two weeks, so I think a little partying is in order."

"It sounds wonderful. I've always wanted to go to Louisiana myself. My mother's ancestors came from there."

"Are you going right back to New York?"

Julie shrugged. "I guess I'll go back next Tuesday, though nothing is urgent. I won't know about a new play for at least a month."

"That means you've plenty of time. Julie, why don't you drive down to New Orleans with me? We'd have a ball, just like the old days. Remember how we used to tool around in your mom's old Chevy?"

"I hope you're not driving an old Chevy?"

"No, of course not! I'm driving a brand-new bright red Miata."

"How, very expensive, "Julie teased. The advertising business must be very lucrative."

"It is, believe me. C'mon, Julie, think about it. Think about that family research you used to talk about doing."

Julie raised an eyebrow. "I can't believe you remember that!" She had always wanted to go to Lafayette Parish. Her mother was a Landry and she wanted to look into her family history.

"I remember lots of things," Kathy said. "What did you used to tell me? Was your mother French?"

"Yes, of Acadian descent."

"Well, think of this as the perfect opportunity to look into it. We can go through Lafayette Parish. Just get me a road map and I'll drive anywhere you want in Louisiana as long as we're in New Orleans for Mardi Gras."

It was spur of the moment. It was totally unplanned. The idea of going somewhere else after she left St. Louis hadn't even crossed her mind. But why not? She was alone and completely unencumbered. Her tiny New York apartment was even without plants. She had no one to answer to; she was the mistress of her own actions. "It sounds like fun."

Kathy clapped her hands. "It will be, I promise you."

"I've never been this—this spontaneous," Julie confessed.

"It's good for you. Give me your room number."

Julie wrote her room number down along with the phone number of the hotel and handed it to Kathy.

"I'll pick you up at nine sharp on Tuesday morning. Be ready to travel."

Julie laughed. "I will be."

And no sooner had she said it, then she realized how few clothes she had brought with her. Well, what did it matter? This was the age of credit cards and she was in a fine shopping city. Yes, Emery, Bird, and Thayer would have everything she could possibly need. And if Emery, Bird, and Thayer lacked anything, there were hundreds of boutiques in St. Louis.

Yes, she thought cheerfully, she would buy a few new summer clothes to augment the two dresses, the evening gown, and suit she had brought with her. She would get clothes for warmer weather—April in New Orleans was bound to be warmer than in New York or even St. Louis.

Suddenly Julie felt her spirits lift. This *would* be an adventure!

The banquet room of the St. Louis Hotel was decorated with alternating relief panels of plain white trimmed with gold and panels of marvelous textured gold-and-red wallpaper. Each of the tables was draped with a red tablecloth had each had a bouquet of white roses at its center.

On the stage at the front of the room the head table was set for twelve. Julie paused at the doorway while one of the several hostesses checked her reservations. "Table two," she whispered as she directed Julie to a table directly in front of the stage but slightly to the left of the center.

She smoothed her dress self-consciously. It was a shimmering iridescent blue with long sleeves and a high neck.

It fit her body like a glove down to the hips, and then it flared into soft folds. She wore a silver bracelet, earrings, and necklace. Her dress fabric glittered, so she felt there was no need for fancy jewels, too. She was inordinately proud of the dress. It was one of her own designs and she'd had it made from her own pattern. Her long hair was pulled up and back, though some golden curls escaped to frame her face.

Table two was set for six, and four had already arrived. She took one of the two empty chairs and sat down. She smiled at her dinner companions. "Julie Hart," she said, introducing herself.

"Myra and Jeff Bonner," a tall, thin man replied as he stood up. "Christy and Jason Henry," the other man said, doing the same. "We're all from San Francisco. And you?"

"New York," Julie answered.

"Are you a nominee, too?" the dark-haired woman named Christy asked as she leaned forward.

"Yes. I think they put all the nominees at the tables in front to make it easier."

"That makes wonderful sense," Jeff Bonner said a little sarcastically. "I'm surprised the organizers thought of it. Last year the winners had to troop down front from the very back of the room."

At that moment a tall, broad-shouldered young man in his thirties sat down.

Jeff stood and shook his hand. "We've all introduced ourselves. I'm Jeff Bonner and this is my wife, Myra. This lovely lady is Julie Hart and this is Christy and Jason Henry."

"Rich Edwards, from Boston."

"As if we all couldn't tell from your accent, my man!" Jason laughed and then reached for the open bottle of wine. "I'm sure no one will mind if we begin the honors." With that, he poured each of them a glass of wine.

"As long as they bring refills," Christy murmured.

"Jason's been nominated for best stage designer in a contemporary drama. I just get ever so tense."

Julie looked around and wondered if they had all been nominated in different categories. If so, it was certainly tactful of those planning the seating arrangements to make certain direct competitors were not seated together. Competition for the medals was keen. Winning was an automatic boost to one's career.

"I've been nominated for best contemporary costume design," Jeff revealed.

"And I for best period costume design," Julie chimed in.

"Best historic set design," Rich Edwards announced. He sipped some of his wine and turned to Julie. "You're very young. This is quite an honor, you know."

"I do know. I envy you. I do set design, too. I'd love to have been nominated for both."

"My, you're ambitious."

"I guess I am," she admitted.

"New York is where the best of small theater is located. And of course, if you want to go on—move out of small theater and summer stock, you have to be either there, in London, or in Toronto," Jason Henry said dryly.

"I thought Boston had lots of theater," Julie said.

"Not as much as it used to have," Rich responded. "You know, the recession and all."

"Ah, here comes the appetizer," Rich announced.

"I can't look," Jason muttered. "Is it four shrimp on an avocado or just tomato juice with a lemon wedge?"

"Tomato juice with a lemon wedge? Why?" Julie asked.

Christy laughed. "My, you are young! When you've been to enough of these overpriced events you can guess the entrée by the appetizer."

"Chicken," Jeff whispered as the waitress set down the tomato juice. "Probably Chicken Kiev."

"Well, we're not really here for the food, are we?" Julie said.

Rich Edwards raised his brow. "Speak for yourself. Personally, I always hope for a good feed."

Julie just smiled. She supposed they were seated together because most everyone else had brought a guest and they were the two singles. Then, as if he had been reading her thoughts, he leaned over. "Are you single?"

"Yes."

"Me, too. I was married, but she ran off with a producer. I'd say she was a social climber, but I guess she was more of a theater climber."

The others laughed at his joke but Julie just smiled. She was very much aware of his eyes on her, yet she wasn't sure if he was admiring the dress or admiring her.

Soon the empty tomato juice glasses were cleared away and salad was brought. This was followed by the entrée which was not Chicken Kiev but Chicken Milano. The conversation was light, meaningless, but not unpleasant. It was the kind of conversation one would expect six strangers thrown together for an evening to have.

Then all the plates were taken away and coffee and dessert served. The master of ceremonies, a white-haired producer named Austin Blakely, took the podium. He told a few jokes, welcomed everyone, and suggested they "raise the curtain" on the 1992 awards.

None of the people at her table won in their categories, but they didn't seem too disappointed. When her category was announced, she was relaxed, even reconciled to losing. It was, she told herself again and again, an honor to be nominated when you were so young and just beginning your career.

Then suddenly she heard her name called and her mouth opened in surprise.

"Wonderful!" Christy said. "Dear, don't look so overcome. Run and get your award."

Julie hurried to the podium amid applause. She felt stunned and more moved than she had thought she would be—not that she had even seriously considered the idea she would win. Then, looking out at the sea of faces, she felt a little tongue-tied. It was strange. She could be aggressive in her work, but now she discovered she was a little shy in front of an audience.

"I want to thank you all," she managed to say and then added, "I want to thank my mother for helping me so much."

She felt her face flush as she went back to the table and she knew her hands were trembling. The medal, a beautiful silver circle hung round her neck on a blue ribbon just below her necklace. The ribbon nearly matched her dress, it was as if someone had known what she would be wearing.

Later, she thought, she would put it on a chain. It was the size of a silver dollar, designed to be worn as a pendant.

Rich Edwards stood up to greet her as she came back to the table. He pulled out her chair and kissed her lightly on the cheek—a theater kiss, Julie thought. Still, it was nice of him to pretend they were together even though they were virtual strangers.

"May I take you out for a celebratory drink after this is all over?" he whispered in her ear.

Julie nodded. He seemed nice enough. "I'd like that very much."

Rich helped her on with her wrap and they took a cab down to Laclede's Landing. There, in a bar overlooking the river, he ordered champagne cocktails.

"Too bad it's so late," Rich lamented. "We could have taken that marvelous river boat down the Mississippi for the evening."

Julie nodded. She did love the river. As a child she had been steeped in Mississippi folklore. "I always liked being on the river. It's a powerful experience and so much a part of American history."

"Ah, of course. A history buff. But then, you do period

theater costumes and sets, so you *must* be a history buff. Naturally I am too.''

"I don't think someone from Boston can have a mind free of history.''

He laughed. "Hardly. Tell me, do you intend to stay in legitimate theater or go into movies and television where the real money is.''

She tilted her head slightly as she thought. It was a difficult question. "Is it either/or?'' she asked after a moment.

"Usually. I'm contemplating a movie offer now. Of course it would mean relocating to California—not really my cup of tea.''

"Nor mine. At least right now. No, I think I'll stay with the theater.''

"How about that river ride tomorrow night?''

"I'm sorry, but I have to see my family.''

"And the next night?''

"I won't have the time. I have to get up really early. I'm leaving for New Orleans.''

"Well then, I guess we'll have to make the most of tonight.''

Julie wasn't sure what Rich meant, so she only shrugged.

They had two more drinks, then he suggested they walk back to the hotel. "I'm not at the Sheraton,'' she explained. "I'm uptown at the Chase.''

"We'll take a cab.''

She started to tell him he didn't need to take her back to her hotel. She knew he had drunk more than she. But the cab stopped and he ordered it to the Chase. On the way, he grew silent, and his arm dropped around her shoulders.

Outside her hotel door she looked up at him and felt a growing apprehension. "Rich, I can't invite you in. I like you, but we don't know each other very well.''

The hall was empty and she suddenly wished it wasn't. Rich's arms were around her and he pulled her to him roughly, kissing her hard on the mouth and trying to force open her lips. At the same time, his hand moved to her breast and squeezed it.

"I thought we were going to make the most of tonight," he slurred.

"I'm sorry if you misunderstood."

"You're a little tease," he hissed. "You're all wrapped up pretty and sexy. What do you think I'm supposed to think? C'mon, honey, let's get it on."

His lips nuzzled her neck and she struggled to free herself from his grasp. How could anyone who seemed so nice at first turn into such an awful person so soon? "Let me go," she said firmly. "Let me go or I'll scream."

He swore under his breath but did not release her. Julie struggled harder, feeling her face flush with exertion. Then to her enormous relief she heard the elevator doors open. "Let me go!" she said, wiggling free of his embrace as he turned toward the men who had gotten off the elevator.

He stared at the men and she turned the key in the lock, opened the door, went inside and slammed the door after her, slipping the dead bolt into place. He banged on the door. Then, a few moments later, she heard him swear again and stomp off.

Julie leaned against the door and breathed deeply in relief. It had all started out so well, and it had turned so ugly. She walked dejectedly to the bed and threw herself across it. She hadn't been the least attracted to him and she wondered why she had even accepted his invitation. Now the memory of an evening that should have been perfect had been taken away.

She touched the silver medallion hanging round her neck. "But nothing can take this away," she whispered.

Sylvia Hart put the pot roast down in the center of the table. "There we are," she said, looking at it with pleasure.

"Frankly, I'm starved," Henry said. He winked at Julie. "How about you?"

"It certainly smells good."

"Well, I wanted to have it for you. I remember it was always your favorite, Julie. And I don't suppose living alone and all that you really eat proper meals."

"Oh, I try," Julie answered. She didn't want to elaborate, though she hardly thought she looked emaciated. The fact was, she was in fine physical condition. She ate a good breakfast and she usually jogged at least a mile every morning. She worked out at the gym several times a week, and while she didn't eat much for lunch, she always tried to have a hot dinner, except in the summer when the New York heat sapped one's appetite.

"Well, I'm glad to hear that," Sylvia said as she sat down. "I'm so sorry your cousins couldn't come tonight, dear. They're just so busy."

Uncle Henry passed the potatoes, then the vegetables, then the gravy. "I think it's kind of nice and quiet without all of them," he said as he carved the roast. "Besides, pot roast is my favorite, which means there's more for us."

"Oh, Henry," Sylvia said with a sigh.

Henry finished his carving and rejoined his wife and Julie at the table. "Ready, set, eat," he announced with joviality.

"So, you're going right back to New York?" Sylvia looked at Julie.

Julie supposed she should tell someone where she was going. "No, actually I'm not," she answered.

"But the other day you said—"

Julie swallowed a forkful of mashed potatos. "I know, but this was all very spur of the moment. I decided to go down to New Orleans with an old friend."

"A girl friend?" Sylvia asked pointedly.

"Yes, a girl friend."

"That's nice. Who are you going with?"

"Kathy Charles. I don't think you know her."

"Kathy Charles—no, that name doesn't ring any bells. Do you know her, Henry?"

Henry shook his head.

"I hope she's a nice girl. Are you staying with her relatives?"

"No. In a hotel," Julie answered. She felt as if she were at the grand inquisition. It was hard to tell if Aunt Sylvia really cared or if she was just trying to make dinner conversation.

"Two girls alone," Sylvia sighed. "Things certainly have changed since my day."

"Yes they have," Henry put in. "They've changed a lot." He grinned at Julie. "We're really proud of you, winning that award and all. I think your dad and mom would be proud, too."

Julie managed a smile. "I wish I'd won it before . . ." She found she couldn't finish the sentence. It suddenly didn't seem like a year since her mother had died. She had thought it sudden, but as it turned out, it wasn't. Her mother had known for some time about the cancer, she just hadn't told anyone how little time she had left. Her note had just explained that she hadn't wanted to waste time in mourning before she died—that she wanted to enjoy her time without thinking about it. Suddenly, Julie's eyes filled with tears.

"Hey, there," Uncle Henry said. "Sorry."

Julie shook her head. "It's all right. It only happens now and again."

He patted her hand. "You have a good time in New Orleans," he urged with a wink.

Julie squeezed his hand. "I will," she promised. "I will."

They headed due south on I-55. Kathy had the top down on the Miata convertible, and her red hair was covered with a bright multi-colored scarf. Large sunglasses partially obscured her face, and she wore white shorts with a low-necked blue blouse that matched her scarf.

Julie wore slacks and a short-sleeved blouse. Her hair

was in a long French braid. She also wore sunglasses. From behind the dark lenses her blue eyes surveyed the land- scape and past memories mingled with present discom- forts.

She loved the rolling hills of southern Missouri and the dramatic flood gates at Cape Girardeau, which they had passed yesterday.

At her urging Kathy and she had lunched in a restaurant near the levee. The river was an awesome sight. It was spring and the Mississippi was at near floodtide. Yes, she loved driving and she had forgotten how much she loved it. The United States was a wonderful country to drive through. She loved the face of the land—the mountains of Colorado and Utah, the desert, then the lush fields and finally the "father of waters." She knew the river near Hannibal well, because in the summer she used to go there with her parents and she knew the river as far south as New Madrid near the border of Missouri and Arkansas. But now she was going to see it all. They would pass through Memphis, Vicksburg, Natchez, and Baton Rouge before they got to New Orleans.

I wish I'd made this trip sooner, she thought silently. And then, sadly, she realized she would rather be alone. She preferred stopping at monuments and museums, while Kathy liked to stop at bars.

They had spent last night on the outskirts of New Madrid and tonight she imagined they would be in Memphis. The rolling hills of Missouri had already given way to the hills of Tennessee. The sun had grown hotter, the traffic slower, and the air heavier.

Julie stole a glance at Kathy. They'd eaten breakfast and lunch in a truck stop where Kathy had taken obvious pleasure in flirting with the truck drivers who eyed her long, shapely legs with sheer lust. It made Julie uncomfort- able. Kathy dressed too skimpily for her own taste and was far too friendly with strange men.

She leaned back in the seat and closed her eyes. Maybe

she was being absurd—too, too careful. I am *not* a prude, she thought. Rich Edwards was drunk and he came on too fast and much too soon. Was she expected to jump into bed with just anyone? She felt annoyed because Rich had as much as said she was a tease, and now Kathy seemed to think she was a stick-in-the-mud because she didn't want to flirt with strangers and invite unwanted liaisons. Had Kathy always been so bold?

Five years. Yes, people could change in five years, and Kathy had changed. Or had *she* been the one to change? No, she was sure it was Kathy. Kathy seemed more forward, her endless chatter seemed pointless, her interests shallow. But it was her propensity for flirting with and then bedding down with strange men that made Julie feel ill at ease. Not that it had happened yet on this trip. But Kathy did have a million stories of her exploits. She talked about this man and that; she talked about the affair she was having with her boss.

"I never thought you'd be so—so virginal," Kathy suddenly said, as if similar thoughts had been running through her mind. "I mean, living in New York and all—being in the theater. I thought you'd be game for some fun."

"I've always been up for fun," Julie said, trying to sound light. "But I don't like to sleep around."

"Aren't we self-righteous. Well, tell me there isn't a lot of sleeping around in the theater world."

Julie laughed gently. "Probably not as much as you might think. It's hard work, you know. The hours are really long. When I come home I'm usually dog tired."

"And here I thought you had the exciting life. Personally, I like messing around."

"It can be dangerous."

Kathy looked over at her. "That's the part I love best. I like the feeling that I'm doing something dangerous. It turns me on."

Kathy seemed to be talking about dangerous men. She

wondered if Kathy thought about taking precautions against diseases. She didn't ask.

Julie bit her lip. "I want to be honest with you Kath . . . I'm not into bedhopping. Am I cramping your style? I thought last night that you wanted to invite that driver back to our room."

"Well, I did. I had hoped you'd be up for a threesome. I'd have liked that, and all the guys dig it. But you came on like an ice queen, so I knew you wouldn't do it. I guess you are cramping my style."

Julie nodded. Better to have it out in the open. "I'll get a separate room from now on. When we get to New Orleans we can go our separate ways. Okay?"

Kathy didn't turn this time. She kept her eyes on the road. "Okay," she said after a moment, then, "Sorry it hasn't worked out."

"Me, too," Julie answered.

For the next few minutes Julie concentrated on the scenery, then silently began to make plans. New Orleans was a fascinating city and she wanted to see it. It was all for the best. Now she could pursue her own interests in history and art. She didn't have to feel uncomfortable and neither did Kathy. Yes, she would be free to do as she wished and Kathy would be free to pursue her sexual desires, whatever they were.

Yes, she would go to all the museums and historic sights, then she would rent a car and go to Lafayette County in search of her roots.

"Aren't you ever going to take chances?" Kathy suddenly asked.

"I've taken a few," Julie answered. "Enough to know what I'm looking for."

Julie's thoughts raced back over time. In her second year of college she had met a young graduate student in history, a teaching assistant. She was just nineteen, he was twenty-five, two years older than she was now. His name has been John Bruns and he was good-looking as well as intelligent. They dated on and off for several months before it became more serious and she surrendered her virginity to him.

For a year they fit their love life into their rigorous schedules. She was a sophomore and he was working on his Ph.D. In her junior year they moved in together to a tiny one-room apartment just off campus. It was hard to study because there was no privacy, but his salary as a teaching assistant and her student allowance didn't permit them to rent a larger place.

Julie thought now that her mother must have been a little disappointed. But she never said anything and Julie remembered thinking that at twenty-one she was old enough to make her own decisions.

At the beginning of her senior year, the beginning of the end of their relationship came in the form of a letter to John. He was offered a teaching fellowship at Princeton. It was too good to pass up.

Reluctantly, she moved back into the dormitory and he left for New Jersey. In the first months he phoned often and they wrote at least three times a week. They made plans to be together at Thanksgiving when he came to St. Louis to be with her and her mother. Then at New Year's she went to Princeton.

Perhaps it was the wrong holiday to visit, she remembered thinking ruefully. There were parties galore and too much drinking. And there was another woman, a woman with whom he was clearly intimate.

Tearfully, they agreed to end it; agreed that their relationship was not strong enough to survive time and distance. She graduated at twenty-two and moved to New York. Two months later her mother died.

Now she was one week shy of her twenty-fourth birthday. She had done the costumes for two off-Broadway shows and won an award for one. Unconsciously, she touched the medal which she had hung on a silver chain round her neck.

"Does your silence mean you will take another chance sometime?" Kathy persisted.

"When the right man comes along," Julie said. "Then I'll take a chance."

Chapter Two

Julie opened the glass door and entered the airy, patio-type lobby of the Maison Chartres. It was a small lobby, intimate and fully enclosed, though it had the feeling of the outdoors. It was rather like a secret hidden tropical garden, a quiet refuge from the busy street outside. Light from a fourth-floor skylight flooded the entire area, and the hand-painted tile fountain bubbled slowly, as drops rather than showers rained on its tranquil lily-covered pool. There were plants everywhere, palms and ferns, lush flowers, and even cacti.

The man behind the desk was plump and round-faced. He smiled cheerfully and ran his hand abstractedly over his bald head. "May I help you, miss?"

"I'm looking for a room."

He grinned. "Isn't everyone! It's four days from Mardi Gras! Every hotel, every bed-and-breakfast, and every rooming house is full up to the rafters."

Julie sighed. "This is fifth hotel I've been to."

"As I said, it's near Mardi Gras. Are you alone? No, how could you be alone? No one comes to Mardi Gras alone."

"I did."

"Well, you are fortunate among room seekers! Most people are couples—I mean, most of our guests are couples. We have one small single room—the result of a cancellation I just received a few minutes ago. But I can only rent it to you if you stay through Mardi Gras." His soft, smooth Louisiana accent flowed lazily like the Mississippi.

Julie frowned thoughtfully. She had intended on taking a room tonight and reserving a room for when she returned from Lafayette Parish. Still, it would give her a base of operations and it meant she need only take an overnight bag on her motoring jaunt up to Cajun country. "Very well, I'll take it."

"I'm afraid it's on the fourth floor and there isn't any elevator."

Julie smiled. "I don't mind."

"It does have a balcony; you'll be able to see the Mardi Gras parade."

"That's wonderful."

"Is that your luggage? I'm afraid I'm alone here—that is, we have no bellboy."

"I can take it up myself, really."

"Well, it's not the way I usually like to treat our guests. We're a small hotel as you can see—very personal and friendly." He shrugged. "But if you don't mind, I would be grateful. It's so difficult to leave the desk since the phone doesn't stop ringing."

As he spoke, he turned the registry book toward her and handed her a card to fill out. She did so even as he took another call. She wrote her name and address and then handed him her credit card. He ran it through his machine while he chatted on the phone, then he handed her a large key from those behind the desk and pointed her toward the narrow, winding staircase that led upward.

After her climb, Julie stood before the door of her room for a moment, catching her breath. Then she turned the large antique-style key in the lock and the door opened, revealing a fairy-tale room right out of a history book. A huge window was covered with sheers and draped with heavy ornate blue brocade. Julie thought with a smile that the drapes would have been suitable for Scarlett O'Hara's ball gown.

At the far end of the room was a dais, and atop it, a single bed with a canopy. The drapes that could be pulled to surround the bed were of the same blue brocade as those at the windows.

The room had three small tables, each one round, each one covered with a crocheted cloth and each one with a hurricane lamp that had modern electrical fittings. There was a large fireplace with a gas-fed burning log. It was obviously intended to take the dampness out of the air, should the evening turn cool. The chairs where spindly-legged and covered with tapestry. The wallpaper was floral and somewhat faded, the rugs thick with muted colors.

Julie thought how motel and hotel rooms in America looked alike, one interchangeable with another. Except for this one. This one was unique. It was a little bit of history, a charming room that carried one back over the centuries.

It even smelled of rosewood. Julie inhaled as she set her suitcase down. The aroma was wonderful! She stood still for a long moment and then walked across the room and drew back the sheers. Beyond closed double doors, a small wrought-iron balcony looked down on Rue Chartres. The Mardi Gras parade would pass right by her! What an ideal spot she had picked and it was all an accident—a providential accident, to be sure.

The rest of today, she decided, would be spent looking around New Orleans, deciding what she wanted to see when she got back. Then, in the morning, she would rent a car and head up the serpentine roads that paralleled Bayou Teche, the heart of Cajun country, the place her mother's displaced and dispossessed ancestors had settled.

* * *

Julie walked along the streets of the French Quarter, the Vieux Carré. "Spring in New Orleans," the concierge at her hotel told her, "is almost sacred. It's cool and fresh. Definitely the best season."

She could not disagree. The greenery was new and fragile, almost lacy in texture. It seemed as if every plant was in wild bud. Here was a sudden array of azaleas in pinks and purples, and above her a riot of petunias and impatiens spilling from the wrought-iron balconies that lined the streets of the Vieux Carré. The huge ivory magnolia trees filled the air with the scent of a woman's boudoir and deep purple wisteria was alive with bumblebees. Green moss grew in the cracks of buildings and down by the water of Bayou St. John and willows seemed to dip into the water and drink.

She felt consumed by the color and aroma of this place, surprised by this city's sensuality and energy. The beckoning smell of gourmet cooking and tantalizing spices mixed with the floral bouquets, making it clear that New Orleans was a city for all appetites.

She paused to look in jewelry shop windows and she passed a candy factory where pralines were made. They filled the whole street with the smell of brown sugar and pecans.

There was so much to see here. She wanted to spend a day in the French Market and at least two or three days going through the museums. Perhaps, she thought happily, she would even take the three-hour Cajun cooking course offered in the Jackson Brewery.

But first, Lafayette Parish beckoned. *And if I want,* she reminded herself, *I can stay in New Orleans an extra week. There is no one to whom I am responsible.* On the one hand, she knew she was free, on the other she admitted to loneliness, to a desire to share the experiences she knew she was going to have with someone else, someone special who was now only a pleasant daydream.

Feeling unrushed and free to follow her own instincts, Julie stopped at Opelouses, a town founded by the French in the mid-eighteenth century as a trading post with the Indians. She toured antebellum mansions that stood at the end of long oak corridors in Gran Coteau, and in Lafayette she visited the museum and the library. Landry, her mother's maiden name, was a common one and she marveled at the numbers recorded as she read the family history.

She went on a swamp tour and visited the Acadian village where houses dating back to the early settlers were located. "The whispering pines and the hemlocks . . ." She murmured to herself thinking of Longfellow.

Then, at Port Bayou Teche, she made a sentimental stop at the Evangeline Oak where tradition held that Evangeline's boat docked at the completion of her long journey from Nova Scotia. Here, she supposedly learned that Evangeline's fiancé, Gabriel, believing her lost, became betrothed to another.

She had been to Nova Scotia, too, and had visited the remaining Acadian communities there. They were a miraculous people who had somehow culturally survived against overwhelming odds and more than two hundred years of intervening history.

The Atachafalaya Basin was a scenic wonderland with hardwood forests, cypress swamps, marshes, and twisting bayous. The boat trip she had taken provided her with what she considered a strange experience.

As she drove back toward New Orleans, she thought about it some more and wondered what had caused it. She had been in the flatboat with other tourists, yet she had felt totally and utterly alone. She looked at the swamp, from which the great cypress grew, and she had the overwhelming feeling that she would come this way again. It was not the usual feeling of déjà vu that people so often had. It was more on the order of premonition, a kind of order to remember it all for future reference. It was so strong, it was almost as if a veil had dropped between her and her fellow tourists. As if they were not there at all.

"I'm alone too much," she said aloud. And with that she turned on the car radio. In another hour she would be back in New Orleans.

Julie kicked off her shoes and removed her dress. She threw herself across the bed, then puffed up the pillows and opened a magazine she spied on the bedside table called *Entertainment in New Orleans*. She had been in the French Market all morning and she was tired.

Lazily, she leafed through the pages. Listings of fine restaurants and intriguing museums were interspersed with sporting events and all manner of special functions centering around Mardi Gras. Naturally there were all the "musts" of New Orleans such as a visit to Preservation Hall to listen to real old-time jazz and a trip down one of the bayous close to the city.

But tonight, she thought, she would venture forth to K-Pauls and sample some of Paul Prudhomme's famous Louisiana specialties. Tomorrow, she would begin visiting various museums and arrange for other tours. She marked several museums, including a dollhouse museum. Then she checked her watch and the small map of New Orleans in the book. The dollhouse museum was not far from the restaurant. If she went there around three, there would be plenty of time to see it before dinner.

"An early dinner and I'll be back here for a good night's sleep," she said aloud, proud of her planned itinerary. "And now for a short southern nap." With that she rolled over on her right side. Weariness had overcome her, as if by setting foot in this city she had already adopted its mores—at least the afternoon siesta.

In moments she was asleep.

Julie turned slowly onto her left side, then flopped onto her back and opened her eyes. The aroma of fresh coffee drifted through the open window as did the muted sound of music somewhere in the distance.

Julie stretched and then looked at her watch. It was two-thirty. She had slept just an hour, but still felt wonderfully refreshed. She sat up and then stood and shook her head. Yes, a cool shower and fresh clothes and she would be ready to go. New Orleans, the city of fine restaurants and exotic architecture beckoned. Even though she was on her own, Julie vowed again to enjoy herself and to make the most of her visit.

For a moment she ran the water, then stepped into the shower and lavishly applied the liquid soap that was supplied by the hotel. It was a fine French soap, pungent and perfumed.

When she emerged from the shower, she wrapped herself in a huge white towel and ventured out into the main room where her suitcase lay open on the luggage rack.

She put on fresh undergarments, then a lightweight blue print dress that was suitable for both the museum and dinner later on. Any manner of dress went in New Orleans, especially now when the city was full of tourists preparing to celebrate carnival. Young people roamed the streets in blue jeans and sweat shirts; older tourists wore slacks and dresses, suits, and some wore their refinery. A few of the Mardi Gras revelers were already on the streets wearing ornate costumes and gaudy masks or heavy theatrical makeup. Last night, when she had turned in her rented car and returned to the hotel, she had passed a group of four men wearing massive wigs and stiletto heels.

As an afterthought, she put on her silver chain with

her award medal which now served as a beautiful silver pendant. On one side there was a set of masks and underneath it read "Best Costuming in a Historic Drama, 1992." On the back, her name was engraved underneath the words, "Presented to Julie Hart by the American Playhouse Academy of Costume and Design."

Julie looked once in the full-length mirror, then slung her purse over her shoulder and left her fourth-floor room, careful to lock the door as she left.

Even though it was early afternoon, out on Rue Chartres and indeed throughout the city, New Orleans was coming to life. Street musicians played on nearly every corner while vendors hawked exotic foods and assorted merchandise.

As Julie made her way down the crowded street toward the dollhouse museum, it once again became obvious to her that even though she was far from miserable, she might have been happier had she been with someone. Experiences were meant to be shared and discussed. No matter how independent she was, she knew she missed sharing new experiences with others—with friends male or female.

That thought caused her to focus momentarily on Kathy. Yes, she had indeed done the right thing. Kathy and she had grown apart. There could be no question about that. In the few days they had been together, she had seen a multitude of changes, most of which she did not—no, *could* not approve. While Julie admitted readily to herself that while the occasional drink was okay, she had no desire to travel with someone whose main interest was drinking and carousing.

Kathy was into things that she herself had never done and knew she never would do. All her life, Julie had avoided peer pressure. Her parents had brought her up as an individualist, and she was glad about that. Sometimes she longed for excitement and adventure, just as she longed for that special man. But the truth was she had a wonderful, exciting job of her own choice. Each day was a challenge; each new assignment a thrill. Everything came into play, her artistic skill, her historic knowledge, her ability to research. And she felt she had a complete life, even if that one important man had not yet come along. There was world enough and time, she thought. There was no need to become involved with every man who showed an interest, and there was no need for her seek excitement in alcohol and drugs. Yes, Kathy had gone one way, while she had chosen a different path.

Better to be alone once in a while, she thought as she pushed through the doors of the dollhouse museum. At least this way she had no one to blame for what happened to her. Her life was very much her own.

"Ah, how nice. You've come to visit our dollhouses. It's quiet this afternoon, what with the preparations for carnival and all."

Julie looked into the face of an elderly woman with intense dark eyes and silver-white hair. She wore a creamy lace dress and a single strand of milk-white pearls. She looked soft and old-fashioned, rather as if she herself had stepped out of a Victorian dollhouse—perhaps, Julie fantasized, from the music room where she might have been playing the harpsichord. Her voice was soft and southern, and her language seemed cultured.

"Dolls are an important part of our heritage. I've always believed our whole history could be told with dolls," the woman said dreamily.

"I don't know if I'll have time to see everything," Julie said, looking about. The museum seemed larger than it appeared from outside and there were few windows, as if its inner sanctums were all artificially lit.

"You can always come back tomorrow. We're open all day."

"I can—yes. Tell me where to begin and where the most interesting dollhouses are located just in case I don't have time to come back."

"You mustn't miss the dollhouses in that room over there." She pointed off into the distance as if to make clear that she was not a guide and had no intention of conducting a tour.

"They're all dollhouses built after the historic homes of New Orleans," she explained. "The most interesting of all is an exact miniature of the house that belonged to one Miss Desirée Coteau. She was a fascinating woman of much influence in New Orleans and early Louisiana. But I don't need to tell you about her. There's a little pamphlet next to each of the houses that tells the story of their owners."

Julie glanced at her watch. "I think I'll start in that room then," she said. She felt intrigued by what the woman had told her and equally intrigued by her idea that all history could be revealed in dolls.

The woman smiled and Julie thought it a strange smile; a knowing smile. "You may not leave as quickly as you think."

"Oh, that I must do," Julie laughed. "For one thing, suppertime is fast approaching, and for another the museum closes within an hour."

The woman's lips parted. "I meant New Orleans. You may like it so much you never leave."

Julie laughed lightly. "I do like it, but I'm afraid I have a job in New York."

"Ah, you young people are so—so organized. You always think things will go just as you plan them. Perhaps a few aspects of your lives are spontaneous, but for the most part I find the young insist on living by some plan—either that or they fritter away everything on the temptations of twentieth-century culture." She sighed deeply. "One extreme or the other. History, my dear is filled with people whose plans were altered by events. Neither you nor I really know what is going to happen. Our past is certain; our future is a mystery to be explored."

Julie felt almost mesmerized by the woman's eyes. They conveyed a dreamy faraway look and her words seemed so definite, and in some way exciting and full of promise.

"Our future is a mystery to be explored," that was a nice turn of phrase.

The woman looked away and passed her hand over her dress as if to smooth it. "Of course the real past, the everyday past, is also a mystery to us. We can't know the hopes and dreams of those who came before. We can't know the trials of everyday life."

"I love reading diaries for that reason," Julie responded.

"Ah, yes. But some do not even tell their diaries the whole truth. I don't think Miss Desirée Coteau told her diary the whole truth. No, no, I don't think she did."

As if suddenly reminded of something, the woman turned her head. "I have things to do before we close. You'd better hurry along or you won't see anything at all."

"Yes, you're right." Julie turned and headed for the room the woman had recommended.

She looked into several dollhouses, mostly Victorian in their design. Though they were exquisite in their detail, they were ordinary as far as dollhouse displays were concerned.

She then turned with fascination to the recommended house, the miniature of the house once owned by Desirée Coteau. It was a rambling southern mansion—not one with white pillars and pseudo-Greek architecture like so many of the antebellum houses, but rather a two-story wooden house with a wide veranda and wrought-iron trim. Like so many French houses of the day in both New Orleans and Quebec, the iron staircases were on the outside of the homes instead of the inside. Romantic indeed, but not for the reasons most suspected. Under French law, a house without an inside staircase was not considered completed, and thus not subject to full taxation. Thus the ever-inventive French built the staircases on the outside in order to avoid their taxes and still have access to the second story of their dwelling.

Near the display, on a small table, was a pamphlet. Julie picked it up and began reading with interest.

"Desirée Coteau was once the most wealthy and influential woman in Louisiana. A stunning mulatto, she claimed to have knowledge of the supernatural, and many called her a voodoo queen. In truth, she was an intelligent and talented woman, who began her career as a hairdresser. Her profession enabled her to learn many of the secrets of wealthy women. It is thought by many that the base of her wealth was obtained by blackmailing her clients, though to have accrued her eventual fortune, she also must have shrewdly invested her funds. Her home was one of the best known, most finely furnished, and most lavish of New Orleans residences in the late 1700's. She owned both a hairdressing saloon and a fashion saloon. At night, her lavish house functioned as a combination hotel, restaurant, and high-class brothel. It was in Desirée's home that the loveliest and most mannered ladies of the night to be found in all New Orleans had dalliances with the rich and powerful men of Louisiana and their guests.

"But it was her successful import business that brought Desirée Coteau her greatest wealth. It also brought her into direct contact with the power brokers of her time. Her intimates were pirates and gunrunners, generals and spies.

"General Bernardo Galvez, who allied himself with the revolutionaries, spent time in this house as did Oliver Pollock and Brady McCormick, well known gunrunners of the American Revolution. Desirée Coteau played a fascinating role during the American Revolution when her home was the center of planning between the Spanish and the American revolutionaries who sought their help. She was clearly a woman of great strength and great power."

Julie put down the pamphlet distractedly as she turned her eyes back toward the dollhouse. The house itself appeared to be real in almost every sense, and its furnishings seemed more complete than those in any dollhouse she had ever seen. Each room was sheer perfection. The kitchen was large and the stone fireplace had been con-

structed of tiny pebbles to emulate the great stone fire-
places found in all houses of the period. There was even
a tiny room adjacent to the fireplace that, had it been a
real house, would have been used as an oven. The miniature wood stove had pots designed to scale and the furniture—a large table and ladder-backed chairs—was as rustic
as they might have been in the period.

Each of the many bedrooms was furnished to perfection
with large canopied beds and there was even a tiny handmade quilt spread on one. There were pictures on the
walls, small lamps, and an extraordinary array of accessories
including combs and tiny brushes on the dresser.

This seemed to Julie a real house inhabited by real people. The more she looked at it, the more she felt drawn
into it, unable to leave it and move on to view the other
dollhouses.

Almost as if she had consciously avoided it till now, she
allowed her eyes to fall on the large drawing room. It was
furnished with brocaded lounges and sumptuous divans.
There was a sideboard covered with miniature silver and
china. Alone, in the center of the room, was a doll dressed
in a sea-blue silk gown trimmed in white lace. It had long
golden blond hair cascading over its shoulders, and for a
second Julie was struck by the resemblance of the doll to
her own image. But then she spied the music box on the
table next to the spot where the doll was positioned. It was
tiny and perfect—so perfect she ignored the sign which
warned visitors not to touch anything. As if directed by
some unseen force, she picked it up, absolutely intrigued
by it. And then, as she held it, a faint sound came from
it—ever so faint, ever so far away. But could this miniature
actually play? What manner of person built this perfect
house and furnished it with such accurate and wondrous
little things? Her lips parted and she held the box closer
to her ear, straining to hear its distant muted sound.

Suddenly, the warm room where she stood seemed to
grow cold—as if a wind had blown through the entire

building. She heard a door slam shut as she took a step forward just as the room was plunged into absolute darkness.

Her thoughts came in sudden spurts, jumbled and strangely incoherent. A storm. Perhaps a sudden electrical storm had caused the sudden cold, the failure of the electricity. And then that thought was chased away as she fought to remember why she had not noticed this room was without windows. Surely such a place, even though it was a private museum, ought to have windows and proper exits in case of fire. But in this room there was nothing but the absolute darkness, utter darkness, and no battery-operated sign guiding her toward the door.

And there was something else. The sound of the music box, had turned louder and quite real. And the box itself! It had grown in her hands and was now full size, as full size as any music box she herself might own.

"I'm hallucinating," Julie said out loud. Then, holding her hand out, she tried to move across the room, aware of a slight faintness, of a strange eerie feeling—eerie, but not really frightening. She felt more curious than anything. She was certain now that she concentrated on the music box, that she was not hallucinating. But she was at a loss to provide herself with any other explanation for what seemed to have happened. Tiny miniatures did not, after all, suddenly become full size. She reached her free hand out and touched a flat surface. Carefully, she set the music box down. Its song was coming to an end, leaving her in the black silence.

Julie took another step and then ran her hands over her clothing. She was not wearing what she had come into this room wearing! She had on a long dress, a silk dress. How could this be? She took several deep breaths, her heart was pounding wildly. Then, carefully, she continued to grope her way toward the door—or at least toward the place where she thought the door was located. A thousand thoughts occurred and reoccurred. Perhaps she had been unconscious. How else could her clothing have been changed?

Was the entire building blacked out? If it were an electrical storm she supposed the whole area, perhaps even the city, could be without electricity. But still she had heard no thunder, nor had the sky appeared threatening when she left her hotel. She bit her lip hard. Nothing explained the music box. What was happening? What had happened?

Then, as quick as a blink, there was a glow behind her. A soft warm orange glow, and Julie turned abruptly, her mouth opening in surprise, a chill passing through her entire body.

Behind her stood the ornate hand-carved credenza that had been in the drawing room of the dollhouse, its two sets of candelabra ablaze with light, illuminating the room, the very room she had just looked upon in miniature.

"Dear heaven," she whispered in amazement.

Her hands fell from her cheeks to her side and for the first time she saw the silk of her gown, the same long blue gown the blond doll in the house had worn—the doll that had stood in a greatly reduced version of the room where she now stood. Yes, she remembered the dress and she was wearing it! It had long tight-fitting sleeves trimmed in lace and a low-cut neckline. The style of the bodice pushed her breasts upward, revealing deep cleavage even as the whalebone in her corset made her waist seem tinnier. Instinctively she reached for her neck. The only thing that remained of her former clothing was the chain with her award medal. She grasped it tightly. It was her only reality.

"How——?" she asked aloud as she reached out to grasp the edge of the credenza. A dream? An incredibly detailed dream. Yes, that must be it. She closed her eyes and shook her head, commanding herself to wake up. But when she opened her eyes, she was, to her shock, still in the drawing room of the dollhouse even though it was no longer a dollhouse but a full-size house.

Julie's eyes focused on the flickering candles in the silver candelabra as she fought to try to understand what had or was happening. For some reason she herself did not understand, she slipped her chain and medal off. She held it, looking at it hard. It was real. She was real. This room and its furnishings seemed real. But how had she gotten here? And again, how had her clothing been changed? Almost as if an inner voice told her to hide it, she slipped the chain and her medal down her dress where it nestled safe and unseen between her breasts.

She jumped when she heard the door behind her open. She whirled around, stunned to discover she was not alone in what she now thought must be either a dream or a hallucination.

A tall, slender but well-muscled man stepped into the room. She took him for twenty-six or twenty-seven. He wore skintight white breeches, highly polished black boots that came to his knees, and a red jacket dripping with ornate gold braid. He stood stiff and straight with an unmistakable military bearing. At his side rested a sheathed sword with a gold handle. She knew her costumes well enough to recognize an eighteenth-century Spanish military uniform.

His hair was not just dark but *black* and his skin was swarthy and smooth, his eyes almost black. He studied her momentarily, then in a sweeping gesture, he bowed from the waist, doffing his plumed hat as he did so.

"Señorita," he murmured. "Governor Bernardo Galvez *servador de usted.*"

Julie blinked at him almost uncomprehendingly. Could a dream or mere hallucination be so detailed? Could a dream come complete with a handsome stranger who spoke a foreign language?

"Governor?" she heard herself saying. As if he were real, as if any of it were real.

The handsome stranger grinned. *"Sí, El Gubeirno del Louisiana. Que es su nombre, señorita."* His well-shaped brow arched as he spoke.

"Julie," she managed. It was as if all the blood had

drained from her head. She felt faint, too stunned to react properly—though she was at a loss to know what a proper reaction to such an imaginary flight would be? Was she losing her mind? In this all too real hallucination she was standing before a historic character, the one-time Spanish governor of Louisiana, the man for whom Galveston was named, and he had asked her name in Spanish.

"Julie?" he repeated, with a look of amusement.

He had given the J that began her name the sound of H which it had in Spanish, she remembered.

"Ah, you must be English," he said, switching languages with ease. In Spanish your name would be Julieta. Julio is a common name for a man, but Julie would be most uncommon for a woman."

Julie nodded as if she had no tongue. She felt as if she had been struck dumb. "I don't feel well," she said after a long moment.

"You look very pale."

"I feel a bit faint," she whispered, "and I must confess, I don't know how I came to be here."

The young governor's face knit in a frown. "I shall summon a countryman of yours. I don't know how you came to be here, either, señorita, but I do know your presence is more than just a mystery—it may be a problem."

Julie started to speak, but instead she maintained her silence. How could this be happening? She did not feel insane. She did not feel as if this were a dream. She indeed felt as if he and everything in this room was quite real. And why might her presence be a problem as he had stated?

Governor Galvez turned his back and, with a wave of his hand, left the room, closing the door behind him.

"What's happening to me?" Julie hurried around the room touching things, feeling them as if her tactile sense would give her a clue of how to explain this occurrence. Was it a trick? She remembered the words of the woman who had greeted her at the door of this museum. She had spoken obliquely about the past and the present, about spontaneity and indeed about history. She had said, "You might not be able to leave . . ." Julie felt a terrible chill. Was it possible? Could it be? Had she somehow walked through a window in time?

Julie leaned against the chair. Was it possible that time warps really existed? Was it possible that she had somehow been drawn into the past?

She was still trying to fathom what had happened, indeed what was happening, when again the door opened. Governor Galvez stepped inside. Behind him was an even taller man, a man of solid build and obvious physical strength. He wore what appeared to be a white silk shirt that tied at the neck, tan breeches, and high brown leather boots. He was without a jacket, but the rest of his clothing indicated he was not, as Galvez was, a military officer. He, too, had dark hair and dark eyes. But his skin was fair, as fair as her own, and when he spoke it was completely without any kind of an accent. He stared at her without friendliness, his eyes intense. She felt as if he were trying to see through her.

"This is Brady McCormick," the governor said. "And this, Brady, is the mysterious young lady I've found. I shall leave you in the hands of your countryman, Señorita Julieta."

She wanted to object but could not. Instead, she watched helplessly as Governor Galvez left. The man he had brought stared boldly at her, so boldly she felt ill at ease, though such a feeling was, she told herself, absurd under such unreal circumstances.

Brady McCormick rubbed his chin and walked around her as if she were for sale. "There are few English women in New Orleans," he said after a moment of circling her.

Was she to comment? She said nothing.

"This is a private home. You don't live here and I have never before seen you anywhere in this city."

"Well, I didn't break in," she said indignantly. "I don't

even know how I came to be dressed in these clothes or why you people are all dressed up. Is this a play of some sort?''

Brady glared at her. "Do you take me for a fool! You are the stranger here, not I, my woman. You had better be able to explain yourself! As for our clothing, we are dressed as we always dress."

Julie stared at him as cold reality began to creep into her thoughts. What on earth was going to happen to her? She really did feel faint as all the possibilities surged through her mind.

Everything seemed to be circling, not just this man who acted as if she were merchandise. Gray, everything was gray. She gasped slightly and felt her knees buckle as she fell.

Brady stared at her, then lifted her in his arms, laying her down on the divan. She was beautiful! Her skin was exquisite, her hair like yards of spun gold. She was seemingly soft and womanly. Exactly the type of woman the British would send as a spy.

He took two strides toward the door. "Carmelita!" he called out.

The woman he had summoned appeared immediately, her skirts lifted as she ran down the hall toward him.

"Fetch me some smelling salts, please."

"Sí, un momento."

She hurried away but then returned quickly. Brady undid the bottle of rock salts soaked in ammonia and passed them under Julie's nose.

Julie coughed, then blinked open her eyes and looked around. It was the same room and the same man but there was a strange woman standing near him. "You may go," he said to the woman who scurried away without a word, closing the door behind her.

"How did you come to be in this house, in this room?" he asked.

Julie shook her head. "I don't know," she answered honestly.

"Would you be so kind as to follow me?" he asked, bowing ever so slightly.

"And if I said I did mind?"

"Then I should be obligated to carry you."

His voice seemed hard to her, his eyes most definitely penetrating. There was no softness about him and indeed he seemed nothing short of unfriendly.

Julie wondered if she could even walk—her legs felt like rubber.

"It would seem I have no choice," she said.

"None at all," he replied.

Julie pulled herself upright and then stood up. When he opened the door for her, she went through, into what only moments before had been a miniature hallway in a miniature dollhouse.

Why was this man she followed so utterly cold? He did not smile or try to put her at ease. In fact, he seemed almost angry, and most certainly suspicious of her.

Chapter Three

The only light in the hall was provided by fat candles set into iron candle holders that hung on the walls at either end. Brady McCormick cast a long shadow in this narrow, dimly lit corridor down which he strode so knowingly. Julie followed as if sleepwalking, though she was aware that all her senses were now alert and functioning. The entire house was filled with the aroma of perfume, or perhaps, she reasoned, some kind of potpourri. Yet there was a mustiness, a reminder that the lushness of New Orleans coexisted with rot, with the prevailing dampness of the nearby swamps.

A dream? A hallucination? Some crazy reality? No, it seemed as if there were no other explanation but that she had somehow been transported back in time. She forced her mind back to what she had read about this house—if indeed this were the same house, though she readily admitted it appeared to be the same house. With a sudden chill she recalled that Miss Desirée Coteau provided mistresses to wealthy men. If this were real—if somehow she had been transported back in time—could it be that this Brady McCormick person had taken her for such a woman?

He stopped in front of a closed door and she was so lost in thought she almost ran into him. He opened the door and stood aside. To her everlasting relief, it was not a bedroom.

The room was smaller than the one they had just left. It had comfortable-looking chairs in front of a fireplace. In one corner there was a big desk with a quill pen and a box of parchment. On top of the desk a flickering lamp provided the room with its only light.

Assorted leatherbound books were on the shelves that lined one wall. Two other walls held landscape paintings. The third wall had a glass door that seemed to lead out onto a small balcony. Yes, that was right. She could envision the dollhouse in her mind. In fact, she knew just what room she was in. It was a small library.

"Julie," he said, letting her name linger for a moment in the silence. "Have you a last name to go with the first?"

"Hart. Julie Hart."

He raised his brow. "Interesting," he muttered, as he again rubbed his chin thoughtfully. "Well, Miss Hart, may I get you a glass of madeira? You seem upset and disoriented."

"Yes, please," she murmured. Perhaps some wine might clear her head. At the very least it might help her calm down. She felt like a taut, too tightly drawn string on a violin.

Brady walked to a table adjacent to the desk. She hadn't noticed it before, but now she saw it held a crystal carafe of wine and some glasses. He proceeded to pour two glasses of the rich dark madeira.

I really do seem to be in the dollhouse that I was looking at, she mentally conceded. Then, still questioning her own sanity, she asked herself if this could be some kind of Mardi Gras game. A game like one of those plays where the audience participates directly by mingling with the actors?

But no, how could that be? The lights had gone out, and when she turned there was only candlelight. She was not taken anywhere; at no time was she unconscious.

I have to concentrate! She stared at Brady, taking in the details of his clothing and trying to place it more accurately in terms of time. Then she looked at her own clothing. How was it possible to have been wearing an ordinary outfit one moment and be dressed in this manner the next? A room or a set could be changed in the darkness but not her own clothes! Absolute panic swept through her. How could she return to her own time if in reality she had been whisked away? Was it even possible to return? What was happening to her—what *had* happened to her—must be real. It seemed alarmingly clear. She really must be in the eighteenth century. If so, what was the exact date? She needed to know.

She took a large gulp of the madeira. *It* tasted real enough.

"So, Miss Hart, if that is truly your name, where are you from?

Julie felt indignant. "Of course it's my name. New York," she replied. "I'm from New York."

She knew full well that at this time even St. Louis was little more than a trading post.

"I see. How did you come to New Orleans?"

She knew full well that sea was the only plausible answer, but could she invent a story good enough to be believed? She knew the raw history, but there were a thousand and one things she didn't know, little things that could trip her up and prove her a liar. And surely he would ask on what vessel she traveled. She knew of none. There was nothing to do but lie and she knew that the most convincing lies were those that stuck closest to the truth.

"You were quite correct, Mr. McCormick, I am disoriented . . ." She bit her lip for effect. "Perhaps worse." She tried to assume a look of bewilderment, even of fright. In reality her strongest feelings were disbelief and curiosity.

Strangely, perhaps because it was all so new, perhaps because she still doubted her reality, fear had not yet crept into her consciousness.

"Has something happened to you?"

He seemed matter-of-fact and not terribly concerned, but there was nothing to do now but persist with her act. "I confess, Mr. McCormick. I seem to know my name and the fact that I come from New York. But I do not know how I came to be here in this house, or even in New Orleans. Worse yet, Mr. McCormick, I do not know what day and year it is." Vaguely, she doubted if the word *amnesia* were yet known. Nor, she assumed, was trauma—at least not in the mental sense. She could hardly claim to have a condition that had not yet been named.

He looked at her critically, almost with exasperation.

"It is Monday night, April 13, 1779. This is New Orleans on the eve of Mardis Gras, and it is a Spanish territory governed by Don Bernardo de Galvez whom you just met. The colonies, New York among them, are two years into a protracted fight for our freedom."

As soon as he gave the date, she had known the rest. But she had no choice but to continue playing the absolute innocent. "Oh," she replied, trying to look even more distressed.

"And so, Miss Hart, I must know how you came to New Orleans and most especially to this house. I must know your sympathies and the sympathies of your family. I must know with whom you traveled."

She looked at the floor and shrugged helplessly.

"Is your father a supporter of revolution? Or does your father work for the English?"

"My father is dead," she answered softly. It was true, unfortunately.

Brady moved close to her, bent down and looked her straight in the eye. His eyes were not only dark but had a hypnotic quality. At this moment they were without kindness. They were the eyes of an interrogator.

"Where are you staying?"

He did nothing but spout a barrage of questions she could not answer. Her mind raced. "I don't know that, either."

"Did you arrive on the *Maria*? She made port this morning."

Julie took a sip of madeira. "I do not know. I only know I've not been well. I've felt faint and had dizzy spells."

He could not deny that she had just fainted, but everything about her seemed suspicious to him. "I shall have to check with the captain of the *Maria*. In the meantime you will stay here."

He turned and left her, closing the door behind himself. Even as her eyes settled on the door, she saw the movement of the lock. He had locked her in!

Julie pressed her lips together and closed her eyes. Was she being held prisoner? How long did they intend keeping her here? She picked up the glass of madeira and slowly sipped it. It was annoying to be held prisoner—to be treated like some sort of criminal, but she knew she could put this time to good use. She needed time to think, she needed time to try to summon her historical knowledge and remember all she could about this period in time.

For a moment Brady McCormick stood and looked at the door he had just locked. Should he believe her? Could someone really just lose their memory? She did not look as though she had been mistreated, and certainly she appeared the picture of good health. He shook his head at the mystery which her appearance had created, then he headed back to the parlor where Galvez and the de Vega brothers waited. For a moment his thoughts left the woman and turned to his compatriots.

Don Carlos de Vega was like Bernardo Galvez, a visionary who believed in the ideals of democracy and supported the revolution. But Don Fernando de Vega was more skeptical, perhaps, Brady thought, more evasive. He was certainly more jaded. Of the two brothers he liked Don Carlos most and reserved his opinion of Don Fernando. Still, he accepted both as comrades. Galvez was doing everything possible to help the rebels even though Spain remained neutral and the De Vega brothers had declared their willingness to follow Galvez's lead.

But for the moment he had to concentrate on the woman. Much had been discussed at tonight's meeting. She had been found in the adjacent room and the walls were far from soundproof. Had she overheard? Who was this woman Juliet Hart who had mysteriously appeared in the house of Desirée Coteau? As if they did not have enough problems without a lost and disoriented female— if indeed she were lost and disoriented and not a British spy planted in their midst.

Not that under other circumstances he wouldn't have enjoyed her presence, even her helplessness. Who would not? She was exceptionally good-looking. Her hair was splendorous and she was breasted like a swan even though her waist was tiny. Her eyes were the color of blue morning glories, deep, and seemingly filled with secrets. And surely beneath her long skirts were long milk-white thighs and shapely legs leading to ... He shook his head. It was a night for business; the pleasurable aspects of this woman, who might well turn out to be a dangerous spy, would have to wait.

He entered the parlor and bowed from the waist. The intriguing Desirée Coteau had joined Bernardo, Don Carlos, and Don Fernando. Oliver Pollock, his compatriot, would have been here, too, but important business had taken him away for a few days. Dinner would be served soon and most of the guests were now in their costumes.

Desirée was dressed as a bird, a magnificent bird of tropical plumage. She was bedecked in feathers of bright green and red. They were sewn on a net material that fit her body like a stocking, so that in spite of her feathers, her excellent figure was quite evident. Don Fernando, never one to be conservative, was also dressed as a bird, but he had chosen to be a bird of prey, and his costume was jet black. His brother, Don Carlos, was dressed more conventionally as a devil, and he himself had no costume at all. He was dressed as he usually dressed around New Orleans in an open silk shirt and breeches. When it was not too hot, he added his leather vest.

The intriguing Desirée was taller than most women and if one commented on her height, which was done frequently, she recited a kind of litany: "My ancestors were of the Fon," she claimed proudly. Then she went on to explain the Fon were the people of a territory called Cameroon, on the continent of Africa. "My mama was taken to Haiti and there was made the mistress of a Frenchman named Coteau. From my mama I learned all the secrets of the Fon." At this point she would lower her voice to a whisper for effect, her golden cat eyes flickering with excitement. "I learned the secrets of the supernatural, the mysteries of life and death, and the enigma of the darkness."

Brady did not believe in the supernatural, but he would have been the first to admit that Desirée had benefited from the beliefs of others. She was the essence of showmanship, a woman to be admired and to be watched.

As he looked at her, he thought that she was beautiful in a unique way. A woman whose actual age was a mystery, her skin was the color of milky coffee. She had full lips, high, wonderful cheekbones, and a long, graceful neck. Her hair was thick, dark, and rich. Her body was shapely, even sinuous. She reminded him of a beautiful snake— lovely, graceful, and lithe. All in all, she was a woman you wanted with you, not against you. She had power, but not power derived from the supernatural. Her power derived from her intelligence and wealth. Above all else she was shrewd.

Like virtually all the other men of his acquaintance he

had once succumbed to her sexual charms. It was an enjoyable and even educational liaison but not one that was destined to last.

Desirée was not a woman to tie herself down, not to any man.

"And what of our lovely unknown visitor?" Don Fernando asked, touching his mustache and smiling with gleaming white teeth. "Only you and Bernardo have had the pleasure, but Bernardo says she's a beauty. Am I to be denied all night?"

Desirée's smile was filled with innuendo and her perfectly shaped brow was arched. "Come now, darling. You are to be with the wonderful Marguerita tonight! I hardly think you shall be denied."

He looked at her and smiled what Brady thought was an alligator smile. Brady admitted he did not like Don Fernando's smile. It never seemed truly genuine. Perhaps, he reasoned, that was why he did not completely trust Don Fernando. And again he wondered how two brothers could be so dissimilar.

"What do you think, Brady? Is she a spy?" Don Carlos was earnest and concerned.

"If she is a spy she is most badly briefed and very confused," he answered. "Still, we must know more about her. She was in this house during our meeting, in the room next to the one in which we met."

"And could easily have overheard," Desirée suggested. "I could talk to her. I have ways of learning the truth."

Brady shook his head quickly. Whatever Desirée's "ways," he thought his own were more desirable. "I've locked her in the library. I'm going to make some inquires about her. She can stay there till I return."

Desirée shook her head. "No, not in the library. It's downstairs. What if she begins to scream? No, take her to room five upstairs. Its walls are thick and the lock on the door is strong. Yes, that would be much better."

Brady nodded and stood. As if there weren't enough to

do. Now he had to find out about this girl who had seemingly materialized out of thin air.

He flung open the door to the study to find her looking at the books. "What are you doing?" he demanded roughly.

"Trying to find a book to read," Julie answered in annoyance. "You did lock me in. I'm bored."

"Are you trying to tell me you can read?"

"Of course I can read." The words escaped her mouth before she even had a chance to think, to remember how limited literacy was in this age.

"I'll look into that later," he said. "For now you're to come upstairs."

Julie looked at him in surprise. Upstairs? There were nothing but bedrooms upstairs. "I think not," she responded.

"Are you arguing with me?" He scowled at her, and to his surprise, she scowled back.

"I am, yes."

He looked at the set of her jaw. If she could read, she was a hundred times more dangerous than just a simple female spy listening for pillow talk. Obviously she was prideful and stubborn, too. He could see it in her expression. But he hadn't the time to waste in discussion. He strode across the entire room in four strides. Before she even had a chance to object, he seized her by the waist and tossed her over his shoulder. "I hardly have time to argue with the likes of you, missy. As if you weren't enough trouble already!"

"Let me go!" she screamed, but to no avail. His grip was like iron and he had to bend slightly to pass through the doorway. As he carried her shrieking down the hall. A door opened and two men peered out. One of them laughed.

He reached the stairs and he bounded up them and down another long hall till he came to a room marked "five." He kicked open the door with his foot and took her in. She was still screaming and kicking and pounding his back. He felt thoroughly irritated as he dumped her unceremoniously on the bed.

"Get away from me!" she cried.

He looked at her for a long moment. "Hellion," he muttered.

"Don't you dare come near me, you—you rapist!"

He put his hands on his hips and stared at her for a long moment. My God, is that what she thought? Then he broke into peals of laughter. "I have no need of rape," he said after a moment. "My women wait for me."

He moved close to her and she moved away, scrambling to her feet. "What *are* you doing?"

"Preparing to search you."

His hand had been on her! Did he intend undressing her to search her?

"Remove your dress," he ordered. "And shake it out for me."

"You're out of your mind!" Julie said, taking a step backward. "If I am to be searched, send for a female maid to do it."

"I think not," he replied. He moved to the wardrobe and from beside it, withdrew a screen. He set it up. "I should not want to insult your modesty, my woman. Now step behind the screen and undress. If you do not do it, I shall be forced to do it for you."

Even though his tone was one of bemusement, she knew he meant what he said—he wouldn't hesitate to pull the clothes right off her. Reluctantly she stepped behind the screen and began to undress. For a single moment she clutched the medal and chain in her hand. He couldn't see it. But perhaps he wouldn't examine something in plain sight. She laid it on the dresser while her back was turned.

"Throw out your clothes as you disrobe. I must search the hems and check for secret pockets," he called out.

"You're absurd," she fumed.

Brady sat on the side of the bed. The lamp was on the dresser behind the screen. With growing delight he watched her silhouette. This quite erotic shadow show seemed a fitting payment for the scratches and kicks he had endured.

Her dress crumpled round her feet and she tossed it to him. He searched it, and returned his eyes to the screen just in time to see her removing the chemise.

He had to control himself not to make some utterance of pleasure. The shape of her breasts was quite evident, as was the shape of her whole beautiful, desirable body as she moved gracefully, a nude shadow. She threw over the chemise.

"Your shoes, too!" he ordered, watching with tremendous pleasure as she bent over, the curve of her buttocks obvious. He smiled; clearly she did not realize the light was behind the opaque screen. Watching her was like watching a tantalizing, if somewhat ethereal, dance. She was perfectly formed, a delightful vision. But he forced his eyes away from the arousing spectre and searched everything.

"Hurry up," she said with irritation.

"I'm almost done." He looked again at her naked silhouette and then he tossed her clothes back to her.

Soon she came out fully dressed. Then she turned and looked at the screen. At that moment she must have realized he had been watching her. She whirled around, a look of ferocity on her face.

"You bastard!" Julie felt anger and embarrassment. How dare he do such a thing! She turned and slapped him, then ran for the door.

But he reached out and grabbed her long blond hair and pulled her back. "You're to stay in this room!"

He looked at her hungrily, his eyes seeming to burn through her flesh.

"Leave me alone!"

"Gladly. I'll have some food sent up to you, and then

after I've made some inquiries, we'll decide what to do with you.''

"You're despicable!'' she raged, finally finding her voice. "I'm lost and confused and you have taken advantage of me!''

Suddenly he laughed. "Taken advantage of you! If that were true you would be writhing in my arms with pleasure!''

She screamed and stomped her foot, then picked up a vase and hurled it at him. But he ducked as it fell against the door.

"Desirée will make you work off the value of that vase,'' he said, shaking his finger at her.

"Get out!''

He laughed again. "Gladly.''

He left and again locked the door behind himself. He smiled as he descended the winding staircase. What a delectable creature! She was like cream and strawberries—milk-white skin and no doubt ruby-red nipples. And what a temper! He congratulated himself on not having taken her there and then.

But he did wonder at her haughtiness. He grinned and again looked at the scratches on his hand. Surely no spy would be so purposefully irritating. A good spy, especially one so lovely, would have encouraged seduction in hopes of prying secrets from him during lovemaking. For a second he thought of making love to her and it caused him to smile again.

"I rather hope you're not a spy,'' he whispered to himself as he admitted silently that this was a woman he really wanted to know.

Julie collapsed onto the bed and trembled as the anger drained out of her. What was she to do? She didn't know how she got here, or even for certain if this were real. But it certainly seemed real and she had no choice but to accept the fact that she was locked up in the bedroom of an eighteenth-century whorehouse in New Orleans.

Julie lifted her hands to her cheeks and found her face was hot and flushed with anger and embarrassment. No, she admitted to herself reluctantly, it was not just anger and embarrassment that made her blush. She had felt a second of excitement when she saw the lust in Brady McCormick's eyes. Yes, there had been a fleeting moment of desire for this man who had watched her disrobe. And certainly if he had intended to harm her, he would not have stopped just because she screamed and lost her temper. She sat on the edge of the bed and tried to think about him and about her situation. She shook her head. What was she to do? She didn't know how she got here or even if all this was real.

"Damn," she muttered. "And damn that arrogant man!"

After a few minutes Julie looked around the room. It was quite elegant. The wall was covered not in paper but in a silklike fabric in a soft pink rose pattern—velvet relief style. She ran her hand across it, feeling the velvet of each cluster of roses.

The furniture consisted of a mahogany wash table with a porcelain bowl on it for water, a dressing table with a mirror, and a huge four-poster double bed on a raised dais. A locked captain's chest was at the foot of the bed. Two windows provided light and French doors led to the balcony. The doors, she noted, were also locked. In one corner there was a fireplace with two gentlemen's chairs on each side. In front of the fire was a large fur rug. In one corner there was a table with a carafe of wine and glasses, probably madeira, the same as downstairs. And of course the screen behind which he had made her undress. In an adjacent room there was a large metal tub for bathing.

Was this just an ordinary bedroom? It seemed more than that as she looked about. Most certainly it was one of the rooms where Desirée's ladies of the evening entertained. The rug, the chairs, the large bed, the wine—everything seemed to suggest the room was used for more than sleeping.

She pulled herself off the bed and walked around carefully examining her surroundings some more. On the dressing table an array of items were laid out. Perfume bottles, powders, a silver comb, and a hand mirror.

She picked up the mirror and held it so she could see the back of her hair. It was a tangled mass of blond curls. Then she sat down on the little stool and studied her image in the larger mirror. Her clothes were the clothes the doll in the dollhouse had worn, though she had no idea how they came to be on her body.

She stroked the fabric. It was real silk and a lovely shade of powder blue, almost the same hue as her eyes. Its sleeves were three-quarter length, and beneath them were fine chantilly lace ruffles. The same lace covered her low-cut bodice. She stood up, lost in fascination. Her career was costume design. She had supervised the making of costumes like this, but those costumes were made of modern fabrics and sewn on sewing machines. This dress was the real thing, hand sewn of natural fabrics and ever so much more flattering to a woman's figure than she had imagined from her replicas. The lace was more delicate, and the silk clung to her, falling gracefully from her hips.

Her eyes fell on her neck and her own cleavage. It was deep and revealing. Her face flushed as she remembered how Brady McCormick had stared at her. His lust-filled eyes had fallen there. She shook her head to dispel the memory of his eyes. If he was interested in her at all, it was as an object. And if he wasn't really an eighteenth-century man, he certainly acted like one.

Again she tried to think. How could this be anything but real? She thought once more about the possibility of a play within a play, of some sort of trick. But no. It was all far too elaborate. The unthinkable, the imaginable, seemed to have happened to her. Somehow, someway, while looking at the dollhouse, she had found a window in time and moved through it. Was it possible? Or had her imagination simply run amok? Had she been watching too many episodes of the *Twilight Zone*? And if she had stepped through time, how was she to get back?

Apprehension and curiosity were the twin emotions that fought for Julie's attention. If it were real, she would have to be careful, but what a wonderful opportunity! This was a world about which she had only read. Now she could experience it. A part of her felt a certain thrill, a fascination with the unknown. *Yes,* she thought. *I must use this time alone wisely. I must think of a believable story to explain myself. And I must win over Desirée because she can help me.*

She then closed her eyes, trying to think of all the things that might give her away. Abstractedly, she touched her fingers to her neck and remembered the chain and medal she had left on the dresser in plain sight. He had searched her clothes thoroughly, but he hadn't seen it, and as her back had been turned, he hadn't noticed her putting it there. She sucked in her breath. She had been lucky. Where could she hide it? She prodded around under the covers of the bed until she found in one corner a small hole where the mattress stitching had come loose. She poked at the mattress which was stuffed with Spanish moss, commonly used for stuffing furniture by the inhabitants of Louisiana at this time. She forced her chain and silver medal into the hole and then pulled on the thread to tighten the hole back up. It would be safe there, she thought. And she could retrieve it when necessary.

Brady McCormick made his way through the milling crowds at the dockside market. Soon the festivities would begin and costumed revelers would parade through the streets till dawn. As always, it would be a night-long orgy of dancing, eating, and lovemaking. As always, the Caribbean rum would flow freely, at first releasing the inhibitions, then dulling the senses till sleep crept upon the partygoers. New Orleans was a hard place for the outsider to imagine. It was peopled with freed black slaves, mulattoes from the islands of the Caribbean Sea, most especially from exotic Haiti, Frenchmen from the highest and lowest echelons of society, Cajuns who had been dispersed from Acadia in the most northern part of the British Colonies, Spaniards of all castes, and of course American revolutionaries like himself—men who fought to overthrow the yoke of British colonialism. Brady McCormick dreamed a heady dream. He dreamed that his sons, if there were any, would be the first generation to live free—they would be Americans.

New Orleans was an exciting, exotic place. A tower of Babel where even the language of the city was a unique patois composed of Spanish, French, English, and words from African languages.

The *Maria,* a Spanish galleon whose mast had been damaged in an April storm, was tied up to the dock. Her proud white sails were folded, her decks devoid of activity save for the lethargic watch officer.

"Yo!" Brady called out from the bottom of the gangplank.

The guard moved his ungainly rifle and stood at the top looking down. *"Como se llama? Que es usted negocio?*—state your name and your business," he ordered from on high.

"Brady McCormick. *Hay que con su capitan!"*

The guard did not answer only turned and called out in Spanish. Another guard appeared instantly, showing that they had left a skeleton crew aboard.

The two men spoke rapidly, and finally the man who had been summoned disappeared. A few minutes went by, and then a large heavyset man with a handlebar mustache and thick black beard appeared. He was uniformed in white cotton trimmed in red and gold braid. He wore a three-cornered black hat, also trimmed in gold. His uniform clearly identified him as the captain.

"English?" the man shouted down, hands on his ample hips.

The Spanish, on the whole, were no more fond of the British than the French. Indeed, Galvez believed that one day soon Spain would enter the war on the side of France, a country that had allied herself with the revolutionaries.

"Colonist! A revolutionary!" he shouted.

The captain dropped his hands from his hips and motioned Brady aboard. The designation of revolutionary obviously made him more acceptable.

Brady bounded up the gangplank. "Do you speak English?" he queried.

"Yes, but not by choice. I learned when I was a prisoner."

Brady said nothing. Regardless of how the captain knew English, the fact that he did understand made things easier. His own Spanish was passable, but perhaps not good enough for questions of import.

"Come, we'll go to my cabin." The captain led the way and Brady followed. "I'm surprised to find you aboard on such a night," he said, making casual conversation.

"I will go ashore soon. I stayed only to finish a manifesto."

"It is a night of much gaiety. New Orleans is full of beautiful women."

The captain chuckled as he opened the door to his luxurious suite. "I'm looking forward to them. A glass of rum?"

"Thank you," Brady said, seating himself.

"And what brings you to the *Maria*? Why are you not enjoying the beauties of New Orleans?" He poured rum into two mugs and handed one to Brady.

"It is about a beauty that I come. Perhaps you can help me."

"Perhaps." He took a swig of rum, then ran his tongue round the rim of his mouth, making sure every drop was taken from his mustache.

"There is a woman, a very beautiful woman. She has

thick golden hair and blue eyes. Her skin is like milk and her figure perfect. She appeared this evening in the home of Desirée Coteau. She knows not from whence she came and knows nothing but her name. She does not even know how she got to New Orleans. Yours is the only ship to have arrived in the past few days. I wondered if you transported her."

The captain laughed. "Had I seen or transported such a vision she would be tied to my bed even now! No, my friend, I am deeply sorry to say I have seen no such woman."

Brady nodded. He had known it was unlikely that a Spanish captain would have let so beautiful a woman go. He finished his rum. "Thank you for your hospitality," he said, bowing slightly.

The captain nodded. "Have you been in New Orleans long?"

"Six months," Brady responded. He might have added, "this time," but he did not. Many knew his sympathies were with the revolution, but the fewer who knew the details of his business, the better. New Orleans was awash with spies; likely even his mysterious beauty was a spy. And if she was, she had come to the right place.

"You've been here long enough!" the captain said, slapping his leg. "Tell me where I should go tonight for the best entertainment."

Brady thought for a long moment. If this captain wanted one woman and would treat her well, Desirée's was the place to go. But he sensed from the conversation that this was not what the captain desired.

He thought of El Gato, a Spanish inn where the waitresses were stunning golden women with long sinuous legs. They wore no tops on special nights like Mardi Gras. Their bare full breasts were rubbed with aromatic oils and they danced close to a man, touching him and arousing him. For a fee a man could take one or more away with him—

that was definitely the place for the captain. "El Gato," he returned. "You will enjoy it there."

After spending a few more minutes with the captain, Brady then left the *Maria*, and hands thrust in his pockets, walked back toward Desirée's. Juliet Hart, or whomever she was, awaited him there.

He vowed he would get the truth out of her.

As Brady McCormick approached Desirée's house light seemed to pour from every window and he could tell the Mardi Gras celebration had begun.

It was Desirée's custom to wine and dine her specially invited guests, then, costumed and ready for a night of revelry, they would all leave her house just before midnight to party in the streets till the first rays of dawn were apparent in the eastern sky.

Brady went in and followed the red-carpeted hallway to the winding staircase. In the main dining room some twenty persons were being served a sumptuous sit-down dinner presented on heavy silver trays. The aroma of steamed shrimp, chicken, and hot meat in some sort of spicy sauce and rice assaulted his nostrils as he climbed the stairs.

Brady paused before the door which Julie was locked behind and then unbolted it.

At his entrance Julie turned suddenly, her blue eyes wide. Clearly he had startled her. Still, she did not look frightened, only defiant.

"I've been to the *Maria*. You did not come to New Orleans on that vessel."

"Well, I came here somehow," she answered.

He closed the door. "I think you're a British spy."

"I am not a spy." She pressed her lips together. "I know there's no way I can convince you. I believe I was kidnapped. I may have been brought here some time ago—I only remember being held in a dark place and then walking till I came to this house.''

He looked into her eyes. He certainly wanted to believe her, but lives depended on his being careful.

"I have nothing to hide," she said. Immediately she thought of her medal and chain which she had hidden in the mattress. How glad she was that she had thought of that!

"You will stay here till you have convinced me of your innocence."

"Are you the law of the land?" she snapped.

"Be grateful, woman!" He narrowed his eyes. "I could have you thrown into the jail. I don't fancy a woman like you would come out the way she went in! Worse things could happen to you than to be locked in this room till I have satisfied myself that you're not a spy."

Julie scowled at him, but this time she kept her silence. She knew enough of history's realities to know he was probably right.

"If you remember anything or decide to tell the truth, knock on the door and one of the maids will come. You can have me summoned."

Julie did not answer him. She did not even look up when he closed and locked the door from the outside.

After leaving Julie, Brady smoothed his unruly hair and went downstairs to the dining room where he joined the other guests.

"What of our lovely visitor?" Don Carlos asked.

"I've decided she should stay. But she bears watching."

"I shall question her before we leave," Desirée said, lifting a glass of wine to her full lips. "I shall have to see how best this woman can make herself useful. I have no use for idle hands. She must earn her own keep even if she stays here against her will."

"So that is how you became so rich," Don Carlos laughed.

"I became rich because I know what others want."

Don Fernando also drank some wine. He turned to Desirée and half laughed. "You became rich because you know secrets."

Desirée smiled enigmatically. "Secrets are always worth money."

"Tonight is a night for secrets, my dear Desirée." Don Fernando leaned over and kissed her ringed fingers. "Trysts will be made and vows broken."

Desirée laughed throatily. "It is, my dear, a night for listening and learning."

With those words, she stood up. "I'll return in time to go out with all of you onto the streets of New Orleans. But now I must visit my newest guest. Perhaps I shall even bring her down."

"For now she is in your care," Brady said.

Desirée took her mask and left. Eyes lingered on the doors she passed through, ears listened for her footsteps in the hall.

Desirée opened room five and went in.

Desirée Coteau introduced herself with a graceful bow of the head to Julie.

"I want to leave," she said firmly.

Desirée shrugged. "But of course you do. Tell me, where would you go?"

Julie looked into Desirée's ever so slightly slanted golden eyes. They were wonderful eyes, knowing eyes. Desirée's question lingered. Where *did* she want to go? This was not a place she knew. This was not her world nor her century. She guessed that many dangers lurked beyond the walls of this house.

"You hesitate," Desirée whispered. "I suspect that I have asked a question without an answer. If you are truly alone, there are few things a woman alone can do to earn money. And one must have money in order to live."

That much was the same, Julie thought. One always needed money to survive. "I am truly alone," Julie answered. Even as she said it Julie wished she would be whisked back to her own time. At first she thought it might be fun to be here, but now she began to see the complications. Was this adventure permanent? What would she do? She certainly knew one thing: Desirée was right. There were very few things she could do to support herself. This century, far more than her own, belonged to men.

"Come downstairs. You will join us for a brandy."

Desirée led, and Julie followed.

In the library, men and women mingled. They were all drinking and laughing. Julie's eyes moved from one to another. The women appeared to be Desirée's women and the men were a mixed group of military officers and civilians. In one corner she saw Governor Galvez and across the room, Brady McCormick.

Desirée poured her a brandy and then took her to Don Carlos. "Don Carlos speaks your language," she said by way of introduction.

Don Carlos bowed from the waist. "Señorita."

Julie smiled at him. He seemed to be a gentleman.

"You're very beautiful, señorita."

Julie blushed. She was not used to such compliments from men. In her own time it seemed they confined themselves to meaningful looks.

"I am told you are from New York."

"Yes, it is all I can remember."

"What a terrible pity. We are all hungry for news of the rebellion and its successes."

Julie had to concentrate. His words reminded her that news traveled slowly and that she must be cautious about what she revealed.

"I pray for their success," Don Carlos said earnestly. "I would willingly discard this uniform which denotes my rank and station. I dream, my dear, of a world ruled by republics, a world where all men are treated fairly and equally."

She held her tongue and did not mention all the oppressed minorities. "May your dreams come true," she said, sipping some of the brandy in her glass. Its heat filled her chest with warmth.

"Drink up!" a male voice called out. "Drink up! It's time to go out and celebrate!"

"I daresay we've kept ourselves from the revelers long enough," Desirée added.

In a second she was back at Julie's side. "Come my dear. I'm afraid you must stay in tonight. It's so confusing out there. We wouldn't want you to get lost." She looped her arm through Julie's and Julie did not resist. They moved to the room down the hall, the smaller study where Brady had first interrogated her.

"I must ask you to stay here," Desirée said softly. *"Adieu.* And as I am trusting you down here, please do not scream."

Julie stood for a moment in surprise as Desirée locked the door. Somehow she had hoped her ordeal was over. Did this mean she was still under suspicion?

She strained her ears to listen. She heard most of the revelers depart, but there were still voices in the adjacent room. She pressed her ear to the wall and listened.

"We must keep her here for now," she heard Desirée say.

"I do not think she is a spy," Don Carlos whispered.

"If there's the slightest chance she works for the British we must keep her where Desirée can watch her." The other man spoke, Don Fernando.

Julie backed away from the wall. Suddenly she felt very unsafe, more unsafe than she had felt before. She looked around the room in which she was held prisoner. But this time she looked not because she was amazed or bewildered by her surroundings, but because she wanted to escape. Perhaps if she just got out of this house she would be returned to her own time. Perhaps the house was enchanted or magical or—

She went to the window and forced it open. It had iron bars. She grasped them and suddenly realized two were loose. The bars were more for decoration than protection!

She examined them more carefully and saw they were loose at the bottom and that if she pushed upward, she could take them out. She did, and the space created was quite enough for her slim body to push through. She glanced around the room one last time, then she squeezed through the bars and pulled the drapes shut behind her.

For a single second she inhaled the damp night air. It was slightly foggy, and in the distance she could perceive only eerie flickering lights.

She ran across the garden and through another, then she emerged onto the street. Hearing music and singing, Julie walked through the night and hurried toward the sound.

Chapter Four

"*Mon Dieu!*" Desirée said in dismay as she looked about.
"I must have left my mask in the room upstairs."

"All New Orleans awaits you, my dear," Don Fernando
said with a flourish. "But I suppose you too must have a
mask even though no costume could possibly hide your
beauty."

Ah, nothing like being the only truly sober person in a
room full of those who had been drinking, Brady thought.
He almost laughed. It was obvious everyone else had par-
taken of ample liquor while he had been gone. Not as
much as they would drink before the sun came up, but
enough to loosen the tongue and turn men into fine actors.
Don Fernando, usually the more sullen of the De Vega
brothers was full of gaiety and his mannerisms, more often
dismissive, were tonight as full of flourishes as his words
were laden with adjectives.

"I shall only be a moment." Desirée hurried upstairs
and down the hall to room five. She opened the door
and checked for her mask. She shook her head and
then it occurred to her that she must have left it in the

study, the room in which she had ultimately locked the prisoner.

Still, just to make certain, Desirée's sharp eyes surveyed every corner of the room. She frowned as she observed the end of the bed. It looked as if someone had removed the sheet—it was not as neat as the other corners.

She moved quickly to examine it and she felt around as she lifted the corner of the sheet. The heavy thread that held the mattress together had been tightened but not knotted. She loosened it again with her long nail, then poking a finger inside the mattress, she felt something— something strange. She pulled the object out, holding it down under the lamp so she could examine it. What strange thing was this? It was clearly a silver pendant and chain. And there was writing in English! She squinted and held it still closer to the light.

The words jumped out at her. "Best Costuming in a Historic Drama, 1992." On the back were the words, "Presented to Julie Hart by the American Playhouse Academy of Costume and Design."

"Nineteen ninety-two." Desirée whispered the words and even her steady hand began to shake ever so slightly. This coin was like no other she had ever seen. It was small, yet clearly it was a coin of real silver. 1992! Two hundred and fourteen years into the future! The woman could be nothing less than a time traveler!

Desirée dropped the chain and the silver medallion as if it were red hot. Then she picked it up and stuffed it back where she had found it, pulling the thread together again, leaving it just as she had found it. Miss Juliet Hart would return for her coin, of that Desirée was certain. For the moment it would be more advantageous if the young woman did not know she had found the pendant. A time traveler! To what uses could her special knowledge be put? Many, Desirée concluded. She felt wonderful! For into her possession had fallen a woman who knew the future for certain. Desirée smiled. It did not matter if this were the devil's work, or simply a quirk in the universe. It would be worth a great deal. Yes, she thought, a great deal.

She composed herself, went back downstairs and opened the door of the library—the room in which she had left Julie Hart locked. She opened the door and for a moment stood in its entrance. The girl was gone! She hurried to the window and pulled aside the drapes. Two iron bars were missing. She immediately surmised they were on the ground below, no doubt in the bushes. The little minx!

Silly girl, Desirée thought. What difficulties would be caused looking for her! But she must be found. At least the girl's disappearance was quickly noted and her head start reduced. If her absence had not been discovered before morning, they most certainly would never find her. Still, it was enough of a problem. This was Mardi Gras and that would surely complicate matters.

"I see you've retrieved your mask," Don Fernando said when she returned.

Desirée did not even look at him. "We've lost our prisoner! She found two loose bars on the window and seems to have escaped. I want her recaptured!"

"And we shall have to search for her. Who knows what she might have overheard before we found her," Don Carlos said.

Don Fernando stood up. "Who indeed! Well, my friends, you join the revelers and I shall institute a search for the young lady. I will alert my personal guard. She cannot have gotten far."

Brady frowned only slightly. "I'll search the eastern part of the quarter and you take the rest. We'll meet in two hours at the church."

"Fair enough," Don Fernando agreed.

"And Don Carlos and I shall go to the square and keep our eyes open, "Desirée assured him. "I am sure if she is to be found, we will find her. And if she is telling the truth, which I believe she is, she will have to make inquiries because she will be lost and unsure of herself."

Brady nodded. It seemed clear that Desirée believed the girl was not a spy, but he did not know what to think. He only knew that no matter how lovely she was, caution had to be taken.

Desirée led her flock away, and Don Fernando launched out on his own. Brady himself headed in yet another direction. Miss Julie Hart, if that was her real name, certainly could not have traveled far.

Julie kept to the shadows, her mind rerunning the events of this afternoon and evening. Perhaps she would round the corner onto Bourbon Street and find it once again lit by electric lights. Perhaps beyond the French Quarter, which would have been closed off because of the parade, there were cars and streetcars. Perhaps all this was a dream from which she would soon awaken.

The noise of the merrymakers grew louder as Julie rounded the corner and saw that nothing had changed. The light from the windows of various buildings clearly came from candles, and where Bourbon intersected with what in her time was the main street of New Orleans, there was nothing. No cars sped along, no streetcars traveled their tracks. Indeed, there were no tracks.

She sighed and once again accepted what seemed her new reality. She had been whisked away, carried through time and left here to experience those things about which she had only read.

Bourbon Street was absolutely full of people. She stood in the shadows and watched, taken aback by the sights and sounds of the carnival.

Beautiful, scantily clad mulatto women danced in the street. Their costumes were minimal and clearly designed to show off their bodies. They wore grotesque makeup rather than masks. Many had chalk-white faces, painted eyes, and mouths made large and ruby red.

The men, for the most part, did not seem to be in costume, though they certainly did wear masks.

Those were the street revelers. But there were other sorts of celebrants. There were huge floats drawn by horses, and fine carriages as well as gaily decorated wagons. The women on the floats, wagons, and in the carriages were elegantly dressed in what she imagined was the most expensive refinery available in this century, and no doubt imported from Paris. They wore powdered wigs and their delicate manicured fingers gripped the more common hand-held mask.

The men who accompanied these women were costumed. They wore crowns and elaborate capes. Their shirts were ruffled and many of them seemed to be wearing articles of clothing that composed some sort of uniform.

She hurried on, turning a few corners and still keeping to the shadows.

Suddenly, as if on cue from some invisible leader, music filled the air and the crowds parted as dancers came down the middle of the street—shocking dancers filled with more than the spirit of Mardi Gras.

There were twelve huge African men dressed in loin cloths. In the lantern light, their skin glistened with perspiration as they danced. Some turned cartwheels, others did hand stands. Everything was in rhythm with the drums. Then with a startling shriek, they were joined by bare-breasted women whose dark skin looked like soft velvet and gleamed with the oils with which they covered themselves.

These dancers were watched, but not joined by others. Suddenly, Julie felt fingers enclose her arm. She turned and looked into the eyes of a man whose face was covered with stubble and whose breath smelled heavily of rum.

"A blond princess," he slurred even as he smiled. "What luck have I tonight. Let me see that shoulder. 'Tis it really as white as it appears?"

He jerked down the sleeve of Julie's dress, baring her shoulder.

"Let go of me!" She struggled and was surprised at the strength of his grip.

"Pretty," he muttered. "Do you like the voodoo dancers, my pretty?"

Julie summoned her strength and kicked him, even though such a movement was difficult when one was wearing such cumbersome clothing.

He winced and in surprise let Julie go. She lifted her skirts and began running. It was apparent, as it should have been from the beginning, that this was no place for a woman alone. The women on the floats were all escorted and removed from the crushing crowds. Even the half-naked voodoo dancers had escorts. Apparently there were only two kinds of women on the streets. Those who were with escorts and those who were looking for a sexual liaison.

Julie kept running, staying close to buildings where no one would notice her, speaking to no one and stopping for nothing.

Juan Antonio Martinez was twenty-six years old. His father, and his father's father before him, had all been in the employ of the aristocracy. It was a comfortable life since close personal guards and confidants of those who ruled were the receivers of many favors.

Like his friend and employer, Don Fernando de Vega, Juan Antonio Martinez did not believe in the principles of the American Revolution, nor the changes it might well bring to Spain and France. He saw in such radical idealism an end to the system under which he and his family had flourished for centuries. How could such ideas succeed? How could they end in anything save utter chaos? In his eyes liberty for the masses meant license as well. And the very idea of "electing" rulers struck him as both humorous and dangerous. After all, those who elected a leader would be supporters, and supporters would surely be rewarded with power and position. Well, he was a supporter of royalty and he was rewarded with power and position. Thus, all this republicanism, with its far-flung and most dangerous ideas, would simply change those persons in power without really altering a system as old as human nature. Cream, he reasoned, always rose to the top.

If only Don Fernando's brother, Don Carlos de Vega, felt the same. But he did not. Don Carlos, like Bernardo Galvez, was a passionate convert to republicanism. Both favored Spain entering the war on the side of France and the colonies.

Of course a man could not always be open about his beliefs. Neither he nor Don Fernando agreed with Galvez even if he was aristocracy, and even if he was the governor. Nonetheless, they pretended to be republicans. They did so to find out what was going on and to subtly thwart each move the young republicans made before the effect was too great. They informed those who agreed with them in Spain, and they informed the British, too. As an aside, a pretty penny was to be made from the British. They were willing to pay, and pay well, for information.

Don Fernando had other reasons as well, reasons well known to Martinez. Don Fernando and Don Carlos were twins. Not identical twins, but rather fraternal twins. Indeed, they looked nothing alike. Their father was Gabriel de Vega, a first cousin to Don Juan de Sepulveda whose family had received a land grant from the king of Spain for nearly all of the glorious territory comprising what was known as southern California to the few English settlers who had made their way west. The de Vegas and the Sepulvadas were among the wealthiest families in New Spain. Those who were the inheritors were to be envied, and hence the difficulty. Each family must have a single heir, estates such as the de Vegas' were not divided. The first son inherited, while the second had certain defined rights. In the case of twins there was no clear inheritor, especially since at birth the midwife had become confused and didn't know which child had entered the world first.

All of their lives, Don Gabriel de Vega had made his favorite clear. He adored Don Carlos. Some said that Don Gabriel chose Don Carlos because of the two he was the best looking. Of course, that was true. Don Carlos was tall and suave. He had fine features and dark hair. Don Fernando, on the other hand, had swarthy skin and sharp features. Over all, there was a lupine quality to his appearance.

Others said that their father chose Don Carlos because he was the more intelligent of the two. Juan Antonio Martinez found it hard to differentiate. He did feel that Don Fernando was the most shrewd. Perhaps in the raw, rough world of reality he was the most likely to survive.

Juan Antonio Martinez looked about and to his relief he saw Don Fernando approaching. As promised, he was alone.

"You're late," Antonio admonished.

"I had difficulty getting away from the others. Of course I'm supposed to be looking for some young girl."

Antonio Martinez smiled a dirty smile. "Aren't we all."

"Not this one. She was found in the house of Desirée Coteau. She is a stranger, and a most lovely one."

"What's the problem?"

"They thought perhaps she was a spy. But she isn't."

Antonio laughed. "Why would they need more than they have?"

"Only we know that, my friend. In any case, when we are finished I must go look for her. I will say she was a tasty morsel."

"Perhaps I should help you."

"I fear you shall be otherwise occupied. We met tonight with Brady McCormick. Galvez, that fool, is providing a ship. It will leave New Orleans tomorrow night, laden with arms for the rebels."

"What ship?"

"*El Dorado.*"

"I know that vessel. She used to be a treasure ship. She's fast."

Don Fernando drew a sheath of papers from inside his cloak. "This is her route. You must take these to Romero tonight and have them copied. I need them back by tomorrow. When her route has been copied, pass it to our English friend, Benson."

"As you wish, Don Fernando."

Don Fernando smiled. Yes, even his sharp pointed teeth had a lupine quality. Especially his teeth, Martinez thought.

Julie crept along, still trying to keep in the shadows, close to the buildings. She tried each door she passed, hoping to find one that was open. What she wanted most was a place where she could get off the street and be safe. But she realized she was wandering aimlessly and that although most of the revelers were in the street, almost all were drunk by now. She cursed herself for having left the house of Desirée Coteau. In spite of their suspicions about her, she now realized that she would have been safer there. Perhaps, she reasoned, she could find her way back and get in the same way she had gotten out. It was even possible that she had not yet been missed.

She paused for a moment and tried to picture a map of the French Quarter in her mind. It was not laid out on a modern grid, but it was not so complicated, either. She cursed the darkness.

"What's this!"

Julie was spun around by the huge dark man who had grabbed her arm. He shouted out in a patois she did not understand, and she found herself propelled out of the darkness and into the torch light.

A cry went up from the crowd. Julie looked around frantically. Surely she had wandered to a part of the city in which she should not be. At least not in the year 1779.

The crowd parted magically as the big man jettisoned her forward into the center of a circle, which immediately closed around her.

In the center of the circle a naked drummer began to beat his drums and the circle of people around her all began to dance. It was a wild frantic dance, a frightening dance. Men were stripped to loin cloths, and women wearing only cloth skirts danced around them.

She stood still, mesmerized by the rhythm and frightened by the sights around her. Then she suddenly saw the circle open ever so slightly, and a man entered it. The circle again closed behind him.

He was a horrible-looking man, old and scrawny with shoulder-length white hair and long yellow teeth. His face was skeletal and his eyes bloodshot. He waved his hands at Julie and she shrank back instinctively because his fingers were long and his nails, like his teeth, were long and yellow. He was dressed in long purple robes trimmed in gold.

He raised his hands toward the sky and made a terrible sound from deep inside his throat. She wanted to bolt and run, but she knew she could not. She was absolutely surrounded.

Suddenly the old man withdrew a chicken from his cloak. He threw it on the ground and it ran around frantically, fenced in by the circle the same way she was. And then she saw the old man had a knife, a long, sharp, glistening knife.

Julie's blood ran cold. She had the sudden feeling of being near pure evil, and she realized that this had to be a voodoo ceremony. Most certainly they intended on sacrificing the chicken, but what of her?

As the old man grabbed the chicken she covered her eyes and screamed. Then she jumped as gunfire rang out. When she finally dared to open her eyes, the circle had dispersed and all who had been in it were running.

A strong arm pulled her up off the ground and onto a carriage.

"Looks like I found you just before the devil himself!"

Julie looked at the driver and recognized her rescuer as one of the men who had been at the home of Desirée Coteau. She recognized him because of his fine costume. Adorned in black feathers, he was dressed as a large crow. He wore no mask over his face.

"Thank goodness you came," she breathed. He quickly moved the carriage away as the crowd parted to make way for the big stallions. Many in the crowd looked angry while others were screaming and shaking their fists. "Did you fire the shots?" she asked anxiously.

"I fired into the air. To disperse the crowd."

"I'm fortunate that you came along."

"Yes, you are. They were very drunk and when drunk they can be dangerous. Ignorant and superstitious people live in this area. I'm afraid my timely arrival may have deprived them of a sacrifice."

"A sacrifice—my God."

"A fate worse than death, they say. They practice the ancient art of voodoo. They have drugs, powerful drugs, that can make the living appear dead. Once you have been forced to take the drugs you never recover. They say you walk among the living dead."

Julie did not dare look at him. Was he telling her the truth or was he intentionally trying to frighten her? In her own time she knew weird crimes had been committed by those who presumably practiced a strange religion related to voodoo called Santeria. And she had read an article once about the practice of voodoo in Haiti and how a serum derived from a poisonous shellfish was used to produce a drug that induced a zombielike state. Yes, she decided, these people had that ability. And most certainly he was right. She had strayed into a strange neighborhood, a place away from the French Quarter. Yet wasn't Desirée Coteau said to be a voodoo queen?

"It is true that I do not know how I came to New Orleans

or to the home of Desirée Coteau, but I do remember
being told that she was a voodoo queen."

Don Fernando looked at her and grinned. "Ah, yes.
Well, she is not the sort of voodoo queen or practitioner
you just met. There is voodoo and there is voodoo. Desirée
is a master of magic, of theatrics, of grand illusion. She
uses superstition to her advantage; she knows the magic
of making money. She is also a respected businesswoman."

Julie nodded. She had suspected as much from what she
read.

"Where are you taking me? Back to Desirée's house?"

He shook his head. "No, to my house. Where you can
relax and refresh yourself. Where you will be safe."

"Thank you. I am sorry to say I don't remember your
name."

"Don Fernando de Vega."

"You have a brother, don't you?"

"Don Carlos. But we don't live together."

Julie studied the man who had taken her away from the
threatening mob. He was not as good-looking as Brady
McCormick nor as cheerful as Don Carlos, his brother.
Indeed, had the circumstances been different, he would
be the kind of man whom she would avoid because there
was something about him—perhaps a shifty appearance.
He seemed to avoid eye contact, but there was no denying
she was glad he had come along, and she reminded herself
that one could not tell a person's worth by their looks.
After all, Brady McCormick was very good-looking, even
charming when with others. But he had watched her
undress! He had tricked her. Though, she admitted reluctantly, he had not actually touched her. And he had
searched her clothing very thoroughly. But surely he could
have gotten a woman to search her if indeed such a search
were necessary. On the other hand, perhaps he was justi-
fied in being suspicious. After all, he was working for the
gunrunner and American revolutionary, Oliver Pollock,

and she had appeared out of nowhere and without explanation.

She reminded herself that her fear in the street had been real. That the old man had hurt her and that the chicken's blood had flowed. No one could have such a nightmare and yet not wake up.

It is true, she thought, wondering if she would ever be able to go home again. *I have traveled back in time.*

"You're quiet," Don Fernando noted.

"I was just trying to remember."

"Well, whether you remember or not, you must learn to be careful, señorita. There are those men a young woman can trust, and those who are utterly untrustworthy. Great danger lurks in the dark streets and in the bayous. Especially for a woman without the protection of a man. There are pirates, unscrupulous men who kidnap women, use them, and then sell them into slavery."

He half turned to her and his expression was something of a leer. It made Julie feel uncomfortable, as if the threats he described somehow excited him.

"You, my dear, would fetch a handsome price. I have heard of lovely blond concubines kept in sexual servitude behind the Great Wall in the Forbidden City in Peking across the sea in China. Or you could be sold by one captain to another and end up in the slave markets in Constantinople. This is a seaport. A woman taken here can end up anywhere."

Julie said nothing. He did seem to be enjoying his speech on the dangers of the city. It was true that she had not really considered them. That he knew so much about what could happen to a woman made her wonder if she had gone from the frying pan into the fire. Perhaps the man who rescued her might be more dangerous than the voodoo devil who had threatened her. Or perhaps he thought if he frightened her she would turn to him for protection. That, she decided, was more likely.

"And you have already had a taste of local dangers. They

say there are zombie slaves kept in secret houses in the bayous for the entertainment of the living.''

"I'm sure the dangers are many.'' She tried to sound unafraid.

He drew in the reins as he turned the carriage into a winding drive that ultimately led to a large house.

Don Fernando sprang down and then lifted her to the ground. His hands held her waist firmly as he set her on the ground. He didn't let go.

"You are most beautiful,'' he whispered, leaning over to kiss her.

Julie stiffened and turned her cheek. His breath was heavy with rum.

"Now, now. Is that any way to treat a man who has saved you?''

He ran his hands over her hips and his eyes were fastened on her breasts. "I do want to feel you struggle beneath me.''

"I think not, señor. I should like to be taken back to the home of Desirée Coteau.'' Julie wriggled free of him and stepped back.

He looked a bit confounded, then a frown covered his face. "I do not allow women to say no,'' he said, lurching toward her.

"You will allow this one to say no,'' Brady McCormick's even voice said. He stood framed in the doorway of Don Fernando's own house. "Fortunately I dropped by to see if you had any luck finding our runaway.''

"I had no real intention of harming her,'' Don Fernando stuttered.

It seemed clear to her that Don Fernando *had* no intention of taking on Brady McCormick who was, after all, a massive man, not only tall, but broad chested and well muscled.

"I shall return her to the home of Desirée,'' Brady announced.

"And have her for yourself no doubt." Don Fernando swayed ever so slightly.

Brady walked toward him. He grasped his shoulder. "You're drunk, my friend."

Don Fernando accepted the way out gracefully and simply nodded. Then, with a bow, "You may use my carriage."

"Thank you. I suggest you sleep a few hours before drinking more."

"But 'tis a celebration!"

"You began drinking much too early, my friend. Much too early."

"No harm done then," he muttered as he staggered toward the house.

Brady lifted Julie up, then climbed beside her, taking the reins in hand and urging the horses gently forward.

"I wouldn't trust that man were I you," she said after a moment.

Brady looked at her and nodded. "I don't. But then, I trust no one, not even you. Or perhaps I should say, especially you."

"I told you everything I know. Whatever you think I am, you are wrong."

"I hope so," he replied as they turned a corner. Suddenly Desirée's house appeared, its windows still bright from the burning candles and lamps within.

He pulled up out front and guided Julie into the house. "Are you hungry?" he asked.

She shook her head. This man before her was arrogant and sure of himself, but still, for some reason, and in spite of his having searched her and watched her undressing, she felt safe with him.

"I don't know what to do," she said softly. Suddenly it was as if all the events of the past twenty-four hours closed in on her. She hadn't slept much before this had all happened, save for a short nap in the hotel. Then she had this experience—this experience that she could not begin to explain and the reality of which she still questioned.

After the shock of finding herself in another century, she had been locked up and searched. Then she had run through the streets and been captured by horrible people practicing some form of witchcraft. Lastly there were the advances by Don Fernando . . . Tears filled Julie's large blue eyes and she began to cry.

Brady looked at her in discomfort. She was a tigress, but even a tigress could be driven to far. Her tears seemed genuine enough, though he did not consider himself an expert on female sincerity. But her sobs seemed wrenching and he could see she was becoming hysterical.

"I'm so tired," she sobbed. "And I want to go home, but I don't know how."

He lifted her into his arms and carried her up the stairs to the room in which she had been locked before. He laid her on the bed and left, returning to her only after a few minutes. He held a glass and urged her to drink.

"A trifle bitter, but it will help you sleep."

She nodded, not fighting nor even arguing. In moments she felt incredibly relaxed and she drifted off into a deep sleep.

Brady undid her dress and slipped it off, leaving her in her filmy chemise. The night was warm, so he did not cover her, though he pulled the mosquito netting around the bed. Then he extinguished the lamp and turned to leave.

He paused in the doorway and stared at her beneath her gauze prison. Her hair was a mass of blond curls, her body slender yet curvaceous. He did not have to imagine her without clothes—he had the memory of her silhouette, which had revealed an entirely desirable body. Now, curled up in the massive bed, beneath the white gauze, she looked like a sleeping angel. How easy it would be to take her now. How easy and how enjoyable to kiss her breasts and arouse her sufficiently to welcome him. He bit his lip and turned quickly, shutting the door and locking his lovely vision in for the night.

The sight of Julie amid the pillows and beneath the netting reminded him of a tale he used to read to his sister Mavis, who was seven years younger than he. Their father had given them the book for Christmas. The tales were French fairy tales written by Perrault but recently translated into English by Robert Samber. *Sleeping Beauty*—that was the title. No doubt it would be better to win her than to take her, he decided. He smiled. Wherever she came from, spy or innocent, she had no equal in all of New Orleans. He would have to guard her carefully from now on.

Julie moved among her pillows and then tossed on her side. In a moment she opened her eyes and then she sat up, pushing aside the gauze netting.

Sleep had not ended her dream nor sent her forward to her own time. She was still here, locked in this room. She was here where Brady McCormick had brought her, here in the home of Desirée Coteau in the year 1778. Last night she had thought that leaving this house might enable her to return to the twentieth century—but she had almost been killed.

1779

She looked down and ran her hand over her arms. Then, more completely awake, she realized that Brady McCormick had removed her dress! Not that she would be a mystery to him, she remembered bitterly. But was that all he did?

She remembered the potion he had given her to drink. Her face flushed as she recalled some vague memory of desiring him, of having him kiss her. He had lain down beside her and removed her clothes, all the while caressing her gently. His hands had been soft on her skin, his movements urgent and demanding. She had yielded and drawn him close. They made love on a bed of scented flowers with soft breezes floating over them. No. That just wasn't possible.

Julie touched her hot cheeks and shook her head. No,

it had not happened. She strained to separate her dreams from reality. She thought of his hands on her body, hands taunting her and lips caressing her till she moaned in sweet delight. But did he? If he had taken her in her drugged sleep, why would he have bothered to put her chemise back on? Moreover, if he had been with her and it had been as pleasant as she recalled, why was he now gone? She could not be certain if indeed he had taken her or if she had experienced an erotic dream—probably the result of the potion, or whatever it was. "Damn," she murmured as she pulled herself from the bed.

She went to the window and pulled the heavy drapes. To her surprise, the sun was high in the sky, as if it were noon or even later.

She was staring outside when she heard the door latch turn and the bolt unfasten. She turned quickly, Brady's name on her lips. Yet it was not Brady who entered but Desirée.

Dressed considerably more plainly than before, Desirée sailed into the room, bearing a silver tray.

The mistress of the house was dressed in a bright yellow print dress trimmed in white. Her ravishing thick dark hair was pulled back with a ribbon. Her face was made up, but not as excessively as last night. Heavy gold hoop earrings hung from her ears. She had an incredibly long neck and Julie again noted her magnificent cheekbones and flawless coffee-colored skin.

She knew from what she had read that Desirée was nearly forty, but she looked at least ten years younger.

"I imagine you will want fresh clothing, my dear. Such can be found in that chest and in that wardrobe. I believe they will fit you without a problem."

Julie looked at the tray and for the first time it struck her that she was really very hungry. "Thank you. Is that for me?"

"Yes. A little breakfast."

"Would it be possible to take a bath after I eat—before I dress in fresh clothing?"

"But of course. I shall see to having the bath filled." Desirée set the tray down on the small table. She pulled up a chair for Julie and then one for herself.

"I shall have a cup of coffee with you. We must discuss your situation."

Julie stirred her coffee. It smelled wonderful. She took a big gulp. The tray held breads and coffee, fruit, and some kind of hot gruel.

"You're welcome to stay here as long as you wish," Desirée said, "but this is not a hotel. A way must be found for you to earn your room and board."

Julie nodded. "I don't expect something for nothing."

"Well, I have a number of girls who entertain in the evenings. They make a good living."

Julie shook her head. "I won't do that. I just can't."

Desirée arched her brow. "Very well. Perhaps I should tell you that Desirée has given you much thought. That in the night a vision came to her—a vision of a lovely blond-haired woman traveling through space, through time." Desirée moved her hands dramatically and her eyes were half closed as if she were indeed remembering a vision.

But it was not her looks or motions that struck Julie dumb. It was her words!

"I know about you. I know you're a time traveler."

Julie felt the blood drain from her face. How did Desirée know? How could she possibly know? Maybe she really did have psychic ability. Perhaps she really could read minds.

"Your expression tells Desirée her vision was divine insight. You are a time traveler."

"I don't know how I came to be here, but it would seem you might be right."

"Yes. I know you don't yet accept your own situation. Tell me, what did you do in your own time? To make a living."

"I was a costume designer. I made costumes. I can sketch and make patterns and sew."

"I could make use of such talent. I need someone to supervise my seamstresses. I own, among other things, a shop where all the fine ladies are outfitted. But of course your most valuable asset is your knowledge of the future. Yes, Desirée can make use of your knowledge of the future."

"If you know I am a time traveler, if you have such visions, you should know the future. Why do you need my knowledge of things to come?"

Desirée smiled critically. "One does not see everything."

Julie frowned. Did this woman know or had she guessed? If she did know, was it because of her visions? Perhaps she had given herself away somehow. It was all very perplexing.

"Are you willing to work supervising my seamstresses and to help me make money *forecasting* certain events?"

"I have no knowledge of specific things. I know general things—actually, I am quite ignorant of everyday life."

"As I am sure I would be of life in your time." Desirée's eyes grew large. "Knowledge of the outcome of the war would be worth a fortune, however."

Julie could easily see why certain knowledge could be valuable, yet she readily admitted that she could not imagine how to use such broad general information in this world. At the same time she felt hesitant. Surely it was important for her not to alter history, to be careful how and with whom she shared information.

"I'm sure it would be," she said slowly. This was a clever woman. She would have to be equally clever if she were to stay alive and benefit herself.

"So, tell me, how does the war turn out?" Desirée asked.

"The time is not right for you to have such information," Julie replied. *I can be as mysterious and as cryptic as Desirée,* she decided. "We will begin a little smaller. Perhaps with some battles. Besides, I must think of myself."

Desirée again arched her handsome brow. "I like to deal with shrewd people. Very well, we shall begin slowly."

"And make sure it is understood that I am in the fashion business and not the sex business. I will not be one of your ladies of the evening."

"Too bad. You are a loss to my business in that respect. You would have done well."

Julie did not answer directly. "What room shall be mine?"

"You may stay here. Carmelita will be your maid. I will send her to you as soon as your bath is filled."

"Thank you," Julie replied.

Desirée turned. "Tell me a little thing. Tell me if a maid would fill the bath in the time from whence you came?"

"There would be no need. Water comes to homes through pipes. One only need turn it on."

Desirée's expression was one of ever so slight disbelief. Then she smiled. "It does sound wonderful."

"Not all changes are good," Julie confessed.

Desirée nodded. "I understand," she said thoughtfully.

Chapter Five

Carmelita Landry was petite, less than five feet in height and weighing no more than one hundred pounds. Her hair was reddish brown and her eyes large and dark brown. Her skin was rare indeed, also a reddish brown, almost the color of light rust. She was both attractive and unique in appearance.

"Carmelita? Are you Spanish?" Julie asked.

"I am many things," Carmelita replied with a shy smile. "My grandmother was a Cajun woman from Acadie. Now they call it Nova Scotia—New Scotland. The English sent my mother's people from that place, from their home."

Julie had asked the question casually, to make pleasant conversation. But now she felt her interest rise because of her own Acadian heritage. "Was that your mother's mother or your father's mother?"

"My father's mother. Her name was Marie Anne Landry. She had no husband—which is to say I do not know who my grandfather was except that he was Spanish. My father, also named Landry, had many brothers. My own mother was a full-blooded Choctaw woman."

Julie smiled. "My mother's maiden name was also Landry."

Carmelita looked dubious. "Are there Acadians in New York?"

Julie knew she must be careful. "The Acadians are a scattered people. My mother did not come from New York." Her explanation seemed to satisfy Carmelita for the moment. Certainly no one could argue with the fact that the Acadians had been scattered to the four winds.

"Perhaps we are related," Carmelita allowed. "There are many Landrys, but maybe we're family."

Julie sensed in Carmelita a quiet intelligence and a certain loneliness.

"Perhaps we are. Where is your family now?"

"My parents are dead. I have one brother. He's gone north to fight with the colonists against the British. I have many uncles and aunts who live in and around the bayous, but no other brothers and sisters."

"You must be lonely."

"I keep busy."

"Do you—are you one of the women who entertains men at night?" Julie asked. Carmelita was certainly attractive enough to be one of Desirée's women.

"Oh, no! That is why I work as a maid. Like you, I do not chose to make my living in such a way."

"Desirée told you of our arrangement?"

"Yes. Desirée is very good, you know. I mean good as far as women are concerned. She is very against women being forced to sell their bodies. She is against slavery, too. She tries to help as many women as she can, giving them jobs. Of course, New Orleans is renowned for its brothels and many women like to make money by sleeping with men. Desirée lets her women keep almost all they earn, except what is needed for room and board. And here," Carmelita added, "the women are safe."

"Do you have friends, beside the people who live here?"

"Oh, yes. I have good friends like Brady McCormick."

Julie tried not to react at all. Was Carmelita involved with Brady McCormick? She shook her head slightly in annoyance with herself. What would she care if she were? Still, she could not bring herself to ask any more questions.

"Your bath is ready by now," Carmelita informed her. "I almost forgot to tell you."

Julie nodded. She wondered if this girl could even guess how much she was looking forward to a bath. She erased all thoughts of Brady McCormick from her mind and replaced them with fantasies of hot water. "And I am more than ready for my bath."

Julie looked at the metal tub in awe. In her time it would have been considered an antique but here, in this time, its purpose was entirely utilitarian. It had been filled with hot water heated on the stove. The water steamed up.

"There is a robe for you on the chair," Carmelita said. "I took the liberty of scenting the water."

"Thank you." Julie began to undress. When she was naked, she stepped gingerly into the water, submerging herself in its fragrant waters.

"Oh, this feels wonderful," she said, sinking down into the water. Vaguely she wondered how often baths were possible. Surely this was a luxury.

"Here is the soap."

Julie took the soap and began washing. It, too, was fragrant, a perfumed French soap. Then she looked up at Carmelita. "You needn't stay. I can manage by myself."

Carmelita curtsied ever so slightly. "Very well," she said and left immediately.

Julie lay back against the tub and closed her eyes. Again Carmelita's comment came to her. Could it be Carmelita was involved with Brady McCormick? Was she perhaps his mistress?

Julie opened her eyes and for the second time in as many minutes chastised herself for even wondering about Mr. Brady McCormick. Without further thought, she plunged her hair into the water and began washing it, too.

Whatever happens, she thought, she might as well try to make adjustments, to get used to the idea that she was now living in the year 1779. But there were so many adjustments to make!

The large kitchen held a gigantic fireplace with walk-in ovens on either side. Great pans hung on large wrought-iron hooks from the low-beamed ceiling, and an ever-burning pot of coals smoldered away, waiting to be used to light the cooking fire if needed. The sink was a huge iron tub, and the counters were made of wood. Above the counters in high cupboards, dishes, bowls, and glasses were stacked and put away. One door led outside to the back of the house, one door led to a large pantry where food was stored, and one door led to the root cellar.

At one end of the kitchen there was a large wooden table surrounded by chairs, the backs of which were woven cane. Brady sat at the table with Carmelita, a mug of coffee in front of him.

"Where is she now?" Brady asked as he leaned over whispering conspiratorially.

"Taking a bath. I have been assigned by Madam Desirée to be her personal maid."

"Good. Did you ask to be her maid?"

"Yes, but I think it aroused no suspicion."

"Have you spoken with her yet?"

"Oh, yes. We had quite a long conversation. Her condition is most perplexing, but somehow I feel she is telling the truth. She remembers many things, but not how she came here. She had told Desirée she is a clothes designer. She made some sketches to show Madam Desirée and Madam is putting her in charge of the seamstresses."

Brady took in the information. His first reaction was mild regret that Julie would not be one of Desirée's women. Had she been one, he had intended to avail himself of her charms often. His second reaction was pleasure. Perhaps he could avail himself of her and have her to himself. He surprised himself with the thought and knew this was a new feeling for him. Yet he admitted that if he had such a woman, he would not want to share her.

But there was more important information in Carmelita's words than simply the information that Juliet Hart would not work in the evenings for Desirée. He turned to the meat of the matter. "Not just a seamstress, but in charge of them?" he said, seeking to confirm what she had said.

"Yes, in charge of them."

It seemed a lofty elevation considering Desirée had hardly had time to know Juliet Hart. She certainly had not had time to see her sew or look at many designs. But Desirée was too shrewd to make irresponsible decisions. He wondered if Desirée knew something about this woman he did not.

"So she remembers how to design clothes, but not how she came here."

"Yes. She also remembers her family. All that is blank is her journey here. She tells me her mother's maiden name was the same as my name, Landry.

"Really?" Brady felt suddenly more interested. The Landrys were of Cajun descent, and the Cajuns were almost all anti-British to the core. They had all been harshly treated by the British, uprooted and deported from their home, Acadia, in 1755, some twenty-three years ago. Families had been separated, and many had died. Cast away, many Acadian men had married Indian women. Carmelita was the progeny of such a marriage, but how strange that a woman whose mother was Acadian should come from New York? To his knowledge, almost all the Acadians had ended up in the South—first in the Carolinas and then migrating onward to Louisiana. Nor, he thought, did Juliet Hart look Cajun. No, it was probably all a lie to make her more readily accepted.

"Do you believe her?" he pressed. Carmelita had a wom-

an's intuition. She was bright and anxious to help the
cause. He trusted her implicitly.

"Yes, I do believe her. But why not take her up the bayou
to meet my third cousin, Philip Landry. He knows all the
Landrys. Perhaps he can help identify her."

Brady smiled. It was a great suggestion on more than
one count. He himself wanted to meet Philip Landry, about
whom he had heard many stories. Landry was a kind of
family patriarch, a man of many talents and much knowledge. But his original reason for wanting to meet and talk
with Landry had nothing to do with Juliet Hart. He wanted
a team of Cajun volunteers to help transfer the arms that
he and Pollock had secured. The arms were to be sent to
George Rogers Clark. Secondarily, he agreed with Carmelita—it would indeed be a good way to find out about
Miss Juliet Hart. Yes, a trip up the bayou could serve two
purposes. He could further investigate Juliet Hart and he
could make the initial overtures concerning the recruit-
ment of Cajuns.

"Can you make the arrangements, Carmelita?"

She smiled warmly at him. "But of course. I shall send
a message right away. But you had better speak to Madam
Desirée."

"I will. Keep your eyes open and watch our Miss Hart.
I am not yet as certain of her as you."

The war and the women of New Orleans provided the
topic for endless conversations in the coffee houses and
bars that lined the docks of New Orleans. When discussing
women, there was much bragging and when discussing war
there was much talk and no news.

La Paloma was a quiet ordinary bar and coffee house.
It was frequented by gentlemen and ruffians alike.

"*Amigo,*" Don Carlos said with a genuine smile. "Please
join us.

"By all means," Don Fernando added.

Brady pulled out a chair and sat down with Don Carlos and Don Fernando de Vega.

The barmaid came immediately. She wore a red print cotton dress and a black apron. Her hair was completely hidden beneath an elaborate African-style turban. The bodice of her dress was cut very low, and her full, high breasts were more than half exposed as she bent over the table to take their orders.

All three men ordered rum, but it was Don Fernando who insisted on paying. He took the coin from his pocket and deposited it down the woman's cleavage, then with a leer he ran his hand over her breasts and smiled knowingly. "Irresistible," he muttered under his breath.

But it *was* resistible, Brady thought. Not that Don Fernando's actions made him a villain. He was hardly the only man who acted as he did. For the most part the women of New Orleans had a reputation for lustiness. Still, Brady knew that Don Carlos would never have done such a thing. He knew that on matters such as these, Don Carlos thought as he did: that women—all women—should be accorded a certain respect.

He thought back on Juliet Hart. He had looked at her, but he had not touched her or forced himself on her in spite of his desire. Don Carlos would have restrained himself as well. It occurred to him once again that Don Carlos and Don Fernando were very different.

But the two brothers did not differ just on the matter of women. They differed politically as well. Don Carlos believed in the revolution. He was a dreamer, and yet he worked incredibly hard. He had made a great success of growing sugar cane along the Mississippi. He not only harvested cane, but produced rum. He wanted to expand his land holdings in order to increase his production. He also wanted to obtain additional river frontage. In this way, he believed he would have not only cane and rum to market, but a means of transportation via the barges. He was convinced that the liberated American colonies would be a trading market for rum as Britain was not. Britain got all the rum she needed from the Caribbean. He also knew that due to certain family rivalries, Don Carlos kept his business plans secret from his brother Don Fernando. Brady knew his friend's plans, but he respected his confidence and did not discuss those plans with anyone.

Don Fernando, on the other hand, seemed to live primarily off his inheritance, though he, too, owned a farm where he grew cotton. But his farm was managed by an overseer; Don Fernando himself would never become involved. He professed to believe in the ideals of the revolution, but he did little to promote it. Indeed, in Brady's eyes Don Fernando was naught but a charming dilettante.

"Will you be at Desirée's tonight?" Don Carlos asked.

"Yes, the room I rent is small and cramped. Besides, the landlady serves no meals."

"You should perhaps move to Desirée's. I am sure she would rent you a room," Don Fernando suggested.

"I fear our friend would never rest there. Not for a moment," Don Carlos remarked good-naturedly.

"You mean you think he would avail himself of beautiful women all day and all night?" Don Fernando laughed.

"No, only that it would be distracting."

"And you are right," Brady said. It would be much too distracting. I fear I would indeed spend all my time with the women."

"Now, now," Don Carlos said, "one does not need to eat only candy just because one lives in a candy store."

"Ah, but what a candy store it is!" Don Fernando said, raising his brow. "Listen, I have only just talked my brother into visiting Esmé."

"Esmé?" Brady said after a moment.

Brady smiled. He was used to such talk. Not that he too hadn't visited many of Desirée's women. He had done so because he was lonely, because the atmosphere was different from other such places, and because some of the women were genuinely interesting.

He had met Carmelita while visiting another woman. They had become friends, and he would not sleep with her now because he knew her and she knew him and they had agreed to be only friends.

"The red-haired wench," Don Fernando replied.

"Ah, yes," Brady answered. Esmé was indeed a beauty, although he himself did not feel attracted to her. He preferred women with softer looks but whose spirits were strong.

"Why don't you move to my house," Don Carlos suddenly said. "I have many rooms. You can still eat at Desirée's, but you won't have to, and you can have your privacy."

"That's very generous of you."

"Not at all. It is my pleasure to house a revolutionary."

"Then I shall take you up on it."

"What have you heard, if anything?" Don Fernando asked. "About the war, that is."

Brady shrugged. "News is slow to travel. I do expect to hear something tonight or tomorrow. I know Pollock has dispatched a messenger."

"We look forward to news," Don Carlos said. "And please, move in anytime."

Don Carlos relaxed in a huge chair, his feet on a stool. He sipped a drink Esmé had made him, and watched as she disrobed for him. It was an arousing sight. She slowly undid her skirt and let it slip to the floor. Then she took off her bodice. She turned quickly, her long loose hair spinning with her, and when her spin was complete, she faced him only in her filmy chemise. She came to his side and dropped to the floor beside his chair. "Loosen me," she whispered. "Free me."

Don Carlos felt beads of perspiration break out on his brow. His fingers trembled in eager anticipation as he fumbled with the ribbons on her chemise. When they were undone, he pulled it aside. He took a long, deep breath;

her breasts were quite wonderful. His eager hand flew to one and she moaned in happiness.

"Carry me to the bed," she whispered.

He gulped down the rest of his drink and did what she asked. He quickly disrobed himself and was aware of feeling drunker than he ought to have felt, but no less enthusiastic. He lay down beside her on the huge bed and she ran her hands over him seductively.

He kissed her neck, her ears, and her breasts. Everything in him wanted her, but somehow he could not make himself firm.

"We have all night," she whispered. "Tell me about your property on the river. I have heard it is very large and very beautiful."

"Profitable," he mumbled. "I want to buy my brother's property as well. He has no sense of its worth. I know the Americans will win; I know the river traffic will increase." He was unaware of how his speech sounded, but he slurred his words now.

"And so you really want the Americans to win?"

"With all my heart. The ideals of the revolution are seductive!" Now he could hear himself beginning to miss words and it seemed hard for him to speak. It was as if his lips were paralyzed.

He looked at her glistening naked body, yet in spite of all the desire she made him feel, he could do nothing. It was as if he were inert, dead, unable to move.

"There is always morning," she said, a crafty look in her eyes. "Let us continue talking."

Julie lay in bed and listened. The walls were thin and she reminded herself to remember that fact. Esmé was uncommonly beautiful with her fine skin and red hair. Esmé, she knew from Carmelita, was a quadroon, one whose genes had given her red hair, golden skin, and large dark eyes.

She wondered what man graced Esmé's bed. Somehow his voice sounded familiar. But more important, it seemed to her that the man was either drunk or drugged and that Esmé was questioning him. His words were unclear, but she knew Spanish was his mother tongue. Perhaps it was one of the de Vega brothers, she thought. But had she heard their voices enough to recognize them? Besides, the accent alone was hardly enough.

Still, something strange was going on here. Esmé was questioning someone. And Brady McCormick was a revolutionary and thought her a spy. Perhaps Esmé was a real spy, Julie thought. Perhaps that explained her questions to this strange man. And perhaps Brady had good reason to be suspicious. Perhaps information was being sent to the enemy.

Brady McCormick drew his carriage to a halt in front of a large white building across from the church. Julie sat silently beside him. He had insisted on her coming with him to see New Orleans, to see if anything at all would jog her memory.

The carriage ride confirmed her previous belief that New Orleans in this year of 1779 did not extend much beyond what in the twentieth century would be known as the Vieux Carré—the French Quarter. And not even all the blocks of Vieux Carré were filled with houses or other buildings. Outside the boundaries of the Quarter, there were some houses scattered along the riverfront above and below the town. There were a few more fronting on Bayou St. John.

The Palace d'Armes, known in her time as Jackson Square, was the center of the capital. The Church of St. Louis faced the river while the house of the Capuchin Fathers stood to the left of the church. On the other side of the church the town jail and the guardhouse were next to one another and on each side of the square was a row

of soldier's barracks. In front of the town there was a low
levee cluttered with goods of all sorts and beyond the
church, on the other side of the barracks, was the French
Market, which consisted of a series of wooden stalls and
benches.

The most imposing building was the Casa Capitular in
front of which Brady had just stopped. This was the seat
of Spanish government in Louisiana.

Julie looked around, her eyes wide with curiosity. She
had walked through this square on her way to the dollhouse
museum. She had only recently stood in this very spot two
hundred and fifteen years hence! She felt awed at the
thought, overwhelmed with knowledge of what would happen here, of how things would change, of what the next
fifty years would bring. Facts from the tourist books she
had devoured filled her head.

The actual square, which was now only dirt covered, was
rather muddy from the rain last night. In her time it was
grass covered and there were monuments, benches, and
a plaque that told the history of the place. From previously
reading the plaque Julie well knew that all she now saw
would be destroyed by a terrible fire in 1788—nine years
from now. As she recalled, the second oldest building in
the city was built in 1789, still eleven years away. The oldest
was the Ursuline School. It stood now, and parts of it would
survive into the twentieth century. All else had been badly
damaged or destroyed in fires, floods, and hurricanes in
the years that would follow.

"This is the Casa Capitular," Brady announced.

Julie said nothing, not wanting to betray her foreknowl-
edge. She knew that in seventeen years this building would
be rebuilt in stone and called the Cabildo. The Spanish
would rule Louisiana from here until the colony was again
ceded to the French and then sold to the United States
in 1803.

"I daresay the buildings of New Orleans are not as
impressive as those of New York City," Brady commented.

Julie suppressed a smile with difficulty. She wondered how he would react to the buildings of New York City as she had left them, or indeed how he would react to the city she knew New Orleans would become. It was not simply a matter of buildings, but of tremendous population growth. In this year of 1779, the population of blacks, Indians, Acadians, Spanish, French, English, and American frontiersmen numbered only a few thousand, but one day it would expand to six hundred thousand.

"No, they aren't as impressive," she answered, and then added, "but it is a different architecture and a very different climate."

He laughed. "I daresay."

"Where are you from?" she asked. Certainly his accent was far different from all the others to whom she had spoken. Yet she could not place it among modern-day American accents.

"My parents live near Fort Pitt, my brothers are fighting in the revolution. I believe them to be somewhere near Philadelphia."

She nodded, thinking again how slowly news traveled. It was April, and fierce battles had been fought in the East. In spite of his arrogance, and the fact she was irritated with him much of the time, she hoped his brothers had survived.

"I have to see Bernardo," Brady said as he climbed down and secured the horses to the hitching post. "You can come inside and wait. It will give you a chance to see the building. My meeting is confidential but won't take long."

She allowed him to lift her down. They walked on something like a cobblestone sidewalk toward the Casa. But she was still obliged to lift her skirts. What cumbersome clothing! she thought. It was pretty enough, and the dress she wore was nicer than many day dresses. It was a light-brown dress consisting of corset, sleeves, chemise, and skirt. It was layered with a bodiced overskirt of cream lace, and with it she wore a large shawl of lace woven with ribbons.

She was also obligated to wear a mobcap of lace and trimmed with the same yellow ribbon with which her shawl was interwoven. Her flaxen hair hung loose, curling at the ends in the ever-present dampness of the New Orleans morning.

They passed the guard and walked through large double doors into the foyer of the Casa Capitular. It was a big, empty area furnished only with a few desks, some lamps, and a rug runner which led to the winding staircase. In spite of the year, it had the feel of a government building, even the smell of one, she thought as Brady guided her toward the winding staircase. Again she lifted her skirt as they climbed the stairs.

The hall on the second floor was more lavishly furnished. There were busts and paintings as well as lamps. Brady opened the door and they entered another large room. This one held flags, a considerable number of pieces of heavy mahogany furniture in the massive Spanish style, and still more paintings.

A wizened old man with a pointed goatee sat behind a cluttered desk.

Brady took her to a small velvet-covered chair. "You will wait here."

He went to the desk, leaned over and spoke to the man, and in seconds the doors to an inner chamber opened. He passed through them and they closed as if swallowing him up.

Julie remained seated for only a moment, then began to walk around the room, studying with interest the various artifacts it held. The ceilings were beamed and the walls were whitewashed and made of stucco. A large iron candelabra was suspended from the ceiling's center beam. She examined two distinctive lamps and then turned her full attention to the paintings.

One in particular caught her eye. She wandered over to it and read the small plaque next to it. How utterly strange! A chill ran through her. The painting was of

Columbus. It was one she never recalled seeing and now she assumed it must have been destroyed in the fire. Was this perhaps a painting for which he had posed? Or was it like others which were painted long after his death? She looked at it for a long while, then returned to her chair, her eyes fixed on the large doors behind which Brady had disappeared.

Brady stood opposite the governor inside his lavish office.

"Brady, I did not expect to see you this morning."

"Nor I you," Brady said, leaning across the expansive desk to shake hands with his friend.

"And what brings you here?"

"*El Dorado.* Bernardo, I'm worried. In case, just in case, the girl is a spy and overheard something, I think we should change the route by which *El Dorado* will sail. It is not too late for me to change the rendezvous."

"I cannot believe she is a spy. And I saw her. You seem to have her in tow."

"Yes, I brought her to see if any sights jarred her memory. But then I got to thinking, why not be doubly safe?"

Galvez nodded. "You do not trust Don Carlos or Don Fernando either—what about Desirée?"

"I trust Don Carlos implicitly. I am less trusting of Don Fernando, but I shall reserve my judgment. As for Desirée—well, I think she can be trusted, but I do not wish to test that trust. In any case, I should rather have her with me than against me."

Galvez smiled. "That is wise of you, my friend. All right, I shall have the route changed and you shall have the rendezvous changed as well. Only the two of us will know."

Brady nodded his approval as Galvez went to his strong box. He returned with a map which he spread out on his desk. He traced a new route and wrote it down. Brady chose a new rendezvous and wrote that down.

When they were finished, Galvez folded the map and they shook hands. "To a successful venture," he said, grinning.

"Yes, to a successful venture," Brady answered. He turned and again passed through the double doors. Bernardo was in a difficult position. He wanted to help, but his own government was torn. Many influential Spaniards wanted to join the fray and fight the British, but many others feared for their own monarchy and decided to protect the status quo. Toward that end, they firmly rejected an alliance with the revolutionaries.

Julie stood up as Brady walked toward her. "Did you take a look around?" he asked.

"Yes, of course. There are some fascinating paintings in this room."

"Yes, it's quite a collection. Have you seen anything that sparked your memory?"

Julie shook her head. How could she say that far from helping her remember, all she saw sparked a vision of the future? As they walked from the Casa Capitular, she looked across the square. One day the famed Cafe du Monde would sit on the opposite corner. It would be crowded day and night and it would gain a world-wide reputation for the world's best coffee and *beignets*. And that was not all! What could she say now?

"One day this will be a beautiful square," she finally said as she left all other thoughts unspoken.

"Only if New Orleans can defeat its greatest enemy."

"Which is?"

"Pestilence. Surely you have noticed the mosquitoes. There are many plagues here. Fevers and the like that attack and kill."

She knew he was right. Malaria was a problem, and no doubt so were other illnesses brought in from the Caribbean aboard the ships that docked here. She reminded herself to be careful of what she ate and drank. And somewhere, somehow, she knew must find some quinine or a reasonable substitute. This was not the season for malaria, but when it came, she knew she would be as vulnerable as anyone else.

"Come along," he said. "I'll drive you around some more. You must tell me if you remember anything—anything at all."

Julie followed. History had always fascinated her, but living it seemed a trifle more uncomfortable than she had imagined.

Esmé threw her light cape around her shoulders and ventured out into the sunlight. Her long hair was loose, and she walked along with a sense of purpose, looking neither to the left nor to the right.

Brady turned the carriage onto Chartres. "Look, there's Esmé. She lives at Desirée's, too. Have you met her?"

Julie looked at Esmé and immediately thought of last night. "No, not exactly."

"What do you mean, not exactly?" Brady asked.

Julie glanced at his handsome, rugged profile and wondered if she should tell him the essence of what she had overheard. He seemed so interested in spies, maybe he would be interested in Esmé and her conversation with Don Carlos.

"I mean we have not been formally introduced, but I know she has the room next to mine."

Brady smiled. "I hope you shall get some sleep. Esmé is very popular and she sells her favors."

Sells her favors—what a lovely way to put it. "She was with Don Carlos last night," Julie imparted. "At least I thought it was Don Carlos. He was very drunk—or possibly drugged. It may be favors she sells, but it was information she was after last night. I heard her questioning him."

"Esmé?" Brady said in surprise. "Questioning Don Carlos? You must be mistaken."

Julie shook her head. "I am not mistaken. I heard what I heard."

"Why are you telling me this? Only Desirée would put Esmé up to such a thing. Now I must also consider whether you have been sent into our midst to divide us."

Julie didn't know what to say. She had been trying to help, but if he could not see it, well, then that was his fault. She decided then and there that there was no use telling him the truth about herself. If he didn't believe what she had told him about Esmé, he most certainly would not believe the truth about her.

"You're absurd," she replied antagonistically. "As well as bull headed and stubborn."

Esmé saw the carriage and she waited till it turned the corner before she took the road that led to the home of Don Fernando. She did not want Brady McCormick to see her. He would be suspicious and wonder why she was going to Don Fernando and not the other way around. But she had to go. Don Fernando had summoned her.

She rang the bell and a maid answered the door. She did not wait to be announced, but rather hurried into the reception room. Don Fernando was behind his desk, writing with a quill pen and looking uncharacteristically businesslike.

The reception room was one of her favorites. It was large and airy, with many sofas and divans, paintings, and wall hangings. It was a room from a castle in Spain, she imagined, a room such as would be found in one of the fine homes of Europe. Don Fernando could afford fine imported things. It was her dream to be able to have such furniture and a beautiful home. It was her dream to be the mistress of such a home rather than simply one of Desirée's women.

Surely if Desirée could have such things she could have

them, too. But it was not just lovely things she wanted. She wanted the love of a gentleman.

Don Fernando looked up and smiled, his sharp teeth glistening in the sun. "You are a morning vision, Esmé my dear."

"Thank you," she replied with a curtsy.

Don Fernando looked at her critically. He got up and came over to her. Her dress was red silk, hardly the thing a lady would wear during the day. Poor Esmé, she wanted it all, but she would likely never attain her dreams. Her taste was all in her quite delectable mouth. Still, she was an ambitious little tart, and ambition properly channeled had its uses.

He pulled her to him roughly and just as roughly passed his hands over her suggestively. "Did you enjoy my brother last night?" he asked her, pressing her yet closer.

She wriggled free. "Of course not. He was drugged."

"And in the morning? When he awoke in your bed?"

"I was gone. He thought we had made love. I assure you he had sweet dreams."

Don Fernando raised his brow. "Sometimes you're clever. Now tell me what you discovered."

"That he is negotiating to buy a large plot of land adjacent to that which he already owns. The plot he desires is right on the river. He wants to expand his sugar plantation and obtain river frontage to prepare for increased trade with the colonists and settlers to the north. He most certainly believes in the revolution." She finished speaking and found herself feeling guilty because, in truth, she liked Don Carlos.

"And in sugar and rum," Don Fernando sneered. "Well, cotton will be the crop of the future! My brother is an idiot."

Esme frowned. She wasn't quite sure that was true, but Don Carlos had confessed to her that he had given money to the revolution and she had thought that a great waste.

"He is helping to buy arms for the revolutionaries," she added.

Don Fernando made an unpleasant face. The very thought made him angry. He thought of telling their father, Don Gabriel, how his favorite son was wasting money, but he knew in his heart the effort would be wasted. Their father would probably approve. He, too, would probably give money and he himself would be fortunate indeed if there were anything left to inherit.

"You seem upset," Esmé ventured.

He nodded. He had known his brother was a supporter of the revolution, as he himself pretended to be, but he had not known about the money. His brother rarely spoke with him about money or about his investments.

"Is there nothing you can do?"

"Not at the moment," he said coldly. Then, as if consumed with emotions he could not express, he reached out again for Esmé, pulling her into his arms. He kissed her mouth, then her neck roughly. "I must have you now," he whispered.

She opened her mouth to protest slightly because of his strange mood, but then she simply closed her eyes and gave in to his rough caresses.

He removed her clothes quickly and efficiently, then took her without so much as unbuttoning his own ruffled shirt. When he finished, having found his own pleasure with no concern for her at all, he all but threw her aside. Then he withdrew a gold coin and laid it between her breasts.

"For your efforts," he said, leaving the room and leaving her in tears.

Esmé wiped her cheek after Don Fernando left, mad at herself for crying. She pulled on her clothes angrily. Don Fernando was a wretch! He had treated her horribly.

Esmé hurriedly gathered up her scattered clothing. *Why did I agree to help him?* she asked herself again and again as she dressed. Then her thoughts strayed to the night before, to Don Carlos. Don Carlos had not made her feel ashamed. He had treated her as if she were a fine lady and he had been kind and gentle. Suddenly she began to cry anew, not because Don Fernando had treated her badly, but because she had helped him to spy on his brother, who was, she decided, a much finer man. In fact, there was no comparison.

Desirée stood by the entrance to her garden. The air was heavy with the threat of a spring rain, perhaps even a thunderstorm. The skies overhead were an ominous gray, and the wind was still as if it were waiting for some signal to begin blowing across the land.

Desirée inhaled deeply of the aroma of magnolia blossoms. They lined her garden, giving off their heady perfume, a perfume she found sensuous and full of promise.

Julie pulled her shawl around her and hurried up the path, glancing upward as she headed for the house.

"Best you come in now," Desirée said. "A big storm is coming, Desirée feels it. Tonight the wind will howl."

"I think you're right," Julie said, closing the door behind her. Carrying a sheath of paper and a some pencils, she set them down, telling Desirée, "I've some sketches for you."

Desirée sat down at the long wooden table. "Let me see them."

Julie handed them over and leaned back. She sniffed the air. "Is that coffee on the stove?"

"Yes, help yourself."

Julie poured herself a cup of coffee and sat down, too. It was chicory flavored, and took some getting used to.

"These are good," Desirée said, nodding, after she had studied the sketches. "Yes, very good. You will go over them with the seamstresses tomorrow morning."

"I'll be glad to do that."

"You went out with Brady this morning."

It was not a question but a statement, one to which Desirée clearly expected her to respond. "Yes, he drove me around New Orleans to see if anything jogged my memory."

"Ah, he still believes you can't remember. Well, it is good you do not have to pretend with everyone. You can be honest with Desirée. I will keep your secret."

"Thank you" was all Julie could think of saying. It wasn't so much the fact that it was a secret, of course; it was more what people would think, or were willing to believe. This was a superstitious place filled with superstitious people. Some might believe her, but most would not. Most would think her mad and she would be persecuted. She was not enthusiastic about Desirée knowing, save for the fact that she was such a strange, shrewd woman Julie was certain she would keep it to herself because it suited her to do so.

"And how do you like Brady McCormick?"

It was a question out of the blue and Julie hardly knew how to answer. "I think he is overly suspicious and very arrogant," she replied.

Desirée smiled without showing her teeth. It was an odd, knowing smile. "You are a very beautiful woman. I think he likes you."

"I doubt that," Julie answered. "He seems very preoccupied."

"No man is ever so preoccupied that he does not take notice of a beautiful woman, least of all Brady McCormick."

"You seem to know him very well."

"We were lovers for a time," Desirée revealed. "He is a masterful lover, a very handsome and strong man."

Julie tried to read Desirée's feelings. Did she still care for Brady? Was she jealous? But why would she be jealous? Desirée was a real beauty, an unusual woman in whom any man would be interested.

"Do you still love him?" Julie asked.

Desirée shrugged. "I love many men."

Julie realized this was not the answer she hoped to hear. "What about Brady?" she asked.

Desirée laughed throatily. "I suspect he is interested in many woman."

Julie straightened. All this talk was silly. She had no intention of becoming involved with anyone. After all, she might be whisked away at any moment, sent back in time. In any case, she had no intention of becoming one of Brady McCormick's many lovers.

She drained her coffee cup and stood up. "I think I shall go to my room for a while before dinner."

"I, too, must freshen up. But first I must remind you of the other half of our bargain. You must think about events. I should like to know at least a few details of the war that might be useful."

Julie nodded. She headed up the back stairs toward the second floor. What could she tell Desirée? Two things came immediately to mind. One was that Spain would soon enter the war, the other that Charleston would fall to the British. British consolidation in the South had been going on for many months and would not end till the peace treaty was signed; the other was about to happen. She chose Charleston.

Chapter Six

Desirée appeared for dinner wearing a stunning gold silk gown that made her yellow cat eyes seem even larger. Like all her dresses it was cut daringly low so that one could see her heaving bosom under its black lace bodice. Her hair was piled high, yet three thick curls hung down the back. Her makeup was artfully applied to emphasize her high cheekbones.

Brady sat mid-table where he could feast his eyes on either woman. They were, he concluded, both incredible beauties, though there were other women present who were far from ugly.

Desirée Coteau and Julie Hart were complete opposites. One had an exotic dusky beauty, the other a blond strawberries-and-cream beauty. One had all the experience in the world, the other exuded an intriguing innocence which was oddly combined with a high spirit, sharp tongue, and quick temper. Both women were tempting, but one was known and the other was not. The mystery of the unknown added to his desire for Julie Hart.

Brady sipped his wine, glancing now and again at the

two beauties. There were other men there, of course, but none of his intimates. Don Carlos had gone up river to his sugar plantation and Don Fernando was at home. Bernardo was at sea, but would be back later. In fact, Brady expected to meet him in Desirée's parlor for cognac sometime after dinner.

Tonight's dinner guests were all from outside of New Orleans. One was a man called Jason Hurley. He was a farmer up river, a man who seemed uncommitted to any cause save his own prosperity and survival. Another was a young man, a Spanish commander on his way from Cuba to Texas where he was to take up a new post. The third was a visiting Cuban plantation owner, a large man dressed in white. It was evident that each of these men, would spend the night with one of the women. And just so there would be no misunderstandings, the women had been assigned ahead of time and Desirée had made it clear that Julie was not among her "working girls."

"New Orleans is so interesting," Jason Hurley drawled. "It seems populated with lovely women of uncertain virtue."

"How fortunate for us," the large Cuban laughed.

At that moment, the doors to the dining room opened and the governor of Louisiana stepped into the room. He was dressed as properly as ever, but he seemed out of breath and a trifle agitated.

"Bernardo, how wonderful that you could join us," Desirée cooed.

"I cannot stay," he replied. "Brady, I must have a word with you in the study. I know I was expected later, but I've come now instead."

Brady did not hesitate. He excused himself, and closing the doors behind them, he followed Bernardo to the study.

"What's happened?" Brady asked. "Not only are you early, but you are certainly upset."

"With good cause, my friend. With good cause."

Brady poured them both a cognac. "Sit down, tell me."

"*El Dorado*. You were right, there must be a spy in our midst."

"Has the ship been sunk?"

"No. But had we sent it on its original route it would have been. I have just learned three ships were set to intercept her—British ships."

Brady let out his breath. "Thank God we changed her route."

"You, my friend. *You* changed her route. You have saved me great embarrassment. I do not have to tell you how serious it would have been had a Spanish vessel been caught carrying arms to the rebels when we are not yet allied."

"We can no longer take these chances, Bernardo. Our arms must go overland. I have a plan. I want to engage a team of Cajuns to help us. I want to go up the bayou and raise a contingent of volunteers.

"A brilliant idea. I think they will help you. God knows they have no lost love of the British."

Brady nodded. "And we must find our spy."

"Do you still think it is the girl?"

"It would seem so, though I hate to admit it."

"We really have no proof, you know. But I suppose you must question her again."

Brady nodded. "More important, I intend to take her with me. If she is with me all the time, she will have no opportunity to pass on information. Besides, she claims to be a Landry. Perhaps Philip Landry can identify her. Carmelita suggested I try that approach."

"A good idea. Well, my friend, I must leave you on your own for a short time—just to let things cool off. You understand."

"Of course."

Bernardo Galvez gave him a great bear hug which Brady responded to with gusto. Bernardo was one man he really liked. He was honest and upright. He was strong and had the makings of a hero.

Brady returned to the dining room and took his seat. Desirée was as calm as calm could be and he detected no nervousness in Julie, either. For a moment he looked longingly at her and hoped again that she was not what he suspected her of being.

Julie lifted her long skirts and prepared to climb the stairs toward her room. Tonight Esmé was not engaged, so she reasoned she would get a good night's sleep, undisturbed by the strange sounds that so often emanated from the redhead's room.

"I must talk with you," Brady said seriously as he intercepted her at the foot of the stairs.

Julie looked up into his face. He was, she reluctantly admitted, handsome. His features were rugged and he exuded a raw masculinity. She felt drawn to him, yet afraid of him because of his erratic behavior. Sometimes he was kind and pleasant, at other times he was brash, belligerent, and suspicious. At the very least he was, as the saying went, a diamond in the rough.

"Here I am. Talk to me."

"Not here. Either in the garden or in your room."

"There's a storm coming up, but I guess it will have to be the garden because you're not coming to my room."

"The garden it shall be."

Julie stopped for her shawl, wrapping it around her shoulders as they slipped out the back door.

The only light was from the lamps in the house and from the small lantern Brady carried. The moon and stars were hidden behind the swirling, threatening clouds. The dampness was pervasive, and a low fog seemed to hang in the still air. It was almost ghostly.

He led her down the long winding path away from the house till they were deep in the garden. The only illumination was the small amount cast by his lantern. Its light bobbed ahead of them as they walked. In the darkness a thousand insects sang their songs, not the least of which were the katydids. It was discordant music, like an orchestra warming up for a concert.

"Now," he said, setting down the lantern before a bench, "I want you to sit down and tell me everything. I want to know who you are, how you came to be in Desirée's house that night a week ago, and for whom you work. It will all go easier on you if you tell the truth."

Julie did sit down, but it was with exasperation. He still did not believe her! What was she to tell him? And what did he mean by "go easier"? She could not see his face, and she didn't like that. Whenever she talked with someone, she always liked to look into their eyes.

"I have told you the truth. I do not know how I came here. I am not a spy."

"I am afraid I have good cause to disbelieve you, my dear."

Julie felt irritated. It was struggle enough to adjust every day to the hardships of this century without having to put up with this man's suspicions. "I am not 'your dear.' And frankly, I don't give a damn whether you believe me or not!"

"What ladylike language! Ah, you are a little tart, aren't you?"

He yanked her up off the bench and shook her. "Last night a trap was set for a ship carrying arms to my countrymen. Had I not changed the route at the last moment, it would have been captured and our cause would have suffered a serious setback. The original route for that ship was discussed the very night you appeared from out of nowhere. I, my sweet, do not believe in coincidence!"

Julie was stunned at his anger. She wrenched herself away and started to run down the path in the darkness. But before she could get away Brady reached out and grabbed her long hair. He wound it round his hand and roughly pulled her back. Then he spun her around and he held her hard against him—so hard she could feel the outline of his body against hers and feel his hot breath on her throat.

"Let me go!" she demanded. "Let me go!"

"I shall not let you go till I know the truth!"

"I have told you the truth! Look elsewhere for your spy! I told you about Esmé questioning a man I am sure was Don Carlos. Why is she not under your suspicious eye?"

He released her ever so slightly and looked into her face, which was only partially illuminated by the lantern that now flickered slightly in a breeze that had just come up. God, she was spirited and beautiful. He bent down and pressed his lips to hers.

Julie doubled her fists and started to hit him, but his kiss was deep and passionate and the heat of him against her caused an unfamiliar feeling she could not even define. Their mutual anger seemed to melt.

She could only feel the maleness of him as he pressed against her, his mouth moving hungrily on hers. It was a wild, wondrous kiss, a kiss like none other she had ever had. It was a kiss taken, and at least for the moment it was a kiss that conquered. And then, as if nature responded to them with equal passion, the small breeze turned to a cold wind, a wind that could only be the hallmark of the storm. In less time than it took them to break their embrace, the wind had turned to near gale force.

Her hair golden hair blew tangled and wild and the lantern flickered out just as a wall of rain began to fall. Brady grabbed her hand and pulled her through the darkness. Her skirt billowed and caught on a nearby bush. She heard it tear, but she was wet and cold and frightened. Was this a hurricane? She could not even catch her breath as he pulled her on.

The storage hut in the back of the garden was suddenly visible as a bolt of lightning crackled across the sky. Brady pulled her toward it and together they staggered in, seeking what small shelter it offered. He slammed the door against the wind when thunder suddenly shook the ground.

Julie all but fell into his arms, her mass of wet blond curls falling over bare shoulders. Her body gave off a sweet aroma and he held her tenderly now, stroking her hair gently because she seemed vulnerable and afraid. How he wanted her. He fought to keep himself from further disrobing her, from kissing her cool, wet breasts, from knowing the magic of her long white legs. But he could not sleep with a woman he did not trust, and though he wanted to trust her, he had to be sure.

"I am not a spy," she suddenly sobbed. "I am not!"

"We're going up the bayou," he said softly. "I'm going to take you to Philip Landry. You told Carmelita your mother was a Landry. He knows all of them. Perhaps he can identify you."

Julie did not pull away from him. Had he tried to take her, she knew she would have been too tired to struggle. She realized perhaps, she would not *want* to struggle. But the fact was, she did not think he would do anything. He seemed calm now, calm and reasonable. But this trip might only add to his belief that she served the British. After all, Philip Landry would not know who she was, even though she might learn something of her own ancestry. If only she knew more of her mother's people, but they were a mystery and in any case, those she knew about were far into the future.

There was another clap of thunder and she cringed. Brady continued to stroke her hair. She listened and it seemed the wind was blowing less furiously now.

"I do have obligations here. I have work to do for Desirée," she said.

She shivered once again and he held her closer. She inhaled the sweet smell of his wet buckskin and wondered if it were waterproof or if he was as wet as she beneath her clothes.

Then, after a few minutes, he stood up and lifted her

to her feet. "I think the wind has died down and the rain tapered off. We can go back to the house now."

He led and she followed in the darkness. Then the flickering lamps of the house came into view. She looked down. Her skirt had been ripped off and her thin chemise was soaking wet.

Brady turned and looked at her just before he opened the back door. She felt him devouring her with his eyes and her face flushed.

"You better go upstairs," he said, "or you'll catch cold."

He squeezed her hand and they looked into one another's eyes. It was as if she could feel his lips on hers, as if they kissed good-bye mentally. She broke away and hurried up the stairs. Her emotions were at war as desire, judgment, anger, and even fear fought within her. She was apprehensive and still a bit angry with him. But there was no denying the first flush of longing, too. There was no denying this man's appeal or that she had been alone too long. She sighed and flung herself across her bed. Dreams were so much safer than reality.

The morning sun streamed through the window, causing Julie to toss in bed, then sit up suddenly, her eyes open. As she did each time she awoke, she looked about to establish her whereabouts. Something inside her still rejected what seemed so obvious and she knew that each time she closed her eyes she half expected to wake up in the twentieth century. And then the memory of last night washed over her in the morning sunlight and she wondered if she still wanted to be returned to her time and place. She conceded it was certainly something she would have to think about.

Julie pulled herself from her bed and sat before her dresser. As she brushed out her hair, she suddenly realized she was humming. Brady McCormick? The memory of his kiss would not leave her lips and she blushed even though she was quite alone.

She turned away from her mirror when she heard a knock on her door. "Who is it?" she called out.

"Desirée."

"I was just dressing," Julie said as she let Desirée in.

"So I see." Desirée's eyes quickly surveyed the room.

No doubt, Julie thought as she watched Desirée taking a mental inventory, she was looking for signs that Brady had spent the night, or part of it, here in this room with her.

As if to confirm her thoughts, Desirée commented, "You and Brady disappeared last night."

"We went for a walk in the garden and got caught in the storm."

"Ah," Desirée said, letting her breath out slowly and not bothering to disguise the knowing look that crossed her face.

"We got soaked," Julie added unnecessarily.

Desirée laughed under her breath. "I imagine you did."

Her words were laden with innuendo which Julie decided to ignore. "Are we still meeting with the seamstresses this morning?" she asked cheerfully.

"Yes. Come along downstairs when you're finished dressing and we'll have some coffee together. I must know some information about the war. It is time for you to help me."

Julie nodded. However clever, and regardless of whether or not she still cared for him, Desirée could not disguise her curiosity concerning Brady McCormick. *She wants to know about our relationship,* Julie decided.

But Desirée's request concerning the war forced Julie to turn from thoughts of Desirée's concerns with Brady to Desirée's demands for information. She had already decided to tell Desirée about Charleston but not about the Spanish declaration of war. That was far too dangerous.

"Here, have some fresh bread," Desirée offered as she poured a cup of steaming hot coffee when Julie entered the kitchen. "We are quite alone in here and so we can speak privately."

"That's good," Julie said.

"Now you tell me about the war—"

"There are many details I don't know," Julie said slowly. "You must understand that what I know of the war I read in books and you know how much can be left out."

"I read," Desirée revealed. "I learned secretly. I have businesses, I need to know certain things—I need to know because people would cheat me otherwise. Desirée is not stupid."

Julie felt pleased with Desirée's revelation. Certainly it must have been very hard for her to learn to read. She wondered if she were entirely self-taught or if she had somehow obtained help.

"I would never think you stupid," she assured her. "But to learn to read! In this time, in this place—that's a real accomplishment."

Desirée looked pleased with Julie's praise. "First I learned to read Spanish. It's easier than French and English. When I learned to read English I hired a teacher. He came to live at my house and everyone thought he was my lover. We kept it all a secret."

"What have you read?" Julie asked, hoping Desirée's answer would provide her with a clue of how to deal with her problem of providing ongoing information.

"Many books. I have read many books, but I continue to read the Britannica—a Scots book, By *a Society of Gentlemen in Scotland*—a dictionary of the arts and sciences. Three books, big books. I do not understand all these books say—they say much. But I read them."

Julie was stunned. In her mind's eyes she could see the books. They were thick leather volumes in old English script, published in 1769 and reissued in their original format two hundred years later for collectors. She owned a set herself and had found it endlessly useful, in gleaning details to ensure the accuracy of the costumes she designed and also for when piecing together everyday life two hundred years ago.

"I know these books," Julie said.

"All knowledge is contained between their covers," Desirée said with surprising reverence.

"Have you read about the Romans?"

"Yes, of course," Desirée replied. "But more about the Greeks. They had oracles. If you tell me what the future is, I can be an oracle."

Clearly oracles appealed to Desirée since she desired to be one without benefit of divine powers. "But you could not tell me on what day or month this or that happened to the Greeks or the Romans, could you?"

Desirée frowned and shook her head. "No, I could only tell you general things."

"It is so with my knowledge of the Revolution." To some extent she was lying. In fact, her knowledge of the American Revolution had been superior to that of most of her contemporaries in the 1990's.

She had majored in American history and she had toured many battle sights. Colonial history fascinated her. Yet she knew there were many details she could not supply and much information she did not want to supply for fear of somehow changing history. She decided to be honest enough to impart her fears to Desirée.

"Please try to understand that I must be careful, Desirée. I want you to think about this carefully. History as it happened must not be altered."

Desirée looked surprisingly thoughtful, even impressed. "Did you know of me?"

"You are recorded in the history of Louisiana."

Desirée smiled.

This information pleased her, Julie observed. So she continued. "You became very wealthy and influential. Even more so than you are now."

"And how did I become so?"

Julie frowned. "You made shrewd investments." She

spoke softly, for only now did she recognize Desirée's trap. A trap of pure reason.

"Perhaps I made these shrewd investments because I had information from a time traveler." Desirée smiled with absolute satisfaction, her point well made.

"I am trapped by my own caution," Julie admitted. She felt no small admiration for the woman who sat across from her. She nodded, then said softly, "Charleston will be taken by the British shortly. I am not certain of the month, but I know it will happen soon. The British will hold most of the South till the peace treaty is signed."

Desirée smiled. "Good enough. It is good enough."

Julie drained her coffee cup. "I should like to meet with the seamstresses now."

"But of course. I shall take you myself."

In moments they were on their way, off in the carriage to the shop where Desirée employed a dozen women whose job it was to make fine clothes, trimmed with accessories imported from Madrid and Paris.

As the carriage sped along, Julie once again stared at the sights of New Orleans. But this time her thoughts were not filled with history but with the present. How much could she tell Desirée? And how could she make herself truly useful to the business? She lacked the technical expertise to create machines—the key to rapid production— but perhaps even assembly-line techniques would be a sufficient innovation. Silently, she began making a plan which she would present to Desirée. There was no doubt in her mind that if she was to survive in this time period she would have to find a way to become financially independent. She deemed the first rule would be to make herself indispensable.

The carriage pulled to a halt in front of Desirée's shop on Bourbon Street. It consisted of a number of small fitting rooms and one roomy work area. There were large cutting tables but no machinery of any kind—not that Julie had expected any. Nothing, she thought but scissors, pins, and talented fingers.

On a long rack in the back of the workroom half completed gowns were hung and there were rows and rows of shelves filled with bolts of cloth, laces, and various accessories.

"Take me step by step through the whole process of making a dress," Julie requested.

"I have seen your drawings. Surely you know how it is done." Desirée seemed a trifle annoyed.

"I think I do, Desirée. Still, I want you to show me what is done now." She paused for effect. "You know, my knowledge can help in other ways. After all, in my time dresses were all sewn by machine."

Desirée's eyes widened. "Can you make such a machine?"

Julie shook her head. "In just over fifty years from now a Frenchman will invent this machine of which I speak. He will use it to make military uniforms."

"Men are such peacocks," Desirée said with disdain. "How will this wondrous machine work?"

"The fabric will be run under a needle on the top which will interlock the thread that comes from the bottom. At first the needle was made to go up and down with a wheel, then a treadle which the seamstress operates with her feet."

"Ingenious," Desirée said in awe. "It is a great pity you can't make one."

Julie nodded, thinking that she might be able to make something similar if she had a metal worker with whom to work. She certainly understood the principle of how the sewing machine operated. But doing such a thing would constitute a major interference with history. "Even without the machine, Desirée, you can use some modern production methods. Now tell me everything and I will explain."

"First the customer comes in and is measured. Then she is shown a variety of sketches from which she selects. Then a pattern is made and cut. The pieces are sewn together and the accessories added. Of course there are many fittings.''

"Of course," Julie said.

"And what do you suggest?"

"That we begin with four patterns only—patterns taken from four basic designs. Each dress may have different accessories and different fabric and will therefore be unique. But the advantage is that many pieces can be cut in advance and each of the seamstresses can become expert on part of the gown. One, for example, will sew only seams, another only sleeves, yet another hems, and so forth. A written record shall be kept of the sizes needed, and production will go much more quickly."

Desirée looked thoughtful. "It's true that Fifi makes far better collars than Evette."

"Then Fifi should make all the collars."

Desirée smiled. "Yes, this is a good idea."

Julie smiled. She could not introduce modern machines, but she could introduce modern methods.

"Come," Desirée said. "We will explain this to the seamstresses together."

It was early evening and the sky was clear and the air fresh. It was as if last night's storm had washed the humidity and heaviness away so that the fresh air of spring could once again envelop the city.

Brady hurried along toward Desirée's house. Usually he took the carriage, but tonight he felt a brisk walk was in order. He thought of himself as a frontiersman, a fighter, a man to whom living outdoors was second nature. But of course he had to admit to himself that he had not been reared on the frontier nor had he grown up outside the city. He had adopted the frontier philosophy, though, and all things considered, he had become adept and able to hold his own with any man.

New Orleans, he realized, was spoiling him. The food
was too rich, the beds too soft, the women too tempting.

His thoughts settled on the women, specifically Juliet
Hart, the woman with whom he had almost slept last night.
Now, in the setting sun of yet another day, he wasn't sure
why he had not taken her. But something had stopped
him. The reason he had given himself was his suspicions
of her. Again he wished that Oliver Pollock would return,
so he might be able to relax a little. But as long as Pollock,
America's agent in New Orleans, was away, he was in
charge. It was a responsibility he felt strongly.

Responsibilities such as he had could tolerate no distrac-
tions. And the woman was a distraction. Her origins were
a mystery, her strange and sudden appearance a cause of
suspicion, her whole being—a growing temptation. When
he thought about her he could be stronger and more
rational than when he was with her. Rationality slipped
away all too easily when he smelled the aroma of her body
and saw her white, unblemished skin. Then he immediately
envisaged her silhouette behind the screen—the curve of
her perfectly shaped breasts, her long legs, her slender
waist and rounded buttocks. Everything about her beckoned him and when he was without her he now hungered
for her, thinking only of how much he wanted her. So
what had stopped him? Her vulnerability? Her confusion?
Or the fact that he was afraid she might be a British spy? He
wasn't certain, so he settled on his need to be responsible.

He stopped short. He had nearly walked past Desirée's
house. Darkness was rapidly overtaking the Crescent City
and in the parlor men and women met for conversation
and drinks. For a moment he turned and looked at the
houses and buildings of the city as they were outlined
against the sunset.

What a city! Brady thought as for a second he wondered
how it would look to future generations. The tallest building and the most substantial was the Ursuline Nunnery
and School, where the nuns who taught the children of

New Orleans lived and worked. They were a teaching order, and he knew from one of their number that an identical structure stood in Quebec City.

His eyes fell on the house of Jean Claude. New Orleans had a kind of society, men and women who designated themselves elite. In 1769, when he was still a young man growing up in western Pennsylvania, there had been a Creole uprising—but not an uprising caused by a desire for freedom such as the one in which his countrymen were now involved. The cause was much more typical of New Orleans and he loved the story for that reason.

The then governor of Louisiana, Don Antonio Ulloa, had married a Peruvian heiress who arrived in New Orleans with a huge entourage and all her belongings. She refused to invite the Creole elite to her parties and did not attend theirs. In no time they grew angry at the slight, and the Creole women urged the Creole men to rise up in revolution. There were no lofty ideals, simply the allegation that Ulloa's wife was a mulatto, and so were all her friends. In the meantime, Jean Milhet, the richest merchant in the colony, returned from France. He had gone to try to persuade the French to take New Orleans back and not to abandon the French city to the Spanish. The combination of the French refusal to reconsider, and the antisocial behavior of Ulloa's Peruvian wife gave way to cries of "Liberty!"

The Spanish responded by sending Don Alejandro O'Reilly. He proved a hard, but essentially just, taskmaster and soon things were in hand in spite of the fact that even now poor O'Reilly was known as bloody O'Reilly for putting down the rebellion. Some people were jailed, but generally life had returned to normal quickly. Vaguely he wondered if, given that history, the people of this city would rise up again and demand to be part of the new republic, the republic he hoped to help build when the British were defeated. It seemed to him to be inevitable. In fact, in his heart he believed that one day the republic would encompass all the land between the oceans. Was he a dreamer? He couldn't answer his own question. He waited for a moment, then turned and went into the house.

Brady walked into the parlor and helped himself to a drink. The hum of various conversations filled the room.

"Ah, you have come," Desirée cooed and she floated up to him. As usual she was a color-filled vision who did not hesitate to display an expanse of desirable flesh above the daring neckline of her passionate red gown.

He kissed Desirée's hand, but his eyes strayed to Juliet. She was in the corner talking with Bernardo and his most beautiful Creole companion, Felice de St. Maxent d'Estréhan. Felice was a young widow, and it was well known that Bernardo, who was just twenty-nine, a year older than himself, had petitioned the king of Spain for permission to marry her.

He looked for a long moment. Juliet and Felice complemented each other. Felice had black hair and dark Spanish eyes. Juliet was blond with blue eyes.

"You're distracted," Desirée observed. "There was a time when you would not look away from me."

He looked at her and smiled. "I think you understand." Yet he admitted that it made him feel guilty. Vaguely he wondered if Desirée had told Juliet about their liaison. Did women talk about such things? But surely Desirée was not jealous. It was she who had broken with him and not he who had left her. Desirée was quite wonderful, but she could not be loyal to any man. On the other hand, if Desirée were jealous, why would she have given Juliet such a good position? Why would she seem so protective of her?

"Desirée, I must speak with you. Perhaps we should go to the library next door."

Desirée nodded her agreement. They left and went to the library, closing the doors discreetly.

"Pollock is coming back in three days time," Brady confided. "As soon as he returns I want to take Juliet up Bayou

Teche to meet with Philip Landry. She says her mother was a Landry."

"Well, she does have responsibilities here," Desirée said hesitantly.

"It is important to our cause, Desirée. I have already obtained the governor's permission."

Desirée pressed her full lips together. He could tell she was not happy.

"If you have Bernardo's permission, there is nothing much I can do or say. Naturally I would not go against the governor of Louisiana."

"I'll take her next week then. When Pollock has returned."

"Very well. But I do hope you won't be gone long. She is quite a gem, you know. Absolutely invaluable to me."

"I'm glad," he said, surprised by her praise for another woman.

Oliver Pollock was a businessman, a former resident of Pennsylvania, a revolutionary, and Irish to the core. He was a fine businessman and very shrewd, but when he spoke it was with a soft Irish lilt.

When he was only twenty-three he had begun a trading company that dealt primarily with the Spanish West Indies and seven years later, in 1768, he moved to New Orleans where he became, partly because of their shared heritage, a close friend of Governor O'Reilly.

By the time the revolution began, Pollock had already made his fortune, and so became the purchasing agent for the revolutionary government in Louisiana. He sent much-needed supplies to his friend, George Rogers Clark, and since no compensation was possible, he borrowed money from the king of Spain when his own funds were exhausted. Even Bernardo Galvez had helped, giving a small fortune to the cause.

"Did you have trouble getting through British lines?"

Brady asked as he sat in Pollock's study sipping brandy, an apt question as the British controlled the forts up river.

"I skate on thin ice with the British, you know that. I certainly hope Spain will enter the war soon," Pollock admitted.

"I feel certain they will," Brady said. "But tell me the news."

"So much," Pollock said, pressing his lips together. "Some very bad, some good—some intriguing."

"Is the fighting going badly?" Brady asked.

"In the South, yes. Elsewhere I feel the tide of battle has truly turned. Clarke has captured the British commander, Hamilton. The Northwest is his."

"And in the East?"

"A hell of a lot better than last year at this time. The addition of French vessels and German troops has made a real difference."

Brady thought of his two brothers. In truth, he didn't know where they were posted. In a sense, he felt undeserving of his easy life in New Orleans when he knew they were in the thick of battle.

"You're thinking you have it too easy, aren't you?" Pollock said. "Listen, my friend, your work is important. Supplies are the lifeblood of the army."

Brady nodded. Perhaps the troops had it easier now. Pollock's news might be the most recent news he had heard, but all news was old—even when it reached Pollock's ears. Sometimes those who traveled the rivers knew more because they encountered couriers. He longed to go up Bayou Teche—the Acadians had good couriers who often met Canadians who traveled the river system south.

"And for intrigue, I must tell you we have company," Pollock said. "A fellow named James Willing. You may have heard the name since he's from a rather well-known Philadelphia family. His brother is a partner to the banker, Robert Morris, and a member of First Continental Congress."

"I know the name of Willing," Brady said, nodding. Willing was an upstart, sometimes a troublemaker. "He lived in Natchez for a time. He tried to start a store, but he spent all his time and money carousing."

Pollock smiled. "Yes, the same man. He was given some approval by the Congressional Committee on Commerce—a committee that seems to know nothing about commerce. In any case, he left Ft. Pitt with thirty men on an armed river boat, The *Rattletrap*. He burned and pillaged farms and plantations, then he moved on Natchez proper. He's headed down river—"

Brady frowned and then swore under his breath.

Pollock laughed. "You never hide your feelings, Brady McCormick. You should like this man Willing—he's a revolutionary who has won battles."

"And stolen money, I'll wager."

"We have all stolen money."

"Ah, and used it to further the cause of the revolution. Willing won't do that. He'll spend it on wine, women and song. I know him."

"I'm afraid you do," Pollock said thoughtfully. "Well, my friend, when he reaches New Orleans we will have to deal with him."

"*Must* deal with him," Brady corrected. "He'll do our cause no good."

Pollock nodded his agreement and turned to pour himself more French cognac. "What's been happening here?"

Brady leaned back, preparing to give his friend an abbreviated version of the discovery of Miss Juliet Hart and of the more important but not necessarily unrelated fact that *El Dorado* had a near miss. The attack had been based on the original plan, and it would appear that they did have a spy in their midst, even if it were not Juliet Hart. Pollock was a man of even disposition who never jumped to conclusions. He would not immediately think Juliet a spy— though he, too, would no doubt agree there was a spy on the loose.

Chapter Seven

Julie sat on the end of her bed feeling both apprehensive and curious. This was not the twentieth century, she kept reminding herself as she wracked her brain making a mental list of what she should pack. In the meantime, she sewed furiously. Enough was enough. She was not wandering off in a pirogue—a dugout canoe—wearing some flouncy dress trimmed in lace. Nor, she vowed, would she go off unprepared and unarmed. The swamp could be a dangerous place even in the twentieth century, never mind its hazards in the eighteenth century!

"Come in!" she called out, without glancing up from her sewing, after hearing a knock on her door.

Desirée came in and looked at the garment that covered Julie's lap. "What on earth is that?" she asked, lifting her shapely brow.

"Culottes," Julie replied. She did not care if she changed the history of fashion. It was surely time that women learned clothing should be practical, not just pretty.

"Culottes?" Desirée repeated. "I do not know of these."

Julie shook them out. "A divided skirt," she announced

proudly. "For riding or for some activity for which today's clothes are unsuited."

Desirée took the garment from Julie and held it in front of herself. It was full and, fell exactly like a skirt, even though it was divided. "Very clever," Desirée praised. "Very clever indeed. I shall want you to make some of these when you get back."

"I will," Julie promised. Then, looking more seriously at Desirée, "Tell me what you know of medicines," she requested." I have little desire to go off on this trip with nothing should I fall ill."

"Desirée smiled enigmatically. "Desirée knows about potions and powders from her grandmama and mama. The Fon are wise people. But surely you know of future medicines."

"Sanitation is the biggest lifesaver. Boiling drinking water, Desirée. That's very important. And sterilizing wounds and washing one's hands—these things are very important."

Desirée nodded. "Since you told me, all the drinking water here has been boiled."

"I know. And see, there is less illness. But I know there are important medicines that people know about now. I must take medicines with me. I must have something for fever and something for pain if necessary."

"Ah, the bark of Chinchoa tree. I have that among my powders. It is for fevers."

"And something for the stomach."

"Desirée will give you what you need. She will pack it for you. You're a smart woman. And not just because you are a time traveler. Desirée will tell you one important thing. When you get to the village of Philip Landry, go and visit old Angelique. Everyone in that village will know who she is. She is the smartest medicine woman in all the bayous, in all Louisiana. You must go and talk with her."

"Thank you," Julie said with a smile. "For both the compliment and the information." Desirée probably did not pay compliments all that often, especially to her competition, Julie thought.

"When do you leave?"

"Brady says in the morning," Julie answered.

"Take a dress, too," Desirée advised. "The Cajun people like to sing and dance."

Julie agreed. She intended on taking her mosquito netting as well. In fact, she had sewn some onto a bonnet in order to keep insects from her face.

She looked at the small pile of things she intended to pack and felt reasonably proud. It would make, even including a dress, a small, neat bundle.

Desirée went to the door. "I will go for your medicines," she promised. Then she added, "I hope your journey will not be too difficult."

That night Julie lay in bed and tried again to imagine the route she and Brady would take up Bayou Teche. But it was no use. She could not bring a map of Louisiana into her mind and visualize the complicated river system, even though she had studied it endlessly when deciding where to go and which villages she would visit.

How strange it all was! It had been only been a few weeks since she had rented the car and driven to Lafayette Parish. But now it seemed far, far away. What she could remember vividly was flying one year to Mexico. Her plane had flown over Louisiana and it had been one of those truly rare days without clouds. She remembered looking down on the maze of bayous that drained, together with the Mississippi, into the Atlantic. The enormous delta was a mass of green interspersed with blue. The thin lines of water were like snakes on the land. From aloft she had seen a view no person in this century could even imagine. The variegated beauty of seemingly virgin forest intersected by thousands of waterways was a sight to behold, a sight she knew she would never forget. And she remembered thinking then— wondering really—how the early settlers found their way.

Even in the twentieth century she had been told there were places where a stranger could easily become lost.

Now, she thought, with a tremor of excitement, she would find out what it was like when the forests still were virgin and when the land was virtually unsettled.

It was early morning and a light fog floated over the river beneath the gray sky. A variety of aromas from the market filled the air. The mouthwatering smell of freshly baked bread mixed with the odor of fish being smoked.

Julie climbed down off the carriage carrying her bag. It was not a basket case such as most women carried but a duffle bag she had made herself.

Brady was facing the long dugout, handing bundles down to the Indians who would paddle. He stood up straight and turned at the sound of the carriage halting. When he saw her, his lips parted in surprise.

"You're a most unusual vision," he commented.

"I've chosen to make clothes which are practical for such a journey," she replied. She knew she must look strange to a man of this time, though she had decided to dress as she felt necessary. She wore a light-brown divided skirt, a leather vest, and beneath it a sort of overblouse. Around her waist she wore a man's leather belt. She carried a knife in a leather sheath and a holstered pistol. Her long full divided skirt fell to her ankles, but she did not wear shoes. Rather she wore men's boots which rose to her knees beneath her culottes. On her head she wore a hat with a net that fell to her shoulders but which was presently tied on top. Her long blond hair was braided.

"Your clothes do indeed seem practical. I have never seen garments like them."

"I made them," she announced in order to end further discussion. "Especially for this journey. Women's clothes are simply no good in a dugout canoe."

He laughed. "You'll get no argument from me. I like

your dress, even if it is less revealing than that normally worn.''

''The better to keep insects away.''

''Is that your satchel?'' He pointed to her duffle bag.

''Catch!'' she said, eyes twinkling.

''Whoa!'' He caught it, but nearly fell backward into the water.

''Sorry,'' she said, smiling.

''You will have to sit still. We shouldn't want the boat to tip—and all the more care must be taken on the bayou since the water is full of gators.''

''I'll be careful,'' she promised.

''Come then. I'll help you into the boat.''

His hands around her waist were strong and warm, and when he set her down, she felt her face flush ever so slightly. The sight of him, the feel of him, brought back memories of the other night in the garden—a night when passionate kisses had been truly interspersed with the roar of thunder and the flashing of lightning; a night when she now admitted she had wanted him.

Yet the desire she had felt then—and now—frightened her and raised questions she could not answer. Was it right for her to form liaisons in this century when she might only be a visitor? Then their eyes met and she knew he, too, was remembering the other night and she wondered if this liaison could be avoided.

She sat down. This was not a canoe in which she would have to kneel, but rather a large dugout. She was allowed to stretch her legs in front of her. He climbed in beside her and in a moment they were joined by the four Indian paddlers.

The tether that secured them to the dock was untied, and with silent skill the paddlers guided the boat through the water and upstream against the current. But they did not have to fight the river for long. After a short time, they turned.

''We're entering the first of bayous we'll travel on,''

Brady told her as she looked about. "It parallels the river, yet it has no strong current to battle."

Strange, she had not thought of that. She had simply assumed they would go up river till they got to what in her time was Baton Rouge and that then they would turn west toward Lafayette and Bayou Teche, known by all in this time as the transportation route that connected the villages and towns of Louisiana. The Teche was a great river; it could be navigated for a hundred miles upstream from its mouth on the Atlantic. But before they could reach the Teche, they had to parallel the Mississippi and then head east. She assumed they would join the Teche somewhere in what was in her time Lafayette Parish, up river from Morgan City.

Now and again they would pass cultivated land, but no houses were visible. Later, she thought, this would no doubt change. When they reached the Teche, there would probably be houses along the Teche, the French having seeded as many arpents of land back from the river as a settling family could clear.

"What do you think? Does the sight of the bayou bring back memories? You might have come here by boat or by barge."

She shook her head slowly. The bayou did not evoke memories, but rather a vision of the future and future problems. In her time, many of the waterways were crowded with water lilies. They had been introduced to Louisiana in the early 1900's at the World's Fair, and the state spent millions trying to eradicate them so they would not clog the water and take all the oxygen, thus ruining the shrimping. But the absence of lilies was only one difference in the face of the land. When she had passed this way in the car, stumps stood in the water where now giant cypress trees reached for the sky. During Louisiana's boom years, before people realized how precious these great trees were, too much harvesting had taken place. It was with some sadness that she looked at the cypress. What was truly familiar was the Spanish moss which hung from the trees like northern moss. It gave these wonderfully tall trees an otherworldly appearance. It was as if they were inhabited by giant spiders who had spun magical webs from great heights.

"It seems funny to see the waterways this way," she said abstractedly. As soon as she said it, she knew she had allowed her thoughts to break through into idle conversation.

"What way?" he said, turning.

She shook her head and avoided looking into his dark demanding eyes. "I don't know—I seem to have memories of a place like this where flowers grew on the water."

Brady laughed. "Not here. Perhaps you remember some similar spot."

"Perhaps," she allowed, closing her eyes and letting the smells of the bayou and the sounds of the ever-singing birds sweep over her. The air was heavy, perfumed with the aroma of flowers while the motion of the dugout was slow, gliding. The sun, where it shone through the tall, lacy trees was warm.

She felt him reach over and take her hand. She did not withdraw it, but rather let him hold it. He began tracing small circles on her palm, playing with her fingers. Never before had she thought of her palm as being an erogenous zone, but surely it was. His touch sent little ripples throughout her system, like a pebble thrown on still water. A chill passed through her followed by the flush of heat she knew all to well was excitement. Then, almost furtively, he kissed her fingers.

Again she wondered what to do, wondered if a liaison with him would be right. But then she wondered if she could stop him in any case—not now while they were with the paddlers, but if they were alone, totally alone, as they had been in the garden.

The thoughts she was beginning to have about Brady were outrageous and she reminded herself that they were out of character. Never had she thought about a man so much, let alone dreamed wild erotic daydreams.

"When do we reach the first Acadian Village?" Julie asked.

"Tonight."

She stared off into the distance, taking in the scenery but thinking of their kisses in the garden and wondering what would happen that evening.

It was twilight when the first Acadian village came into sight. It was a large semi-circle of log cabins with an expansive green lawn that came right down to the water's edge. In the middle of the semi-circle there stood a stone church, its simple wooden cross reaching heavenward. There was one large barn used by all, and a blacksmith's shop.

The whole population of the village assembled at the water's edge to meet them. Julie counted some forty people in all and she assumed there were more away hunting or fishing.

"We'll be sleeping in the home of the LeBlancs," Brady told her.

As soon as the boat was secured, Julie hurried ashore. As she had been sitting all day she had to suppress the desire to run across the grass. It was especially inviting, like a village green. During their voyage they had drunk only water from a flask and eaten only bread. She hadn't minded at all, but now that the sun was going down and it was cooling off, she felt hungry and more than ready to eat.

Julie felt incredible enthusiasm and more than a little awe as they walked toward the houses.

What a wonderful experience! These people were her ancestors—or like them. They were displaced Acadian farmers from Nova Scotia. They were fun-loving yet devout, hard-working, and modest. There were no low-cut gowns here. The women wore long-sleeved white blouses under long, heavy cotton pinafores and they covered their heads with white caps. Yet they did not look surprised or shocked by her dress, which was, after all, quite modest by New Orleans standards.

Julie found the inside of the one-room houses both surprising and interesting. The fireplace with its wrought-iron utensils and the long table laden with fresh vegetables caught her eye immediately. Half a log upended made a chopping block, and spices hung and dried from the rim of the round candelabras that were suspended from the ceiling. All the furniture was handmade and the more comfortable pieces were gaily covered and stuffed with Spanish moss, as were the mattresses. These women, she well knew, did not live idle lives. Their days were probably busy from the time the sun rose till it set. In this century simple chores were involved and time-consuming.

Brady had come with her into the home of Pierre LeBlanc and his wife Amélie.

As gifts, Brady had brought bolts of cloth, a few tools, and a few books.

"We'll have a celebration tonight, eh?" Pierre suggested. "We get few visitors here."

Julie listened when they spoke. Their French was already disappearing, to be replaced by something distinctive. A new language, a combination of seventeenth-century French, eighteenth-century Spanish, and English with Indian words thrown in for good measure. One day, she thought, it would become Cajun, the distinctive language of the Louisiana Acadians in their exile.

"What brings you here?" Pierre asked.

Brady pulled a stool up to the big table. Amélie was already setting out mugs and big hunks of homemade bread and cheese.

"I want to raise a team of Acadians to help the revolutionaries. We need to move arms north in order to defeat the British."

Pierre grinned.

"And I am seeking my family," Julie said, knowing as soon as she said it that he would wonder about her speech, which was certainly not like his or his wife's.

He did indeed frown. "Are you Cajun?"

"My mother's name was Landry. But I was brought up in New York."

"We're headed up to see Philip Landry," Brady added.

"He would be the one to ask about the Landrys. He would also be the man to contact about raising a force. He is our leader."

"Do you think some of your men would be willing."

Pierre laughed heartily. "You know we have no love for the British. We would see them defeated at any cost. They've decimated our people and scattered them to the four winds."

Brady nodded and looked at Julie. Maybe there were reasons for her lack of memory. Yet, as Pierre had noticed, her accent was not Cajun. In fact, she sounded like no one he had ever heard before.

Pierre laughed. "Yes, we shall have a celebration! And with it much homemade wine."

Julie remained silent, afraid of revealing herself to these kind people in some accidental way—not that anyone would believe she was from the future. How could she ever possibly explain the truth? But ancestors were not family, so she did not want them to look too hard for those they believed to be her relatives. She cursed herself for admitting her Cajun heritage in the first place—surely that admission was going to raise questions for which she had no answers. She did not look particularly Cajun and she didn't sound Cajun. True, she spoke French, but it was modern Parisian French.

"Is something the matter?" Pierre asked.

Julie quickly shook her head. "No, not at all. Perhaps I am just a bit tired."

"Understandable. It is a long journey."

Julie forced her apprehensions aside. The more preoccupied she appeared, the more suspicious she would seem. She decided that no matter what, she would concentrate on enjoying herself. Partaking in a real Cajun celebration would be a wonderful experience.

The church, Julie soon learned, had many uses. When the priest came once a month, it was a church and only a church. But the rest of the time it doubled as a meeting hall and tonight it was a place to hold a party. The altar was put away, the benches moved to the sides of the room, and tables set out with food from every house in the village, as well as the promised homemade wine.

And it seemed that no Acadian village was without a fiddler. This one was a man with a white beard who wore buckskins and a old misshapen hat. But when he picked up his fiddle he became young again and everyone, including old men and small children, took to the dance floor to step dance. It was a vigorous dance which seemed, as more wine was consumed, to get faster and faster, if not louder and louder.

At first Julie only clapped. But it was as if the sound of this music aroused some primordial instinct in her and she could not even sit still. She had seen the dance performed by an Acadian group once, but the performance had not been like this. And now she was no spectator; now she was a part of it.

Brady was on his feet and dancing, too, and the two of them where whirling about and drinking rich red wine and whirling about some more. The feel of his large hands on her waist was wonderful and the smile on his face enchanted her. For the first time since her journey back in time she laughed, truly laughed. For the first time she let herself go entirely and enjoyed the moments as they flew by to the tune of the infectious, colorful music.

She was hardly aware when he danced her right out the door and onto the wide expanse of lawn. He whirled her and twirled her to a small building at the very edge of the water, and then he swooped her into his strong arms and carried her inside, depositing her on sweet-smelling soft hay.

His hot lips were on the back of her neck even as he undid her long golden braids, loosening her mane so it fell over her shoulders. Then his lips were on her lips and she felt as if she would cry out with happiness and desire.

How quickly he moved as he slipped off her vest and removed her blouse, belt, and skirt.

"You are beautiful beyond words," he said, kissing her shoulder. His fingers flew to her remaining bit of clothing, a light chemise. In seconds it, too, was discarded and his hands played round her full breasts even as the moonlight poured through the window of the little barn. "I've seen you in silhouette, but only now in the flesh, my lady." He touched her breast almost reverently before he lowered his lips and kissed them both gently at first, then with increasing passion. He kissed them in a way that made her burn for him.

She was naked and lying in the moonlight, her skin white and smooth. He stood for a moment and quickly shed his own clothes, then lowered himself beside her.

"You are like an angel," he whispered as he kissed her neck and then her lips.

She felt him hot and strong and she moved against him, running her hand through the hair on his broad chest, feeling his muscles tense and strong beneath his salty skin. His breath was heavy now, as was hers. They rolled together, reaching for one another, touching each other in ways meant to tease and taunt.

He was firm but gentle as he held her tightly, his mouth holding her now-hard nipple while with his other hand he teased her other nipple, rubbing it gently between thumb and forefinger. It was sweet, sweet torture and if she had for a single moment thought this man dressed in buckskins, this backwoodsman who claimed to be a revolutionary, did not know how to please a woman, the thought was now unthinkable. He knew exactly what to do, how to do it, and, most important, how to prolong her torment.

She writhed in his arms and encircled him with her legs, whispering urgently, begging him.

But he laughed at her and continued his explorations. His lips now were in the valley of her breasts, then lower and lower till she gasped and struggled against the most intimate of all caresses, a caress she had never had from another man, a caress that stabbed through her and made her moan and beg him to fulfill her. But he held her on the edge, kissing and withdrawing, his lips and tongue magic instruments of divine pleasure.

Her skin glowed hot beneath his movements. Again and again she raised her hips to him and finally he slid his hands beneath her to grasp her round, firm buttocks.

When he entered her it was slowly, allowing himself to sink into her a little at a time, slowly even as he returned to nurse her taut pink nipple.

Her legs were as long, lovely, and lithe as he had imagined. She was moist and soft, the smell of her skin arousing, the feel of her like no other with whom he had coupled. He drove into her now and she moaned slightly and clung to him.

Beneath him she throbbed and thrashed, clinging to him, prolonging the wildest most wanton pleasure she had ever known. She lifted herself to him with a noise of satisfaction, her whole body trembling in his arms.

And then together they fell into the abyss, each clinging to the other.

Brady held her tightly and could only think how she was perfect, so perfect that all others ceased to exist for him.

She trembled in his arms wondering why only here in another century had she found a man who finally awakened her fully.

That night they slept in a single bed in the house of the

LeBlancs. They slept drugged with wine, lovemaking, and weariness from a long day.

Early the next morning as the sun streamed through the window, Julie lay awake happily listening to the serenade of the wildlife on the bayou. It was a sweet song of happiness and satisfaction to her ears. Beside her, Brady lay with his leg across her. Though he slept, she could still feel his arms wrapped around her, still feel the warmth and comfort of his body. She snuggled closer to him and closed her eyes. She was no longer alone in this strange world!

It took them two more days to reach the second Cajun village, which was their ultimate destination. It was much larger than the first. The church was bigger, and there was a separate meeting hall and more than forty homes.

The home of Philip Landry was the largest. It was a stone house with log additions to accommodate the many members of his immediate family.

He was a short man compared to Brady. Julie took him to be five foot seven inches or so. But he was nevertheless a bear of a man. His arms bulged with muscle and his chest was broad. He had brown eyes and a gray mustache and beard. His skin was toughened by the outdoors and by the life he had led. He was, she realized almost at once, a precious being, a man whose mind was a repository for family history and for the tragic events that had shaped the history of a whole people. Moreover, from the beginning she knew he was a consummate storyteller, a man with a velvet voice, an ability to imitate, a man of great and good humor.

She had learned Landry was seventy-eight, a venerable age to have reached in the year 1779. He had been fifty-four years old at the time of the expulsion twenty-four years ago, and from what she knew of the brutality of that event, he was surely one of the oldest survivors.

Brady bade her to sit across from Landry who occupied

a handmade rocker, while he himself perched on the mantel. Landry paused and studied them, but before he even spoke she knew he was a treasure of a man, a man whose words ought to be preserved.

"I was born in Nova Scotia," he said slowly. "South of the Great Port—very far south of the fortress of Louisbourg on Cape Breton Isle."

Julie nodded and tried to conceal her pleasure. She knew the area well. The Great Port was, of course, Halifax. And the fort was still called Louisbourg! It was indeed a great fort, won and lost many times during the wars between the British and French. In her time, it had been historically restored and she had visited it a few years ago.

But what Landry didn't know was that all the players in North America also warred elsewhere. The same generals who fought in America fought in India and the Orient. The kings and queens moved their men about the giant colonial chessboard with ease so that in the century from whence she had come the name Cornwallis was as familiar in New Delhi as it was in New England or in Canada.

Soon the French, believing Louisbourg to be the most valuable of their possessions, would trade their holdings in India to the British in order to keep Louisbourg. What an irony! What a mistaken choice! More so since they would lose Louisbourg, too, in yet another war. In the end the French ended up with neither a foothold in India nor a significant colony in North America. The French in North America would survive both here and in Canada, but they would have to fight to retain their culture and their language.

St. Genevieve, the town near where she grew up in St. Louis, was the first French settlement west of the Mississippi. It still existed in her century and the descendants of its original families gathered at Christmas to sing songs in a language they did not understand. The language was seventeenth-century French.

She leaned forward. "Did your village in Nova Scotia have a name?"

Philip Landry nodded. "Pointe-de-Église, Church Point."

Julie felt her excitement surge through her. She could not say she had been there, that she had walked the peaceful campus of the Université Sainte-Anne. She could not tell him that Acadians still lived there—descendants of those who escaped the deportations, or those who managed to return.

"We are peace-loving people; we wanted no part of the war. Most of us left France because we were tired of endless war. But it followed us, and when France and England went to war, the English saw our settlements as a threat even though we had lived under English rule since I was just a boy in 1713. So they came. We weren't all taken at once, and some were left or even made their way home."

He did know, Julie thought silently. Somehow she was glad. If only she could tell him about Acadians in the twentieth century. Of course it was out of the question.

He continued. "But most of us were loaded on ships and dropped off along the way, scattered to the four winds from the Carolina coast to the Louisiana bayous."

Brady took her hand and leaned over toward Landry. "This woman came to us in New Orleans. She appeared at the home of Desirée Coteau with no memory of how she came to be there. She says she is from New York, she says her mother's last name was Landry, but that her father's name was Hart."

Pierre rubbed his chin. "She is from no Landry family in Louisiana. But what she says is still possible. Some by that name were taken from Acadian settlements farther east. They were taken to the Carolinas and then began the trek home. Some stopped or married along the way, staying with their new families. It is quite possible her mother was taken to the Carolinas and, on her way home,

married in New York. She looks to be twenty-three or
twenty four—"

"Twenty-four," Julie said.

"Ah, then she was born the very year of the expulsion.
Probably her mother stayed in New York because she was
pregnant. Likely, she married there."

"This does not explain how she came to New Orleans."

Pierre Landry smiled. "*Oui,* it does not."

Brady looked at Julie, whose eyes were still on Landry.
He felt frustrated, because he had hoped Landry would
know exactly who she was. But instead all he had done
was explain that the heritage she claimed was hers was
plausible. Still, he could not believe she was a spy. Certainly,
given the way he felt, he did not want her to be one.

"Thank you for trying to help," Brady said.

Julie did not turn to look at him, but rather continued
to look at Landry. "I would like to write down some of the
history you know—the history of your people."

"You write French?"

"No, I will listen and write in English."

Landry nodded his agreement. "But we will have to talk
later. Brady has asked to speak to me on other matters."

"Privately," Brady said.

Julie stood up. How could he not trust her yet? She had
slept with him. Yet how could she blame him? She had yet
given him her trust; she had not yet dared to share her
secret with him. She smoothed out her skirt. "I shall go
now and return later."

"I look forward to it," Landry replied.

Julie paused. "Is there a woman called Old Angelique
about?"

Philip Landry smiled knowingly. "Ah, yes. She lives in
the third row of houses. Ask one of the children to take
you to her door."

* * *

The little boy who took her to Old Angelique's door left her there and ran away. Julie knocked lightly and in a moment the door opened a crack.

"Are you Angelique?" she asked shyly.

The old woman opened the door a little wider and peered at Julie. She was a tiny woman with long scraggly gray hair and swarthy weathered skin. But her eyes were remarkable. They were sea green with golden rings, and though the woman was old, her eyes were young. They were clear and sharp and Julie felt thoroughly examined in one long look.

"I am Angelique Dupuis," the woman answered. Her voice was gritty, like sandpaper.

"My name is Julie—I am a visitor to this village."

Angelique opened the door wider. "Come in."

"I have heard you are the wisest medicine woman in Louisiana. I'm interested in medicine."

"And where have you heard this said?" Angelique questioned.

"I heard it from a woman in New Orleans."

Angelique smiled. "I did not know my reputation had traveled so far."

Julie could hardly take her eyes off Angelique to look about her tiny cabin—a cabin filled with drying leaves, herbs, and jars and jars filled with mysterious ingredients.

"Did you collect all these in the bayou?"

Angelique shook her head. "No. Some come from other places. But it is true, most of what one needs is here."

"If you had a sick man whose skin was dark and whose teeth were loose, what would you give him?"

"A weak man?"

"Yes, very weak."

"Tea made from rose hips," Angelique replied.

Julie almost smiled. She had described scurvy and Angelique had prescribed vitamin C. Even in her century English mothers still gave their babies rose hip syrup.

But scurvy and its cure were all Julie was able to describe

and know if she was getting a correct answer. Still Angelique did know what to give for scurvy and that alone indicated her expertise.

"What would you give for stiffness in the joints?" Julie asked.

"Powder from creek willow bark."

"Asthma?"

"Smoke of jimsonweed."

"Mild pain," Julie asked.

"The boiled bark of the willow."

Julie again almost smiled; Angelique had just given her a prescription for a crude form of aspirin.

"You are a wondrous woman," Julie said in admiration

Angelique came over and took her hands in hers. She turned them and examined them. "These are good hands for a medicine woman. If you learn the plants of the forest, you could be a medicine woman."

Julie wondered to herself. She loved sewing, but surely given her knowledge she could be doing more in this century to help people. Perhaps if she learned what Angelique knew and combined it with her knowledge of first aid and knowledge of sanitation she could find a new career.

"Sometime in the future I would like to return here," Julie said carefully. "Perhaps you would teach me."

Old Angelique nodded her head. "I can teach you," she said slowly. "I think you can learn."

"Thank you." Julie turned and left. There wasn't time now, but maybe in the future there would be time. The whole idea fascinated her. Filled with a sense of purpose she walked slowly back to Philip Landry's house.

"You're a strange woman," Brady McCormick said as he walked with Julie through the fields that seemed to stretch forever behind the village. "And now I find you've been talking with medicine women."

"Does that make me strange?"

"You're beautiful and delicate looking, yet I suspect you can use the pistol you carry. You ask questions to which you already seem to know the answers."

"I can use the pistol. I do not always know the answers." She did not elaborate. She could hardly tell him she lived alone in New York, a city far different than he knew it to be. She could hardly explain she had gone to a firing range and learned to use a gun. Nor could she tell him about the whole world of twentieth-century medicine. Instead, she laughed gently. "How else am I strange?"

"You read and write and you understand and speak both Spanish and French."

She almost told him how difficult it had been for her to understand Philip Landry, whose French was mixed with other languages and was, in any case, seventeenth-century French, far different from today's modernized Parisian French which she had studied. But of course she could not tell him that either.

"I had no brothers," she answered. "My parents felt I should have an education." It was certainly not a lie, though she imagined that if she had brothers her parents still would have wanted her to have an education.

"Very few women are educated," he replied.

She looked at him and tilted her head ever so slightly. "I think I am not the only strange one, Brady McCormick. You dress in buckskins and tell me you are from Fort Pitt, yet I suspect you, too, are educated. You speak as one educated. I have also noted that you also read. Fewer women may read, but not so many frontiersmen read, either."

He grinned at her disarmingly and slipped his arm round her waist. "I suppose we are just a strange twosome then."

"You have no intention of explaining yourself?"

"I went to Harvard like my father who is a doctor. I didn't study medicine, but rather philosophy. We moved west, and then the revolt against the British began. My family never believed in taxation without representation in British rule. We believe this country will only develop and grow as an independent entity.''

''Regardless of what you believe of me, I, too, know that to be true.''

He nodded. ''I want to believe you because you are like a lovely flower and I want to have you again and again.''

His eyes lingered on her and he stopped talking. She could actually feel his unspoken desire, see the exciting lustfulness that filled his eyes.

Suddenly he turned and gathered her into his arms. His lips sought hers with an urgency as he kissed her neck, her ears, then her lips.

Julie trembled in his arms and marveled at both his rough edges and cultivated center. He was such a large man, a man whose hands could easily span her waist. And what a lover this man was! He was torturously slow and deliberate, and even now as he held her, his hands roaming freely over her, she could relive the moment he had first awakened her, that incredible delicious moment when he had first taken her.

''We agreed to wait till we leave here,'' she breathed.

But it was too late. He had bent her until she lay on the grass with his huge form leaning over her. His hands held her wrists as he ravished her with seductive kisses and entangled her with his legs.

''Say no, my woman. Say wait. Tell me when to stop and your wish is my command.'' His large hand plunged down her dress and his knowing fingers caressed her breasts and then slowly he began to toy with her nipples, gently rolling each in turn between his thumb and forefinger.

Her face grew hot and her breath was beginning to come in quick pants. She knew that now, in the daylight, he could well see the heat in her face, the agony of expectation and desire in her expression. There was no hiding her excitement, no way of trying to play coy.

"Say no," he again challenged. He was smiling at her; no, leering. She wriggled as once again he rubbed her nipples, teasing her with the promise of so much more.

She opened her lips and he kissed her. His tongue was hot and probing while his hands explored her.

"Ah, you shan't say no, my woman."

She felt his other hand beneath her skirts, moving slowly between her legs.

You're moist with excitement." He breathed in her ear even as his fingers unlaced her bodice and freed her. "Even lovelier by daylight," he whispered as he lowered his lips to her now-hard nipples.

She did writhe in his arms, and never so much as when he reached beneath her skirts to caress her thighs and then her most intimate place. She cried out for him and he opened his breeches and teased at her entranceway while she tried desperately to raise herself to unite with him.

"See, you cannot say no," he teased.

His fingers flew to her area of greatest sensitivity and he played there till she groaned and tossed in his arms, till she whispered, "Please," breathlessly, wantonly.

Then with a long kiss he entered her. As slowly as before, sinking bit by bit into her as she seemed to fold around him. His mouth nursed her breast as he moved within her and then, unable to wait, she felt her pleasure pour over her as he moved faster, pleasuring himself as well.

He held her tightly in his arms. "No waiting for us, my woman. No. We cannot wait."

Chapter Eight

All her life the word "bayou" had caused Julie to conjure up images of a sinuous, shadowy waterway with overhanging limbs that looked as if the trees from which they sprung were drinking from the mirrorlike waters. And beyond, into the distance on either shore, the huge trees would fade into the darkness of the green velvet swamp with oak and cypress draped in their weblike clothing of Spanish moss.

Certainly parts of Bayou Teche and its tributaries filled Julie's every expectation, bringing her conjured-up images into the realm of reality. But there was so much more! So many things that had not been here when she had traveled this way by car.

In places, there were fields of waving sugarcane such as Don Carlos had told her he grew on the banks of the Mississippi. Waterways were the roads of this century. As they traveled farther downstream toward the Gulf Coast, the bayou seemed to come alive with commerce. Pirogues, skiffs, and flatboats appeared, traveling in both directions.

Julie smiled to herself. It was this bayou, the Teche that

Longfellow would immortalize when he came to write
"Evangeline," the story of the Acadian deportations. It
was from this bayou that long oak corridors would eventu-
ally lead to huge white antebellum mansions. In fact she
had read that Cretian Point Plantation, off this bayou and
built in the early 1800's, had the wonderful curving staircase used in the film, *Gone With the Wind*.

How odd it was! Before this trip, Bayou Teche had been
a dream. Now she had seen it in two centuries. She had
marked all the historic places she wanted to see in her
guide books. But now she had seen the bayou, traveled its
length, and many of the places she had visited had not yet
been built.

She leaned back in the dugout and watched Brady who
was taking a turn paddling. His shirt was off, and his tanned
skin glistened with perspiration.

Julie smiled at him and he returned her smile. She
leaned back and closed her eyes. They were almost to the
coast, almost to what in her time was Morgan City. From
there, they would travel overland to New Orleans.

She was so relaxed in the warm sun that she was skirting
the rim of sleep when the gun shots rang out.

She jolted upright in terror. "Brady!" She shouted his
name at the moment she saw blood gushing from his
shoulder.

"Pull ashore! Pull ashore!" She looked up disbelievingly.
The shore was lined with British troops, their long rifles
pointed directly at the dugout—at her and Brady, at the
frightened Indian oarsmen.

"Don't shoot!" she called out. "We'll come ashore.
Don't shoot!"

She crawled forward carefully on her hands and knees.
"Go ashore!" she said, motioning to the Indians.

She reached Brady. His face was contorted with pain.
She fumbled in her bag for her chemise, and when she
found it she withdrew it and tore it into a wide strip. As

the dugout was paddled to shore, she bound his shoulder, trying desperately to stem the flow of blood.

"Out of the dugout!" a British officer demanded. Soldiers dragged the boat out of the water and before she could protest a soldier grasped her roughly and pulled her out of the boat.

"An added prize," one of the officers said, his eyes roaming her body.

"And dressed so charmingly," another commented as he disarmed her.

"Get out of that boat, you traitor!" One of the men kicked Brady viciously in the side.

"Leave him alone! He's hurt!" Julie protested.

They dragged Brady half conscious from the boat. Another soldier viciously kicked him again. He groaned and seemed to slip into complete unconsciousness.

"Get him on a litter and take him to the rowboat. He's a traitor and we'll take him back to Mobile and hang him!"

"No!" Julie screamed. Then suddenly she remembered where they were. "This is Spanish territory, you have no jurisdiction here!"

The officer in charge, a round man with a red nose, laughed heartily. "Our guns give us jurisdiction, my lady. But you can stay here and fend for yourself. We're going to take Mr. Brady McCormick, traitor to the Crown and gun runner, back to Mobile to dangle from the end of a rope."

Brady groaned and looked up at the officer. "Mistaken—" he muttered. "I'm John Andrews out of Natchez."

His words seemed to come painfully and his eyes were focused not on the British officer, but on her. They seemed to beg her not to betray him.

"And I am Mrs. John Andrews," she said indignantly. "We're British supporters, loyal to the core. You and your men will pay for this miscarriage of justice, for wounding my husband."

The officer narrowed his eyes. "We're here because we were told Brady McCormick was on his way down the Teche. You fit his description."

"I don't care what you were told! He is my husband and his name is not Brady McCormick." Julie glared at the officer in charge.

The look the officer gave them was less sure but nonetheless harsh. "Row them out to the *Exetor* and lock them in a cabin. We'll take them to Mobile where there are people who know Brady McCormick."

"And what will you do when you find you've made a mistake?" she asked, still looking at him defiantly.

"Allow you to go free," he answered dully.

"You had better be careful with my husband," she warned.

The officer looked at her meanly. "You had better hold your pretty tongue or we'll leave you here for the pirates to find."

Julie said no more. She sat in their rowboat and held Brady's head in her lap as they were rowed offshore toward the armed vessel that flew the British flag.

Julie squeezed Brady's hand. All she could think was that she hadn't traveled back over two hundred years in time to find a man she could love just to lose him to a hangman's noose. Fate could not be that cruel. But just in case it was, she decided she had better begin making plans to get them out of this mess. She pressed her lips together. Whatever else was true or not true, one thing seemed obvious. There was a spy. Someone had told the British of their trip up the bayou. That person must have figured out the route by which they would be coming back to New Orleans and more or less the hour they would return.

Don Fernando walked toward Desirée's home. Inside he felt mildly triumphant. Not that he could be certain of the outcome of his little plan, but assuming all went well, Brady McCormick would no longer be about. He would not return to New Orleans to aid Oliver Pollock or influence Bernardo Galvez. In fact, Brady McCormick would either be in irons in a British jail or buried six feet under the ground.

Don Fernando seethed inside when he thought about the fact that Galvez and his brother had given Pollock and McCormick huge sums of money to aid the rebels, had helped them raise funds and had turned a blind eye on arms shipments. And Spain was not even at war! Control, he thought to himself. He must control his temper or he would never succeed with his plans.

He stopped in front of Desirée's house. To his surprise she was on the veranda looking almost as if she had expected him.

"Dear Don Fernando," she greeted him. "Have you come to visit?"

"To drink in your beauty," he replied, bowing from the waist.

She smiled what he felt was an inviting smile. "Come, walk with me, Don Fernando."

Don Fernando walked beside Desirée in the moonlight. He had hoped for months to be invited to her bed, but the invitation had not come. He could not, he reasoned, be upset that Esmé, had turned to his brother since he paid her to pry information from Don Carlos's lips. As for the beautiful Miss Hart, she unfortunately seemed as smitten by the American, Brady McCormick, as he was with her. Alas, there had been no way for him to have Brady captured without also having the lovely Señorita Hart captured as well. But perhaps the British wouldn't hold her— they were all such gentlemen. Perhaps they would allow her to return to New Orleans.

He glanced at Desirée. Her profile was magnificent. She was like a willow, tall and graceful. He could only imagine *through*

the wonderful treasures hidden beneath her somewhat modest dress—modest for Desirée in any case.

Bravely, he slipped his arm around her tiny waist as they walked. He could feel the motion of her hips swaying and it sent a chill (though) him. He let his hand drop slightly lower to cover her surging buttocks. She did not react.

"If the revolutionaries defeat the British," she said softly, "I will wager that one day Louisiana will be theirs."

"Do you think so?" He could barely speak he was so aroused by just the simple undulating movements of her walk. How could she discuss politics at a moment like this?

"Yes, I do. Tell me, Ferdie, do you believe the British will win?

She was the only woman who had ever dared to call him Ferdie and he could not think of how to react. He certainly did not want others to take such liberties, but from her lips he could forgive it. "Yes, yes," he answered.

"Really? Does that mean you support the British cause or do you just think they will emerge victorious?"

"You know I support the revolutionaries—as Galvez does, as my brother does." He sputtered out his words, though his mind was on her.

"I know you say you support them. But remember, Desirée can see into men's hearts and minds. I think you have other loyalties."

He was taken aback. "I have no idea what you mean."

She turned suddenly and faced him. Her smile was wonderful, warm and radiant. She grasped his wrist and directed his hand to her full breast. He seized her and stood staring into her hypnotic catlike eyes. Surely this brazen action meant she was willing.

"Come to my bed," he stuttered. He had slept with many of her women, but he had always wanted her. She was exotic, mysterious—it was said that she could do things no other woman could.

"I will and we will talk more. Go to your bed and leave

the door unlocked. I shall join you when the moon is full in the sky. Desirée must think now.''

He almost stumbled as he hurried back to his own home several blocks away.

Don Fernando lay in his bed waiting, aware that in spite of excessive drink he was ready.

He did not even hear her enter the house, nor did he hear her footsteps on the stairs. She came like an incubus in the night. She came dressed in a transparent gown and seemed surrounded by a fragrant mist. She lay down on top of him, surrounding him, as it were, covering him with the length of her lithe body. Her movements were snakelike as she seemed to engulf him. He touched her and she eluded him even in the moonlight. Yet she was there moving across him, over him, beside him. When she told him to close his eyes he did so, and then he felt her take him into her moist depths. She moved atop him and he felt the tips of her soft breasts brush his cheeks. He fulfilled himself with a sudden uncontrollable burst while she seemed to hover in mid-air above him, taking his seed silently.

Then she was beside him, her voice soft as her knowing hand caressed his damp body. ''You are such a dilettante, Ferdie. I can't believe you are really a revolutionary.''

''Would you forgive me if I weren't?'' The words fairly spilled out of his mouth though he had never intended telling her his true feelings.

She touched his lips with a long finger. ''I could forgive you anything except lack of greed. I know you're greedy, it's why I have always liked you.''

''You have always liked me?'' He felt incredulous. He had thought she liked everyone else. Why had she never slept with him before?

''Oh, yes. Always.''

''My brother is an idiot,'' Don Fernando declared drunkenly. "He wants to raise sugar, but cotton will be king. He wants to support a revolution that will destroy us and our kind!"

"Your brother will inherit, is that not so?"

Don Fernando cursed under his breath. "I should kill him," he muttered.

Desirée leaned over and kissed him deeply. "Not yet," she whispered. "You will do nothing without consulting Desirée."

Silently he reached for her and nodded. "Nothing," he promised.

Desirée brushed out her rich dark hair and contemplated her liaison with Don Fernando. Without question he was the spy that Brady knew existed. It all seemed quite obvious to her. Don Fernando was jealous of his brother and afraid he would make the right investments. He was afraid the Americans would win, and he was working against them as a matter of self-preservation.

Desirée decided Don Fernando was an idiot. She felt certain the Americans would win, but she also knew the British would take Charleston. Frankly, she admitted to herself that she did not care one way or the other who ultimately won, except for the fact that generally she found the British boring. The important thing, she reasoned, was to make a profit. Her dilemma involved no matters of ideology, only those of practicality. What was she to do with Don Fernando? Clearly his usefulness was limited by time, but for the moment he was obviously in touch with British forces, and that could make him useful. The trick would be to disassociate herself from him at just the right moment. And when should she tell Brady? Not that he was here to tell in any case. She felt annoyed. They had been gone longer than anticipated.

Then her thoughts turned to Julie. The girl was really very beautiful and, alas, smarter than average. She was a worthy opponent, Desirée decided. If she were going to lose Brady, it ought to be to this girl who was at least deserving. In any case, the girl's knowledge of the future was absolutely necessary. Even though she had felt a pang of jealousy at first, she would ignore it. She would encourage Brady's obvious infatuation. She would combine the girl's knowledge of the future with Brady's knowledge of the present and with his access to the soon-to-be-powerful new American Republic. It behooved her to play the revolutionary role. It was in line with the governor's wishes and it would be, in all likelihood, the winning side.

But she could also keep Don Fernando on hand. She could feed him bogus information and she could find out from him what he was planning. Through him, she would have access to high-placed British sources. That was the best plan. The tide of battle had not yet turned; there was still money to be made from the British.

She would let the British know that although her house was the center of revolutionary activity in New Orleans, she allowed it only so Don Fernando could keep them abreast of developments. She would, in the meantime, continue to help the rebels, and if Don Fernando were discovered—indeed, she toyed with turning him in at the right moment—she could claim to have known and to have taken steps to neutralize his activities.

She would divulge certain information to Carmelita whom Brady trusted implicitly, and that information would serve to keep her in the clear later on. With that in mind, she set off to see Carmelita.

"Oh, madam, I was not expecting you." Carmelita opened the door of her small room.

"I was passing, otherwise I would have summoned you, my dear."

Carmelita was dressed in a modest white dress trimmed with red. Her hair was pulled back neatly. She stepped aside. "Would you like to come in?"

"Yes."

"I'm sorry there is no place to sit."

"Never mind. You were not the one who furnished it. But I shall see to it that you are given a chair."

Carmelita felt mystified. "That would be very kind," she answered.

"Brady is late returning. Have you heard anything? I know you are friends."

"No, madam." Carmelita was surprised. She and Brady had always been discreet. Sometimes Carmelita felt Desirée did indeed have certain powers. She always seemed to know everything about everybody.

"I suspected not. Well, I have not come to talk about Brady who I am sure will be back soon. I've come to confide my suspicions to you and to ask for your help—or rather your sharp and observing eyes."

Carmelita said nothing and she wondered if her expression betrayed her surprise and curiosity.

"It is Don Fernando."

"Ah, yes," Carmelita murmured.

"It shan't take long for everyone to know he adores me and that we have become lovers."

Again Carmelita said nothing. Desirée was never without a lover and while Don Fernando did not seem her type, he was wealthy, and generally wealth was the woman's main criteria in a man. Brady had been an exception.

"Does that surprise you?" Desirée asked.

"No, not really."

"Good. Naturally I'm very fond of him but I am also troubled. There is no question about Bernardo's convictions and desires to help the revolutionaries; there is no question about Don Carlos, either. But I sense something about Don Fernando—I sense he may bear watching."

"Have you spoken to Brady or Oliver Pollock about your suspicions?"

"Heavens, no! It is far too soon. What if I am wrong? Not only would it end our affair, I would destroy a friendship, come between brothers—no, no, one must be certain.''

"What may I do?''

"Just keep your eyes and ears open. See what you can find out of his connections, his other activities. I know you have friends, Carmelita. Nothing escapes me.''

Or very little, Carmelita thought silently. For the second time in as many minutes she wondered if this woman did have unusual powers. "I shall do as you wish," she replied. "But watching does not seem much.''

"There will be more later. Perhaps you should get to know Don Fernando's friend Martinez. It might prove fruitful.''

"Yes," Carmelita agreed.

Desirée smiled as she turned to go. She thought to herself that within hours of Brady's return Carmelita would have talked with him and the seeds of her concern for the cause would be firmly planted.

The two British sailors tossed Brady on the bunk roughly and then shoved Julie inside the tiny cabin, bolting the door behind her.

Julie set down her bag which the British officer had reluctantly allowed her to bring. Then she went to Brady who opened one eye and looked at her, a smile creeping across his face.

"You were not unconscious!" she said, tilting her head in mock anger.

"Shh, my love. This is a far better place than the hole and a far better way to travel than in irons. Besides, it is no fun kicking a man who does not groan.''

Julie felt like crying. He was so brave. His shoulder must hurt terribly, but his humor was still intact. "You must be serious. You've lost a lot of blood, Brady. And I'll have to take that bullet out of your shoulder or else it will fester.'' There was no denying the fact that she would have to act quickly. The heat was a guarantee that an untreated wound would go septic.

"Are you now a doctor, too?"

She shook her head thinking of her recent visit with Angelique. "How I wish I were."

He reached out for her and she let him grasp her hand. "We really have little time to lose," she warned.

"Ah, such concern. Well, one good thing has come of this. You didn't betray me, my woman, so I know you are not a spy."

She leaned over and pressed her lips to his. With his good arm he encircled her shoulders. "We must make the most of time. I may well be hung."

She shook her head. "No. I'll never let that happen." She kissed him again and then pulled herself away. "Now, Mr. John Andrews of Natchez, you need to have the bullet removed and then you need a proper bandage."

He smiled up at her. "Yes, Mrs. John Andrews. Ah, my woman, when you said you were my wife, relief surged right through me. But there is no doubt now, there is a spy. One who knew our route."

She agreed. "Close your eyes, Brady. I have to summon someone and I want them to think you're still unconscious. I will need a few things."

He did as she bade and she went to the door, banging on it and shouting, "I want to see the captain! Immediately!"

For a time her cries went unheeded and then the captain appeared with a guard behind him and the same red-nosed officer who had been on shore.

"This is outrageous!" she said, drawing herself up. "Absolutely outrageous. We are loyal British subjects, loyal to King George the Third! When we get to Mobile we will be vindicated and all of you will be reprimanded—perhaps even punished."

The captain glanced at the arresting officer. "Was there anything on them to prove this man is the suspect?"

The officer shook his head. "But he does fit the description."

"Many people do," the captain muttered.

"My husband needs help. He has been wounded."

"We have no doctor aboard. We don't even have a barber."

She all but shivered at the mention of a barber. "I shall do what has to be done, but I demand boiling water and and—" she could hardly say it, "pliers."

"Pliers?" the captain repeated dumbly.

"Pincers—I mean pincers," she said, quickly correcting herself.

The thought almost caused her to be ill. But she knew that bullets in this day and age were large. She knew infection was the clear and present danger.

"In case you are wrong," he said, turning to the officer with the red nose, "I think we should err on the side of caution." Then he turned to her. "Very well, madam. But you will have to stay in this cabin, we have no other."

"You will have our meals delivered," she said haughtily.

"Yes, madam."

They started to leave. "And I want the hot water and bandages right now. And a bottle of your strongest white rum. There isn't a moment to lose."

It was no more than ten minutes before a steward returned with the things she had requested.

Julie set everything out on a tray. Then from her own kit she took soap. She washed her hands in some of the steaming water and then she washed the wound. Brady winced.

"Aren't you going to give me some of the rum?" he asked.

"No, I wanted it because it is alcohol. Alcohol is a stimulant. If you drink it it will just make your heart beat faster and you'll lose still more blood. I want it to clean the wound with."

"A barber or a doctor would take out the bullet and

then cauterize this wound with a hot iron, searing the skin closed."

"My God," she breathed. "No, I shall have to do this my way and you shall have to trust me."

She sterilized the bandages in the hot water, then washed the wound with the rum while he again grimaced.

It was at that moment that she remembered Desirée's powders and potions. She went to the small kit and opened it. She read the hand-written labels carefully till she came to one labeled, "painkiller."

Mercifully Desirée had written directions on a small piece of paper enclosed in the kit. One was to give the patient the entire bottle. She prayed Desirée knew what she was doing. She handed Brady the bottle and told him to drink it.

In less time than she would have believed possible he was truly unconscious. She opened the window so she could see better, then as gently as possible she prodded the wound till the tip of her sterilized knife touched the bullet. She prodded some more and felt about, thrusting the bullet upward. When she could see it, she took the small pincers which she had also sterilized and removed it. Then she again washed the wound with water and then rum. Next she took strong thread from her kit and also sterilized it with rum. She held the needle in the flame of the lamp and then threaded it with the wet thread. Deftly, and in spite of the fact that she hated the feeling of it, she did what she had to do. She stitched up the wound as neatly as she could, drawing the ragged skin in and mending it as she would a torn seam with a slip stitch.

Last, she properly bandaged the wound first with bandages soaked in rum and then with heavier dry bandages.

With great physical effort, she got Brady's clothing off, then covered him and sat down in the chair by the bunk to wait. His sleep was incredibly deep, almost frighteningly deep.

Twice Julie tried to awaken him. But he slept on, and

in time, she too succumbed to exhaustion, falling into a deep sleep.

Julie started at the knock on the door of the small cabin. She shook her head, reorienting herself. Yesterday's events came back to her in a torrent of disjointed memories.

"Yes," she said, pulling herself from the chair and realizing how stiff she was.

She did not go to the door, however. Instead, she turned immediately to Brady and leaned over him. His breathing was regular, steady. And his wound did not appear to be oozing blood, though she knew she would have to clean it again and check it for infection.

Behind her the door opened a crack and a young boy of thirteen or so eased into the cabin and put down a tray. "Tea and kippers, madam."

Julie turned to look at him. "I shall need two buckets of hot water," she said irritably. "And the chamber pot needs emptying."

"Yes, madam."

She forced herself to smile at him. He was, after all, only a child. Probably a poor orphan forced into labor. He took the covered chamber pot and she sat down again and poured some of the steaming tea into the cup. The vessel rolled ever so slightly, but she supposed she should be grateful that the Gulf waters were tranquil in spite of the fine breeze. They were under full sail and moving with surprising speed.

She sipped some of the tea and acknowledged that it tasted good. Then she picked at the kippers and ate some of the bread that was also on the tray.

No sooner had she finished when the young boy returned with a clean chamber pot and the buckets of hot water.

Taking advantage of the fact that he still slept, Julie changed Brady's dressing and inspected his wound.

Relieved it showed no signs of infection, she decided to give him a sponge bath even though he still slept in a drugged sleep.

When she had finished, she gave herself a sponge bath, too, changed into clean culottes, and rebraided her hair. She used the remaining water to wash a few clothes which she hung near the window so the sun would dry them.

She returned to her patient. Should she be distressed that he slept so soundly and for so long? She didn't know what to expect since she did not really know what she had given him. She bent over and listened, her face resting on his bare chest. His heartbeat was quite normal and again she noted his breathing was unlabored. Whatever the potion was, she was grateful that it had worked.

She went to the door and banged on it. In a few minutes the young man came. "I should like to see the captain," she said firmly.

He came within the hour. Peering into the cabin behind her, he saw that Brady slept. "You seem to be doing well," he commended.

"Well?" she questioned indignantly. "Sir, my husband has been shot and we have been kidnapped. Now you have locked us in this tiny cabin. I should like to walk on deck and enjoy the sea. It is the very least you can do. I have never been on a vessel under full sail."

"Never?"

"I was born in this new world. No, never."

"You're prisoners."

"Mistakenly," she insisted. "And where pray would we go? My husband is wounded, we are at sea. Do you think I would leave him and jump into shark-infested waters? In any case, I can't swim," she lied.

He frowned and rubbed his chin. "Very well. I shall leave the door unlocked. But you will have to stay on this deck."

"That is agreeable."

She glanced again at Brady, then followed the captain

outside and left the cabin door open so the small room could air out. She walked around the deck ignoring the staring eyes of the sailors. The sails unfurled were beautiful! Were Brady not wounded, and were the circumstances different, she thought, she would be dancing around the deck. All her life she had wanted to be on a real sailing ship. Now, here she was!

Julie leaned over the rail for what seemed a long while, watching the swelling green-blue waters of the gulf and the bubbles of white foam as they washed against the side of the vessel.

Then she heard her name being called and she spun around and hurried back into the cabin, closing the door behind her.

"Oh, thank God! I thought you might never wake." She flew to Brady's side and knelt by the bunk.

"Don't call me by my name," he said, shaking his head, then, "By heaven woman, what did you give me?"

"Desirée's painkiller potion. I had to give you something."

He looked at his shoulder. "I don't know where you learned such things, but my father could have done no better."

She smiled at him. There was no way to tell him that completing an advanced first-aid course in her century probably taught one as much about medicine as doctors in this century knew. "I'm a seamstress," she joked. "I stitched you up as best I know."

He propped himself up on his good arm. "My woman, we have much to discuss. Lock the door."

She did as he told her, this time locking the door from the inside.

"You will tell me about Mr. John Andrews of Natchez, won't you?"

He grinned. "Precisely what we must discuss. But first some of that tea, even if it is cold. And some bread, too."

She poured him tea and tore off a chunk of bread for him. He ate it with some hard cheese he had in his pack.

Then, whispering, he began his tale.

"I've been a thorn in the side of His Majesty's forces for some time. Pollock and I have been running guns to John Rodgers Clark. Clark has been magnificent. So, my woman, I fear there is a price on the head of Brady McCormick. For that reason, I established another identity. John Andrews of Natchez owns a farm on the banks of the river. He is away often, but his neighbors know him to be a loyal British subject as are many of those in Natchez."

"But they said there is someone in Mobile who can identify you."

"If that is so, then I may well hang from a rope. But if it's bluff, then we must not let down our guard."

"You must tell me about Natchez, I've not been there." She could not tell him that she did know that a few months from now Natchez would be taken by Galvez.

"It's a haven for loyalists expelled from the colonies. I tell everyone I was expelled from Boston."

Julie nodded. "What do we grow on our farm?"

"Cane," he replied. Then, grinning, "Come, woman, give us a kiss. I may be wounded, but I woke up hungry for you."

She leaned toward him and kissed him tenderly.

"Ah, too much nursing," he muttered. "Undress and come to me."

She looked at him teasingly. "Are you strong enough?"

"You shall find out how strong I am."

She stood up and slowly began to discard her clothing. His dark eyes clung to her, caressing her with looks of desire. "I do lust for you," he said as she lay down beside him.

She undressed him gently while he toyed with her, teasing her with his fingertips, touching her in forbidden places.

With his good arm he nudged her toward him and then,

realizing what he wanted, she straddled him as he had always straddled her.

Her full breasts caressed his face and he took one of her already hard nipples into his mouth. The sensation was new and strange, and as she moved above him, her own hands reached for him. He continued flicking his tongue on her nipple while he played with her other breast. Then, knowingly, he moved his hand over her back, down over her curved buttocks, down the back of her thighs. He lifted himself slightly, allowing his swollen manhood to tease her entranceway even as his hand moved from her back to her front, even as he touched her most sensitive area, causing her to cry out and squirm delightfully above him. He repeated all of his movements again and again until she bit her lip and begged him. Then he moved upward, filling her completely, even while touching her in such a way that she moved to a magical rhythm only the two of them could hear. She cried out and fell upon his chest exhausted as they both fulfilled themselves. He held her close, his hand on her buttocks, his lips on hers. Then, when both had caught their breath, he whispered, "Not bad, my woman. Not bad at all."

She slithered down next to him in the narrow bunk, stretching out. "Nor are you bad, either," she returned. "For a one-armed man."

"And now on to Natchez," he whispered. "Our farm is on the east side of the river," he told her. "Listen now, I'll describe the house—everything. You must remember it all. Every detail."

"I shall, I promise." Then, after a moment, "How long will it take to get to Mobile?"

"That depends on the prevailing winds, but this vessel will take a wide berth around New Orleans. If all is well, perhaps we will get there in three days time."

Julie digested the information. "Three days," she murmured.

He reached over and caressed her gently. "And three nights."

The full moon over New Orleans hung in the summer sky like a great orange ball. It was a harvest moon, though this was not the season of the harvest nor the time of year when such a moon normally appeared. Nonetheless, it was there, reflecting the sun's light and sending that reflected light back to the dark side of the earth.

Carmelita was dressed in a dark dress with little fullness. She wore a lightweight dark cape in spite of the heat, and she hurried along keeping to the shadows, a silent ghostlike spectre on the streets of the sleeping city.

She reached Rue Dumaine and paused for just a moment to look at the river. The moon's light sent a shimmering bridge of light across the water, making it appear peaceful and romantic.

Carmelita moved on, stopping at a house on Decatur. She went around the house and knocked on the back door.

In a moment a round-eyed boy opened the door a crack and looked out at her questioningly.

"I've come to see Mr. Pollock," she whispered.

"Him be in his bed," the boy replied.

"Rouse him," Carmelita said in irritation.

"He be mad."

"No, he won't be mad. Do as I tell you and hurry!"

He opened the door, admitting her. "Stay here," he said, summoning what authority he had.

Carmelita waited in the dark kitchen, listening to the unmistakable sounds of the marauding night mice in the pantry.

Then the light from a lamp filled the room and she looked up into the face of a sleepy Oliver Pollock. He held the lamp in his left hand, and Julie could see he was clad in pajamas and a long robe. The boy who had answered the door peered out from behind him nervously, "She say you no be mad," the boy whispered.

"No, no. I'm not angry, Joshua."

"That be good," the boy said.

"Carmelita, what brings you so late?"

Carmelita bit her lip. "Something of import. Something private."

Oliver Pollock nodded. "Come into the study. Joshua, make us some tea."

"Yes, Mr. Pollock."

Carmelita followed Pollock down the corridor and into his study. It was a large room and on the wall was a large map. She looked at it curiously. It was not the first map she had ever seen, but it was certainly the largest.

Pollock smiled. "A gift from George Rodgers Clark."

Carmelita knew that Clark was a military leader, the man to whom the arms Brady and Pollock arranged for were sent.

"But you did not come here in the middle of the night to discuss maps, did you, Carmelita?

She shook her head.

"Sit down, my dear. Joshua will bring us our tea and then you can tell me what urgent information has brought you out in the middle of the night.

She nodded and sat down. In a moment the boy Joshua appeared at the door with a tray. Oliver Pollock took it from him and closed the door. He set the tray down and poured them some tea. "We are quite alone now, you can begin."

"As you know, Brady has not yet returned," she said softly.

"Of course I know. He's weeks late. I was expecting him some time ago."

"Miss Desirée is beside herself. I don't understand. She seems more concerned with the girl Julie than with Brady."

Pollock sipped the steaming tea. "You have heard something, haven't you?"

Carmelita reached down inside her dress. From between her breasts she withdrew a small cylinder such as was used to transport parchments containing written messages. "I received this today from a friend of my uncle who made certain inquiries."

Pollock read the message carefully. After a time he let the parchment drop into his lap. "This is not good," he muttered. "Not at all."

Carmelita leaned forward anxiously. Then she softly whispered, "I cannot read."

"No, of course not. I'm sorry. It seems that Brady and the woman left your uncles many weeks ago. It had been reported that a man and a woman were taken by a British patrol at the mouth of the Bayou Teche and transferred to a British man-of-war in the bay."

Carmelita covered her mouth with her hand. "They've been captured," she whispered.

Pollock nodded. "It would seem so."

"I pray for them."

Instinctively Pollock reached across the distance between them and covered her hands with his. "Brady is most resourceful," he said, trying to reassure her. He did not mention the price on Brady's head nor on his own.

"But what were the British doing in Spanish territory?" Carmelita asked. "It is as if they were watching for him."

Pollock nodded. "That may be so. And if it is, then there is a spy among us, a spy who is not Miss Juliet Hart."

Carmelita did not know whether or not to reveal her conversation with Desirée. Desirée thought Don Fernando bore watching; she herself, however, was not sure of Desirée. She decided for the moment to say nothing to Pollock about Desirée or Don Fernando. She picked up her teacup and drank every drop of the hot liquid. "I should get back now," she said. "Before it is known that I am gone."

"Will you be all right?"

"Yes, I'll be fine."

He squeezed her hand. "Thank you for coming, Carmelita. I shall see what I can do."

Carmelita left by the front door this time. She hurried along, returning to the house of Desirée Coteau by the same route as she had come.

Chapter Nine

Carmelita bustled around the house. Each of the rooms had been restored to perfect order and, as Desirée directed, each had been scented by the burning of an aromatic potpourri. "I cannot tolerate lingering cigar smoke," Desirée proclaimed, "but men cannot seem to do without it." Hence the morning ritual of the potpourri. Carmelita had paused in the study to dust and to gather glasses from the night before.

"May I speak with you?"

Carmelita turned in surprise to see Esmé who had once again been with Don Carlos last night and who usually did not rise till later in the day.

"Of course," Carmelita replied. She noted that there seemed to be something different about Esmé—a hesitancy, a new shyness. Even her clothing seemed more modest. She was wearing a long russet-colored cotton dress trimmed in eyelet. Her long red hair was tied back, but wisps of it caressed her forehead. Her skin was a wonderful golden color and her eyes a soft doelike brown.

"I would rather we speak elsewhere," Esmé said. "If we stay here, someone will surely interrupt us."

"Then come with me to my room," Carmelita suggested.

Esmé agreed and together they climbed the stairs to Carmelita's room.

The expression on Esmé's face was serious. She perched herself on the end of the bed after Carmelita took the one small chair in the room.

Esmé got to the heart of the matter. "I must speak with someone and I know not with whom I should speak. You and I have not been close, but I know you are friends with Brady and Brady and Don Carlos are close."

Carmelita betrayed nothing, but Esmé's words were curious. She could see that Esmé, for all her appearance of worldliness, was not the sophisticate she had imagined her to be. She looked truly concerned and upset. "I don't know if I can help you, but I shall be glad to listen."

"I've come to confess something to you. To ask your advice."

"I see."

"It is Don Carlos. He took me to his bed some time ago. We have been together often. I think I am in love with him."

Carmelita looked into Esmé's face and eyes. She felt a little sad. Esmé was not the first to fall in love with one of Desirée's customers. Sometimes such a love turned out all right, but most of the time it did not. It was true that the women of New Orleans were known for giving freely of their favors, but it was equally true that many men demanded wives who were virginal or, at the very least, women they could believe were virginal. A woman with Esmé's past could not pretend, and certainly she could not pretend with one of her former customers. Still, she had noticed that Don Carlos seemed smitten with Esmé, so perhaps a permanent liaison was possible.

"How is love a problem?" Carmelita asked, even though she knew there were any number of possible answers.

"He seems to care for me, too. He is good to me." Tears began to well in Esmé's large brown eyes. "And I have betrayed him."

Carmelita reached over and took her hand. "Betrayed him? I don't understand." Now she was truly perplexed. Esmé's sadness was caused by a matter entirely different from that which she had imagined.

"His brother, Don Fernando, paid me, to find out certain things—matters concerning Don Carlos's business. And then, when I went to Don Fernando in New Orleans, he took me to his bed. I did not want to go. After being with Don Carlos I wanted no other. I don't know what to do! I cannot live with what I have done, but I am afraid to tell Don Carlos. I am afraid he will never want to be with me again."

Instinctively Carmelita put her arms around Esmé. "Tell him," she urged. "He may understand everything. If he is as kind as you say, he will take you back. I am sure of it."

Esmé looked into her eyes even though tears continued to run down her cheeks. "Do you think he might?"

"You must try," Carmelita urged.

"Thank you. Now I must go or someone will wonder where I have gotten to."

Carmelita nodded and watched as Esmé hurried away, closing the door behind her. She felt most perplexed. Why would Don Fernando want to pry information from his own brother? What was going on that she did not understand? And what, if anything, did Don Fernando de Vega have to do with Brady's kidnapping? Could it be that Don Fernando was a spy?

It was high noon when the British vessel dropped anchor in Mobile Bay. Julie peered at the shore, on which there was little more than a wall of a fort with a tower flying a British flag.

Brady stood beside her, one arm still bandaged and in a sort of sling she had fashioned, the other arm round her waist. "Try to look a bit more cheerful, Mrs. Andrews."

Julie turned to him and forced a smile. "I'm worried."

"And I'm anxious to get off this rat-infested British tub, my dear."

"It took two days longer to get here than you thought."

"It will take us considerably longer to get back to New Orleans—if we escape." Then he leaned close and whispered in her ear, "You were magnificent with the captain. Just keep on being a perfect British colonial bitch."

Julie smiled. "I shall try."

The captain approached them. "Have you your belongings? I'm having a boat lowered to take you ashore."

"We are quite ready," she replied. "I trust *you* are ready to face the consequences for having made this terrible mistake."

"If a mistake has been made," he muttered.

Listening to the captain's words, Julie could tell that over the past week he had begun to question his information and question the arrest. He seemed more solicitous with each passing day and more penitent with each of her many indignant protests. Their food improved and he had even taken to asking after Brady's wound.

They both watched as the longboat was lowered into the water, then Brady, because he could not climb down the rope ladder with his wounded shoulder, was lowered to the boat as if he were cargo.

"We'll put you in the longboat the same way," the captain told Julie.

"I can perfectly well go down the ladder," she returned.

He looked at her culottes and let his heavy shoulders fall in a deep sigh. "As you wish," he said, now preferring to avoid all arguments with her.

She scrambled down the ladder thinking that her backstage training stood her in good stead. In moments they were being rowed across the choppy waters of Mobile Bay toward Fort Charlotte.

Captain Elias Durnford sat at a massive oak desk. Behind him there was a map and to one side the British flag. Captain Durnford had been schooled in the best British schools and as a result, he was fastidious and gentlemanly.

He looked at Julie and then at Brady. He studied them in silence and then looked down at his well-manicured nails. "We had information that Brady McCormick would be traveling to the mouth of Bayou Teche with a blond woman. You fit his description perfectly, yet you deny you are he."

"Vehemently," Brady said firmly. "There has been a mistake. God knows how many dark-haired men there are, though I readily admit that women as rare as my wife are hard to find.

Durnford lifted his brow. "I couldn't agree more." He turned his eyes to Julie. "I have never seen such clothing," he said thoughtfully.

"Frills and ruffles are not practical when traveling on the frontier, though I was quite at home in them in Philadelphia."

"You're from Philadelphia? Our information was that you were from New York."

"Captain, my husband and I have already told Captain Garnett that we were arrested in error. We are loyalists driven from the East by the war. We have a farm in Natchez."

Brady smiled. "I thought there was supposed to be someone here who could identify me?"

Durnford raised his brow and looked at Captain Garnett.

"I thought it would make him admit who he was," Garnett stuttered.

Julie felt relief surge through her. Indeed, this new bit

of knowledge made her feel bolder. Certainly they would
not hang a man when there was no one to make a positive
identification.

"That we have been kidnapped, my husband wounded
and beaten is a grave and serious matter," she said, leaning
across his desk. "We are utterly loyal to the British Crown.
Do you have the slightest idea who I am?"

So wild was her next planned line that she could not
even look at Brady.

"I had thought you were the woman who was accompa-
nying Mr. Brady McCormick, a woman named Julie Hart.
But now you claim to be Mrs. John Andrews of Natchez."

"And so I am," she said proudly, "Does this mean nothing to you?"

Captain Durnford's expression said it all. He was dumb-
founded.

"My name now is Elizabeth Andrews, but I am the former
Elizabeth Shippen of Philadelphia—and we Shippens are
known to be a loyalist family! Loyalist, wealthy, and most
influential!"

Captain Durnford's face flushed bright red. He turned
on Captain Garnett. "You're a dunderhead!" he muttered.

Captain Garnett looked down at the floor. When he
returned to his ship he doubtlessly would turn on the
red-nosed officer who had arrested them just as Captain
Durnford had turned on him.

"My humble apologies," Captain Durnford said as he
stood up. "I shall see to it that you're returned to Natchez
as soon as possible." He paused, tapping his fingers on
the desk, then added, "But I must warn you, there's been
trouble around Natchez. A revolutionary named Willing
has been burning and pillaging the area. He's gone, but
some of those who were with him remained, a murdering
gang of renegades. Natchez, indeed that whole area, is
quite dangerous."

"We'll stay here for a while and rest," Brady said. "At
least until my shoulder has healed. But danger or no, we

still want to go home. If you give us supplies, we'll make our way back.''

"You will be afforded every hospitality Fort Charlotte has to offer," Captain Durnford said with a sweeping bow. Then he walked to his door and summoned his aide. "Take Mr. and Mrs. Andrews to the empty officer's quarters. Make them at home and see to it they have everything they need."

"As you say, sir."

Julie smiled. "Thank you captain."

"Anything to rectify such a dreadful error."

Julie and Brady followed the young aide in silence. She felt like bursting into laughter, but she knew even as they walked across the compound that her bold assertion would cause problems. In all likelihood, Brady knew who the Shippens of Philadelphia were, though he would not know all that she knew.

The house they were taken to had one large room which served as kitchen, living room, and dining room. It had a huge fireplace for cooking and was furnished in frontier fashion with handmade furniture. The only exception was an overstuffed sofa clearly imported from England.

The second room was a bedroom which had a real bed, a dresser, and a chest. The third room held a great luxury. It had a tub for bathing and a toilet which was emptied from the outside. Hardly wonderful, but better than the outhouse she had imagined, or the ever-present chamber pot under the bed.

No sooner had the young aide to Captain Durnford left them alone then Brady turned to her. "You stunned even me, my woman."

"And it surprises me you want to stay in a British Fort for even five minutes. Surely the sooner we leave, the safer we'll be."

"Quite true, but there are other considerations. How

can I pass up this opportunity to assess this fort? By God, we're on the inside."

She nodded. History would not be changed or altered. Fort Charlotte would be taken by Galvez in a few months time. "The larger fort is Pensacola," she said.

Brady came to her. "My woman, I want to know about you now. Your memory is suddenly very good indeed, and your knowledge vastly superior to any female I have ever known. You say you are from New York, yet you know the name of Philadelphia's most influential loyalist family. You know, too, that the Shippens had daughters, beautiful blond daughters. Are you really a Shippen? If not, you lie well enough to rouse my suspicions yet again."

She shook her head. "I am who I told you I was. I have not lied to you. Brady, I lied *for* you and there is a great difference. I am from New York as I told you."

"Then how do you know of the Shippens and how do you know about the strength of a British fort in West Florida?"

Julie felt a trifle indignant. She wanted to shout she had been acting a part and that she had done so to save him from the noose. That she had succeeded should please him, instead, he turned it all on its head and now voiced his suspicions of her once again. For a moment she had toyed with telling him she was a time traveler—with telling him the absolute, though doubtless unbelievable truth. Would it matter to him? Would he even believe her? No, this would not be a good time to tell him, she decided. Unhappily, she admitted that there might never be a good time.

Nor could she tell him why the Shippen name popped into her head. It was because she knew that Peggy Shippen had married Benedict Arnold and that Arnold had, or would, betray the revolutionaries. She knew that Arnold's betrayal had happened in the year 1779, but she did not remember in what month—indeed, since news traveled so slowly, even if it had already happened, it would not yet have reached here. If only Brady knew! She had come close to betraying them both in the captain's office. She had almost said something about Benedict Arnold and his loyalist stand but the captain also wouldn't know yet that the best of the revolution's generals, Benedict Arnold, had just, or was about to switch sides.

"I'm waiting for your answer, my woman. Is it taking you so long to think one up?"

"No, Brady. I was thinking how sad it makes me that after all our lovemaking, after how I have taken care of you, that you are still suspicious of me." What she said evaded his question, but it was true.

"You might care for me and still be a spy."

"I am not a spy and you will just have to believe me. As for the Shippens, they are well known. Philadelphia society is not unknown in New York. And I read, remember? I have read that Pensacola is an important British fort. It is all quite simple. As for my ability to lie—though I prefer to think of it as acting in this case—it is made easier by the thought that it might spare you from the noose."

He smiled at her and pulled her toward him. "I shall have to trust you," he said, looking deeply into her eyes.

"Yes, you will," she said steadily. "But please, do what you must do and let's get out of here. I feel we should get back to New Orleans as quickly as possible."

Again she stopped short of telling him everything. Spain was about to get into the war and when it did, it would be infinitely harder to get back.

For three days the sky had been utterly cloudless and the merciless sun had beaten down unrelentingly without even the relief of an occasional cloud or mild sea breeze. Now, even as the clock was about to strike midnight, the heat of the day could still be felt.

Esmé turned from her boudoir table to face Don Carlos. She had been expecting him and was dressed only in a chemise of ecru lace. Her rich thick hair hung long and loose over her bare shoulders.

"You're more lovely each time I see you." He bent over her and kissed her. She looked at him in her mirror. He was so tall and handsome, straight as an arrow, with an erect military bearing. And yet his eyes were soft and kind.

"It's cooled off a bit," he said as he discarded his red jacket trimmed in heavy gold braid. "Had it stayed as warm as it was this afternoon, I fear even our lovemaking would have suffered."

"It does not seem to have cooled off much." Her voice cracked slightly. She forced a smile and then turned to him, her eyes filled with tears.

"My little Esmé, my sweet flower. What troubles you?"

Esmé trembled and then stood up, letting him embrace her, hold her tight. "Something—I know not how to tell you."

"You must tell me, my darling. You must trust me." His hands roamed over her body, but she did not move against him as she usually did. Instead, she began to sob softly, and he could see she was truly distressed.

"Tell me," he prodded.

"It's such a long story, I don't know where to begin."

He kissed her hair and smoothed it, even as he held her against him. "Begin at the beginning, Esmé. Lovers should not have secrets, especially secrets that cause tears."

"When I tell you, you may not want me for a lover. You may never want to see me again."

"I can think of nothing that would cause me not to want to see you."

To see her. She had hoped he would say he loved her. She had hoped he would say, "I love you so much I can forgive you anything." But he had not said those words she so longed to hear. There was no stopping now. Even if he discarded her she would have to be truthful with him. The weight of her deception burdened her.

"Tell me," he prodded.

"Many weeks ago, before you came to me the first time," she began slowly, "your brother, Don Fernando, came to me."

Don Carlos smiled. "Esmé, I knew you had other lovers. It was Don Fernando who told me of your charms. I can't understand why he was willing to give you up. But I have thanked him ever since."

She shook her head and more tears fell down her cheeks. "You don't understand."

He held her by her shoulders and she stood in front of him, tears running down her cheeks. "Are you going to tell me that you are still his lover?" Don Carlos asked.

"Oh, no. I see no one but you.

"Ah, then what can be so terrible, little Esmé? I know your past. It is your future that concerns me."

"This has not to do with love or lovemaking, Don Carlos."

He bent slightly and sought her moist eyes. "You're torturing me, Esmé. I cannot bear your sadness. Tell me."

"He instructed me—Don Fernando, that is—to get you drunk. He supplied a potion for me to put into your brandy so you would tell me things—things he wanted to know about your business."

Don Carlos stiffened. "That first night. I remember being intoxicated, I remember—I remember that in the morning I couldn't recall much of anything except your beauty."

"You were not intoxicated. You were drugged. And the next day I went to tell Don Fernando all that you told me and he—he threatened me. He took me, too, roughly and meanly." Her hands flew to her face to cover it. "I do not know how to ask your forgiveness for this terrible deception. I don't know how to tell you how I feel, how I have changed. Your brother frightens me, Don Carlos."

He wrapped her protectively in his arms and drew her close. "Oh, Esmé, I wish you had told me sooner."

"I'm sorry. It was so difficult."

"I understand, and Esmé I forgive you completely. I adore you. I love you."

Esmé leaned against him. How long had she wanted a man to say these words to her? Always, it seemed. And now it was not just any man, but it was Don Carlos, a man she truly loved. A man she truly admired.

"How can you love me?" she asked. "I'm a lady of the night, a whore."

"It is easy my darling. I want to take you away from here and make you the mistress of my household. I will seek permission to marry you and you will no longer be one of Desirée's women, but a grand lady. Together we will have children and a long and happy life."

"And if permission is not granted?"

"Then I will treat you as my wife and demand that others treat you as my wife, too. I want you to leave here tonight and come home with me. I should duel to the death any man who lays a hand on you again, even my brother."

Esmé felt at this moment as if she could fly. But she also felt it necessary to warn the man she loved. "You must be careful, my darling. Your brother is filled with envy. He does not wish you well."

Don Carlos nodded. Long had he suspected his brother's envy, his plans, and his desires to inherit everything. The next months would be difficult indeed, and he would have to be very careful if he wanted to prosper.

"Come," he said, leading Esmé toward her closet. "Take what you need and come with me now. We'll make love when we get home. Tonight, Esmé, is the beginning of a new life for us both."

Julie lay in bed listening to Brady's regular breathing. In a few hours he would awake but for now he slept peacefully, deeply. She wasn't sure what had awakened her, but she

knew she was fully alert even though it could not have
been more then five in the morning.

Outside, the fort was coming to life. The guard on the
ramparts was changing and in the mess hall tea and bread
and fruit was being served with gruel.

But it was not the distant sounds of the fort awakening
or even the birds in the woods behind the house that had
roused her. Her own thoughts had forced her from sleep,
her pressing need to try to remember every detail she
could of coming events. Of all her historical knowledge
she was more familiar with this period than with any other,
and yet there were vital details that escaped her.

She searched her memory, though she knew far less had
been written and she had read far less about the revolution
on this part of the continent.

Spain had signed a secret convention with France some
time in April—last month, but when in April she was not
sure. She was quite certain that the final declaration of
war came in mid-June, but that news did not reach Galvez
until August. But when in August? And did the British
learn of the war before the Spanish? No, that hardly
seemed possible. If they had, they would not have been so
easily defeated at Baton Rouge, which she was quite certain
was taken before Fort Charlotte.

She knew that General Galvez was immensely popular.
He had helped refugees from British Florida, refugees
whose lands had been burned with James Willing. He had
also been fair with the Choctaws, which prevented them
from allying themselves with the British. Dates slowly began
to come back to her.

Then she turned her thoughts to where they were. Surely
Mobile was not much more than a hundred miles from
New Orleans—nothing in modern terms, but probably a
long and dangerous trek in this century.

Julie turned on her side and looked at Brady. His shoulder was getting better by the day, and his strength had

returned. *We must leave here,* she decided. Historically, time was growing short.

She took a deep breath, then she jostled Brady's sleeping body. He groaned and opened one eye. Then a smile she knew well crossed his face and he moved his hand to her breast, kneading it gently.

"Brady!" she whispered sharply. "Wake up!"

"Move closer," he said, reaching for her again.

"No. We must talk. Brady, you must listen. We have to leave her today, this very day. I feel it. Please listen to me."

He blinked both eyes open and sat up.

"And I thought you had awakened me to make love."

"Please listen to me. We must go back to New Orleans. It is dangerous for us here and something is about to happen. Something important."

"Desirée is the soothsayer."

"I am not trying to foretell the future. Please trust me. When we get back to New Orleans I will tell you everything. But we must go."

He looked into her beautiful blue eyes. They were alert and intent, pleading and commanding at the same time.

"Are you confessing that there is something to tell?"

"Not what you think. Or thought. No. But yes, there is something to tell, though I cannot tell you till we are back in New Orleans and I can prove it."

He felt perplexed, yet she had saved him and brought him this far. "I could use just this one day," he said earnestly. "I want to examine the west wall."

She nodded. "This day only."

"We should in any case go by night. Tonight if you like."

"Yes, tonight. Brady, what day is it?"

"'Tis mid-June—perhaps the seventeenth or eighteenth."

"I see." She climbed from the bed and slipped her feet into her slippers. But to her surprise he pulled her back roughly.

"You woke me. I should like to start the day right."

His grip on her wrist was like iron and she was his willing prisoner, excited by the glint in his eyes, the promise of his roving hands, the heat of his knowing lips.

He was insatiable, and she never knew how he would take her. Sometimes he was slow, gentle and deliberate—torturing her with long, sweet kisses and caressing her into total acquiescence. At other times he was rough and demanding, bending her to his will and exciting her beyond belief with his ability to hold her, toy with her till she begged him, and then fill her with urgent and commanding completeness.

This morning he was in his commanding mood. He took her and held her fast, his lips on her hot flesh, his leg moving hers apart. Surrendering herself to his strength, she allowed him to ravish her with his heated kisses and urgent desire.

Oliver Pollock paced back and forth slowly, his pipe clenched firmly between his teeth.

Governor Galvez sat on the edge of a chair across the room, leaning forward, his elbows on his knees, his fingers on his temples as if deep in thought. The silence between the two men was heavy. Both of them were men of action, yet neither could think of exactly what action should be taken given the circumstances.

"There can be no doubt about it," Pollock finally said. "Brady is missing. It's a terrible loss. I can only think that Carmelita is right and that he was kidnapped."

"I hope she isn't right. There's a price on his head."

"The British won't hesitate to hang him. If they knew he was going to be there, then surely they set a trap. This was not random."

"We shall have to be doubly careful," Galvez said.

"As if we wouldn't soon have our hands full with other matters."

Galvez looked at Pollock steadily. Pollock, like everyone else in New Orleans, had heard the rumors that plagued the city. From the dockside to the far outskirts of town, every single person was laying in stores, hording for the coming battles, preparing for the war to come to them.

Galvez's aim, and indeed the Spanish aim, was to drive the British from the Gulf of Mexico and the banks of the Mississippi where their settlements were prejudicial to Spanish trade and commerce as well as a threat to the most precious of their possessions—Mexico. The British aim, on the other hand, was an opportunity to strike a blow against the "Dons" and to expand British interests.

"The British in the Floridas are preparing to attack New Orleans," Pollock said.

Galvez nodded. "So one rumor goes. The other is that the British will launch and attack down the Mississippi out of Canada."

"And what do you believe, Bernardo? Will the British come across the sea from Florida or down the Mississippi?"

"If at all, I believe they will come across the sea from Pensacola. It is my aim to see to it that a mission such as that will be thwarted." He rubbed his chin thoughtfully. "I cannot pretend to be asleep; I cannot ignore what I know is happening. Declaration or no declaration of war, I would be remiss in my duty as governor if I didn't make this colony secure. Mobile and Pensacola are the keys to the control of the Gulf of Mexico."

"Surely you cannot move against them without a declaration of war, Bernardo."

"No, and I would not. But that does not prevent me from making plans and being ready to execute those plans the moment I am free to do so. It does not prevent me from making plans to secure New Orleans and protect her from wanton attack without a declaration of war, Pollock."

"I couldn't agree more."

"Then first you must send an urgent message to the Continental Congress," Bernardo said, looking at his friend. "You must tell them the truth about James Willing. He has caused nothing but trouble—more for you than for me, though I readily admit that with war coming your trouble will soon be my trouble."

"I shall pen the message now. I shall tell them that his party is without discipline, order, or subordination."

"Add that he's piling up expenses—governments always hate that; they're the only ones allowed to pile up expenses."

Pollock laughed. "I will say that because it is true. Do you think a government responsible to the people will build up as many expenses as a monarchy?"

"They will spend as much as they are allowed."

Pollock nodded. "It's true I've heard General Washington's expense accounts are very high indeed."

"Be sure to write that James Willing and his men have thrown the whole river into confusion and created a number of enemies for the revolutionary forces. Please add that he has left a murdering renegade gang behind."

"I shall write all those things," Pollock promised.

"I shall move ships into the river below New Orleans and send emissaries to the Choctaw nation. I will also begin to raise a local army to attack Mobile and Pensacola when war is declared."

"And Baton Rouge—"

"Baton Rouge first," Galvez assured him.

"Surely I can do more than write letters," Pollock said as he sat down.

"You will have your hands full, I promise you. I am negotiating for a ship full of arms to be delivered to George Rogers Clark so that he can secure the upper Mississippi."

"When do you anticipate its arrival?"

"I have not yet heard. It will come directly from Cuba. I'll let you know as soon as possible."

"I'll send a message to Philip Landry to make sure his men are ready to transfer the cargo up river."

Galvez drew in his breath. "I hope to God that Brady

escapes if he's been captured. We could use a man of his experience."

"I'll send out inquiries. Perhaps one of our informants has heard something," Pollock suggested.

"Good. I'll meet you on Wednesday at Desirée's."

Julie walked briskly across the parade ground of Fort Charlotte. She had walked nearly a mile to the market on the waterfront for needed supplies and was now on her way back to meet Brady. Tonight they would be off. Soon she hoped they would be out of British territory.

"Mrs. Andrews! Mrs. Andrews!"

It was only because the parade ground was deserted that Julie turned. She remembered suddenly who she was supposed to be. Captain Elias Durnford walked swiftly toward her.

"Good afternoon Mrs. Andrews!" He bowed and Julie curtsied ever so slightly. She always had to remind herself that in this century men and women did not shake hands.

"Good afternoon," she returned.

"I see you've been to market."

"Oh. I just needed a few things. But you know how it is, one always buys more than one intends. Mostly I went for the walk, such a pleasant day." She hoped he would not take her basket and realize how heavy it was.

"And where is Mr. Andrews?"

"In the house. His shoulder still pains him. He must take every opportunity to regain his strength." It was a lie, of course. Brady had been walking around the perimeter of the fort. Each time he returned, he made sketches. She in turn sewed the cylinders holding the sketches into the pockets of her culottes.

"Yes, a great pity. But I have splendid news. Some neighbors have arrived from Natchez. They were driven out of their home by James Willing. I want you and your husband to come to my quarters tonight for dinner. You can have a reunion.''

Julie struggled to keep calm and retain a placid facial expression. Neighbors from Natchez! They would know who Brady was—or more precisely who he was not. Did Captain Durnford already know? Or was he simply being polite? Or did he realize this was his opportunity for a positive identification without taking a chance beforehand that he might be wrong and she would be further thrown into a temper? And what if Brady were not back when she got there! They would have to leave right away. When they didn't show up for dinner, half the fort would be out looking for them.

Julie wondered if Captain Durnford could see her heart beating within her chest.

''Mrs. Andrews, are you quite all right?''

She smiled as devastatingly as possible. ''Oh, yes. Just a little tired from my long walk. Dear Captain Durnford, your invitation is so kind. It will be wonderful to talk with people from home—from Natchez. What time shall we come?''

''Will seven suit you?''

Julie touched his arm lightly. ''Could we make it eight? I'm afraid I really must wash my hair and it does take so long to dry.''

''I would certainly want you to look as beautiful as possible. Eight is perfect.''

Julie smiled again. ''I must hurry then,'' she said as she waved good-bye to him. She walked as rapidly as she could. Each step was punctuated with a wish for Brady to be there—for him not to accidentally run into the captain . . . What if? Oh, she could not think of the possibilities. She quickened her pace yet again.

After running up the steps, she flung open the door of the house. ''Brady! Brady! Where are you?''

Silence greeted her. He had not yet returned. She stood

with her hands over her face. Each second would be agony. Her heart pounded, but there wasn't a second to waste. She began packing immediately. When Brady did come back, if they were not already compromised, there would be no time to lose.

Chapter Ten

Julie looked at their supplies. She had packed everything and prepared the food. She had gotten ready to travel right down to braiding her long hair. But that had been over an hour ago and Brady still had not returned. She now stood by the door, each second seeming as if it were an hour. "Oh, please," she murmured to herself. Worry mixed with irrational anger. It wasn't as if he could call. But where was he? Should she begin looking for him or stay here? The sun was starting to set. Time was slipping away, their lead time was disappearing. Then suddenly, from out of nowhere, he rounded the house and stood, poised in the doorway.

She threw herself at him and his arms went around her. "Here, here, I wasn't gone that long."

"Don't laugh. Don't talk. Listen," she begged. "People have come from Natchez. Durnford expects us at eight. When we don't come, they'll know. Brady, the whole fort will be looking for us."

He looked at her steadily. Her face was ashen and her

words were coming in short gasps. He could see the tension in her eyes.

"We'll go now," he said, looking around. "Good, I see you're ready."

"Surely it's dangerous traveling by night."

"We'll have to keep to the coast for a while until I'm on familiar territory. Come, my woman. As you yourself said, we haven't a moment to lose. We'll have to circle behind the fort while there's still light."

He led and she followed, her bag slung over her shoulder. He carried everything else in his back pack which she had tried to fix so that it would not lean heavily on his wounded shoulder.

Now and again, he moved off the path they followed and marked a tree.

"What are you doing?"

"If they use Indian trackers, they'll think we went that way," he indicated. "Just misleading signs for those who follow."

The woods were thick and it was darker then it was on the shore. "What time do you think it is?" she asked.

"Around seven. I'd say we have another hour and half before a search party is sent out. Durnford's such a gentleman he would expect us to be fashionably late."

She felt as if she could not walk fast enough. But the heat was prohibitive. Beneath her netted hat beads of perspiration formed on her forehead. "This is a miserable way to travel," she muttered.

"It will soon improve," he promised.

"How can we walk the whole way? They have horses. It's over a hundred miles. It will take us three days at least."

"Oh, my woman, I would not make a beauty such as you walk a hundred miles in this tropical forest. We're just going to have to acquire some horses. In any case, it may be a hundred miles to New Orleans, but it is not a hundred miles to Spanish territory."

She let out her breath. There were certainly things she

did not know. One of them was where the dividing line between British and Spanish territory was located.

"I must say you're intuitive," Brady remarked. "You seemed to know this morning that we had to leave."

"I've felt it for days." This, she thought to herself, had nothing to do with knowing the future. It *was* truly intuitive.

"There," Brady whispered. "It is a farm. No doubt there are horses."

"We can't steal them. What would the farmers do?"

"My woman, I have every intention of paying for them."

Without hesitation, Brady went to the door of the farmhouse and knocked loudly. In a few minutes a man answered. Julie stayed back, waiting for Brady to consummate his deal and all the while she watched as the sun dropped from the sky and was replaced by an orange glow. It was June, and the days were longer. It must be nearly eight, she thought anxiously.

Brady took off his boot and to her surprise he paid the farmer with gold coins.

"Come," he said, hurrying her along. "We've two horses. But you'll have to ride as a man rides."

"It's no problem," she laughed. If only he knew that she could ride no other way.

"It is well you are wearing whatever those are."

"Culottes," she answered.

The farmer brought the two horses round the side of the house and Brady helped her on. How long had it been since she had ridden? Years. She thought of how sore she would be the next day.

Brady himself mounted and then they were off, this time headed for the coast which they could travel along till they came to the entrance to Lake Pontchartrain. There, a series of islands cut the lake off from the coastline which reached like a serrated knife into the gulf below New Orleans.

They rode side by side along the sand. Her hat had blown off and was now round her neck, held by its strap.

Her hair was free, the wind whipping through it. It was exhilarating. "They'll be after us now," she said.

"That farmer is no friend of the British. He'll not tell them we have horses. "Come, my woman, I know this coast. I know where to stop and where to water the horses. I know my way home."

Julie smiled across at Brady, feeling almost comfortable for the first time all day. She only hoped he was not over-confident.

Downstairs, in the drawing room with its rich wall hangings and imported furniture, Jonathan Pollock met with Governor Bernardo Galvez and Don Carlos.

Galvez swirled the brandy round in his glass and smiled. "I have good news, señors. Yes, I think you will be pleased."

Don Carlos nodded. "Good news is always welcome."

"Are you going to keep us in suspense all evening?" Pollock asked.

"Ah, you Americans are so impulsive. So anxious to know everything right away."

"I confess you're quite right," Pollock answered cheerfully. He and Galvez and Brady had spent many a happy hour discussing their cultural differences and varied temperaments. He knew full well that of the three of them, Brady's temper was by far the hottest. But Brady wasn't here, and it saddened him.

Galvez looked around the room, then closed the large heavy oak door that led to the hall. When he spoke it was with a lower voice, a kind of half whisper. "A ship, *La Mira*, leaves Havanna this very night. She is laden with arms for you, Pollock, arms for the new Cajun recruits you've organized.

"And there is a second vessel as well. Those arms are to be hidden till needed. The time will come when we'll want to move against Baton Rouge."

Don Carlos slapped Pollock on the back. "Soon we'll be allies."

Pollock nodded. "I am grateful, gentlemen. And were Brady here, he would be grateful, too. But first we must rid ourselves of this James Willing."

"Have you sent the message?"

"I have indeed. But I have no desire to wait. I'm having the order forged. We'll send him on his way home by ship."

Galvez laughed. "You are less conservative and more inventive than I imagined, Pollock."

"He is naught but an opportunist and a man of little or no honor," Pollock said.

"I'm glad you've taken care of this. He is certainly not welcome in New Orleans. I am afraid that, American or not, I will have to make it known that he is not welcome," Galvez added. Then he leaned over. "Now you must understand that *La Mira* docks five days or six days hence. She must be unloaded and her cargo temporarily warehoused. All this must be done with stealth."

"Of course," Pollock agreed.

"Then I shall leave all the rest to you and Don Carlos."

"Who has an important assignation," Pollock revealed.

Galvez smiled. "We know who she is, my friend. Dare we guess this liaison may become permanent?"

"I will be making an announcement soon," Don Carlos said. His swarthy complexion did not easily show a flush of embarrassment, but now it seemed quite evident.

"Trust me, my friend. Married life can be quite blissful," Galvez said.

In the next room, a room to which the door was locked, Desirée carefully replaced the small painting of the Spanish countryside that hung on the wall and stepped off her blue brocade footstool.

The replacement of the painting covered a small peephole in the wall, a peephole that allowed one to not only see into the next room but to hear what was going on.

She smiled with unusual satisfaction. A tidbit of information. Even though in the long run she certainly favored the revolutionaries, she did want to see to it that her little investments paid off. Those investments were made on the premise that Charleston would be held by the British. She intended playing both sides toward that end, until forced to choose. She needed to know what was happening on both sides and that meant holding on to Don Fernando for a time. And what better way to hold on to him than give him some information he dearly needed to have? She felt pleased with herself, but entirely put out that her time traveler had disappeared.

"And just when I need to know what will happen," she complained.

James Willing's head pounded from the rum he had drunk last night. He rubbed his unshaven chin and looked about for somewhere to spit the tobacco he had been chewing. Seeing no spitoon, he simply spit it on the floor outside the huge doors that led to Governor Bernardo Galvez's office in the Casa Capitular.

He had expected better treatment; he had expected adulation. After all, he had conquered the Mississippi, burning and looting British homes and he had entered New Orleans triumphant. But no one had come to greet him. Not that bastard Pollock who claimed to run the show and not the greasy governor. And now this! It was the final insult. He had been "escorted" here by armed soldiers and treated as a criminal. His men had been rounded up and put in the local jail. Who the hell did Galvez think he was? And what game was Pollock playing?

No sooner had he silently posed the question than the large doors to the Casa Capitular's inner sanctum swung open and a formally dressed aide looked at him witheringly down his long nose. "The governor will see you now," the aide said.

James Willing pulled himself up. As he passed the aide, he swore under his breath and stomped into Galvez's office.

"This is an outrage," he grumbled. It was then that he saw Pollock sitting placidly to one side of the governor's desk. He turned his rage on him. "I'm under orders from the Continental Congress! I'm a hero! What the hell am I here for and why the hell have my men been rounded up?"

Galvez whirled about, his chin set, his dark eyes ablaze. "Your Continental Congress has no jurisdiction here! This is Spanish territory, and I am the governor!"

"Then go screw a señorita, you lousy Spaniard!" Willing's mouth twisted meanly.

Pollock shifted uneasily. The idiot would be fortunate if he didn't end up being flayed alive. Indeed, had Galvez been a different type of man, one could have guaranteed that would be the outcome.

Galvez stared Willing down. "You are no revolutionary. You're a drunkard, a looter, and a thief. You are extremely lucky that I don't hang you. There's a ship waiting, your men are being put aboard even as we speak. You and your men—the ones we caught—will sail this ship to Philadelphia and under no condition return to New Orleans or to the Louisiana Territory. If you do, my soldiers will fire first."

Willing's mouth twisted and he was about to speak when Pollock stood up. "By order of the Continental Congress you are to return to Philadelphia, Willing. Immediately." Pollock handed Willing a scroll and Willing looked at it dumbly. Then, as if to check its authenticity, he fingered the seal.

"It's real," Pollock said brazenly. It was not, of course, but an answer to his message would take another month. There was no time—Willing had to be gotten rid of so that he and Galvez could get on with more important business.

"When I get home the Continental Congress will hear about this," Willing muttered darkly.

Pollock did not respond. He had taken another step, a step that was rare indeed. He had let all the information on Willing's vessel be known to a British agent. Willing was no revolutionary. He was by all accounts a thieving, murdering criminal. With any luck, the information he had planted would be passed on and acted upon. If it was, then James Willing would sit out the rest of the revolution in irons. To Pollock's way of thinking, it could not happen to a more deserving fellow.

Desirée alighted from her carriage. She was dressed in a rich white satin dress that clung to the curves of her body, pushed her ample breasts upward, and flared out from her rounded hips. It was trimmed in seed pearls and lace. Her hair was a masterpiece. It was pulled high up and then fell in long perfect corkscrew curls to caress her long neck.

Don Fernando held out his hand and helped her down. "What brings you to my lair?" he asked, smiling.

She looked at him impassively and thought, not for the first time, that he did indeed have sharp pointed teeth. In fact, all his features were pointed. He was, in many ways, to her thinking, a dismal man. But he was a dismal man with money and influence. One simply had to put up such people—more than put up with them. *But my time will come,* she told herself. In the meantime, she would allow him to make love to her. It did not bother her as long as she retained the upper hand, and as luck would have it, Don Fernando seemed to crave a certain domination. In time, she thought, not that she intended spending the time, she could turn him into a proper lap dog.

"Invite me inside and you will find out why I am here."

"But of course, Desirée. Come in and make yourself at home."

Desirée allowed him to escort her into his drawing room. The large house had belonged to his father. It was in the Spanish style with indoor fountains, and rooms with adjoining terraces. It was all built around a patio on which lovely tropical flowers bloomed.

She sat down on a gold brocade settee. "I have always admired your home, Don Fernando."

"Everything in it comes from Seville."

She smiled, knowing full well that even some of the flowers on the patio were of Spanish origin. That was one thing about the Spanish, they did import a variety of items. Even plants. In California they had planted cork trees and olive trees. Such would not grow here, but other plants flourished, and sugar certainly seemed to be the crop of the future. The English settlers, on the other hand, unlike the French and the Spanish, for the most part made due with what they found. She knew that there were fine families in Boston with imported furnishings from England, but on the whole the settlers were satisfied with hand-hewn wooden furniture, and local silversmiths labored over silver from Mexico to make unbearably plain dinnerware devoid of all the flowers and curlicues she adored. Puritans still, she thought with a sigh.

"May I offer refreshment?" Don Fernando asked.

"Cognac."

He smiled at her. Another woman would have asked for wine, but not Desirée. Not only did she think like a man, she drank like a man. He gazed on her high full breasts and leered. Apart from her mind and her drinking, she was all woman.

"May I ask the reason for your unexpected visit? I can't flatter myself that you have come just to see me."

She smiled. "You're right, you can't."

"Your tongue is so sharp! I'm hurt."

"That I doubt. I've come to tell you that this night a

ship has left Havanna with arms for the rebels. They will unload them here and then store them till the time is right to send them up river with the Cajuns."

"Do you know the name of this ship?"

"*La Mira.*"

"*La Mira,*" he repeated thoughtfully. Immediately his brow furrowed. His mind raced ahead. With those kinds of arms he could take a group of men and capture his brother's lands. He could burn the cane and ruin his brother. Then he could move on and deliver the arms to the British in Baton Rouge. It was all there before him, a glorious plan. His brother would lose everything and their father would see who was the more powerful of the two of them. The rebels would lose, too, and he would be a hero to the British.

"I see your mind working even now," Desirée said. "I trust you will use this information wisely."

"I shall use it very wisely."

Desirée looked at him with annoyance. "I still do not have my cognac."

"Oh, forgive me!" He went immediately to the crystal decanter and filled a snifter. "To success." He touched her glass with his and the crystal tinkled.

"To success," she replied. Then she sipped from her glass. "There is one other thing."

"Tell me."

"Your brother will seek permission to marry Esmé."

"Esmé? He intends to marry her?"

"So it seems. She has already moved to his house."

Don Fernando now looked nothing less than triumphant. "I shall have to tell my father. He will not be pleased to have his beloved son marry a woman of Esmé's profession."

Desirée kept her silence. She would have to tolerate him a little longer for gain, but she hoped it would not be too long. He really was a dreadful person. A man of little sense.

"Will you stay?"

"Desirée must visit all her businesses tomorrow. I shall have a most busy day indeed. Perhaps on the weekend, Don Fernando."

"I am your slave. I await your summons."

"You're full of sweet words and evil plans. You do not fool Desirée."

"It is why I like you."

Don Fernando watched Desirée's carriage as it pulled away. It was just as well she didn't stay, he thought to himself. There really wasn't a moment to lose.

He put on his jacket, slipped his sword into its sheath, and ordered his horse brought around. No time for cumbersome carriages, either. In any case, a carriage would not travel well where he had to go.

Martinez was quartered in a military encampment south of the city. Ostensibly, he served under Governor Galvez, as did all Spanish soldiers in the colony. But he was not loyal to Galvez nor were the men he had chosen to serve with him.

At the insistent pounding on his door, Martinez rose from his bed and went to the door. "Who's there?" he called out, annoyed that he had been awakened.

"Don Fernando. Open up!"

Martinez unbolted the door. "Wait, I must light the lamp," he cautioned.

He went to the stove where the coals burned, took a hand-twisted candle and held it to the coals till its extra-long wick caught on fire. Then he used that to light the lantern.

The room contained only a crude table and some handmade chairs. In one corner was a bedroll where Martinez slept.

Don Fernando barely looked around. He did not expect soldiers to have fine homes. "I've learned a ship comes from Havana laden with arms. We must intercept it," he said urgently, "and store the arms for our own use."

Martinez only nodded. He did not need a lecture on the use to which these contraband arms might be put. "I have a map, let's take a look."

"Good," Don Fernando muttered.

In a moment Martinez had the map unfolded on the table. "And where will Galvez be? Do you know?"

"I stopped and made inquiries. As luck would have it, he'll be at sea."

"And you know the name of the ship that will be carrying the arms?"

"La Mira, out of Havana."

"Ah, yes. Well, I would suggest an intercept in the river south of the port. Perhaps around Chalmette. That's quite far enough away from the barracks."

"I daresay. But then what?"

"Sail her down Bayou Barriere and hide her there until the arms are removed. Then load her up and pay the captain to sail on."

Don Fernando pulled on his sharp goatee. "How do we intercept her?"

"I can round up forty men loyal to me. We'll surprise her. Let's see, if she leaves tonight, she will have entered the river in four or five days. It can be done quite easily."

Don Fernando agreed. The only problem was the money. He certainly did not have sufficient cash to pay the captain for his cargo. But then he thought of Desirée. She would most certainly have enough. And he thought of something else as well. He thought of Esmé. Perhaps the captain of the vessel would like a comely wench. Yes, that would be good. His brother would be utterly distracted looking for her. And, he thought, she might just be the icing on the captain's cake. Perhaps with sweet Esmé he would not ask for quite as much money.

* * *

Desirée hurried into her salon. It was early morning and as yet the matrons of New Orleans had not begun to filter in to have their hair done or to try on wigs imported from Spain and France.

"Colette, Miranda, Jeanne! Come now. I haven't got all day and I shall require your reports. Come, come."

The three women appeared instantly. Desirée smiled radiantly at them. She was proud of them; she had trained them herself in the art of hairdressing and information gathering. They were experts at both.

"You first," she said, indicating Colette. "What have you for me today?"

"I heard from Captain Gomez's wife that Governor Galvez is going to sea and expects to receive orders soon to aid the American rebels."

Desirée smiled knowingly. "You mean orders to aid them more than he is already doing."

"Yes, m'am."

"That wasn't a question. What else?"

"Madame Laroquette is pregnant and fears it is not her husband's child but rather the child of Monsieur Beaudette. She told me they have slept together many times while his wife was visiting her relatives up the river."

"Ah, that's good. Madame will not want her secret revealed." Desirée marked down the information for future reference. It never paid to try to cash in too soon. People would be suspicious. But months later when they had forgotten they had confided in their hairdresser— then she would go to them and say she had a vision. She would describe the lovemaking—easy enough since people had limited imaginations—and the man's appearance. Guilt would quickly win out. They would confess and pay her not to tell their husbands. Not that their husbands didn't have secrets, too. And of course this bit of information was doubly useful since it enabled her to collect a modest sum from both parties.

"Anyone else?"

The girls looked from one to the other. Sometimes there were many bits of information, sometimes there were less.

"Never mind," Desirée said patiently. "Profits build over time."

She then toured her other businesses and, satisfied that all was well, she returned home where, unfortunately, she found Don Fernando waiting anxiously.

"What brings you this time of day? I must say you look as if you haven't slept a wink all night."

"Barely that," he confessed. "Desirée, we have a problem."

"What do you mean, 'we'? I have no problems."

"Hear me out. I must have money to pay off the captain of the vessel, the one that brings the arms for the rebels."

"I'm sure you have money."

"No, not that much money. Desirée, you must help me."

"I must do no such thing. I don't want a shipload of arms."

"We can sell them for a profit to the British in Baton Rouge."

She frowned. What he said was true enough, although this was not really the sort of thing with which she wished to become involved. "If we're caught we could be killed," she reminded him.

"You are already involved, Desirée. You told me about the vessel. If I tell Galvez that he'll have you arrested. You'll lose everything."

She was taken aback. She had not considered Don Fernando either this smart or this devious. "So would you," she muttered darkly.

"I have nothing to lose. I have everything to gain either way. If I turn you in, I am a hero—perhaps even in my father's eyes. If I get the arms, I will make money and will have the opportunity to destroy my brother's cane fields in the process.''

Desirée looked at him darkly. She was not used to feeling trapped. But she felt trapped now, and she didn't like it.

"I will give you the money," she agreed.

"No, you will come with me. You will make the payoff.''

Desirée grimaced. The situation was intolerable. He had tricked her.

Julie's legs ached from riding. It was unbelievable that a hundred miles could seem so far and could take so long to travel. As she and Brady galloped on, all she could think of was the fact that in her time this distance could have been covered in a matter of hours by car, less than that by train, and in minutes by plane—give or take the amount of time it took to get to the airport.

Again she contemplated how she would tell Brady about herself. She had made the promise to herself that she *would* tell him, but she still wondered if he would believe her— proof or no proof.

"Look!" Brady called out. "There!"

Julie looked into the distance. It was water, and it looked like any other river. They had forged so many rivers she had lost count. The area was just one huge drainage plain into the Gulf of Mexico.

"What is it?" she asked, drawing in her reins so that her horse was even with his.

"The narrows," he answered. "That way is Lake Pontchartrain," he said, pointing to what seemed like the northwest. "That way is the sea."

They guided their horses closer to the shore. In the distance she could see land and she knew that land was the jutting end of the crescent. They were almost back to New Orleans. Her heart leapt within her. Soon they would be safe.

"We'll have to follow the water for a mile or so," he said. "There's an old man who will take us across."

"I'm glad we're not going to swim," she replied.

"You jest, my woman. It is far too deep."

She followed as again he led, sure of himself in this veritable wilderness.

It was not like riding and camping in the twentieth century. The woods were deep and there was no population. The dangers were many and ranged from poisonous snakes and voracious insects to quicksand and uncertain, rugged terrain. There were no motels, hotels or inns; no restaurants or even stores. One lived off the land and made do. As she watched Brady atop his horse she knew that with a less experienced woodsman she might have perished. This man had taken care of her, guided her, seen to her survival in every sense of the word.

They had eaten mostly fish which he caught fresh daily and greens which they picked in the forest. He knew all the edible growing things, even which mushrooms could be eaten and which would cause illness. Sometimes they had berries, and he had brought sugarcane on which to chew.

Each night he built a small lean-to; he watered and tethered the horses. He rigged the netting which they slept beneath, and he rubbed her body with the juice obtained from crushing the leaves of a plant he said repelled the insects. He built a campfire on which to cook the food he either caught, picked, or shot. Time and time again Julie marveled at his varied skills.

She gazed at the narrows and knew that on the other side New Orleans waited. Oddly, with all of its drawbacks in this year 1779, it seemed as if civilization was waiting there across the water.

"There!" he shouted back to her. A short way down the trail there was a wooden cabin and in front of it a dock. Tied to the dock was a dugout.

As they drew in their reins, an old mulatto rounded the house, a shotgun slung casually over his shoulder.

"We need to cross the narrows!" Brady called out.

"Have ye the fee?" the man answered.

"Yes."

"Come along then."

Brady dismounted and signaled Julie to do the same. He led the horses to a hitch and tethered them. "We'll get fresh ones on the other side."

The old man loaded them into the dugout and he and Brady rowed across the narrows. On the other side, fresh horses awaited.

Brady helped Julie out of the dugout and then onto her horse. He paid the old man and once again they were off.

"It wasn't so far across. Couldn't the horses have swum?"

Brady smiled at her and laughed. "Alligators, my dear."

Julie turned and looked out at the water, seeing a pair of cold, beady eyes staring at her. Julie shivered. She had forgotten that gators were plentiful.

"Now on to New Orleans," Brady declared.

"And a blessed hot bath," Julie added.

The sun was setting and the sky was a brilliant orange gold as Brady and Julie rode into New Orleans. She rode by his side down Decatur and people stared at them, especially at her in her odd dress riding as a man rode rather than side saddle.

"Are we not going to Desirée's?" she asked.

"Not right away," he replied. "I have more important business, my woman."

She did not question him further. He drew in his horse and dismounted. He helped her down and tethered the horses outside of number 23. It was a rambling two-story house with a widow's walk that faced the river.

He knocked impatiently on the front door.

Pollock answered it and his eyebrows lifted in a combination of surprise and joy. "Brady!" he shouted even as he grasped his hand. "My God, man, I heard . . ." He did not finish his sentence, instead he looked about warily. "Come in, come in."

Brady reached back and took Julie's hand, pulling her inside. "This is Julie Hart," he said. "She is not a spy as I once thought."

Pollock only nodded as he led them into the study. "You look in need of brandy."

Brady grinned. "I think we are both in need of brandy."

Pollock quickly poured three snifters of brandy. "I heard you had been kidnapped, man. Carmelita had a message from one of her kin. She believes someone tipped off the British as to your route. By heaven, Brady McCormick! I am glad to see you. I thought by now you might be swinging from a rope."

"I might be were it not for this resourceful woman."

"Then let me thank you, Miss Hart."

Julie said nothing. She just smiled and sank into a chair. It was wonderful to sit somewhere comfortable. It was wonderful to taste brandy.

"Tell me everything," Pollock urged.

"We were indeed kidnapped. The British were waiting at the mouth of the Teche, as if they expected us. I was wounded in the shoulder."

"My God, man, should I summon a doctor to look at it."

Brady shook his head. "It's healing well." He glanced at Julie. "I had the best of care. She's quite remarkable. There's no infection."

"A miracle."

"In any case we were taken aboard a British vessel to Fort Charlotte at Mobile. My woman here told a delightful story, and as no one could identify me, we were held under house arrest. We escaped and here we are."

"I can't tell you how glad I am to see you."

Brady laughed. "Ah, Pollock! As an added bonus, we

bring the full plan of Fort Charlotte. I had plenty of time to look about.''

Pollock roared with pleasure. "Galvez will be anxious to see those plans, I'll wager.''

"Has something happened? Have the Spanish joined us yet?''

"Not yet, but Galvez is certain they will. We have begun to make preparations. Galvez is at sea now. He is gathering Spanish ships from all the Gulf ports. He readies for war, and when that war comes, Mobile and Pensacola will be among the first attacked.''

"What of up river? In Fort Charlotte I heard much of James Willing. He's made us no friends.''

"Willing's on his way home, though I doubt he will make it. The sea is so full of British ships.''

The smirk on Pollock's face said more than his words. Brady did not ask because he did not care. All he cared about was the essential fact that Willing was out of their hair.

"Is there more?''

Pollock again glanced at Julie.

"Speak in front of her. I have trusted her with my life.''

Pollock nodded. "There is a ship headed here from Havana. It should arrive here in two days time. It is loaded with arms for the Cajuns to transfer. We'll store them here till arrangements can be made.''

Brady drained his snifter of brandy. "Best I take this woman back to Desirée's. She longs for a hot bath and a comfortable bed.''

"We will meet tomorrow," Pollock said.

"I'll turn over the plans to Fort Charlotte then. My woman has them sewed in her clothing.''

Pollock laughed. "I look forward to seeing them." Then, as a second thought, "Why not leave your horses here and take my carriage? I'm sure you are both tired of riding.''

Julie smiled and whispered her thanks. He was quite right. She was tired of riding. And Brady was right, too.

She longed to soak in a hot tub, she longed to make love with him in a proper bed, she longed for a good night's sleep without insects. At the same time, she knew she had benefited from this experience. If she hadn't fully understood before, she understood now what living in this century meant. Danger was everywhere and nature was both a friend and enemy. In one sense she knew much more than many, in other ways she was totally ignorant. But it did not matter. She wanted to stay here with Brady. She would learn from him all she needed to know.

Chapter Eleven

The house of Desirée Coteau was ablaze with light when they arrived. It was a place of endless gatherings that often went on late into the night.

Brady helped Julie down from Pollock's carriage.

"I'm so stiff," she confessed. "It's been years since I've ridden."

"It is how you ride that is the miracle, my woman. I have never known a woman to straddle a horse."

Julie only shrugged. "It's easier." In her wildest imagination she could not envisage wearing a cumbersome dress and riding side saddle through the wilderness they had just crossed.

He carried his own pack as well as hers. They climbed the steps to the veranda and he opened the door, which was unlocked. "I suppose we'll make an entrance that will be talked about for some time."

Julie smiled up at him and they went inside. They walked directly into the reception room where a large number of people were talking and drinking. They stood for a long moment in the doorway and slowly, as they were noticed, all conversation ceased.

"Brady McCormick!" Don Fernando turned about. His sharp features twisted slightly as he smiled, hoping to cover his surprise. Inwardly he cursed. Somehow Brady McCormick had survived; he had hoped never to see him again.

Desirée floated toward them, her hand held out toward Brady.

"Desirée is much relieved to see you! And to see you have returned my most valuable employee."

Brady kissed her hand. He could not remember Desirée ever having been pleased to see another woman before—indeed, when Julie had first appeared she had seemed less than thrilled. Again he wondered why Desirée had placed Julie in charge of one of her businesses. Not that Julie was not talented. He knew she was, and he most certainly admired her riding outfit—her culottes, as she called them.

"You were supposed to return weeks ago," Don Fernando said, "Whatever happened to you two?"

"We were captured by the British." Brady's tone was nonchalant. He looked into Don Fernando's eyes expectantly.

"And you escaped?" Don Fernando asked incredulously.

"Obviously."

Desirée made a motion with her long, graceful arms. "Desirée knew you would escape. She knew you would be safe, that you would be delivered back to New Orleans. Desirée interceded with the dead on your behalf. She read the signs and knew you would be returned."

"And so we have been," Brady replied without comment on her alleged powers. "And now Desirée must know—because she knows all—how much we would like water heated and a tub filled."

Desirée laughed throatily. "One tub?"

Everyone laughed and looked at them. Julie felt her face hot with her blush.

"Aye, woman. One tub."

The men laughed and the ladies turned away. Desirée did not laugh.

"Are you making fun of me? Of Desirée's powers?"

Brady shook his head. "I respect your power," he replied.

Desirée nodded. "I shall have the tub filled."

Julie shed her clothes with pleasure. She climbed in and Brady, who was already there, pulled her down in front of him. "It's the only way we'll both fit," he said with joviality. "And I can wash your beautiful backside."

He reached for a pitcher of warm water which he poured over her golden mane, working it in with his fingers till her hair was soaked. He washed it with soap, then rinsed it with warm, clear hot water. It felt wonderful! Then he washed her back, lifting her long mop of wet hair, kissing her neck now and again as he scrubbed. When he was finished, he reached round her, and with the washing cloth, he washed her breasts, her neck, and between her legs. The water was warm, his movements slow and sensual. She groaned with deep pleasure even when he paused to wash himself before returning to rinse the soap from her.

Then he stood. He was a massive man and the water fell from his well-muscled body in sheaths. He was wet and naked and his skin glistened in the candlelight. He lifted a dripping Julie from the water and wrapped her in a great towel, drying her as if she were a precious object instead of a flesh and blood woman.

Then, still damp, he bent and kissed her, holding her close to him. "You are bright and beautiful and inventive. I have never known a woman like you."

He carried her to the bed and set her down. She looked at him and thought that she had never known a man like him, either. Her only previous lover had been John Bruns, a reticent man of few words. She could hardly recall ever having actually had a long conversation with John—at least one that had to do with her. If he talked to her at all it was to lecture her, to impart knowledge to her as if she were one of the students he taught.

But this man was different. At night they had sat by the campfire and talked. She talked to him about things she had read and he asked her about her designs. She had even confided her desires to learn more about medicine. They lay on the ground and looked up at the stars and both made up stories to tell the other. He discussed philosophy and asked her what she thought. When they talked, it was give and take. But they had not yet discussed their feelings for one another. Their love was too new, she decided. It was still too much in the realm of animal desire. When they were together she could feel the heat from their bodies, feel their mutual energy and shared physical pleasures. Together they were wind and fire, raw heat and desire. She had never felt so intensely before, nor had she known the satisfaction they experienced at the end of every stormy encounter. But if she told him the whole truth about herself? What would he do if he knew about her? The time was here and now. She could no longer keep secrets from him. Julie inhaled and drew on her inner courage.

He reached out for her and touched her cheek gently. "I see you are distracted, my woman. Your eyes are reliving some memory. You are hiding something from me."

His sense of her moods was as incredible as their lovemaking. "You know me too well, yet not at all."

He laughed gently. "And now, my woman, you speak in riddles."

"I promised myself and you I would tell you everything. I am ready now."

He propped himself up on one elbow and looked into her eyes. "Tell me your secrets, Juliet."

"I am who I say I am. And I am not a spy. But I did come to this house in a strange manner."

"You remember?"

She shook her head. "Not in a way you mean. I will try to tell you straightforwardly, though it will not be easy."

The look on his face was now one of interest mixed with distress. He sensed her hesitancy, her fear that he would not believe her story.

"I came to New Orleans with a friend. I was in a museum—"

"A museum?"

She drew in her breath. "Yes. A place where items of value from the past are collected."

"I have never heard of such a place in New Orleans."

Now she noted his expression had changed from distress to mystification. "The museum had dollhouses. One of them was an exact model of this house."

"No. I know there is no such place in New Orleans," he said firmly.

"Not now—not yet." She said the words in a whisper. "Brady, I am twenty-four years old. I was born in the year 1969. I was standing in the museum looking into this house—a replica of this house, in the year 1992."

His mouth opened slightly and a frown creased his brow. "Your words are too fantastic, my woman."

She shook her head. "Brady, I am a historian—was a historian. I designed costumes for historic plays. I don't know how it happened, or why. I only know that the lights were extinguished and the next light I saw was the candle-light in the drawing room downstairs. I turned and Gover-nor Galvez was in the doorway. Brady, I swear to you, I am a time traveler."

"And I am a rational man."

"I'll show you. When I came here, I had only one object from my own time. I hid it here, in this room where you first searched me."

She got up off the bed and went to the corner of the

mattress. She felt around and tore the thread a little. Then she removed her award medal and took it to him. "I won this," she said, handing it to him.

Brady took it and turned the silver medal in his hand. His brow furrowed more deeply as he read the inscription and studied the manner in which the medal was made. Then, still biting his lip, he rolled over on his back and exhaled deeply. "I must think on this."

Julie took the medal and looked at it herself. Could she blame him for his disbelief? She had not believed what had happened to her, either. How she wanted him to hold her now, to tell her it didn't matter, to make love to her. But he seemed stunned, to stunned to reassure her in any way.

Then, as if he were in a trance he asked her, "If you are a time traveler, you know what will happen in my future, in the future of this country and this place."

"Yes, I know general things."

"Do we win this revolution?"

"Yes, but the war lasts for a long time and there is another in 1812. We become a free nation, the strongest nation on earth."

"And the Spanish?"

"They enter the war."

"If only I could believe you. I want to believe you."

"It is all true, I swear it."

"Either that or you are clever beyond belief."

She wanted to scream *How could I lie to you after all we've meant to each other,* but now she wondered if she really meant anything to him. Perhaps it was all in her own romantic mind. Had he told her he loved her? No, he called her "my woman," but it was just a figure of speech. She felt spent, defeated. She had told him the absolute truth. She had shown him the only proof she had, and yet he did not believe her.

"Have you told anyone else this fantastic tale?"

"Desirée guessed."

"Did you show her this?"

"No, I told you, she guessed."

"That is even more fanciful. I have never believed in Desirée's so-called powers. She is simply a good listener and a splendid information gatherer."

"I do not presume to know how she guessed."

"Have you told her anything of the future from which you claim to come?"

"Only that Charleston would be held by the British. Nothing else. Brady, it does not matter if you believe me, but you must not repeat things I have told you. You could change history."

He stood up and began to dress. "I must go home to my room at Don Carlos's house. I must think this out."

Julie sat up, her long wet blond curls tumbling over bare shoulders. He looked at her for a long moment. It was, she felt, a sad look. She fell back against the pillows. Why was he leaving her? Why didn't he believe her? And most important of all, did he not love her?

Julie felt miserable as she lay down, turning on her side. She watched Brady's shadow on the wall as he dressed, then he blew out the lamp and the room was plunged into darkness. She trembled and curled up in her bed, wondering if this was how her long adventure would end.

Alone.

Without Brady.

Forever.

The following morning Esmé came flying into Julie's room. She was terribly excited. "Oh, I'm so glad you're all right. I'm so glad you're back."

Julie rubbed her eyes and looked at Esmé. Nothing had changed. She was still here in this house in this century. But Brady was gone from her side. He had not even spent the night.

"I have so much to tell you my head is spinning," Esmé

announced. "I've moved into the house of Don Carlos. He has asked to marry me! I'm so happy! I'm so in love!"

Julie looked at Esmé and thought that only a short time ago she had felt the same. But now her dreams had vanished. Stolen in the night, traded for the unbelievable truth.

"Hurry, hurry!" Esmé implored. "This is the first vessel in ever so long to come from Spain! It docked this morning. It's filled with wonderful things, and they'll all be for sale in the dockside market. You'll see! Desirée has already left! She'll be buying bolts of fabric and all manner of goods, but then all the Creole women of New Orleans will be there!"

"Is it always this way when a ship comes?" Julie spoke as she got out of bed and began to dress. Perhaps the distraction would do her good.

"No. Most of the ships that come these days are military vessels. That's what makes a merchant ship so exciting. This one is from Barcelona so it will have goods from France as well as Spain."

Julie tried to share Esmé's enthusiasm, though it was difficult. But she supposed after a long while in this time period, events such as this would be far more exciting.

Esmé urged her on and they hurried downstairs and into a waiting carriage.

"We could easily walk," Julie said as they climbed in. Now that she had come to know New Orleans, she knew where she could go and where she could not go. Nearly all of the Vieux Carré was quite safe, and it was a small area really. Desirée's house was on Dauphine and Dumaine, only five or so blocks from the market.

"The streets are muddy from last night's rain," Esmé replied. "If the sun dries them, we could walk back."

Julie accepted the assessment and reminded herself that the clothing she was obliged to wear in town was not at all practical on muddy streets. Without further protest, she climbed into the carriage.

* * *

"It's crowded," Esmé said as they approached the market.

Julie looked around. True, New Orleans was home to only three thousand, but it seemed as if all of them were here, in the market, at this very moment.

"Everyone comes to see what is being offered, "Esmé explained. "Oh, I do want some tortoiseshell combs for my hair. I hope I shall find some."

The market was a long wooden structure, open on all sides. Merchandise of every variety was spread out on roughly hewn tables and presided over by members of the crew.

There were many bolts of cloth—fine brocades and taffetas. There were bolts of laces and ribbons, and there were even jewels. Shoes, mostly impractical for the climate, Julie noted, made up a large section of the market. There was also a large section of metal products—pots and pans, cooking stoves, and even axes. As she looked around, Julie could see why the colonies were in full revolt. Their artisans had the skills to make these products here, in the new world. They no longer needed European imports. Always before she had thought of taxation as being the main cause for the revolution; now she experienced the economic reasons for the revolution as well.

Of course New Orleans was not Boston. Blacksmiths who did metal work on the frontier could not make the quality pots and pans available in the East during this century, and silversmiths and furniture makers were not as plentiful. Nor were those who would take the time to carve a fine tortoiseshell comb, she thought with a smile.

No sooner had they left the carriage then she and Esmé had separated. Julie went to look at the bolts of cloth and Esmé wandered off in search of her precious combs.

"Julie!" Desirée called her name and Julie went to her. "Help me to pick out some fabrics," Desirée said without looking up. She was fingering various cloths, deciding on its real value. "I'm glad Esmé brought you."

"Are looking for something specific?"

"Not really. I have decided to take your suggestion, however. I will let you set each of the seamstresses to work on a different section of a dress. Whatever we buy, we must buy fabric in sufficient variation to make ten or twenty dresses."

"If we use the pattern I made before I left, we shall need six yards of each fabric."

"Yards? What is a yard?" Desirée asked, her brows raised.

"A means of measurement—"

"From the future?" Desirée whispered.

"Yes, one yard is approximately one arm length from fingertip to shoulder. Here, let me show you." Julie picked up a bolt of fabric and measured it out. "See?"

"Very clever," Desirée said, obviously impressed.

In a different part of the market Esmé wandered. Then, seemingly from nowhere, a man appeared. Esmé looked into the face of Martinez, whom she did not know and indeed of whom she had never heard.

"Are you looking for something special, señorita?"

"Combs, tortoiseshell combs."

"Ah, yes. There are none out, but I have a pair in which you might be interested. Come with me and I'll show them to you. They're in my wagon which is round that building."

Esmé glanced once at the crowded market. Julie was nowhere to be seen. She smiled at Martinez. "Very well." She lifted her skirts and followed the stranger away from the crowds of the market and round the side of the warehouse. There, in the deserted alley, was a wagon with two men atop it.

A feeling of unease crept over Esmé and she turned instinctively to hurry back to the market, back to the crowds. But Martinez grabbed her arm and spun her around quickly, covering her mouth as he did so.

"She wants to look at combs," he said, smirking.

Esmé struggled, but one of the men quickly clamped her hands behind her so she could not scream. Another bound her hands behind her and then tied her feet. They then tied a bandanna round her mouth and tossed her in the straw-filled wagon and pulled a blanket over her. Soon they were off, clattering down the rutted road that led out of New Orleans.

Back at the market Desirée completed her purchases while Julie looked around for Esmé, who was nowhere in sight.

"There," Desirée said with absolute satisfaction. "I do believe we've purchased the best of the lot."

"I'm sure." Julie continued to look about. The crowd had thinned out and most of the desirable merchandise carted away. But Esmé was still nowhere in sight.

"Are you all right?" Desirée asked impatiently.

"Yes. But I came with Esmé and she seems to have disappeared."

"Perhaps she tired of waiting and went home to Don Carlos."

"I think she would have said something."

"Not necessarily. In any case, I don't see her anywhere either."

Julie still looked about, but she couldn't spot Esmé anywhere.

"I'm quite certain you'll find her at home with Don Carlos enjoying her siesta," Desirée concluded. "Come along. We'll take my carriage."

Julie nodded and followed. From the height of the carriage she took one more look around. But Esmé was nowhere to be seen.

* * *

Julie went directly to Don Carlos's house. He was not there, having left alone earlier. She began in the garden, then she methodically went through the house asking all the servants if they had seen Esmé. Dejectedly, Julie returned to Desirée.

"I'm very worried," she confided to Desirée. "Esmé simply has not returned."

Desirée frowned. "It is a bit mysterious," she allowed. "But perhaps we should not be too concerned yet."

Julie could not agree with Desirée. No matter how disturbed she was about Brady, she had to find him. She took the carriage and returned to the home of Don Carlos.

She knocked on the huge door and a male servant answered.

"Is Don Carlos here?" she asked.

"No, señorita. Only Señor McCormick is home."

"Then I shall see him," she said quickly.

The servant signaled her to follow him and she did. Brady was in the Don Carlos's study, reading.

He looked up when Julie came in and their eyes locked on one another. She tried to read his mood, but, as in the beginning, his eyes seemed like dark pools.

"It's Esmé," she quickly said. "I've come to speak to you about Esmé."

"She's not here, nor in Don Carlos," he responded. He'd been smoking a pipe, and he took the opportunity to strike the bowl against the side of the ashtray.

"Are they together?" she asked.

Brady shook his head. "Don Carlos left early this morning. He was alone."

"Esmé went to the market this morning with me, but when I left, she wasn't there. She is not at Desirée's, either. I'm worried. I have a bad feeling about this."

"It's odd." Brady had stopped fiddling with his pipe. He looked thoughtful and concerned.

"You must believe me, I think something has happened to her."

"I don't want to think so," he said slowly.

He seemed to be studying her and she wondered what he was thinking. Did he think she had made all this up as an excuse to come here and see him? Why was he so cool with her? And why couldn't he seem to bring himself to believe her? As worried as she was about Esmé, she felt equally perplexed by his reaction to her revelations.

Brady pulled himself out of the chair. "I'll go and make inquiries," he said.

He paused, looming over her, his eyes studying her intently as if she were a butterfly pinned to a collector's board. Then, clearly to excuse himself, he said, "I am still thinking on those things which you told me last night."

Julie turned quickly from him, not wanting Brady to see the tears in her eyes. "Think all you wish," she said as she left. "But please look for Esmé."

Brady left Don Carlos's house almost immediately after Julie. He took his horse and rode directly to meet Oliver Pollock.

As mid-summer approached, the nights grew ever warmer. The great muddy river, brown even under intensely blue skies, slowed its flow and rambled lazily down to the sea. It was a moody river, Brady thought. It changed with the seasons and was not even the same year to year. In summer it was slow and ponderous and sometimes, when there was little rain in the territories upstream, it seemed to undress, revealing great sand bars in its huge delta, sandbars that had not been evident before. In winter, it flowed under ice upstream and was fed by smaller rivers and lakes that often froze completely over. Then the river ran cold even through the warmer southern climate. The river ran with moderate swiftness in fall, filled by rains. But in spring the river was a tyrant. It was fed by thousands of miles of tributaries, each clogged with melting snow and ice, each adding to the depth of water. In the spring, the river was a torrent of rushing water that carried whole huge trees, houses, and even drowned farm animals to a final grave in the sea. Sometimes it spilled over its banks and covered everything as far as the eye could see with muddy water. But when the flood receded, the water had deposited rich soil on the flood plain, and from that soil sprang a deeper, richer, and thicker vegetation.

But it was not spring now, it was summer and the muddy brown water hardly seemed to be moving at all. A light mist hung over the far bank, and one had to strain to hear the water lapping at the dockside.

Pollock leaned against the side of a building staring into the darkness.

"Pollock." Brady said his name softly so he wouldn't be startled. Not that Pollock hadn't been expecting him.

"Brady, what kept you? You're late."

"I was reading and forgot the time," he answered honestly. Pollock was not the kind of man to whom he could tell the whole truth. Not the kind of man in whom he could confide, he was in love with a woman who claims to be a time traveler. No, Pollock was too practical, too much the businessman. Brady knew he was without a metaphysical side. He was not a man who saw beauty in flowers unless the flowers had a purpose—such as healing or eating. If you said it was a beautiful day, he would add, "to do business." He might be able to talk about Julie to Don Carlos had he been here, or to Galvez had he been in port. But Pollock would not do.

"Reading. Anything interesting?" Pollock asked.

"Not really."

"Well, it doesn't matter. The ship hasn't come. It's docked nowhere along the river."

Brady drew in his breath. "I don't understand. It should not be this long. It should be here by now."

"Yes, overdue by three days I'd say."

Brady stared at the ground. Time travelers, late ships, missing women. Was anything or everything connected?

"Come home and have a few drinks with me?" Pollock suggested.

Brady shook his head. "I'm going to Desirée's to see Carmelita."

"It's late."

"I know. All the better."

"Tomorrow, then." Pollock turned to leave.

"Tomorrow, unless ^The ship turns up or we hear something," Brady added.

Brady ignored the steps which led to Desirée's front door. It was very late and the house, usually ablaze in light till well after midnight, was shrouded in darkness, its inhabitants asleep.

Instead, he walked round the veranda that circled the entire house and arrived at the back door.

He turned the knob and pushed gently. The door, unlocked, gave way and he slipped inside, through the darkened kitchen and up the back staircase to Carmelita's room. He knocked gently and opened it only when he heard her whispered answer.

"Did anyone see you?" she asked as she admitted him to her small room.

He shook his head.

"Please sit down," she murmured. The small oil lamp on her bedside table flickered, even though the night was deathly still and no breeze came in through her open window. "What news have you?"

"Madam Desirée told me something strange."

"And what might that be?"

"Well, perhaps it was not such strange a thing but only seemed strange—"

Brady frowned. It seemed obvious that Carmelita was trying to find a way to tell him whatever it was.

"Tell exactly what she said," he prodded.

"She told me she has taken Don Fernando for a lover, but that she suspects his loyalties," Carmelita finally imparted. Then, in order to explain herself, "I don't find the part about having taken him as a lover strange—only the part about not trusting him. Should one not trust the person with whom one sleeps?"

He felt at a loss to answer her question. He struggled with that very question himself, yet in a far deeper and more personal way. "Tell me more," he pressed.

"She says it is too soon to tell if Don Fernando is loyal, that she might be wrong about him. But she asked me to help her watch him and to get to know his friend, Martinez."

Brady shook his head thoughtfully. Carmelita's loyalties were unquestionable. But no one beside him and Pollock knew the extent of her activism. Desirée's request suggested nothing less that spying on Don Fernando. "I assume you agreed?"

"Yes, of course."

"Then watch Don Fernando, but stay away from Martinez. I know him to be a dangerous man."

Brady rubbed his chin and thought for an instant of what Julie had told him. She had heard Esmé pumping Don Carlos for information and she claimed Esmé had told her Don Fernando had put her up to it. She further claimed that Esmé had confessed to Don Carlos, who had forgiven her. Was it possible that Don Fernando was responsible for passing on the information about *El Dorado*— the information that almost resulted in her sinking? He certainly knew the original course of the vessel because he had been at the meeting the night it was discussed, the night Julie first appeared. Brady then thought of the rivalry between the two brothers. Yes, it all made a terrible kind of sense. In fact, the rivalry might even account for Esmé's disappearance.

"It's good you have told me this," he said. "Do as Desirée

wishes, but report everything to me first. And remember, avoid Martinez."

She smiled. "You are like my brother. Of course I will tell you anything and everything."

Brady kissed her tenderly on the cheek and then stood up and stretched. He paused and turned back to her. "Have you spoken to Julie today?"

Carmelita nodded. "She is very distressed. She is worried about Esmé. She thinks the girl has disappeared. I, too, am worried about her."

"*Yes,* Julie came to the house of Don Carlos earlier and told me that Esmé had been with her and disappeared. And what of Julie? What do you think of her?"

Carmelita looked at him unblinkingly. "I think she loves you," she answered.

He squeezed her hand and then went out the door into the long corridor. He was being a fool. He loved her as he had never loved another woman. He would have to go to her and tell her so. He would have to beg her forgiveness for doubting her. Surely what she had told him was possible. And now he knew that it did not matter to him. Time traveler or no, she was the only woman in the world for him, and he would have her if she would have him. But right now he had a mystery to solve. *La Mira* had not arrived. Had she been intercepted? But how could Don Fernando be responsible? He did not know anything about *La Mira*. The rendezvous between the ship and Pollock had been arranged between Pollock and Galvez. He would have to go back to Pollock and question him.

Julie stood at the end of the dark corridor in absolute darkness. She had been tossing for hours in the still heat and finally had gotten up and decided to go downstairs and make herself some tea. Just as she had gone out into the dark corridor, Carmelita's door had opened and a sliver of light from Carmelita's lamp fell on the corridor.

Like an actor stepping on to a stage, Brady McCormick stepped into the light.

Instinctively she had stepped back into the shadows. When she saw him, her heart sank. Carmelita! Tears filled Julie's eyes and she hurried back into her room and flung herself across the bed, sobbing violently. Never had she wanted anything so much as she now wanted to be transported back in time! He did not believe her! She had been mistaken about everything—not only did he not trust and believe her, he had not even waited before taking a new lover!

Perspiration covering her and salty tears soaking her pillow, Julie fell asleep at last, wishing only that she would wake up in her own time.

The shack was utterly devoid of any comforts. It kept out neither the vermin nor the insects. Worse yet, it had been a long ride to get here and no decent refreshment awaited.

Desirée looked about in distaste. "What's that noise?" she asked irritably.

"The girl, Esmé," Don Fernando answered without hesitation. "I imagine she will sweeten the pot for the good captain and I cannot, after all, have my brother marry her."

Desirée glowered at him and then her dark eyes roamed to Martinez. Worms both of them, untrustworthy and dishonorable. "I order you to release her," Desirée said evenly.

"Who are you to order me to do anything? You are here with the money to pay for the arms. We are two armed men. I could just as easily sell the both of you to the captain."

Desirée did not flinch. "You think that because you are stupid everyone else is stupid, too. I am not. I would not ride off into the night with the two of you, Don Fernando.

I would not carry so much money. No, Don Fernando, I am a cautious woman. I know how to ensure my safety. No, no. If your captain accepts this deal he will have to take a small down payment. The rest will await him in New Orleans, and it will only be made available when I am home safely.''

"She didn't bring it all with her?'' Martinez questioned.

Desirée shot him a terrible look. Still, his comment revealed he was smarter than Don Fernando.

"She's bluffing,'' Don Fernando blustered, snatching Desirée satchel.

"I never bluff.''

"My God! It *is* empty! There's nothing here but pieces of metal.''

"Of course there is no gold. Now let Esmé out of there immediately!''

"But I cannot let her go! She will tell Don Carlos everything.''

"You're whining,'' Desirée snapped. "I despise men who whine almost as much as I despise men who trick me. Yet you do have a point. Esmé will tell Don Carlos everything and she will spoil everything, too.''

"So I will sell her to the captain—''

"You will not. You will not harm a hair on her head. She will be taken up river to your farm. And I think the other one should be taken, too—Juliet Hart. There they can be held safely till everything is under control. I will arrange it. But understand they are not to be molested in any way. If anything happens to them or to me, letters will be delivered to the governor, letters which will tell him everything about you two. I am not one to take chances, Don Fernando.''

Don Fernando scowled at her but did not argue. He signaled Martinez who went and got Esmé.

Desirée quickly untied her hands and feet and pulled the gag from her mouth. Esmé threw her arms around Desirée. "Thank you,'' she whispered.

"It's all right," Desirée said, pulling back. "I would not let you be sold. However, I am afraid that for a time you will have to go away."

"But Don Carlos—"

"Will have to wait," Desirée said firmly. "Now listen to me, Esmé, there are things I do not want you to know. Things *you* do not want to know. Go back into that room and wait. When we are through making our arrangements you will be summoned. I will see to it that you are kept safe."

Esmé nodded and voluntarily returned to the dark room, closing the door behind her.

Within the hour, the captain of *La Mira* arrived.

Desirée took four gold coins from her bodice and put them on the table. "This is a down payment. You will accompany me to New Orleans with the young lady in the next room. There I will pay you the rest. When you return, under escort, your cargo will be unloaded."

The captain pocketed the coins and smiled. "I am at your disposal, madam."

Desirée turned to Martinez and Don Fernando. "You will wait here." She turned sweetly to Don Fernando. "Desirée does not like men who try to trick her."

Don Fernando shrank back, vowing silently to even the score with this woman who dared to challenge him.

Chapter Twelve

No matter what Brady had advised, Carmelita deemed it imperative that she visit Martinez. She pressed her lips together and then took a deep breath as she stood outside Martinez's office. Rather than her usual modest dress, she wore a cream silk dress that fell over her hips in graceful folds with a dipping and daring décolletage that exposed her rounded breasts and silky tawny skin. Her hair, so often hidden beneath a kerchief, was curled and lifted up so that it cascaded down her back.

"Señorita—" Martinez opened the door to his office in the barracks he commanded and, seeing her, gave a sweeping bow.

"Captain Martinez?" She bent over slightly, giving him a better view of her breasts. Then she stood up and offered him her hand.

Martinez took it and ushered her into his quarters. "We get visitors infrequently out here."

"I'm searching for my brother and I'm told you might know of his whereabouts."

Martinez showed her to a chair. His quarters and his

office were in the same small cramped room, though he tried to keep it neat. His desk, his maps, and his duty rosters were all hung round about his desk which was near the door. There also were three straight-backed chairs— one behind his desk and two in front of it. In the middle of the room he had built a kind of divider and behind it lay the bed he slept in when work compelled him to stay in the office and a chest where he kept his uniforms.

He ushered her to a chair. "May I offer you some wine, señorita?"

Carmelita nodded and returned his look of longing. Then she lowered her long lashes.

From a cabinet Martinez produced some wine and two glasses. He filled each.

"Oh, dear," Carmelita said, standing up." I forgot my satchel. A painted likeness of my brother is in it as well as some vital information. I must have left it on the seat of my carriage."

"Please, señorita. Remain seated. I shall go and bring it in for you."

"Thank you," she said, being sure to touch his hand ever so lightly.

Martinez hurried from the room and Carmelita looked down and quickly slipped the jewel of the ring to the right. It opened and she poured the tasteless powder it held into Martinez's wine. It dissolved quickly and she stirred it with a tiny salt spoon she carried in her pocket.

In a moment Martinez returned carrying her satchel.

Carmelita dipped into her satchel and withdrew a miniature painting. "This is he," she said, handing it to Martinez.

"A handsome lad," Martinez commented as he drank some of his wine. "Good looks must run in the family."

Carmelita smiled in acknowledgment of his compliment. She sipped some of her own wine.

"He's been missing for some time," she said. "There was talk that he had joined the army. That's why I'm here."

"It's a big army," Martinez said slowly as he finished his wine and poured himself another glass.

Carmelita smiled and continued talking softly about her brother all the while watching Martinez's eyes as the drug took effect.

"You're a beautiful woman," Martinez said, apropos of nothing. "I should like to get to know you better."

Carmelita stood up and rounded the desk. "What have you in mind, Captain?" she asked seductively.

Had he been less drugged the look he gave her would have betrayed his desires, but drugged as he was, he simply looked silly.

"Let's lie down, Captain." She took his arm and led him toward the bed.

"More than I'd dreamed," he muttered as he finished his second glass of wine.

He pulled Carmelita with him onto the bed. She allowed him to kiss her.

"You must tell me about Esmé," she whispered.

"Esmé? Oh, the pretty red-haired girl. Desirée came. She got the best of Don Fernando, who is a fool."

"But what happened to Esmé?" Carmelita felt annoyed. In seconds he would pass out.

"Esmé taken to—to—ah . . . Don Fernando's farm and the other girl will go, too."

"What other girl?" Carmelita questioned.

"I don't know," Martinez slurred as he tried to thrust his hand down her dress.

"Wait," she whispered. "I will disrobe."

Carmelita stood up and went to the other side of the divider. She waited for a long moment, then peeked at Martinez. He had passed out.

She gathered up her things and left quickly. There was no time to waste.

* * *

Julie forced herself from her bed. She washed and dressed in the coolest dress she could find, then artfully applied makeup so that no one could tell she had been crying. Over and over she told herself that Brady was not the only man in the world. But her own arguments were unconvincing and she recognized the fact that it would be a long while before she was over him. In the meantime, she reminded herself, there were things she could be doing. Important things.

Julie descended the winding staircase, hurried through the courtyard, and then, without hesitation, took the empty carriage. She drove straight to the Casa Capitular.

Obviously ladies were not supposed to drive their own carriages. The moment she turned onto Decatur she was greeted by amazed stares. As she tethered the horses, she drew comments as well from bystanders.

But it didn't matter. Let them stare and gossip, she thought defiantly. She walked briskly across the square and into the building. She did not pause, but instead she lifted her skirts and climbed the staircase to the second floor. She walked down the long corridor and confronted the two guards outside the formidable doors that separated what she assumed was Governor Galvez's office from the corridor.

"I must see the governor," she said urgently.

They looked at each other blankly. Then one opened a door and went inside. He returned with a shrunken little man in an ornate suit of clothing. He grasped a pair of eyeglasses in one hand and he peered at her curiously. He was clearly a civilian and not a soldier as were the others.

"You're English?" he inquired.

She started to explain but he motioned her inside the room she had not been in on her previous visit here with Brady. This room was as she imagined it to be. It had high ceilings and the walls were covered with paintings. The furniture was sparse but elegant, made of dark, highly polished and ornately carved wood and the chairs were tapestried. It was massive furniture as if designed to dwarf those who made use of it. One chair had a back that was fully four feet high.

"How may I help you?" the man behind the desk asked. "I am Alfredo Rossario, the governor's secretary."

"I am Juliet Hart and I wish to see the governor on urgent business."

"Have you an appointment?"

"No. But I assure you my business is urgent."

"He is in conference with Señor Brady McCormick."

"Good. I wish to see both of them."

"But madam, I cannot interrupt."

"You must," she said, setting her eyes on the doors that obviously led to the inner sanctum. All the better that Brady was here, she thought. Then he could hear everything she had to say! Then he could see that she was not afraid to confide in others. Perhaps then he would believe her! Not that it mattered. He already made love to someone else, and she told herself that she did not want him back now under any circumstances. It seemed obvious to her that he had not cared deeply or he would not have turned to Carmelita so quickly—or perhaps returned to her. The two of them were close before she had come on the scene, she thought. Yes, that was probably it. Their whole relationship had no doubt just been a brief interlude—a change of beds, so to speak. She felt angry at her own conclusions. Probably all the men in this century were like Brady, utterly incapable of being faithful.

"You can wait here. When Señor McCormick comes out, I will announce you."

"I cannot wait," Juliet said, standing up. She breezed past him so quickly he did not even have time to stand up before she had pressed down on the wrought-iron door latch, opened the great door, and slipped inside.

"No! No! You cannot go in there!" the fuming secretary shouted as he followed in her wake.

He looked up, his face crimson, "A thousand pardons, Your Worship! A thousand pardons! This young woman burst in here insistent on seeing you."

Governor Galvez smiled warmly, "Ah, Señorita Hart. How nice to see you again." He turned to his secretary. "It's all right, Alfredo. She may stay."

Brady stared at her. She was wearing a blue dress. Her eyes seemed huge, her hair even more golden than he remembered, her skin more perfect. She looked lovelier than the vision in his persistent dreams. But she did not look at him. Instead, she turned to the governor.

"I suppose Mr. McCormick has told you about me," she said evenly.

Galvez raised his brow and glanced at Brady. She sounded deliberate, possibly angry. "I'm afraid not," he replied.

"Since the moment I arrived in the house of Desirée Coteau, Brady has thought me a spy. He never really trusted me, and when I told him the truth, he did not believe me."

"It's not that I didn't want to believe you—" Brady protested.

"Am I the third party in a lover's spat?" Galvez asked, a smile curling round the corner of his mouth.

Julie flushed slightly but shook her head. "I have come here to tell you the truth I have already told Brady. Actually, I have come to prove myself, to prove to you that I speak the truth."

Galvez walked round his desk and sat down. "Please have a seat," he instructed Julie. Then he motioned to Brady who also took a chair.

"I do not know by what means I came to Desirée's house. It is a mystery to me, something quite unbelievable. As I told Brady, I am a time traveler. I was born in 1969. I came to New Orleans in the year 1992. I am by profession a costume designer and historian. I won an award just before coming to New Orleans.''

She leaned across the table and handed him her medallion.

Galvez fingered it, holding it up and studying it carefully.

"It *is* cast in a way I have not before seen," he said slowly. He looked up at her. "And I do remember your arrival. You seemed so stunned, so unfamiliar even with your own clothing.''

"Brady says he is a rational man. Apparently too rational to believe in such things as time travel. Even though I could tell him that in my century men will travel to the moon and much of the work performed by hand today will be done by machines powered by electricity. I can even show you some things; I can tell you wondrous things—''

"I did not say I didn't believe you. I said I had to think on it," Brady protested.

Galvez smiled. "I like her predictions. Surely such a thing is possible, Brady. Think, man! A short three hundred years ago Europeans did not even know this hemisphere existed. Nor did we imagine the progress—''

"It isn't her predictions I doubt, though this is the first I've heard of them. It is the ability to travel through time I've questioned.''

Galvez nodded. "If you are what you say you are, you must know what our future holds.''

"And great care must be taken not to change that future," Julie cautioned. "Indeed, it is because of something I know that I've come here to prove myself and because I must trust you." Julie leaned toward him. In this case, history was on her side.

"Ah, I am interested. Continue.''

"You will become a great hero of this war for independence. You will take Baton Rouge, Fort Charlotte in Mobile, and Pensacola.''

"If Spain enters the war—'' he put in.

Juliet smiled. "Ah, Governor Galvez, that is how I shall

prove to you that I speak the truth. You and I both know that three days ago you received the Declaration of War and that you have kept it secret together with the fact that you have been promoted from acting governor to governor.''

"Is that true?" Brady asked incredulously.

The smile faded from Galvez's face and was replaced by a look of amazement.

Galvez nodded. "And what, lady, shall I do next?"

"You shall attack Baton Rouge. You shall leave to attack it August twenty-seventh. On August twenty-ninth Jose dé Galvez will arrive from Cuba. He will relay the king's orders regarding Louisiana's part in the war. His Majesty will direct you to attack Fort Charlotte at Mobile and Pensacola. I believe he will state that these are, in his words, 'the keys to the Gulf of Mexico.' He will also state that either before or after attacking such places, you should clear the English from the banks of the Mississippi. He will state that you have been placed in command because you had the foresight to map the area and acquire practical knowledge of the country.''

"And does not attacking before the orders change history?''

Julie shook her head. "The history books state you attacked two days before receiving your orders—no one knows why. Perhaps it was because of a time traveler who advised it.''

"Galvez smiled. "And do you advise it?"

"I must be truthful. You will have two setbacks. I would most certainly change history if I warned you of them. But in the end you will be victorious.''

Brady looked from Galvez to Julie and back again. "Do you believe her?" he finally asked.

"She is right about my promotion and about the Declaration of War, Brady. And the truth is, I have been thinking about moving on Baton Rouge.''

"And there is no way she could have found out?"

Galvez shook his head emphatically. "No. She is either what she says she is or she is a gifted soothsayer. Is one more believable than the other?"

Brady shook his head. "I, too, now find myself able to accept her story. But I think her origins should be kept confidential."

"Of course."

"What about Desirée?" Galvez asked. "Have you told her anything?"

"She guessed. But I have never tried to prove it to her and I have told her only vague things."

"You shall leave her house immediately," Galvez said. "I'll move you into my casa, with my wife. You'll be safer there."

Brady looked at Julie, but she avoided his eyes. "I must speak with you," he said after a moment. "Privately."

Julie avoided his look again. "Later perhaps," she said, trying to sound aloof. It was difficult to ignore him. Difficult not to confront him. Difficult to hide her own torn emotions and conclusions about his behavior. But she told herself to be strong.

"I'll return to Desirée's and pack a few things."

"I'll send a carriage for you and your things after supper," Governor Galvez advised.

Julie paused, then looked at Governor Galvez. "I am truly worried about Esmé," she declared. "She seems to have disappeared."

"Brady told me. We're looking for her," Galvez assured her. "Don Carlos will be home tomorrow and I'm certain he'll want to dispatch some of his own men to search for her."

Brady stood up. "I have my carriage," he said, turning to her.

Julie returned his look icily. "I brought Desirée's," she answered. She turned away from him quickly then so he would not see her expression; so he would not see the torment that lay just beneath the surface of her calm, even forced, demeanor.

Julie stuffed clothing into the same bag she had so recently unpacked. God knew what the governor's wife would think of her bag or of some of her modern clothing. No matter, she told herself. It was better to be comfortable riding than to have an accident. With that thought in mind, she packed her culottes.

She had almost finished when there was a knock on the door. She was surprised to find two men standing there. "Juliet Hart?" one of them inquired.

Julie nodded and opened her lips to speak, but one of the men, the larger of the two, pushed past her into the room. "How appropriate, you seem to have been packing." He lifted her bag and shouldered it. "You will come with us."

"Who are you?" she demanded, looking from one to the other. The one who had demanded she come was tall and thin. He had a mustache which was salt and pepper in color. His hair was the same mixed color, and his eyes were brown. His face was pockmarked, and he wore gray breeches, an open-necked shirt with a vest, and high boots. The other was of medium height and had sandy-colored hair and brown eyes. He was stocky with a ruddy complexion and was dressed in similar clothes.

"Who we are does not concern you. We have orders to take you."

"Take me where? To the governor's?"

"No. You won't be harmed, just come along."

"I will not," Julie protested. "I don't know where you came from or who you are."

"You won't be harmed," the tall one said.

"I still won't come with you. At least not until you explain yourselves."

They glanced at each other, a long, meaningful glance that sent a chill through her.

Julie looked at the door, but the stocky one was in the way, blocking the entrance. She opened her mouth to scream, but the larger of the two grabbed her from behind, clamping his tobacco-stained hand over her mouth and stifling her protest. When the man exchanged his hand for a gag, she managed a slight scream, but it ended with a gurgle in her throat.

Julie struggled with all her strength but they were stronger than she. The stocky one quickly produced rope from his own pack. They bound her hands and feet.

"Just till we get you quietly out of here," the tall one confided.

Then one peered down the corridor and the other tossed her over his shoulder. Julie felt sick as they carried her down the stairs and out into the heat. They dumped her into a wagon and covered her with straw. Then they urged the horses forward. Julie struggled and gasped for breath as the wagon bounced along the cobblestones and then hit the rough dirt road that paralleled the river.

After what seemed an endless horrible eternity, one of them began uncovering her. Then he removed the gag and she sucked in air, filling her lungs. Perspiration ran down her face. "Who are you?" she whispered. "Where am I being taken."

"Undo her feet but not her hands," the tall one who was driving called back. "She's a feisty little thing."

"Answer me!" Julie demanded.

"Call us what you want," the tall one suggested. "You'll be safe where you're going. You'll be treated well, that's all you need know."

"Sit down and be comfortable, beauty." The short, stocky one pushed her down on the hay and then sat down next to her. "Pity," he muttered, "We're under orders not to touch you. Too bad. I'd have liked this job more without them orders."

Julie did not look at him even though her hands were tied behind her. She clenched her fists. It angered her that she wanted Brady so much just at the moment. "Damn," she murmured as the wagon clattered on, heading up the riverbank, heading steadily north.

They traveled for hours and hours before the wagon clattered to a halt and they broke their journey to eat. Julie sat dejectedly, her hands temporarily released so she could eat her soup. It was thin, watery, and relatively tasteless. Her two captives hardly spoke to each other and both rejected questions from her save to comment that she would come to no harm.

Julie leaned against the trunk of the giant cypress and watched as the sun, now a golden bowl of flame, settled in the western sky leaving in its wake streaks of orange against the deep purple sky.

Then the tallest of her captors spoke to the other. "We'll leave the wagon at John's place and take his boat from there."

"Good," the other muttered. "It's faster by water."

"Where are we going?" Julie demanded once again.

The taller of the two shrugged. "No harm telling her now—to Don Fernando's."

Julie frowned. Don Fernando had once tried to force himself on her and she did not trust him at all. If this revelation were meant to comfort her, it did not succeed.

Carmelita was beside herself with anxiety. Desirée was no where to be found. Neither Brady, Don Carlos, nor Oliver Pollock were at home, and even Governor Galvez was gone. Finally, admitted by a servant, Carmelita stationed herself in Don Carlos's parlor to wait. Someone had to come sometime, though she prayed it would not be too late.

She paced and she waited as the sands in the hourglass on the table sifted through slowly. But she did not need the hourglass to tell her when early afternoon passed into early evening nor when the sun dropped below the horizon and left the city in darkness. It was half past seven when she heard a carriage in front of the house. She hurried to the front door to greet Don Carlos.

Don Carlos laughed when he saw her. "My heaven, you are a great improvement on Sanchez."

She forced herself to smile at him. "Please, I've come on serious and urgent business," she confided.

"What is it?" he inquired, and then, looking about, asked, "Where's Esmé?"

Carmelita began to cry. "She has disappeared! Julie came here to tell you herself just yesterday, but today she was kidnapped. I saw two men take her away, take her right away from Desirée's house in broad daylight!"

"Esmé has disappeared? When? How? And how do you know Julie did not go with the men willingly?"

"She was tied up! Esmé disappeared from the market and Miss Julie has been very worried. I know they've been taken by the same men. I drugged Martinez and he told me. He told me Esmé had been taken to Don Fernando's farm and that Desirée had ordered another girl to be taken there, too. I didn't know who the other girl was till I saw Julie being taken away."

"Where's Brady?"

"I don't know. I can't find Brady or Pollock or the governor. I've been waiting here since mid-day when Miss Julie was taken."

"And Desirée?

"I know not where she is either."

"I shall kill Don Fernando if he is responsible for this and if any harm comes to either of them." He took Carmelita's arm. "Come. I'll pour you some wine and we'll wait for Brady. He'll return here, I'm sure of it."

Don Carlos poured Carmelita a glass of dark red wine and sat her down. "Tell me what you think, tell me anything that seems significant."

Carmelita closed her eyes to think. "There was a ship called *La Mira*. It was to have arrived many nights ago and it never came. Brady and Pollock were expecting it even before the governor returned. It was sent from Cuba and carried arms. The arms were to be transferred to Philip LaBlanc and his men for transportation up river to the revolutionaries."

"A ship that did not arrive," Don Carlos repeated.

"And Desirée has been gone a great deal. She left with your brother around noon day before yesterday and returned with a strange man well after midnight. Desirée told me to become friendly with Martinez. She said she suspects your brother of being a spy. But I suspected him of having something to do with Esmé's disappearance."

Don Carlos frowned. Up to a point the various pieces of information had seemed to fit. But now they did not—unless Desirée were playing some sort of double game. But still, what had Esmé and Julie to do with any of it? He did recall Esmé's confession to him that his brother had paid her to find out information about his business. Perhaps, he reasoned, his brother was angry because Esmé had told him or perhaps he was jealous and had taken Esmé to hurt him. But why Julie? Did she know something important? Esmé's disappearance might be explainable under certain circumstances, but Julie's was a true mystery. He shook his head sadly. It was hard for him to think ill of his brother, hard for him to accept the fact that his own brother might do such a terrible thing. Even after Esmé's confession he had put Don Fernando's lies and deceptions out of his mind. Now it seemed he must face them, he must realize that Don Fernando was untrustworthy and greedy, that he wanted to inherit, and that he would stop at nothing.

It was then that he heard the sound of horses outside. "I believe Brady is back," he said, standing up.

Don Carlos opened the door to see all three men, Governor Galvez, Oliver Pollock, and Brady McCormick. They appeared hot and tired.

"Come in," he invited. "I'll have some food prepared, gentlemen. Something frightening and terrible has happened."

"Has Esmé——?" Brady asked anxiously.

"No, she has not returned. According to Carmelita, she was kidnapped by my brother and Martinez. Somehow it has something to do with the disappearance of *La Mira*. Furthermore, though I cannot think what she has to do with it, Carmelita tells me Julie was taken by force from Desirée's house this afternoon by two men."

Brady's features hardened. "Julie?" he questioned. Immediately he thought of Don Fernando and how he had lusted after Julie.

"Julie and Esmé," the governor reaffirmed.

"When I drugged Martinez he told me Desirée had ordered another girl taken for safekeeping? He must have meant Julie," Carmelita ventured.

"I think it safe to say that neither young woman will be harmed. One is valuable to you, Don Carlos, one is valuable to all of us," Galvez concluded.

"I don't quite understand," Don Carlos said.

"It is something we cannot share just now. But trust us, Don Carlos, Julie Hart has valuable knowledge."

"Is she then a spy?"

"No. She just has valuable knowledge. I believe our spy is, and was, your brother, Don Fernando. Indeed, I doubt he will return to New Orleans if he was responsible for *La Mira* being intercepted and for the kidnapping of Julie and Esmé."

"He didn't have enough money to pay off the captain for the arms," Don Carlos interjected.

Brady laughed. "Enter Desirée who also knows about Julie."

"She doubtlessly arranged for Julie to be taken away so that she alone will have access to her knowledge," Galvez added.

"And Esmé? Don Fernando might well harm her to hurt me. I fear my brother is more unbalanced than I believed."

"Desirée is most certainly in charge if she paid for the arms. She would not let harm come to Esmé, Don Carlos. Whatever else she is, Desirée is most protective of the women who live in her house."

"But Esmé did move out."

"Desirée was glad for her. I don't think there was a problem there."

"I still do not trust my brother to be their jailer."

"Nor I for any length of time. But we are raising a force to attack Baton Rouge, so on the way we will stop and rescue our women from Don Fernando's uncertain hospitality."

Don Carlos gave a guarded smile. "Has Spain declared war then?"

Galvez nodded. "And I will leave for Baton Rouge before I receive my orders. The ships are ready in the harbor now. We have been busy since early this morning."

Don Carlos poured more wine. "A toast then," he said, forcing a smile. "To the revolution!"

"To the revolution!" they all toasted.

Brady drank his wine. Galvez had a good plan, and under the circumstances it was the only plan. He was not entirely pacified by Galvez's belief that Desirée would protect the women. He closed his eyes and drank his wine, reminding himself that as well as being beautiful, Julie was strong, brave, and resourceful.

The house they approached was hidden by thick forestation, such as did not exist this close to the river in Julie's time. It was no grand antebellum mansion, either, for such had not yet been built. It was, however, grand for this time and place, a rambling wooden house with stables attached and behind it fields of cotton stretching as far as the eye could see.

The old black man who opened the front door when

the wagon rolled up looked neither surprised nor dismayed when she was marched in.

"Untie her now," the tall one muttered.

Julie rubbed her wrists when her hands were freed. She surveyed her new prison. It was not well furnished, but appeared adequate.

"She's to be kept here with the other one," the tall man instructed the old black man.

"Other one?" Julie questioned. She looked about anxiously. Who else was here with her?

"You're to stay upstairs. You can have the run of the whole top floor. Anything you need will be brought. But don't try to escape. This house is surrounded by guards. If you try to escape you'll be punished."

Julie looked at her captors indignantly. "I want some food now."

"Take the lady some tea and sandwiches," the tall one ordered. "And fetch us some wine and a roasted chicken for our trip back."

"I'll have some wine, too," Julie demanded. With that, she lifted her dress and started up the stairs to go to her prison voluntarily.

As she began walking down the hall, Esmé came flying out of one of the rooms. "Julie! Oh, Julie!" With tears in her eyes, the girl flung herself into Julie's arms.

"Esmé! You're safe. When they said there was someone else here, I prayed it was you."

"Come into my room where we can't be heard. I'll tell you everything," Esmé whispered. Then, she added, "Even though it makes no sense to me."

"What happened? How did you come here?" Julie asked, sitting on the end of the bed and holding Esmé's trembling hands.

"I was kidnapped from the market by two ruffians. I was taken down river and imprisoned there by a man named Martinez and his men. Martinez is a soldier who does not obey the governor's orders, that much I learned. They were going to sell me to the captain of some ship. He would have sold me on the slave market—a terrible fate. Then Don Fernando and Desirée came.''

"Desirée?" Julie said in amazement.

"Yes. Desirée was to pay the captain a large sum of money for his cargo. Apparently Don Fernando intended selling Desirée, too—with me, so the price would not be so high and he could keep some of Desirée's gold.''

Julie waited knowing there must be more. Esmé caught her breath and resumed. "Desirée must have tricked Don Fernando somehow. She did not bring all the gold, only a few coins. She threatened him and ordered me to be brought here for safekeeping. Don Fernando wanted to sell me because Don Carlos loves me and Don Fernando hates his brother. Desirée would never allow such a thing. She said I would be freed later and that you would be brought here so you could be protected because you have the knowledge she requires.''

"Is Desirée really helping Don Fernando?" Julie asked, letting her weary body fall back across the bed.

"I think so, but she may be playing two sides. She is very clever and she does not like Don Fernando.''

"If she were *very* clever, we would not be here," Julie said softly.

"What are we to do?" Esmé murmured. "I want to be with Don Carlos.''

"And I want to be away from here. I don't know, Esmé, I have to think. There are few houses around and no roads to speak of. I know where the river is, but it is miles upstream to Baton Rouge.''

"Which is held by the British.''

Not for long, Julie thought. Yes, that was clearly it. They had to get to Baton Rouge so they would be there when the forces of General Galvez took it. But first they had to escape. There would be a fearful hurricane on August eighteenth that would delay Galvez from launching his men upstream. He would not take Baton Rouge until Sep-

mber 21. They didn't have to go all the way to Baton
ouge, she thought. Galvez would rest nearly a week at
e mouth of Bayou Manchac owing to illness and a long
d difficult march. If she and Esmé could escape—if they
uld meet Galvez at Bayou Manchac, all would be well.

But how? They needed supplies, they needed transporta-
on and, most of all, they needed to know the way. All
e knew was that Bayou Manchac was practically in mod-
n-day Baton Rouge. Time and distance in this century
ere both a mystery to her. Yet she did know one thing—
was difficult to travel upstream and easy to travel down-
ream. Doubtless, given the waterways, the most efficient
ay to travel from New Orleans to Baton Rouge was to
ke boats onto Lake Pontchartrain, parallel the shore and
nter Lake Maurepas. From there, it seemed one ought
be able to enter Bayou Manchac following it nearly to
aton Rouge. On the other hand, that might be possible
nly during times of high water, she decided. If only she
ad a map or could remember better! One fact did stick
ith her—it was only eighty miles from New Orleans to
aton Rouge. Yet she knew from history that it would take
alvez and his men twenty-five days to make that trip with
e week out to recuperate.

"You seem very tired," Esmé said, interrupting her
oughts.

"I'm just thinking. I need to know how far upstream we
re. Do you have any idea?"

Esmé shook her head.

Julie tried to figure it all out. She finally decided they
ould not be more than twenty miles upstream. At least
xty miles lay between here and Baton Rouge and possibly
fteen miles between Bayou Manchac and Baton Rouge.
Manchac were their destination, then it was at least forty-
ve miles. Given the hardships, they could not travel much
ore than five miles a day. That meant they had to leave
ine—twelve to be safe—days before they could rendez-
ous with Galvez and his men. She knew today was August

15. In three days, a devastating hurricane would hit th
area and destroy and damage some of Galvez's ships. Sh
wondered what the hurricane would do here—yet wasn
that the perfect time to escape? Tracks would be washe
away, no one would look for at least twelve hours.

She felt hopeful. If only they could prepare in thre
days!

Julie opened her eyes. "I have an idea," she said slowl
"But you will have to trust me."

Esmé nodded. "I trust you."

"Have you explored this house at all?"

"I've been confined to this floor, but the room nex
door must belong to Don Fernando. The chest at th
bottom of the bed is filled with men's clothing."

"Ah," Julie said with a smile. "How useful. Let's go an
see what we can avail ourselves of—what may be useful.

Most of the clothing was of the type one would wea
away from the city. In another room they found even mor
practical clothing—buckskins and broad-brimmed hat
and breeches and boots.

"A stitch here and a stitch there," Julie said.

"They said the house was guarded."

"I doubt it's guarded well. Besides, they'll be lookin
for two women, not two men."

"We're going to dress as men?" Esmé asked in astonish
ment.

"Yes, it's safer. In any case, we'll go during the storm
No one will look for us right away."

"Storm?"

"Trust me, there will be one, Esmé. We must get ou
clothes ready, prepare some food, and we must have
pistol and some ammunition, netting, and bed rolls."

"Is it possible?"

"I think so. I saw a pistol case downstairs. That may b
the hardest part."

"The food is easy. They're most generous with servings
We'll save bread and such."

Julie closed her eyes. "I must make a list," she finally said, feeling a bit like a Girl Scout on her first camping trip. But it wasn't her first, she reminded herself. She had made the trip from Mobile to New Orleans with Brady, she had some idea what to expect.

"I'll get some paper," Esmé offered. "There's a pen on the writing desk in the other room."

Julie stood up and together they went to the room with the desk. Julie sat down and with the quill pen she began her list, heading it with flint, the most important item she could think of. "Fire," she said almost reverently. "It's essential we're able to make a fire."

Esmé nodded her agreement and tried to smile. "This idea of yours rather frightens me," she confessed. "I've never been in the wilderness."

Julie took Esmé's hand. "It's less dangerous for us than staying here."

"I know you're right."

A fine pair they were, Julie thought to herself. She wasn't afraid of the wilderness, but she was well aware of her lack of skills, even her impatience with having to do everything the hard way. For Esmé the difficulty of starting a fire was something natural, while for her the process was extremely annoying. Vaguely she wondered how many times since the night of her arrival she had wanted a lighter, or even a good match. A thousand, she wagered. No, this would not be an easy trip for two women alone, but she vowed that they would make it.

Chapter Thirteen

Brady stood a top the Casa Capitular with a sailor's glass. He scanned the horizon to the southeast and shook h[is] head. For as far as the eye could see—for as far as he coul[d] see even with the aid of the telescopic glass—there w[as] nothing save banks of heavy gray clouds; still clouds th[at] hung ominously over land and sea, blocking out the su[n] slowly turning day into night.

The absence of a breeze, of cool air, could only be th[e] harbinger of a wicked storm. He was not a sailor, but h[e] knew about such storms. The Gulf was famous for them[.] It was still because the storm had sucked up all the win[d] for itself. It would swirl across the water, an angry Go[d] vengeful as it broke on the land, releasing its winds an[d] waves, its thunder and terrible bolts of lightning. He with[-] drew his timepiece and looked at it. It was barely ten i[n] the morning and was almost dark outside.

In the river, Galvez's river boats were peacefully [at] anchor. But it would not last. Julie had spoken of adversi[ty] before victory. Was this the storm of which she spoke?

Galvez came into the room from the winding narro[w]

etal staircase that led to it. Brady turned and handed
m the glass. "It doesn't look good."

"There's no time to move the ships," Galvez muttered.
No, it doesn't look good. Still, not all such storms do
rious damage. Some go ashore in other places and pum-
el other locales."

"You're a seaman, you know such storms."

"Of course I do. I can only hope that if damage is done
ere, equal damage will be done in Mobile and Pensacola."
Brady laughed. "That seems likely."

"When do you think it will hit?"

"Not till nightfall is my guess. But you're the seaman,
hat do you think?"

"I agree. I've sent forth messengers telling people to
ead for high ground. As for the ships, they are well
cured. I'm going now to check the munitions."

"I'll stay here for a while. This evening we'll meet here.
's the strongest structure in New Orleans."

"Stronger than most," Galvez said. "I'll see to having
rovisions brought here."

Brady leaned back against the wall and lit his pipe. His
oughts immediately went to Julie and Esmé. He could
nly hope that Julie knew of this storm, that she meant
e storm when she spoke of adversity. He thought of what
uch a storm could do on both lakes and rivers. It could
hip up a wall of water, it could turn the placid summer
ver into a seething cauldron, it could cover the land
n both sides of its banks, it could visit tragedy on the
nprepared.

"Be prepared, Julie," he whispered under his breath.
Be prepared."

I want to tell you, he thought. *I want you to know how much
love you, how much I want you*. He cursed himself again
r not declaring himself before, for hesitating in the face
f her fantastic tale, for not trusting this amazing women
e wanted for his wife, for the mother of his children.
/ould she ever forgive him? He could only pray she would.

* * *

Desirée paced the halls of her house angrily. There w
a time when her well-built house would have been t
refuge sought by many influential people in the face
such a storm. But not so today. Brady, a frequent visit
until recently, came no more. No doubt because Julie w
no longer here. Don Carlos did not come because he, li
Brady, was helping the governor, and the governor ar
his wife did not come, either. Instead, they had tak
refuge at the Casa Capitular.

She cursed Don Fernando under her breath. She ha
not intended her involvement with him to become so co
plicated, nor had she expected events to move so swift
There were river boats at anchor and more and mo
men seemed to be arriving daily. What was going on? Sl
needed Julie, but Julie was on Don Fernando's farm wi
Esmé.

She grimaced. If she didn't sell the stored arms soon
might be too late. The thought sent a terrible stabbi
pain through her chest. There was nothing more awf
than merchandise that had become valueless. Certair
the Spanish would not buy them, nor would the rebe
They had paid for them in the first place. Only the Engli
would pay for them.

"Curses on you, Don Fernando," she muttered. Nc
he, too, was gone to his land. But he had not left witho
hearing her threat.

"You will leave the two woman alone," she had to
him. "Or I personally will see to it that you are left le
than a man. Cross me, Don Fernando, and you will ha
sexual desires without means of fulfilling them. I promi
you that."

Remembering his cowering look was all that gave h
joy on this day. As soon as the opportunity provided itse
she would simply have to turn him in as a spy. The tri
was not to be caught herself.

* * *

Julie studied the sky first from one side of the house and then the other. The clouds were gathering, and in her mind's eye she could see what others could not even imagine. No one in this century, she thought, had a view of the planet from space. That first photograph taken from the space ship had, in a real way, altered how men thought. Though regrettably, she knew that twentieth-century perception had not changed the behavior of the average person in the slightest. Nor could a person of this century, the eighteenth century, dream of satellite pictures that would enable accurate predictions of the weather. Were this her century, the people in this house would have seen pictures of this gathering storm out over the Gulf. They would know the velocity of the gathering winds, they would know exactly where the storm would make landfall, they would be evacuating coastal areas.

As it was, these people had only memory. They could not tell if this would be a bad storm or a hurricane. But they were making preparations. They were nailing shutters on the barn closed and putting things away.

Julie felt under the bed with the tip of her shoe. Their packs were ready and their clothes prepared. Earlier she had braided her hair and Esmé's so it could be more easily stuffed beneath a hat.

"When do we go?" Esmé asked as she joined Julie at the window. "I'm not looking forward to being outside during the storm."

"As soon as it's dark. I'm sure all the farm workers will be brought inside the barn for safety's sake. We'll cross the fields to the shack by the river road."

"How do you know there is such a place?"

"I saw it when I was brought here. It seemed to be abandoned."

"It could be blown down."

"Yes. But we'll have to take the chance, Esmé. This will

be our only opportunity to get a good head start. We can travel while it still rains and leave no tracks. By the time they miss us, we'll be long gone. We'll draw the drapes and stuff our beds. If someone looks in, they will think we're sleeping late."

"I'm afraid," Esmé said.

"Not as afraid as I was when I stole the pistol last night."

"I held my breath the whole time you were gone," Esmé confessed. "I do hope we don't encounter any wild animals. I've never spent a night outside."

"It will be difficult, but we'll survive," Julie assured her. She herself was an experienced camper in her own century, and of course she had been with Brady on the trek back from Mobile. He had taught her a lot, and while she knew there were dangers, she was not really afraid.

Julie sat down on the edge of the bed and once again went over her list. Their netting was rolled in their blanket and both were rolled in their ground sheet. They had a lantern and some extra oil for it. They had four loaves of bread and some sugar and salt. Julie had fashioned a line with which to fish, and when she had gone for the pistol she had brought a frying pan, a metal flapjack turner, and two mugs from the kitchen together with a small grate she had stolen from the innards of the stove. She deemed the most important items to be flint and a small woodsman's axe. But the latter sat by the back door and she decided not to take it till they were actually leaving. The flintstone was in the kitchen, too, and that also fell into the category of items that would be missed if taken too soon.

Julie took a long look at the hunting knife she had found in the bottom of the pistol cabinet while stealing gun powder and shot. It was an important acquisition.

"When shall we dress?" Esmé asked.

"Not till after dinner. We must eat well. We'll need all our energy."

Esmé nodded and again stared out the window. Julie was very strange. It was impossible not to have faith in her, not to feel confident, but how had she known this storm was coming?

"Heaven and earth," General Galvez muttered. He could not have imagined the strength with which the hurricane dashed itself against the land at Plaque Mines as it roared out of Breton Sound. Its force was only momentarily weakened as it crossed the bayous, swelling them with wind-propelled seawater and filling them with torrents of rain from the sky. Then it reached the Mississippi, and as if completely renewed by the sight of this broad swath of water, it swirled up the river, its winds blowing mightily and dashing New Orleans in its wake.

The Casa Capitular shuddered and shook. Its storm shutters blew off their hinges and through the air as if thin slats of plywood, crashing against a nearby fountain and splintering into thousands of bits and pieces. But the tiles on the roof held, as did the adobe walls.

But the wind was like a wanton vandalizer. It blew in the windows, now unprotected, and extinguished the lamps. It sent sheets of water across the tile floors to render them slick and dangerous. It caused the heavy drapes to blow as if they were unfurled flags, and then, as if to punctuate its presence, the heavens were split with great bolts of lightning, and thunder shook the ground.

"I hope the vessels survive," Brady said. He echoed each of their thoughts.

"This must be the adversity," Galvez muttered. "I suspect the vessels will survive, but of course their masts are quite a different matter."

"What of munitions? Our powder is bound to be soaked," Don Carlos added.

The three of them huddled on the stairs that led to the cellar. Afraid to descend into a darkness that might soon swell with water, afraid to climb back into the kitchen where normally food for the guard was prepared. Dishes had crashed from the cupboards, and where one remaining shutter slammed back and forth in the wind like a giant clock measuring its force.

"We'll have to organize a team to shoot the rats tomorrow," Brady said matter-of-factly.

Galvez agreed. The storm would cause flooding and the flooding would drown thousands of river rats and force thousands of others from their holes beneath the ground. And with the rats would come pestilence.

"I have faith," Galvez finally said. "I'll summon everyone to the square tomorrow."

Julie finished tucking Esmé's hair beneath her hat which was tied on her head securely. Then Esmé did the same for her.

"These clothes feel so funny," Esmé commented. "But I can see how much easier it will be to walk."

Julie smiled and handed Esmé her pack. "Now," she said, "follow me."

Julie tiptoed down the back staircase and into the darkened kitchen. Esmé stood by the door while she went to the stove and took the flint. Then, as they passed through the door, she took the axe.

Out into the darkness they crept. Then, when they were twenty or so feet from the house, they began running through the cotton fields. The rows were straight; they needed only to stay on a straight path till they were over the knoll and reached the river road. Then they need only follow that road to the deserted shack.

They stopped twice to catch their breath, then began running again. After a time they passed from field to road. It was pitch black, darker than Julie had imagined, darker than any night she remembered with Brady. But then, she reminded herself, there were no stars this night and no moon on this night.

She paused and lit the lantern from the wick lit by the

live coal she carried in a smaller metal container. Such awkward things! They could not be carried like other needed items in one's backpack. Still, she was glad she had taken the coal. It would have been hell lighting the lantern if she had been obligated to light the wick directly from a spark obtained from the flintstone.

She held it up and smiled. They were on the road and from here they could use the lantern. In spite of the fact that light traveled far at night, especially in the pitch darkness, Julie knew the light from the lantern could not be seen from the house.

"Oh, blessed light," Esmé whispered. "I hate the darkness."

"We must hurry," Julie said as she felt the temperature begin to change. "We haven't much time. Run!"

The two of them streaked down the road toward the shack. The wind had come up now. It gusted across the land and sucked through the fields of cotton. It rumbled in the distance threateningly as if saying, "this is nothing yet."

They reached the shack and Julie lifted the latch and threw open the door. She thrust the light in and mice scattered, disappearing into the cracks beneath the floor. Otherwise, the shack was empty. Julie slammed the door shut and latched it from inside. She tried to imagine the storm. Like all hurricanes, it would have an eye. It would be powerful and windy. Then it would go calm and die away. That first calm would be the short period during which they would be in the eye of the storm. But that was the most dangerous time because the wind would again rise and the second half of the storm would hit with the same intensity as the first half.

The sucking wind caused the shack to vibrate, even to sway as if it would break apart. But it was sheltered by a cypress grove and shielded by a wall of shrubbery.

They waited, sitting close to the door, their packs beside them. They waited and held on to each other as thunder and lightning battered the area and as the angry wind blew itself out. Then there was a stillness.

"Can we go now?" Esmé asked after a few moments.

"No. It's only the eye of the storm," Julie told her. "You'll see. We're safe here."

Again they were dashed by wind and pummeled with rain. Again thunder filled the sky and lightning crackled, hitting the tall treetops and starting a quick fire that was just as quickly squelched by the falling rain.

Then, gradually the wind died down.

"We'll have to go now," Julie said. "Even though it is still raining."

They made their way down the muddy road till they reached the river. They walked on the far side of the road as rapidly as they could. "The more miles we can put between us and Don Fernando's farm the better," Julie told her thoroughly soaked companion.

Julie stood in front of him wearing his favorite blue silk dress. He walked to her slowly and embraced her, drawing her close enough to feel the outline of her body on his, to smell her sweet soft skin, to bury his face in her neck, just where her blond curls fell below her delicate, perfectly shaped ears. Then he reached up and loosened her hair, freeing it from its combs and ribbons, freeing it to fall on her bare white shoulders.

He kissed those shoulders and unlaced her bodice, revealing her perfection. He knelt and kissed her pink-tipped breasts, then lay on the sofa and drew her down on him, pushing away her clothing, leaving them both naked in each other's arms. Naked and tossing and turning, naked and fulfilling themselves hungrily, naked and melding into one. Then as suddenly as he felt himself throbbing in satisfaction she was snatched from him and taken shrieking into the darkness beyond the light that had flooded over them.

Brady yelled out and thrashed on his side. Then he sat up suddenly panting, still aware of his heart's rapid beating, aware of the perspiration on his brow and covering his broad chest.

The sun was streaming through the window and the air was unseasonably cool and fresh. The floor was littered with leaves and here and there were pools of water. He was in a room in the Casa Capitular, his bedroll spread out on the floor. It was morning and the storm had passed. A dream. It was only a dream. She was only a dream. A vivid dream to be sure, but still a dream he told himself.

On the one hand, it had been a pleasurable dream, on the other, a dream filled with distress. He felt that Julie was in danger. He felt it strongly and it plagued him even as he got up and hurriedly dressed. There was damage to be assessed and preparations to be made. With good fortune, he told himself, they would be in the vicinity of Don Fernando's farm within a few days of their departure from New Orleans.

"Then we'll be together again," he said aloud. He pulled on his boots and told himself again and again that she would forgive him, that no matter what the obstacles they would be together.

Brady hurried downstairs where he found Pollock, Galvez, and Don Carlos together with Galvez's wife in the kitchen. It was still very early, only a little past six. Both the Casa Capitular and the church had been filled with those seeking shelter—those who feared their houses were not sound enough to stand the high winds.

"Coffee?" Galvez offered.

Brady took the extended mug gratefully. It was dark and rich with just the right amount of chicory. He drank it and ate some bread. Then the three of them set forth to assess the damage.

Galvez did not need to board the vessels at the docks to see that the damage was excessive. He toured all his military facilities and dispatched a team of soldiers to arrest Martinez. At the same time, he had his men set about to kill the rats.

"What do you think?" Brady asked Bernardo.

"I think my final decision will be based on the reactions of the people. Have the church bells rung. I will talk with everyone in the place d'Armes. It is time to enlist the help of the citizenry."

An hour before noon the bells pealed out and word spread rapidly that the governor would speak to the three thousand inhabitants of the city at noon sharp.

By noon the square was filled with people. Bernardo de Galvez stepped out on a second-floor balcony and doffed his plumed hat. The crowd cheered. Galvez was a popular man, well liked by all the diverse groups of New Orleans. Brady was pleased as he listened to his friend the governor.

"I've come to tell you that Spain has declared war on England! That Spain has allied herself with France!" The crowd cheered—the English were not popular here. "Henceforth we will openly aid the Americans in their revolt!" Another cheer went up—the revolution was a popular concept. "I further wish to announce that I have been promoted from acting governor to governor and that I am directed to lead the attack on the British."

The crowd roared again. Galvez called for silence. Then again he spoke. "I promise to do all I can for this province. I promise to defend this province! What do you all say? Shall I take the oath of governor?"

The cheers drowned out his question and he smiled. The people were with him. He turned to Brady who stood just inside the balcony. "Now we'll raise a force to march on Baton Rouge."

The governor's secretary appeared. "Miss Desirée Coteau is here to see you, Governor. She says she has urgent business."

Galvez glanced at Brady, then back at his secretary. "Show her in," he directed.

In spite of everything, Desirée appeared in fine form

and dressed in high fashion. "I've heard your speech," she said with a smile. "And I've also heard that the gun powder stored in the government depot was destroyed in the hurricane."

"By the rain, yes."

"I do believe I can help."

"Your help is always welcome," Galvez said cautiously.

"Don Fernando de Vega has been working against you," she said bluntly. "He intercepted a vessel carrying gun powder and arms intended for rebels, but then he couldn't pay the captain for the cargo. In order to ensure that the gun powder and the arms reached those for whom they were intended, I led Don Fernando to believe I was assisting him. I paid the captain, and I can assure you that the gun powder was not damaged, since it is miles from here and hidden in caves well protected from water."

Galvez fought to contain himself. Then he drew an appropriate phrase out of the air, "Madam, you are a wonder."

"Desirée knew there would be a storm. Desirée knows everything. I shall have my men lead you to this gun powder, which of course you may have. I also suggest you arrest Don Fernando."

Brady drew in his breath. She was quite magnificent. "And what of Julie and Esmé?" he asked curtly.

"Julie and Esmé—" Desirée said their names as if she had never heard of them.

"I believe you know what I'm talking about," he said evenly.

"Ah, yes. Don Fernando had intended selling Esmé to the captain, but of course I stopped him. I would never allow such an act of barbarism. I had him send her to his farm, just for a while till war was declared, until I could reveal his unsavory plans. And I had Julie sent with her, for company. There is absolutely no problem. They are both quite safe."

"How dedicated you are," Brady said sarcastically. He

decided not to pursue her lie. She would not admit to it in any case. Martinez knew nothing of Julie, and even Carmelita was not absolutely certain it was Desirée who had ordered her kidnapped.

"I hope you are not lying, Desirée." Brady looked her in the eye and she looked back shamelessly.

"I am loyal to your cause," Desirée purred. "And much more likely to kidnap you than Julie."

He shook his head. She was impossible.

"Send your men to fetch the gun powder immediately. I'm anxious to raise a fighting force and doubly anxious to get started," Galvez said. "We shall pick up the women on the way to Baton Rouge."

Julie looked at Esmé who was as drenched as she and most certainly as tired.

"It's so slow and difficult," Esmé said breathlessly. "All this mud is hard to walk on."

"Yes, but that same mud will make it difficult to track us."

"If only it would stop raining," Esmé replied.

Julie tried to smile back at her friend. And she realized that she now truly considered Esmé a friend, as much a friend as any person she had known in her own century. And at this moment, her feelings went beyond friendship. Esmé was nothing short of admirable. She was used to walking long distances, used to hiking, to camping, to thinking of wilderness trips as a challenge. In her century wilderness weekends or treks were done for pleasure! She supposed that after a time in this century she would feel as everyone else, indeed that she would recognize the hardships in everyday life. But what was admirable about Esmé was that she was a woman of this century, a woman who never walked anywhere but rather took a carriage. Esmé's life had been hard in other ways, but she was not "in shape" given the twentieth-century use of the word, nor were any of the women she had encountered. Women sometimes carried water and emptied chamber pots, but most of the manual labor was done by men. Women's hardships involved the risks of childbirth and all the difficulties that not having a male protector could bring. Given her lack of physical readiness for this trek, Esmé was plodding along without complaint, though Julie was sure that when they rested, Esmé would stiffen up badly.

Yes, she had gone on many wilderness weekends and she loved camping out, but there were times during her trek with Brady and right now, when she would have enjoyed some of the luxuries of twentieth-century trekking. Decent hiking shoes, Gortex clothing, a lightweight tent, a Coleman lantern, and a good sleeping bag would all have made this forced outing much better. Not to mention dehydrated food. The thought of food made her realize how long they had been walking. In spite of the heavy clouds and continuing rain, daylight was at hand.

"I think we should start looking around for someplace to stop," Julie suggested.

"Oh, yes. I would like to rest."

They walked on in silence, then Julie pointed into the distance. There was a shack, part of which had fallen down. Clearly it had been part of some kind of dockside storage building. The dock itself was in ruin and a small boat had been dashed to bits. But the shack on the river road was only badly damaged. Its front end had collapsed, but the back looked safe enough.

"I think we can crawl in here for a bit," Julie suggested. "At least it's dry. Maybe we can get some needed sleep."

Esmé nodded and they both went inside.

"Everything's too wet for a fire," Julie said. "Help me turn this table over. Its underside is dry, we can lay our bedrolls on it."

"I never would have thought of that," Esmé said as they struggled with the table.

"You don't even seem tired," Esmé murmured as she spread out her blanket. "I can hardly stand."

"I'm afraid when you wake up your body will be stiff, too. But each day it will get easier."

Esmé forced a smile. "I must believe you if you say so."

Julie opened her pack and withdrew some bread. She broke the loaf and gave some to Esmé. She poured a little water from the canteen, had some herself, and then passed it to her friend.

"I'll put out a container for rain water," Julie said. "It's good to drink and doesn't have to be boiled."

"I know, you boil all your water. I have never known a person to do this."

Julie wondered if she should attempt an explanation. She had explained to Desirée who accepted the explanation because she believed she was a time traveler. In fact, Desirée had been so impressed, she had ordered her servants to boil all the drinking water used in the house. It would be especially important now, Julie thought. The hurricane must surely have wreaked havoc in New Orleans and most assuredly wells and other sources of drinking water would be contaminated with bacteria.

"I boil the water to make it safe to drink," Julie said, deciding on nothing more complicated. "I am seldom sick."

"I marvel at you," Esmé said.

Julie squeezed Esmé's hand. Then she lay down and closed her eyes. With Brady it had been easier. And now that she thought of it, he never asked why she insisted on boiling her water. He just accepted it, and indeed boiled his water, too.

In spite of the way she felt about him, in spite of his unwillingness to believe her, in spite of his turning so quickly to another, she wished he were here now. It was unsafe in this time for two women alone. Furthermore, Brady knew this country as she did not. He could track and catch small game to eat. He was a good fisherman.

and he could build a shelter out of almost nothing. She admired his woodsman's skills. She admired them and she missed them.

As sleep was settling over her, Julie could not get her mind off Brady. He was strong and good. He was kind and thoughtful too. She supposed she could forgive his not believing her fantastic story. He was probably right. If he had told her such a story she would not have believed it, either. But how could she forgive him turning to Carmelita the very night after they fought? That was unforgivable. Tears filled her eyes. She missed his voice, his humor, their conversations. She missed the way he made love to her— a knowing way that sensed and responded to all her desires. He touched her in ways that enabled her to respond to him with every bit of herself.

As she dropped off into a deeper sleep, she whispered his name.

"The women! The women are gone!" The servant woman ran down the stairs waving her dustcloth as if it were a flag of surrender. "Where is the master? Where is he master?" she asked, running from room to room, bearing news she knew would upset Don Fernando, who had just arrived.

And suddenly he was looming before her, framed in the doorway to his parlor, his wolflike eyes glowing with anger.

"Who's gone?" He shouted out the question in such a thunderous voice that Hezbeth virtually slid to a stop, her mouth open and her brows raised.

"Answer me, woman!"

"The women are gone. Those two women. They're plumb gone. Not there."

"Are you absolutely certain?" It seemed impossible to him. When would they have left? During the storm? How could they have gotten far?

"Yes, I looked everywhere, master, they're nowhere to
be found."

"I want this whole house searched from top to bottom.
I want the barn searched, too."

"And what else, master? Do you want to send men out
to look for them?"

Don Fernando grimaced. The truth was, he didn't give
a damn about either one of them. Not that they wouldn't
have been pleasurable, but somehow that didn't seem in
the cards. As it was, he had his hands full. If his cotton
crop was to be saved he needed every farmhand he had.
He couldn't spare men to go hunting for two stupid
women. Even less savory people than he would doubtlessly
find them and then they would know that they should
have stayed put. No, he had too much to worry about. He
stomped his foot angrily. "No! Just do as I told you and
then get all the men out to the fields. We've a crop to deal
with!"

The woman backed away. "Yes, master. Just as you say,
master."

He turned away, heading back to his refuge and his
brandy bottle. "Master," he whispered. How I love that
word, he thought. It was ever so much better than Señor
or Sir. It denoted much more subservience. Master was a
title with which he could live, a title he felt suited him. A
title he deserved.

Don Fernando returned to his armchair and picked up
his brandy. Yes, with any luck most of the crop could be
saved.

They had left on the afternoon of August 27 as Julia
had said they would. They were a little army of six hundred
and fifty men of all nationalities. It had not boded well from
the beginning, Brady thought. There was no engineering
officer and the artillery officer was ill. Almost all the men
were without tents and other much needed supplies, and

ie roads proved all but impassable. Perhaps a small party
ould have made reasonable time, but an army could not.
he packhorses and supply wagons got bogged down in
ie mud.

Governor Galvez sent messengers ahead to various river
ommunities and towns on nearby bayous to rally local
iilitia units so that now they numbered more than four-
:en hundred men.

Brady sat by the fire, a bit of meat roasting on the end
f a stick. He turned it slowly, cooking it on all sides. He
iought how glad he was to have the rabbit. He'd been
ating fish for days, and finally he admitted he was growing
red of it.

Galvez came up and then sat down next to him. He,
оо, had meat impaled on a green branch which he poked
ito the fire.

"I'm sure that as commander you have a cook," Brady
iggested.

"I find this relaxing," Galvez answered. "What do you
iink, Brady? Will we be in any shape to attack Fort Bute
hen we get there?"

"I should think whatever our hardships the British have
:n times more."

Galvez agreed, then frowned deeply. "We do have one
roblem."

Brandy laughed. "Only one! Tell me."

"You're right to suggest by your tone that we have more
ian one problem; we do. But we have one problem of a
uman nature which distresses me."

"What might that be?"

"You remember that bastard James Willing?"

"He would be hard for me to forget."

"I've sent messengers ahead of us, as you know. I'm told
iat there is a remnant of his force still wandering about
ommitting crimes—murders. They're evil men and care
othing about the revolution. They simply keep terrorizing
›cal farmers and communities along the river. People who

would support us are terrified and they associate these men with Willing and the revolution, so they believe we're all the same."

"I heard about them in Fort Charlotte. I'm surprised they're still about. I agree, it is a problem. We'll have to round them up as we go along."

Galvez turned his meat slowly and nodded. "And we're losing men by the day to disease. Fever is particularly bad. It's an unknown opponent. I wish I knew how to fight it."

Brady, too, knew the disease to be a formidable enemy. Vaguely, he wondered if Julie knew how to cure the fever that attacked them. If she really was from the future, perhaps she knew something about it.

"You're silent."

Brady voiced aloud his speculation then.

"Julie might just know," Galvez concurred. "I always feel, Brady, that we are on the edge of a wonderful age. I believe inventions and man's genius will change everything."

"A byproduct of the revolution, my friend. Freed bodies mean freed minds and freed minds mean progress."

"We're both dreamers," Galvez chuckled.

Brady laughed. "And schemers, my friend."

"Brady, I think you are a man who needs a woman."

"I have a woman. I only need to find her."

"Soon," Galvez said. "In fact, we should be at Don Fernando's farm tomorrow."

Brady smiled. He'd been putting it from his mind lest he wish for too much. But surely she would forgive him. Surely he could make her believe he loved her.

"Tomorrow," he said.

Julie and Esmé trudged on. They dressed as men and avoided others. At night they camped near the river and slept by their campfire. During the day they trod on.

At last they came to a small settlement. "We'll have to

stop here," Julie told Esmé. "I have to find out where we are and how to get to bayou Manchac."

Julie picked the house at random. She knocked on the door and presently it was answered by a middle-aged man with an unkempt beard and long mustache. He looked at them skeptically, then, stroking his beard, muttered, "I got no work."

Julie tried to deepen her voice, though in fact she had always had a reasonably low voice for a woman. "We're not looking for work. We need directions. Do you know the river? Can you draw us a map showing us where the mouth of bayou Manchac is located?"

"And we need to buy bread," Esmé added. She produced a few Spanish coins.

"Come in," the man said, beckoning them inside. "The wife just made some bread, so I suppose we can spare a few loaves. As for the map, I suppose I can throw that in with the bargain. Travelers don't pass here so often," he said, sitting down at his table. "Got ruffians running loose, though. Got to be careful."

"We're law-abiding people," Julie said.

"And too clean-cut to be with that gang that's been round here shooting it up and drinking and stealing from honest folk." He laughed then. "You two don't look old enough to shave. Got nothing but peach fuzz on yer faces."

"We're old enough to be on our own," Julie replied.

"I suppose these days everyone is old enough."

He went to a chest and rummaged around. They sat at the table and the man's wife brought mugs of hot tea. It tasted incredibly good, Julie thought as she sipped it. "What is your last name, sir?" Julie asked.

"I'm Abner Joseph." He pointed to his wife. "This here is Aggie."

"I'm James Hart and this is my brother Ernest."

Abner Joseph didn't look up but continued to rummage in the chest. Finally, he withdrew a parchment and a quill pen and ink. "This ain't stuff I use every day," he said by way of explanation.''

"You be wanting white, bread or dark bread?" Aggie asked.

Julie looked at Esmé who gave no sign of caring. "Dark," Julie answered, thinking it would be more nourishing.

"You come from New Orleans way?" Abner questioned.

"Yes," Julie replied.

"Heard there was lots of damage there. Lots of damage from that big storm.''

"We left before that," she replied.

He came over and sat down next to her, placing the parchment between them. "Gotta show you, most likely.''

"Thank you."

"Now see, we be here now. This is my house, this is Danville town. Now you follow the river. She twists and turns some, but you just follow her. Then you gonna come to White Castle. There be a sign there on a cross. From there on, the mouth of every bayou is marked with a cross. Manchac is a big bayou. You will know it because there is a British fort there, Fort Bute.''

"You've been very kind.''

"You can stay the night if you want. We ain't got much, but you can stay the night.''

"Thank you kindly, but we should be on our way.''

Esmé paid for the bread which they stuffed in their packs, then, folding her homemade map of the area between here and the bayou, they left.

"How I wanted to stay," Esmé sighed after they'd left the village and were walking alone by the river.

"I, too, would have enjoyed a night inside. But we are not what we seem and it would be dangerous to stay there.''

Esmé smiled knowingly and nodded. "I think I'm getting used to sleeping under the stars. It's not bad if the netting is done right and it doesn't rain.''

Julie looked around. There wasn't a cloud in the sky. "I think we're safe tonight," she said.

"What will we do when we get to this place?"

"Wait," Julie said. "Make a permanent camp and wait."

"Are you sure they'll come?"

"I know they will," Julie answered. Happily, Esmé did not ask how she knew.

Chapter Fourteen

The sun rose slowly in the east, revealing a cloudless sky in the blue-purple early-morning light. The lush countryside of Louisiana was bathed in light and shades of green, hillsides of still trees and meandering brown rivers crisscrossed the land and overhead a flock of geese flew in perfect formation toward their winter home. Their shadows passed over the fields, larger than life, the only movement in the stillness.

The advance guard of Galvez's army moved with stealth through the trees and fields. They fanned out and surrounded Don Fernando's farm as if they expected the entire British Army to sally forth to defend it when, in fact, most members of the household were asleep. Galvez joyfully called it "an exercise" for his enthusiastic but untrained ragtag army of volunteers. They sprang into action on Galvez's order, pouring into the house through windows and doors. Their weapons were drawn, but no shots were fired.

Don Fernando, dressed in a long red nightshirt, was

marched outside, his mouth open and his brows lifted in an expression of permanent surprise.

"What is the meaning of this outrage!" he began shouting as soon as he saw Galvez and Brady who waited anxiously for Julie and Esmé to appear. He had begged to go inside himself, but Galvez forbid it. "You'd kill Don Fernando," he'd said, "who will prove a valuable source of information."

"Unhand me!" Don Fernando ordered as he and his captors reached Galvez and Brady, both of whom were still in the saddle atop their horses.

"An outrage, is it?" Galvez said, rubbing his chin. "It does seem to me that traitors are usually made to pay in blood."

"I am no traitor," Don Fernando blustered.

"We have Desirée's word that you are, and your friend Martinez has talked as well. What do you think, Brady? Shall he be whipped or put on the wheel?"

"No!"

Don Fernando's expression had gone from angered outrage to utter and complete fear.

"Where are they?" Brady demanded. "We know full well you have been holding Esmé and Julie Hart prisoner here. They had better be well and they had better be utterly unharmed. If they are not, my friend, you'll be drawn and quartered after you've felt the sting of the whip!"

"I don't know where they are! You must believe me! I was taking good care of them, ask anyone. I never touched them. They ran away—they ran away the night of the hurricane."

Brady clinched his reins. He had been looking forward for days to seeing Julie. He'd planned everything he intended to say, everything he'd intended to do. Now she wasn't here. She was gone, and to make matters worse, Esmé was with her. Don Carlos, who commanded a second unit half a day behind them, would be as disappointed as he. He let go of the reins and slipped off his horse. He went to Don Fernando and grabbed him roughly.

Don Fernando's dark eyes flashed with pure terror. His face had gone utterly pale. He shook involuntarily and spittle ran out of his mouth and down his beard. Brady doubled his fist and struck Don Fernando hard enough to knock him off his feet and into the mud. Blood trickled from his mouth and he held up his hands and cried like a baby. "I've told you the truth! I never hurt them! They ran away."

Brady thought to hit him one more time. Disappointment mingled with anger. He was so angry he had not noticed Galvez climb down off his own horse. He felt his friend's hand now on his shoulder; it was a firm, restraining grip. "He is too much of a coward to lie."

Brady knew it was so. He continued to glare at Don Fernando for a second, then turned away and let Galvez lead him off. Galvez turned back to his men. "Release his servants and question them about the women. Put this man in irons. He'll be sent down river to the jail in New Orleans till this is over and he can be dealt with."

"No, no! Let me talk to you now, General. I can help you."

The words were music to Galvez's ears. "Bring him to the study after dinner." Then Galvez turned back to Brady. "Come now, my friend. I know you're disappointed, but you yourself said she was brave and resourceful. I'm sure we'll find her. And I'm very sure our friend Don Fernando has a splendid wine cellar. Think, this is our first night inside. We shall eat well tonight and drink well too. And tomorrow we'll be off."

It was after nine when they finished a fine dinner of chicken and crawfish. They were into their second bottle of madeira when Don Fernando was brought in and roughly pushed into a chair.

"Now tell me your information."

"Will I be thrown into prison?"

"Yes, but perhaps you won't stay there as long if you cooperate. Remember, I would not hesitate to shoot you."

"You're only the acting governor," Don Fernando said haughtily.

"I am afraid you are uninformed. I have been promoted. I am on the king's mission and we have officially allied ourselves with the French. We are at war with the British."

Don Fernando twitched. "How can this be?" he muttered.

"It just is," Galvez replied. "I am in full command and I think you know what that means."

"But my father—"

"Is an elderly gentleman whom I greatly respect. As I respect your brother whose fiancée you have seen fit to kidnap."

"I brought her here because Desirée told me to bring her here."

"You brought her here because you were told you could not sell her to the captain of *La Mira*. You are a sniveling excuse for a man, Don Fernando. If I spare your life at all it will be only out of respect for your father and brother. Now quickly, enough of your lies and your excuses, tell me what you know."

"I know that there was a threat to attack Galvestown, but the British have decided not to attack there. Indeed, they have withdrawn some of their men from Fort Butt. The British are not ready, they are too few to defend the land they claim to control."

"Then it would seem you have chosen to ally yourself with the wrong side."

Don Fernando stared at the rug. "It would seem so," he replied.

"Did you search for the women?" Brady asked after a moment, realizing that Galvez was finished.

"It was no use. The rain would have covered their tracks. I had the cotton crop to get in. There was no time."

Brady pressed his lips together. It had been days since

the hurricane. Anything could have happened to them. It wasn't safe for women alone to be wandering around. He cursed himself. This was all his own stubborn fault. He should not have let Julie out of his life. He wanted nothing more now than to find her, hold her in his arms forever and let her know how much he loved her.

"We're almost to our destination," Julie said as she looked at the map she had been given. "I don't want to get too close because then we'd be within range of the British fort."

It was a beautiful day, clear and cooler. There were rolling hills above the river on this the west side, while the other side was low and tree covered. Not the way it looks today, Julie thought as she took in the pastoral scenery.

"Now what?" Esmé asked.

"Now we just wait for Galvez and his army to come. We'll make camp in that grove over there. I'm not certain how long we'll have to wait. Perhaps we can make a sort of lean-to. At least we won't have to be walking long distances every day."

"I'm looking forward to that," Esmé said, sitting down. "Of course, we still have to find food."

"It doesn't take long to catch fish."

"Soon I shall turn into one. Wouldn't chicken be nice?"

"Don't talk about it," Julie laughed. "Come on. Help me with these branches. They're quite large. They must have been shaken off the trees during the hurricane. They're perfect for constructing a lean-to."

"You're very resourceful. I wouldn't have thought of that."

Julie wanted to say she had been a Girl Scout but she didn't reveal that. And in truth it hadn't prepared her for this reality; it only gave her ideas, some of which seemed to work, and others which didn't.

"There, we should both be able to crawl in there," Julie said with satisfaction.

"Right cozy I'd say."

Both Julie and Esmé jumped and turned to face four grizzled-looking men. One was tall with thin gray hair and a white unkempt mustache. The second was short with dark hair and yellow teeth. The third was of medium height and also had long dark hair and a beard. The fourth was completely unlike the other three. He had thin blond hair, strange vacant blue eyes, and was lean and pale. All of them were heavily armed.

Julie looked at the men and at once felt sickened. The danger she had been warned about was at hand. Esmé looked paralyzed.

"Who are they? Find out if they have any gold, Henry." Surprisingly, it was the thin blond who spoke. He had drawn a long, sharp knife and he fingered it ominously.

"Sure, Len. Be careful with the knife."

"We have no gold," Julie said, stepping back as the short man with dark hair approached her.

"Come here, young fellow. I'll find that out for myself."

Henry grabbed Julie with sudden force and jerked her toward him so hard her hat fell off. "Hey, what have we here?" Henry said as he held her arm tightly in spite of her struggling.

"It sure ain't no young boy," the tall one said, looking her over.

Esmé couldn't move for a minute. Their eyes were on Julie and all she could think of was to get help. If Galvez was coming here didn't that mean they were ahead of them? If she bolted and ran—if she kept going—would she run into them coming toward the bayou?

"Let go of me!" Julie struggled, but the man held her wrist tightly. He reached up and tugged at her hair. Her long blond braids fell down.

"A right pretty wench, I'd say."

"Observant of you, Gator," Len said to the tall one.

It was at that moment that Esmé bolted. Julie had never known she could run so fast.

"Get that one!" Len called out.

"Run, Esmé! Run as fast as you can!" Julie shouted. But her shouts of encouragement were cut off by a rough slap across the mouth. She looked up into Len's eyes even as his stared into hers. He was the slightest of the four of them, yet he seemed to be their leader. A chill passed through her whole body as she looked into those blue eyes. He was insane. A killer. She felt it as she had never felt anything before. His naked, half-mad gaze terrified her. She ceased struggling. The other two had gone after Esmé, leaving her alone with Len and the one who held her, Henry.

In her heart Julie was praying for Esmé. *Run, run* was all she could think of—please, let her get away.

"Who are you?" Len asked.

"Julie Hart."

Len smiled a funny smile. "Hart," he said, repeating her last name. "And what are you doing here?"

"Waiting," she said. "We're to meet some soldiers here."

Bluff. What else was there to do? What was there to lose?

"Soldiers? What kind of soldiers?"

"Spanish soldiers and Louisiana militia. And some revolutionaries, too."

Len pressed his lips together and looked mildly disturbed. He moved closer to her, threateningly close.

He took her chin in his hand roughly and held his knife close to her neck. Julie summoned all her inner strength. Was she brought to this century to die this way? She could not accept that.

"Why would Spanish soldiers be coming with revolutionaries and militia? Don't lie to me, pretty lady. Don't lie or I'll slit your lovely white throat."

She looked into his eyes, those pale blue yet intense

eyes. "Put your knife down, Len," she said evenly, slowly, deliberately. "Put it down and I will tell you."

Len smiled without showing his teeth. He looked at Henry. "She's smarter than you, Henry. And gutsier, too."

Len lowered the knife and held it at his side. "Talk, pretty lady."

"Spain has joined France and is now allied with the revolutionaries against England. Bernardo Galvez is governor of Louisiana and he has gathered militia to march on Baton Rouge."

"We've been helping some of the loyalists to see the light," Henry said, laughing.

"You were with James Willing, weren't you?" It came to her suddenly. These unsavory men must have been among those left from Willing's bunch. They had a name, but it eluded her.

"See, she is smart," Len said. "And pretty, too. Tell me why you're so smart."

Julie felt pressed. Why not the truth? It was so fantastic who could know how a mad man would take it? "I'm a time traveler," she said. "From the twentieth century."

To her surprise, Len did not bat an eyelash. He just shook his head knowingly.

"A what?" Henry said. "What's she mean?"

"What she said," Len answered back, waving his knife.

"She got away! The little slut runs like a rabbit! Don't she, Mason?" Gator muttered.

"We couldn't catch her," Mason confirmed.

Len drew his pistol so quickly that even Julie did not see him. The shot startled her and she barely stifled a scream at the second shot. Both Gator and the one called Mason were shot; both fell to the ground. They didn't move. Julie forced herself not to react even though she knew they were dead.

Henry loosened his grip on her wrist. His face had paled and his eyes were large. "What'd yah do that fer?"

"They're slow and stupid and they eat too much," Len said, poking his pistol back into his holster.

Julie's relief that Esmé had escaped was mixed with apprehension. What was this lunatic going to do to her?

Len turned back to her and again his eyes locked on hers. "It's the truth, isn't it? You're a time traveler."

"Yes. Yes. It's true. I wouldn't lie to you."

"Can I have her?" Henry asked. "You let me have the others. Let me tie her up and we can both have her. Then you can kill her the way you like to kill—the way you killed the other ones."

Julie tried to keep her knees from buckling. My God, she had crossed the centuries to find an eighteenth-century serial killer—a madman with a big bearlike stupid accomplice.

"Later," Len said impatiently. "You can wait."

"But if we keep her, we have to feed her."

"So the other two are dead now. She doesn't look as if she'll eat much. I find her entertaining. I want to hear about the future. When she fails to entertain me—then you can have her."

Henry made a strange noise in his throat. Julie didn't look at him. "You can let go of my wrist. I won't run away."

"Of course you won't. Tie her under there. She built a little nest for herself—put her in it and tie her to the tree."

Henry did as he was bid and Julie didn't struggle. All she could do was pray that Esmé would find someone to help; that she would run into army scouts coming toward them.

She watched as they built a fire and brought out whiskey. Henry drank, but Len did not. Instead, when Henry was drunk and falling asleep, Len crept over to her. "Talk to me about the future," he said, taking out his knife and a sharpening stone. "Just talk. I'll work on my knife. Tomorrow we'll head for Baton Rouge. There are farms between here and there."

Julie drew in her breath. She was to play Scheherazade

to this horrific little man and her life depended on her performance.

Esmé ran like the wind until she felt her heart would burst inside her chest. Even then she kept going, slowing only to a rapid walk. Now and again she looked behind her, but there was nothing, no one. She did not trust herself or her judgment. Her instincts told her they had given up their chase, but her fear for Julie told her to keep going and so, only slightly refreshed, she began to run again. She ran until she fell facedown in a field panting, fighting to catch her breath, tears running down her cheeks. Tears of fear for Julie. It was dark now and she couldn't see to go on. Esmé shivered and pulled her jacket around her. She rolled up in a ball and closed her eyes.

It was there, lying on the ground as the sun came up that Esmé heard the sound of approaching horses. She sat bolt upright, afraid to believe that those who approached would be friends. Then she stood and saw the approaching force in the distance. It did not move with thundering speed, but rather plodded along.

She ran toward her vision and saw a phalanx of horsemen riding toward her. She waved her arms frantically and in seconds was surrounded. "Take me to General Galvez!" she shouted. "Hurry!"

One of the men swooped her up on his horse and rode back toward the larger force. The others followed.

"General Galvez!" the rider called out as he approached and the general turned. He saw Esmé immediately.

"This must be one of the women," the rider from the advance guard said as he slid from his horse and set Esmé down.

The general slid off his horse as well. "Esmé, what's happened?" She looked terrible. Her hair was tangled and her face covered with insect bites. Her clothes were men's clothes and they were tattered and torn.

"We escaped from Don Fernando's farm. We've walked for days and days. Then last night we reached a point one mile from Fort Bute. We camped and were attacked by four men. They're terrible men and they have Julie! I ran and ran—she told me to run. They'll kill her." She covered her face with her hands and began crying again. This time her tears would not stop and her whole body shook.

"Tell me what they look like," Galvez said.

Through her tears and sobs Esmé described the men. Her terror of them was obvious.

General Galvez held her tightly and let her sob. Then, even though she was still crying, he ordered her taken to the medical wagon. "Dress her scratches and feed her. Have her sent back to Don Carlos de Vega and Don Fernando's farm. Take two horses and return as quickly as possible. And if you find Brady McCormick, send him to me immediately."

Galvez had left Don Carlos in charge of his brother and the other prisoners temporarily. Tomorrow, Don Carlos was to ride to join the main force. Galvez smiled. He could do without Don Carlos for one night more. Let him be with Esmé.

Then Galvez bit his lip. Esmé was safe, but was Julie? He had heard rumors of this band of men—four in all—who had been with James Willing. One of them was a murderer, a violent man whose crimes were horrendous. He had massacred all the inhabitants of two farms. In all cases the women had been raped first, then had bled to death after their veins had been opened. It was the horror of the crimes that had created the stories that flourished about this gang. It was, in fact, the talk of New Orleans. The opening of veins was sixteenth-century punishment for adultery in France. It was an odd way to kill and meant this gang was more than simply a renegade group of soldiers run amok. Indeed, so prevalent were the stories of this gang that they had been given a name: the Bloods.

"You summoned me?" Brady rode up and tipped his hat ever so slightly at the general.

Galvez frowned, a serious expression covering his face. "You'd better take some men and ride forward to within a mile of Fort Bute. We've found Esmé—"

"Esmé! Where is she? Where is Julie?"

"Slow down, Brady. Hear me out."

Brady looked at him and his heart sank. He could feel it in his bones. Something had happened.

"I believe Julie has been taken captive by a renegade group of soldiers."

Brady's face paled. "Not the Bloods."

"I'm afraid her description sounds rather like them."

"I request permission to take some men and ride ahead."

Galvez nodded. "Be careful, Brady. These men are armed and very dangerous."

Brady rode with his men in silence till he saw the circling vultures overhead. On the knoll he found the two dead bodies. Those birds on the ground took angry flight, their dinner interrupted. Brady shuddered. He hated vultures.

Brady examined the ground carefully. He kicked at the remnants of the fire. It had been out for hours. He examined the lean-to and searched in all directions for tracks. There was nothing.

Weary, disappointed, and fearful for the woman he loved, he ordered the bodies buried. It seemed obvious they had left earlier, probably at dawn. He bit his lip hard and tasted his own blood. She wasn't here; there was no sign of her. That, he told himself, was a good sign. But God, what might the two remaining madmen do to her? Were the others dead because they had fought over her? He shivered and took a silent vow to kill them all if they hurt Julie. He mounted his horse and turned to return to Galvez. Perhaps they had taken her to Fort Bute. Perhaps to Baton Rouge—or, more likely they had taken her with them to some peaceful farm on the river. There they would burn, pillage and murder. He sucked in his breath.

"Dear Heaven, let me find her in time," he whispered.

They'd been slowly marching for days. Everything delayed them. Illness stalked them, mud entangled them, wagons broke. Now, although he had been outside and on the march for days, Brady still had the feeling of a caged animal. And cages, he knew, were mostly mental.

As if reading his mind, Galvez commented, "You're ready to spring, my friend, like a cat on the prowl who has too long been denied the prize."

"You guess my mood perfectly," Brady replied. "The fighting will be easy compared to reaching the target. And everything is easy compared to my own anxiety."

"Tomorrow," Galvez confided. "Tomorrow we'll be at the gates of Fort Bute and we will attack. I've sent the officers to prepare the men. We move at dawn."

A surge of enthusiasm spread through him. Maybe Julie was inside. Maybe the renegade murdering gang had been caught by the British. Certainly they were hunted by the British. "Have we enough men who are well enough to fight?"

"I think so," Galvez replied with a half smile. "To tell you the truth, my friend, my intelligence sources tell me that most of the garrison has been transferred to Baton Rouge.

Brady smiled. "Does that mean I'm not truly needed?"

"You're always needed, Brady. You have something on your mind, don't you?"

"If all goes well in the morning, and if Julie is not inside the fort, I'd like to ride with the advance troops."

"I think I understand that request. Very well, I have no objections. But don't forget, you will be scouting. You will take ten men and each day you will send back one to report. You can cover much ground on horseback that we cannot cover on foot and with the wagons.''

"I understand.''

"Brady, even if you find her you will have to go all the way to Baton Rouge. I need to know what to expect.''

"I will do as you command.''

Galvez slapped him on the back. "Good, it's decided. I hate having a worried man on my hands in the middle of a war.''

"I'm worried because the men who have Julie are mad.''

"It saddens me to say so, my friend, but you have good cause for concern.''

"I'm going to turn in now. Tomorrow will come too soon," Brady said. He headed toward where he had laid out his bed roll. Yes, he would ride ahead. He would feel better if he felt he were trying to find her. If he felt he was getting nearer instead of standing still.

It was still pitch dark outside when Galvez deployed his one-thousand-man fighting force around Fort Bute. Cannons were placed in front of the gates and at two other positions facing the walls of the fort. It seemed to Brady as if no one was even breathing. But it was far from silent. In that precious time just before dawn the middle river wakened with the shudder of wings as birds nested in the trees took sudden flight and as small animals skittered across the ground. Katydids and crickets sang their discordant tunes as the cool dawn breeze swept across the land and the ball of fire in the east broke full on this section of the earth.

Galvez raised his hand and fired his pistol. His men surged forward from every direction, and the cannon fired against the gates of the fort.

It was only moments before the white flag was run up the pole and the gates of Fort Bute were flung open. A

cheer went up among Galvez's men, and then followin
their leader, they poured into the fort.

"How sweet victory," Brady said somewhat sarcasticall
when, half an hour later, he and Galvez were in the cap
tain's inner office toasting the victory with the comman
dant's best brandy.

In all, they had found eighteen enlisted men in the for
and two officers—one quite miserable captain and an even
more miserable lieutenant.

Galvez grinned at his friend. "No matter what one find
victory is always better than defeat."

"True," Brady admitted as he sipped the brandy. H
stood leaning against the captain's desk. He put his brand
down and folded his arms across his waist, turning hi
attention to the two officers who, out of courtesy, had als
been given drink. Galvez would keep the two under guard
but he intended to send them together with their eighteen
men back to New Orleans rather than hold them here
He promised all that if they behaved they would be we
treated and sent to Pensacola.

Galvez was a man of his word, and not a few British
loyalists had changed sides because of his fairness.

"Just a few questions," Brady said. "Not military que
tions," he added. "Have you run across a gang of men
There were four, perhaps more in the beginning and
they're known as the Bloods. They came into this territor
with James Willing, a man who claimed to be a revolution
ary, but who is a criminal."

"Willing himself was bad enough!" the lieutenan
answered through clenched teeth. "He burned and pi
laged many a home and not just loyalists, either!"

"We know that," Galvez said. "He's been sent off i
irons."

"Too good for him," the lieutenant muttered. "Wha
he left behind was worse. We found a farmhouse a fe

miles from here ransacked from top to bottom. Everything of value was taken and everyone in the house murdered. And the women—''

Brady saw the look on the lieutenant's face. It was contorted and his mouth twitched with the memory. ''What about the women?'' He almost whispered the question, wondering if under the circumstances he wanted to know the answer.

''All raped. All bled to death, their veins opened. There was blood everywhere. I've never seen a thing like it in war or peace. Not one of my men could keep from retching at the sight of it. The men who did it are said to be led by a madman. God be with you if you are seeking them.''

Brady wanted to speak but he could not. His voice was lost in his throat, his nerves on edge. He turned to Galvez who also looked pale. Galvez knew he wanted to take his detail of scouts and be gone. He opened his mouth to say he wanted to leave now, but Galvez waved him away, permission given without the need for words to be spoken.

Brady rounded up the detail and they rode off within the half hour. If Julie was still alive, time mattered a great deal. He fought to remain optimistic.

''Now there's a nice-looking farm,'' Henry said as he pointed off across the fields of sugarcane.

Len looked at it, his glassy eyes staring off into the distance as if he were hypnotized.

Julie, her hands bound to the saddle horn, rode on one of dead men's horses. The horse was tied to Len's horse so she could not in any way escape. They had even taken the precaution of gagging her so she could not call out.

''Shall we take it?'' Henry asked.

Len nodded and smiled ever so slightly.

Julie looked at the little cabin and wondered who lived in it. She felt sick inside. They would be killed.

"Tether her horse to that tree," Len muttered. "I don't want her with us."

Henry dismounted and untied her horse from Len's. He tied her horse to the tree and then he and Len rode off toward the cabin in the distance.

It was torture. If only she could warn the hapless inhabitants of the cabin. If only she could somehow get this loathsome gag out of her mouth. She struggled, but to no avail. Len knew how to tie a good knot and there was no slack in the gag.

She looked down at her hands. The same was true of them. She was bound securely and any struggle seemed to make the knots still tighter.

She jumped at the sound of gunfire and stared into the distance. She saw two men running; she saw them shot, gunned down by Len, whose pistol crackled in the morning stillness. She heard shouting and cursing and then more shots. She strained to see, and then she saw Len and Henry, unharmed. They were torching the house, setting it ablaze.

The flames shot upward, no doubt fed by some potent alcohol. The smoke was dark and curled high into the sky, dark black smoke, smoke that would be seen for many a mile, she thought. For the first time she felt hopeful. If someone saw the smoke maybe she would be rescued.

When she looked up again, Len and Henry were galloping to her side. Both were drinking and grinning.

"There weren't no women in that house," Henry said.

"Pity," Len replied.

"Why can't I have her now?" he whined. "Bet she's pretty naked. Bet her skin is white and soft."

Len swigged a drink and looked at her.

Julie felt her skin crawl under his gaze. His eyes were so strange, almost as if he were drugged.

Then Len shook his head. "I like her stories. Gonna keep her a while. Then we'll have fun with her. Be patient, don't get all excited."

Julie knew the color had drained from her face. These

men would stop at nothing. They were dangerously insane. Murderers. Had she not been gagged she would have screamed to the heavens. Who could guess what they would do to her before they killed her? She trembled and then forced herself to stop thinking, to stop feeling, to remember that as long as Len found her entertaining, he wouldn't kill her. But time was running out. In her mind's eye she could see an hourglass and see the grains slipping downward one by one.

It was mid-afternoon when Brady looked upward and saw the vultures circling and then one by one swooping down on the carrion. But the carrion need not be animal, he knew that. Only days ago he had found the bodies of the two men. What would he find today? A dead farm animal? More victims of the Bloods? Julie? His heart pounded as he spurred his horse on and signaled his men to ride faster.

He reached the bodies of the two men and judged from what was left of them that they were probably brothers. He hurried to the ashes where once a cabin had stood. He could see the footings and some of the unburned logs. Here and there were metal household items that were charred but had not burned. He kicked the ashes, beginning at one end of the house and walking up and down carefully. To his great relief there were no other human remains. He glanced upward. His men were burying the bodies and no more vultures circled. He knew there were no more bodies in the woods. The dead were all here.

He left a detail to finish the graves, took the rest of his men and moved on.

A light soft rain fell from the skies. It was a gray day with banks of silver clouds overhead and misty rain covering the ground.

Don Carlos prepared to return to New Orleans where he had agreed to act as magistrate and chief keeper of the law in the absence of the governor, Bernardo Galvez.

He had assembled a veritable wagon train of items from his brother's house which he intended to take with him. There was no point in returning here till the war was finished, until Mississippi and Louisiana had been totally secured. And he thought, Don Fernando would not be returning at all. He was thoroughly disgraced and, as well, had been charged with treason. Don Carlos did not expect Bernardo Galvez to exact the maximum sentence on his brother, but he did realize that Don Fernando, when freed, would be forced from the territory.

He gave the signal and the wagon train began to move. He himself intended to travel by horseback.

As the wagons clattered down the narrow road, he looked up to see men on horseback coming the other way. Galvez's men! Or at least a few of them. With them was another rider, a rider who looked like a young boy. It was only when they got closer, having edged past the wagons, that he realized the young boy was Esmé, her magnificent mane of red hair hidden.

"Esmé!" he shouted out to her as he ran up. He held out his arms and lifted her down off the horse. "My darling! What has happened to you? I'm glad beyond words to see you." In spite of her male dress, her insect bites and bandages, he held her close and kissed her with passion.

Esmé leaned against him, listening as the leader of the detail which had delivered her explained her ordeal. Don Carlos seemed to squeeze her tenderly as each outrage was revealed.

"Thank you, Lieutenant. There is little left in the house, but what there is you are welcome to and certainly you should rest."

"No, we must return to General Galvez immediately," he replied. Then, doffing his cap, he turned his horse and he and his men rode away.

"I was so afraid I'd lost you forever, Esmé. You're brave and strong."

She looked up at him and he swooped her into his arms and carried her into the near-empty house. He set her down on the remaining bed and he alone heated water and filled the tub for her. When he was finished he returned to the bedroom. "I've filled a tub for you, Esmé. Come, my darling."

"You should not be waiting on me," she protested. But he ignored her words and carried her to the tub and set her down. Then while she stood submissively, he undressed her.

"I adore you," he whispered as he kissed her tenderly.

"And I you," she murmured.

"Let me be your slave, Esmé. Let me tend your scratches and bites, let me take care of you. I love you, my darling. I want to marry you."

"I have dreamed of this," Esmé whispered softly.

"We will not be separated again, Esmé."

"What of Don Fernando?"

"He's been taken to jail. He did terrible things."

"And Desirée? I know she did some bad deeds, but she did save me."

"Ah, yes. Desirée. I believe the governor decided that since she had to 'donate' the arms she bought from the captain of La Mira to the Crown, she has been sufficiently punished for her ill actions."

Esmé leaned back in the warm water. It felt so wonderful, more wonderful because Don Carlos was at her side. "I do love you," she whispered.

"And I you," Don Carlos said, kissing her with passion.

"I hate the rain," Len said.

Julie watched him as he spoke, as he perused the sky, as he moved. She had tried for days to gauge his insane moods, to be able to predict when he would again burst into violence. But he was totally unpredictable. His moods seemed to follow no pattern whatsoever.

"We're getting mighty close to Baton Rouge," Henry said. "I think we should head down one of the bayous."

Len didn't answer. Instead, he continued to look at the sky and to grimace at the soft rain.

"Then maybe we should make camp here," Henry muttered. "The ground's at least flat."

Len stopped his horse and then dismounted.

Henry took it all to mean they were making camp. He, too, dismounted and pulled the pack off the back of his horse.

"I'm bored," Len said, his eyes falling on Julie.

She looked back at him wondering if her eyes reflected the terror she felt. His words sent a tremor through her.

"Does that mean I can have her now?" He dropped his pack and walked toward her, his mouth half open.

"Get her down off there and tie her to that tree," Len directed.

Henry quickly untied her and pulled her off the horse. She struggled with all her might, but it was no use. He was too strong. In moments he had her arms in the air and tied to a low tree branch. Her feet barely touched the ground, but he tied her ankles with a length of rope so that she couldn't kick even though her legs could be separated.

Len lay down on the grass. "Undress her," he directed, "then unbraid her hair."

Julie wished she would faint, wished she would vanish, wished she could once again be sucked up in time. But none of those things happened and Henry's big bearlike paws were on her. He disrobed her quickly, leaving her naked and shivering as rain droplets covered her. He unbraided her hair. She was utterly helpless. They were going to kill her.

Len gave her his sick, closed-mouth smile. His eyes had taken on an even more peculiar look. Then he turned to

Henry who had taken off his pants in anticipation of having his way with her. "You can have her now," he said.

Henry came to her, his back to Len. His hands moved over her and he actually drooled as he fondled her. He pulled down her gag but she did not reward him with a scream until his hand grabbed her breast and his lips sought her neck. He was rough and cruel and she screamed again. Any moment he would penetrate her. She kept screaming and then a shot rang out and she fell silent, stunned as Henry crumpled to the ground, his seed spilling out of him.

She looked up and saw Len's smoking pistol. Had she expected Brady? She had prayed for him to come.

Len walked slowly over to her. "I couldn't let him ruin you," he said. "You're so perfect. He would have made you all messy."

He took out his knife and the sharpener. "I'll make the blade nice and sharp," he told her. "That way it won't hurt."

Julie stared at him. "What are you going to do?"

"Open your veins and watch you bleed."

She drew in her breath and resisted telling him he was mad. Was this the way her life was to end? She watched, almost hypnotized herself, as he sharpened the knife.

Then he stopped and moved toward her. She shivered as he began to move the razor-sharp blade over her skin. As Henry had touched her sexually, this madman touched her with blade of his knife. As if partaking in a ritual, he moved it over her, not cutting her, just touching her lightly. But he would cut her at any moment. At any moment he would slit her veins. Julie's head felt light as she thought about it. Then, mercifully, she lost complete consciousness.

Chapter Fifteen

Brady spurred his horse and turned toward the screams he heard in the distance. The others may have followed, but he was unaware of them as he moved through the bush, his head down and his hands tight on the reins.

His horse broke into the clearing and what he saw caused him to freeze momentarily. It was Julie, naked and tied to a tree. There was a dead man on the ground and another with a glistening knife.

The man with the knife turned toward him suddenly, his mouth agape. Brady did not hesitate—he drew his pistol and fired. The man's pale-blue eyes bulged with surprise as he grasped his midsection and then doubled over, tumbling to the ground.

Brady turned to the horsemen behind him. "Stay back!" he shouted as he rode across the clearing.

Julie was limp, and only when he had dismounted and come closer did he realize that she was unconscious and not dead. He quickly cut her down and then took the blanket from his bedroll and wrapped her in it.

"Julie, Julie." He touched her gently and her wonderful blue eyes opened and looked up at him.

"Brady," she whispered.

"Yes, my love. By heaven, did they—?"

She shook her head. "One was going to, but the other shot him. He was going to open my veins and bleed me to death. He's a lunatic."

"Yes, I know. He's killed his last woman now." He looked at her longingly and forced himself to remember that there were others waiting. "I'm not alone," he said. "Better get dressed."

Julie nodded, and while he held the blanket in front of her, she quickly dressed in the men's clothing she had been wearing. This time she did not bother to braid her hair or hide it. "Esmé? Did she get away? Did she find someone? Is she all right?"

"So many questions so quickly. Esmé is fine. She's been sent on to Don Carlos who has suffered a thousand deaths since she disappeared."

"Did you suffer so much?" she asked.

"Yes. How did you survive that madman?"

"He liked my stories of the future. But today he decided he had heard enough."

"I got here just in time."

"Yes," she answered back. Then, "All right, I'm decent."

He circled her waist with his arm and kissed her cheek quickly. "A promise of more to come," he said. "God, woman, you scared me half to death. I've been looking for you for weeks!"

"And you didn't have Carmelita to comfort you?" she asked a little bitterly.

"Carmelita? She is like a sister to me. Julie, are you jealous of Carmelita?"

"I saw you leaving her room one night—"

"Ah, yes. She gathers information for me, or did. There is nothing between us."

Julie looked into his eyes and knew he was telling her the truth.

"And yes, I should have believed you," he added.

"Oh, no!" Julie cried as shots rang out.

"Get down," Brady said, pushing her to the ground and shielding her with his body.

There were more shots and then an order was barked to them. "Surrender!"

Brady eased up and raised his hands at the sound of the British voice. Julie followed.

The man in the red uniform rode closer. He circled them slowly.

"Drop your pistol," he ordered. "And explain what we have here—a lovely wench dressed as a boy. Is this Shakespeare? And while you are explaining, explain these bodies."

"The Bloods," Brady said. "The last of a gang which has been terrorizing this area."

"He just rescued me," Julie said defensively.

The officer rubbed his chin thoughtfully. The two dead men certainly fit the description of the Bloods, the gang which he had been looking.

"Are you loyalists?"

Brady nodded. "Our farm was burned."

"I just chased off some Spanish troops. You had better come with us to Baton Rouge. You'll be safe there at the fort." The man then looked at Julie again. "And why are you dressed that way?"

"They took my clothes," she said unblinkingly. "But if we're to ride to Baton Rouge it's all right. Men's clothes are better for riding."

Brady smiled up at the British officer then boosted Julie onto the horse. He mounted himself. "Lead the way."

They rode off and Julie smiled across at him. "This is almost where I came in," she said, thinking of their adventure in Fort Charlotte near Mobile.

* * *

It was night at Fort Bute. Outside, men gathered by the campfire while inside, Bernardo Galvez planned his next move with Oliver Pollock who had just joined him.

"I'm going to stay here a week," Galvez told Pollock. There's barracks and a clinic. Some of my men are really sick with fever. They need to get well, to recover from this mud-bound trek."

"I couldn't agree more," Pollock said.

Both men turned as there was knock on the door.

"Come in," Galvez ordered.

"Jason Wimbley reporting, sir. I am one of the scouts who rode out with Brady McCormick."

"Have you news?"

"Yes, sir. The woman was found and rescued. The Bloods are all dead. But I'm afraid Brady McCormick and the woman were found by the British and taken to Baton Rouge."

Galvez scowled. "Were they arrested?"

"I can't say, sir. We were waiting on orders in the woods when the British came. We all rode off in different directions so as not to be pursued. When we were reunited, Brady and the woman were gone. We tracked the British for a time, and Brady and the woman's horse were with them."

"I see," Galvez said thoughtfully. He rubbed his chin, then reached for his pipe. When he had painstakingly tapped out the contents of the bowl, he began refilling it with fresh tobacco. He looked up at Jason Wimbley. "Was McCormick in uniform?"

"No, sir. He was in buckskins."

"Good. He's probably been taken for a civilian. A heroic civilian who killed the last members of the Bloods."

"Perhaps so, sir."

"What do you think, Pollock?"

"I think it will be useful to have someone inside the walls of the fort at Baton Rouge."

Galvez laughed. "Ah, yes. If Brady is not too busy getting reacquainted with Miss Hart we could have our own Trojan Horse at Baton Rouge."

Pollock laughed, too. "I shall think on what he can do for us."

"It's even more Spartan than Fort Charlotte," Brady said, holding up the lantern and peering into the one-room cabin with its fireplace, bed, three chairs and a table. "You light the fire and I'll find some candles. We'll heat this soup the commandant's wife gave us. I'm starved."

Julie rummaged in her pack and withdrew the candles. She stuffed them into the candle holders and lit them with a wick the commandant's wife had provided along with the bucket of coals.

Brady undid the kindling and, taking small pieces, he started a tiny fire which grew stronger and larger as he put bigger pieces on it.

"It's good to take the chill off," she said, bringing the pot with the soup.

Brady attached it to the iron rod and swung it over the fire. "How did you cook in your century?"

"With gas and electricity mostly."

He sat down and she leaned back against him in front of the fire. "You miss your century, don't you?"

She would be less than honest if she lied. But she wanted to face him, so she turned about and looked into his eyes.

Julie drew in her breath and let it out slowly. "Life is harder in this time, about that there is no question. At first I wanted to go home. I wanted to return to the twentieth century and its comforts and security. I found everything about this world difficult, not the least of which the way men treat women."

"There are no men like Len in your century?" he asked. "No crime, no murderers?"

"There are more, I think. No, one time is as dangerous as another in that respect."

She thought but did not say that in the beginning she had not liked him much. Though she had to admit that he had attracted her in a raw physical way.

"What I mean is, women need men to protect them in this century. Women are sold or can be—women are not supposed to work, to earn money. Women are not expected to be independent."

"Not everyone treats women in such a way. Though most do. How do you feel now? Do you still want to go back?"

"No, Brady. I feel entirely different. Despite the revolution and the changes I know it will bring, despite everything, I could not even consider leaving you, Brady McCormick.

She felt filled with love for this man who was so strong, yet so gentle. "I can do nothing to guarantee the future," she continued. "That much I know, if I know nothing else. But I can hope I won't once again travel through time. I can hope I will be able to stay here in this century and find happiness with you. Brady, I crossed the ages to find you and I know I love you."

He touched her hair and kissed her lips tenderly, then he smiled. "Were you taken back to your time, I would pray to be taken with you. I love you, too, more than I can ever really tell you. The words that might express my feelings do not exist."

They sat for a long while in silence and then Julie pulled herself up and ladled the soup from the now-steaming pot. They ate in silence, looking at one another with new eyes, seeing into each other's souls.

When they had finished dinner, Brady carried her to the bed. "I confess I have thought all day of this. Is that wrong?"

Julie laughed gently. "I have thought of it, too. I have

thought how much I missed you. I have dreamed of you and felt you even when we were apart."

He undid her blouse and freed her beautiful breasts. "Ah, my woman, I, too, had dreams. Dreams of holding you for all eternity. Of locking with you and becoming one forevermore."

His lips, his mouth, his tongue, touched her furtively, gently yet erotically. His hands flew over her and without her even realizing it, he removed her remaining clothing.

His fingers played on her body, his lips caressed her till she felt faint with desire for him, faint with the need for him to be in her, locked together, as he put it.

"You torture me too sweetly," she gasped. "I love you."

"And I you." He said nothing more but continued to taunt her. His skin glistened with perspiration and she felt his taut muscles beneath his smooth skin. The full hardness of him pressed into her slowly, moving ever further inside her. Her arms were around his neck, her fingers on his back. She moved as he seemed to direct her to move, and suddenly he rolled and she was atop him looking down even as he filled her. He took her breast into his mouth and nursed it with just the right tension. His hands held her buttocks and she shivered, then shook above him, crying out in singular delight at the array of sensations she felt as their coupling led them both into pulsating pleasure.

He didn't withdraw from her when once again they both breathed normally. She lay atop him and he kissed her hair. "One thing is clear," he said, kissing her neck. "We belong together, my woman."

"I know," Julie whispered in return. "I know."

The morning sun was strong, though it continued to be cooler. "A fine autumn day," Brady said as he watched Julie dress. "Ah, I know that men's clothes are more practical, but it's good to see you in a dress again. Even a plain dress."

The dress was a loan from the commandant's wife. It was a dull brown, had a white chemise and a stiff starched apron. "Well, it certainly isn't a fashion piece," Julie said. "But Brady, I ride side saddle so badly."

He laughed. "I promise when we're away from the fort you can change and ride as you like."

"Are they simply going to let us walk away?"

"I think so. After all, we are just loyalist settlers. Why shouldn't we return to our homes?"

"Whatever you say," she said, throwing up her arms.

Brady slung his pack over his shoulder and then picked up Julie's. Outside, their horses remained tethered. They had been watered and fed and were now ready to be ridden.

Brady undid the reins. "We'll walk to the commandant's cabin and thank him and his wife for their hospitality."

Brady led and Julie followed. Her eyes roamed the compound. Brady had been drawing pictures since before breakfast. Clearly he had a good idea of what was where and was itching to get back to Galvez.

Brady knocked on the cabin door and the commandant himself answered. "We've come to say good-bye," Brady announced to the sleepy man. "My wife and I wish to return home."

"Travel is not necessarily safe."

"We'll be fine, sir. And thank you again. My wife says she will find a way to return your wife's dress."

Julie watched Brady. He doffed his hat and bowed. She concealed her smile as she thought how much she liked his humor. His eyes often danced with merriment, especially if he was fooling someone or telling a tall tale.

"Have a safe journey," the commandant muttered.

"We will indeed."

Brady returned to her and they left, slowly at first. He led her horse and she rode side saddle. When they were a safe distance from the fort, he helped her down and she quickly changed her clothes. Then she climbed on her horse and they were off at a quicker pace.

*　*　*

Galvez strode out of his headquarters at Fort Bute and looked at the two riders who had just come in. Brady was tall in the saddle, always recognizable even at a distance.

It was Julie he stared at. Her long blond hair was loose and wild, splayed about her shoulders. She wore an open-necked man's shirt and breeches and boots. But even her male clothing did not succeed in covering the curves of her seductive body.

"You look rather different than when I first met you, Miss Hart."

She dismounted. "This is much better, I assure you."

"I shall take your word for it," he replied. "Well, Brady, I take it you've been inside the fort and have news. Pollock's inside. Shall we?"

"May I?" Julie asked.

"But of course. Who better than someone who knows what will happen?"

Brady greeted Pollock and Galvez poured them all drinks.

"It'll be no pushover," Brady said, taking out his notes. "It's well fortified with a ditch eighteen feet wide and nine feet deep. The walls are high and sloping topped with a *chevaux-de-frise,* crowned with some thirteen cannons of large caliber. I've seen those men. They're all veterans and war-tried. But there are only four hundred of them and I would say a hundred or so civilians."

Galvez went to the door of his headquarters, "Call Alvarez!" he shouted out to his guard, "and Captain Don Pedro Favrot as well."

Alvarez and Favrot arrived within minutes. Both glanced at Julie and then turned to their general.

Galvez indicated Julie and by way of explanation said, "A clever and gifted spy who is helping us, gentlemen. Be at ease. Now, Brady, will you repeat what you just told me."

Brady did repeat it and both men agreed it could prove a difficult battle.

Julie knew how this battle had gone and wondered how much she should say. Still, Galvez had won by tricking the British. She waited to see if he had the idea on his own, but while many suggestions were offered, none was the right one.

"There is an orchard," she said slowly. All eyes turned to her. "If you can trick the British into thinking you are placing all your batteries there so they will fire all night at the orchard, you can, under cover of darkness, move your guns to the other side of the fort."

"An interesting idea. I could stay with some weapons in the orchard while you, Alvarez, direct the bombardment on the other side of the fort."

"It also has the advantage of making us appear more numerous," Brady said. "Good mental warfare."

"I like it," Pollock put in.

"It is agreed then," Galvez said. "Tomorrow we move."

Brady walked with Julie in the moonlight. "My woman, you have quite a brilliant mind. Of course, you do know how this battle will turn out in any case."

She said nothing, just squeezed his hand.

"But I must say, I thought you did nothing to change history. Won't this plan of attack change something?"

Julie shook her head. "It is how it happened. I waited and when no one hit on it I suggested it. But it is how it really happened."

He laughed. "Just like leaving before his orders were received."

"Yes. Who am I to say that it didn't happen that way because of me? It must have. Here I am and that is how it happened."

He kissed her quickly before they retired for the night. "I like going into battle when I know how it will turn out."

Julie's eyes twinkled with amusement. "It does make it easier."

During the daylight hours Galvez placed his batteries in the grove of fruit trees and proceeded to fire on the orchard after dark. Sporadically there was more fire at the orchard as, clandestinely, all the heavy artillery was taken to the far side of the fort. Shooting and noise continued throughout the night. The British knew they were under siege but somehow still felt safe behind their ditch and their fortifications.

As the sun rose, Don Julian Alvarez commenced his bombardment. It continued unabated for three long hours and completely destroyed the back wall of the fort.

At nine o'clock, two officers came forth carrying a white flag. By ten, the British had surrendered all of the western section of West Florida.

"You must be generous," Julie advised. "I know you to be generous."

"And how does history record the terms of this surrender?"

"You allow the soldiers to be taken to Pensacola and retain their belongings. The British in this territory will retain their laws till peace is declared. The civilians are not to be punished but are to retain their lands."

"I think I would do this even if I did not know I had," he laughed. "And will most of them remain?"

"Oh, yes. And remain loyal to you for your generosity."

"Very well. This is one battle that is over. Will you come and fight with me at Mobile and Pensacola, Brady?"

Brady shook his head. "I am taking Julie and we're returning to Fort Pit, then onward to Philadelphia."

Julie smiled with happiness even though she knew it would be a long hard journey east.

"Marry us," Brady said to Galvez. "A governor can do such things."

Galvez smiled. "It will be my pleasure."

Julie moved closer to the warmth of Brady's body. They were snuggled in bed rolls inside a small tent. But it was now fall, and they were traveling north, into the cold.

She put her arm around her husband and once again thought of their wedding. They had waited for two days after the fall of the Fort and the subsequent evacuation of the British troops.

Galvez performed the ceremony in a small chapel inside the fort. She wore the same plain dress the commandant's wife had loaned her, and Brady wore his buckskins. When the moment came, he slipped a ring off his little finger and put it on her hand.

"My mother's," he told her as he kissed her and Galvez pronounced them man and wife.

Brady stirred in his sleep and rolled over. "Cold?" he asked.

"No. Well, just a little."

He sat up and pulled another skin over them, then drew her close, so close she could feel him against her. "I love you," he whispered.

The closeness was now a familiar feeling, and immediately she longed for him just as she knew he wanted her. "I love you, too," she returned.

It was always the same with them, always just like the first time, always tender, passionate, and erotic. It amazed her.

"I am a fortunate woman," she whispered, "to have traveled here to you."

"No, my love. It is I who am fortunate."

He kissed her and she buried her face in his chest. Theirs, she knew, was a love for all time.

YOU WON'T WANT TO READ
JUST ONE—KATHERINE STONE

ROOMMATES (0-8217-5206-5, $6.99/$7.99)
No one could have prepared Carrie for the monumental changes she would face when she met her new circle of friends at Stanford University. Once their lives intertwined and became woven into the tapestry of the times, they would never be the same.

TWINS (0-8217-5207-3, $6.99/$7.99)
Brook and Melanie Chandler were so different, it was hard to believe they were sisters. One was a dark, serious, ambitious New York attorney; the other, a golden, glamourous, sophisticated supermodel. But they were more than sisters—they were twins and more alike than even they knew . . .

THE CARLTON CLUB (0-8217-5204-9, $6.99/$7.99)
It was the place to see and be seen, the only place to be. And for those who frequented the playground of the very rich, it was a way of life. Mark, Kathleen, Leslie and Janet—they worked together, played together, and loved together, all behind exclusive gates of the *Carlton Club*.

Available wherever paperbacks are sold, or order direct from the Publisher. Send cover price plus 50¢ per copy for mailing and handling to Penguin USA, P.O. Box 999, c/o Dept. 17109, Bergenfield, NJ 07621. Residents of New York and Tennessee must include sales tax. DO NOT SEND CASH.

ROMANCE FROM JO BEVERLY

DANGEROUS JOY   (0-8217-5129-8, $5.99)

FORBIDDEN   (0-8217-4488-7, $4.99)

THE SHATTERED ROSE   (0-8217-5310-X, $5.99)

TEMPTING FORTUNE   (0-8217-4858-0, $4.99)